It Could Just Happen

by

Robert Perryment

Copyright © Phoenix Film and Publishing Limited 2020

This novel is a work of fiction. Names, characters, businesses, places, events and incidents are either the products of the author's imagination or used in a fictitious manner. Any resemblance to actual persons, living or dead, or actual events is purely coincidental.

All rights reserved in all media. No part of this publication may be reproduced, stored in retrieval system, copied in any form or by any means, electronic, mechanical, photocopying, recording or otherwise transmitted without written permission from the author and/or publisher. You must not circulate this book in any format. Any person who does any unauthorised act in relation to this publication may be liable to criminal prosecution and civil claims for damages.

For permission requests, please contact: info@phoenixfilmandpublishing.com

Find out more about the author and upcoming books online at http://www.phoenixfilmandpublishing.com
Twitter: @PerrymentRobert
Instagram: RobertPerryment5
Goodreads Robert Perryment

Produced in United Kingdom.

Editorial services by www.bookeditingservices.co.uk

Contents

About the Author

Born in London at the outbreak of WWII, Robert commenced his selection for the Parachute Regiment when he was seventeen and a half years old (to the day) in 1957. He successfully passed the extreme selection and went on to earn his wings after a series of parachute jumps. By the time he was eighteen, he was a junior NCO (non-commissioned officer) and in active service with the 2nd. Battalion in Cyprus and Jordan. On returning to the UK, Robert passed a War Office Selection Board (WOSB) and after a spell at Mons Officer Cadet School, was commissioned into the 3rd. Battalion The Parachute Regiment.

Some years later, Robert, now married and with a family, decided to seek a new career. This took him to Africa where he founded an investment and insurance conglomerate in Kenya, Uganda, Zambia and Nigeria. He made regular forays into Bahrein, Abu Dhabi and Dubai in the early days of oil exploration.

Having sold his company to a major international organisation, Robert took his family to live in the South of France where he edited a financial magazine.

The magazine fell on hard times during a worldwide recession, and he decided to bring his family back to the UK.

He took his family to live in the Highlands of Scotland, where he finally decided to look for an alternative lifestyle. He farmed a small croft to see if he could provide all the food that a family of five would need. This he achieved whilst gaining his MA (Hons) in English Language and Literature at Aberdeen University.

After his studies were complete, he managed to buy a run-down hill farm in Aberdeenshire, which he toiled to bring back to a viable concern running a pedigree and commercial flock of sheep, together with his dogs and horses.

He had not long been elected as the Lord Rector of Aberdeen University to carry out a three-year appointment when his first wife, Vicki, was diagnosed with a very aggressive breast cancer. Sadly, she died less than a year later. His children by then had grown up and were either at work or university.

Robert threw himself into campaigning a Scottish challenge for the America's Cup. At the end of the campaign, which had lasted over many months, the challenge had to be aborted because of a lack of sponsorship. However, he used the same crew to participate in the Formula One World Yachting Grand Prix off the west coast of Scotland, then Germany, San Diego C.A., and Fremantle in Western Australia. The Scottish challenge came second in the world. He produced a TV film for his sponsors on both of these events and was soon asked to produce other programmes.

Robert's first love has always been poetry, and he has published a book of Miltonic Sonnets on the Falklands Crisis. It was just before he was due to carry out a one-man show at the Edinburgh Fringe Festival, *To My Pensive Woman*, that he was to meet and subsequently marry his present wife, Maria.

Ever entrepreneurial, the couple created a number of small

businesses and finally moved back south with their son and lived close to Cambridge.

This debut novel has been a long time coming, but it will provide a thrilling and thought-provoking experience.

Robert has now been invited to produce an autobiography, which is to be called *Ready for Anything* ('*Utrinque Paratus*' – the motto of the Paras).

Also, by Author

Falklands '82 28 sonnets. It takes a great deal of history to produce a little literature

Go Get a Life! Seven Meditations That Will Change Your Life

Acknowledgements

I want to thank Alex for her patient editing and for all the guidance that went with that task. Similarly, the book cover designer Rebeca, and all the marketing people and KDP staff, all of whom made this book possible.

To my wife, Maria, who constantly pleaded with me not to tell her the story before she could read it herself. She has always been my sounding board for every crackpot scheme that I've ever come up with since we first met. Thank you, my love.

Si fractus illabatur orbis, impavidum ferient ruinae
(If the world should break and fall on him, it would strike him fearless.)

Horace

The art of life is more like the wrestler's art than the dancer's, in respect of this, that it should stand ready and firm to meet onsets which are sudden and unexpected.

Marcus Aurelius

Chapter 1

Introduction to the Introduction

'Allahu akbar!' The muezzin's high-pitched, reedy, amplified voice pierced the thin mountain air as he called the faithful to prayer. The village seemed drowsy and nothing much seemed to be moving.

From their shell scrape covered in camouflage scrim, two bodies lay motionless, propped up on their elbows, eyes scanning through binoculars at the village below them.

Their focus seemed to be on one particular compound at the edge. A pickup truck was parked just inside the courtyard.

'Yes.' The soft sibilance escaped from Steve's lips as he refocused to capture more detail.

Geordie followed suit. After laying down his binoculars, he reached carefully for the wireless handset.

Steve turned to him and put up three fingers. 'Hello, One, how do you read me? Over,' he softly intoned.

'Send, over,' came back the answer immediately.

'Loading up, ready for the off, three on board, stand by, over.' Geordie looked hard at Steve.

Steve immediately responded with a nod and a thumb jerked in the direction of the road that the vehicle was travelling down. 'Hello, One, birds have flown, over.' Steve paused awaiting confirmation.

'Roger that, proceed as planned, out,' came the reply.

Steve picked up his binoculars and once again scanned the complete panorama below them.

It was going to be a long day. They wouldn't be able to move until sundown, in just about twelve hours' time. Geordie took the first stag; they would each do a two-hour shift. Steve stretched out his legs a little as he lay on his back and closed his eyes. This was not the sort of mission he really enjoyed. Too much hanging about and no bloody action. His mind wandered back over the past thirty-six hours. A chopper had dropped off the two groups at 01:00 hours. They had kept together for the first couple of hours as they tabbed towards their objective. Then, after a quick navigational check, the 'guv'nor' took the other three guys south to their ambush position.

Geordie and Steve had cracked on, reaching their position on the edge of the escarpment with enough time to dig in and cam up before first light. As the temperature soared during the day, the sweat ran in streams washing away the film of dust covering them. Water was at a premium, so careful rationing was imperative. Ration packs were eked out during the day. 'You could live on it.' Crocodile Dundee's quip seemed apt.

The first night in the OP had been bitterly cold, but the next day made up for it by rising into the high thirties. The targets turned up just before nightfall on the second night, just as the guv'nor had predicted. Barring accidents, their job was done. All they had to do now was sit it out and make their way to the second RV, join up with the others and get picked up by the chopper and back to base. Before they vacated the OP, a minute clean-up of the site must take place. Everything they brought with them must go, nothing buried, nothing left.

'And I mean everything!' The guv'nor's voice still rang in his ears – but he knew the score anyway.

Twelve clicks further south, overlooking the bend in the road that would allow a frontal attack on the vehicle, the ambush party lay in wait, camouflaged in the rock-strewn hillside.

Since Geordie's first contact, the tension in the position would only have been felt by other special forces – to all others it would seem as calm and relaxed as a vicar's garden party.

The guv'nor was glassing the bend and acting as spotter for Reg who was in a firing position behind his beloved sniper rifle. Before he settled down, he had chambered an armour-piercing round that would split the block of the pickup and bring it to a halt. His two compatriots were slightly to the right of his position, also in firing positions ready to give backup fire if required.

The guv'nor had briefed them that the passenger in the rear of the pickup was not a target and not to be touched. When the other two emerged after the vehicle had been stopped, Reg would take them out with surgical precision.

It all happened like clockwork; the way it had been planned. It doesn't often work like that. If something can go wrong, it usually does! They heard the bang as the round tore through the engine, and then the vehicle screeched to a stop. The driver and passenger came out looking bewildered. The driver slumped to the ground as the second round passed through his chest. The other passenger, sensing danger but unable to see where it was coming from, hunkered down beside the open door reaching for the AK-47 that was on the seat. It didn't do him any good. The third round found its target, and he also slumped to the ground. Meanwhile, the passenger in the rear leapt over the tailgate and sprinted into the rocks where he dived for cover.

'Reg, Charlie, cover us,' the guv'nor hissed. 'Rhys, come with me,' he called to the final member of the ambush group, a corporal, who was covering their exposed flank.

They ran between the rocks, causing scree to jump down the loose shale, until they reached the parched ground alongside the road.

'Search the vehicle and the bodies. I want all paperwork, wallets, phones, then get them back into the vehicle,' the guv'nor growled before disappearing into the boulders where the last man had disappeared at the start of the engagement.

It took Rhys three or four minutes to carry out the search, and then he hefted the bodies back into the pickup. He had found a grip and was busy stuffing wallets and phones into it when the guv'nor reappeared from the boulders at the foot of the escarpment.

He nodded to Rhys, and they both set off back up the hill to their previous position at a steady lope.

Rhys hissed, 'Did he do a runner?'

'It's what was wanted,' came the curious reply. Once back in the ambush position, the guv'nor called up on the set, 'Skylark One, Skylark One, how do you read me? Over.'

'Copy that, copy that,' replied the American voice of a nameless person in a bunker far, far away.

'Target in position as agreed, go for it. Over.' The guv'nor removed his thumb.

'Wilco. Out.' Silence followed this terse message.

There was no feeling of exaltation, just a wary and continued period of all-round observation.

The Predator drone came out of the sun. Nobody saw the missile as the drone steeply banked away from the hillside. The pickup just disintegrated in a ball of flame.

Back in the ambush position, they quickly packed everything and set off in order to get over the skyline before anyone came to investigate.

Once in a secure position, it only remained for them to wait for nightfall when they, too, could head for the pickup.

The night tab back to the RV was uneventful. The chopper was on time, so in less than two hours they were landing back at the base. Sergeant Jones was there to meet them.

'The IO would like to see you, sir, right away. I think he's got a spook with him.' He chuckled when he observed the guv'nor's face. 'Oh, and, sir, the CO would like to see you as soon as you've finished your debrief. He's in his office.' This time he looked a bit more serious.

The debrief was factual and didn't take long to describe the detail of the observations and ambush. The bag of papers and personal effects were handed over. No mention was made of the third man. If the guv'nor wasn't going to mention it, Rhys didn't think it was down to him to say anything. Two important insurgents killed, and a lot of evidence garnered. The IO looked pleased.

Once the men were dismissed, the spook called out, 'David, I actually came here to see you, but it now seems that you are going back the UK, so we can have a long chat on the flight. I think your CO wants to see you now, but perhaps we can meet up a bit later.'

David (the guv'nor) knocked on the CO's door and entered. It was a shipping container with a bit of threadbare carpet and a desk and a couple of chairs. The walls were covered in operational maps and a whiteboard. There was a set of bookshelves with a motley collection of eclectic titles.

'David, come and take a seat.' He reached in a file draw and pulled out a single malt and a couple of glasses. 'No cold water, I'm afraid. Will you take it neat?'

David felt the short hairs on his neck prickle. Something wasn't right. The boss usually had a distinct twinkle in his eye, but now there was a sadness that could be seen in the way his shoulders had slumped. There was a lengthy pause as he took a pull from his glass and nodded at David to do the same.

'David, I am sorry to be the bearer of bad news… There's been an awful tragedy at home. Your father was on the hill when a sudden storm blew up. David, he was struck by lightning and died on the spot.'

As the import of that statement filtered into David's tired mind, he couldn't grasp it. Must have misheard. He had to do something. He sipped the whiskey. No words would come. His mind had gone blank. Mister Action Man, ready for anything, nerveless in danger, calm under fire, the eternal Stoic.

'David,' the boss cut across the void, 'I've arranged a flight out for you at fourteen hundred hours. When you get to Brize, I've pulled a few strings and arranged for a chopper to take you up to Aberdeenshire. Take whatever time you need to sort out your affairs there and support your mother. Call me when you have time and let me know how things are. I can't tell you how sorry I am to have to be the bearer of this news.'

An important thought suddenly occurred. 'Excuse me, sir, I'm not sure if you are aware, but Corporal Philips grew up with our family and he was very close to my dad. I must tell him—'

But before he could continue, the CO interjected, 'I'll organise it; you go and get yourself ready.'

David nodded a brief thank you and left.

He showered and put on some fresh fatigues (he had no other clothes), chucked some toiletries in a bag with a change of underwear and called for a Land Rover to take him to the airport.

Just as he was about to leave, Rhys came trotting down the track with a duffle bag slung over his shoulder. He came to a halt in front of David. His eyes searched David's face with the same Stoic calm that he had copied from his hero since he first started noticing the quiet but powerful intensity that this man brought to every aspect of his life.

'The boss said I could come with you, but I can only stay for a couple of days,' Rhys explained. David was about to say something, but another voice called out.

'David, can I beg a lift?' The spook moved into the bright sunlight from the shade of the tent canopy where he had been waiting.

'Of course.' David waved a hand as a Land Rover pulled up alongside.

They checked in at the airport and sat down to await their flight being called.

Corporal Philips, realising that the civilian wanted to speak with the guv'nor, asked him, 'Would you like some coffee, sir?'

'Yes, that would be great, Rhys,' he replied and gave him a nod that said thank you.

Once they were alone, the spook looked at David. 'I gather you've had some bad news and are going home to lend a bit of support to the family,' he said. 'Tough that. I lost my old man last year. Brain tumour; not a good death. Look, I know you've just completed a difficult operation, and I guess you've had little or no sleep for the past few days, but I was hoping to chat to you for a while, although now is obviously not the time. However, I do need to have some in-depth discussions about your erstwhile friend who is now with al-Qaeda.' He raised an eyebrow. 'Look, here's my card. I'd like you to call me when everything calms down a bit. I can see you in London, or I can easily come up to Aberdeenshire if you prefer. Either way, we must talk. This is very important in terms of national security.'

David nodded and took the card, glanced at it and flipped it into his top pocket. 'I'll be in touch once things calm down a bit, Peter.'

The spook smiled as he acknowledged that David had noted his name even as the card disappeared into his pocket.

Once aboard the flight, having fastened his seat belt, David closed his eyes and sank into a deep sleep.

He was shaken awake by someone offering food. His stomach rebelled, but his brain told him that this was the first real food to be on offer for a number of days. He forced himself to clear the plate, and then the pudding, and then the cheese and biscuits. He declined the coffee and closed his eyes once more. This time sleep was harder to come by, and it was punctuated with visions, strange dreams and distant memories.

At Brize, he and Rhys were met by Tom Jenkins from the Army Air Corps. David and Tom had been at Sandhurst together.

‘Hi, David, really sorry to hear about your father.’ He paused in the awkward silence. ‘I’ve got to deliver a Lynx to Lossie, so I can easily drop the two of you off at your place.’ He gave a brief nod in the direction of the tarmac and put out his hand to take his grip.

David shook his head, and they both strode out together, followed by Rhys.

The flight itself was fairly uneventful. David was pretty much taken up with his own thoughts, and Tom had the sense to leave him alone and concentrated on his flying. As they made a quick refuelling stop at Catterick, David took the opportunity to call his mother.

She sounded weary and very sad. He gave her their ETA and told her that Rhys was with him and that he would get Tom to drop them off in the home paddock, so she would need to ask one of the guys to move any livestock there. He told her that he loved her and would be with her as soon as possible. Her voice had a sharp, emotional edge as she asked him to be careful.

They soon crossed the Borders and went north following the A9 to Aviemore, then crossing the Cairngorms with Ben Macdui still with a patch of snow on the crest over their right shoulder. The Old Military Road, built by General Wade to subdue the Highlanders, came into view, and David knew that he was almost home. They followed the contour of the hill and side slipped in a perfect landing.

‘Thanks, Tom, I owe you a pint next time we meet up,’ David called out as he swung himself out and turned to retrieve his grip.

‘Think nothing of it,’ Tom replied. He then waited as David and Rhys moved under the rotor blades before he gently lifted off on his way to RAF Lossiemouth.

Three people were standing just inside the gate. Sarah was wearing her old Barbour with a heavy wool scarf wrapped around her neck with her face half hidden. She looked as though she wanted to run towards him, but her feet were lost in her green wellies which seemed to be superglued to the muddy track. Next to her were Dai and Glenis Philips.

Sarah put out her arms; her eyes filled and then overflowed as she reached David. He held her close, stroking her hair and kissing the top of her head. She seemed so small and vulnerable all of a sudden.

They walked back through the gate and down the hill to the small house that had been David's home since he was a small boy. Rhys and his mum and dad followed them.

Inside the house, the open-plan room with a kitchen at one end and a comfortable sitting/dining area was warm. A wood-burning stove gave off the scent of pinecones as well as keeping the room at a comfortable temperature.

Sarah, ever mindful of her son's insatiable appetite, asked if he was hungry.

David shook his head. 'No, I ate on the plane. Wouldn't mind a cup of tea, though,' he replied. His mind was somewhere else: Marcus Aurelius' *Meditations*... '*It is not death that a man should fear, but he should fear never beginning to live.*'

David's father had planted a seed that had been forever in his head: to grow things, to build things, to care for people and animals, to live a joyful life. *Now, for everything there is a season*, he mused, *a time to play a different part, for the lesson here is that this life is just a fleeting moment in time – a bolt of lightning.*

The funeral would take place on Wednesday – in two days' time. Meanwhile, Mo's body was at the funeral parlour in Elgin. Joshua would take the short service. No eulogies needed, for everyone knew everything about Mo. He would be buried next to Sophie and Benjamin, in that beautiful spot which looked down into the valley. He had often said that he would like to be buried in a biodegradable coffin made of willow withies, and have a Gean planted above him, looking down towards the valley that he had loved and cared for so much.

A whine at the back door and a slight scratching had Sarah on her feet. She opened the door and a small, thin-coated Border collie entered the room. The bitch lifted her head and scented the room. She moved directly to David, sniffed his outstretched hand and suddenly came alive with excited swirling and whining that could not be mistaken for anything but pure joy – her olfactory memory had registered that this absentee member of her family had returned home. The crippling sadness of the past few days had almost been more than she could endure. She had been with Mo when the lightning struck, but she had been bringing in some stragglers some two or three hundred metres away. Floss was still lying beside him when they finally found his body.

'Mary has made a meal for us all, and they all want to see you. They just thought we should have some time together first,' Sarah said in a rush as her eyes filled up once more.

'Are you sure this is what you want to do?' David asked, putting his arm around her again.

She nodded. 'They've been wonderful. I don't know how I might have managed without them.' Sarah picked up her Barbour and scarf and started to prepare to go out.

David stood up. 'I'll need to borrow one of Dad's coats; this is the only stuff I've got with me.' He shrugged himself out of the lightweight camouflage smock.

Sarah went to the back door and took a parka off the hook. Without thinking, she lifted it to her face to acknowledge the man's scent she remembered so well. She passed the coat to her son and picked up a large torch by the door as they quietly let themselves out.

It was pitch dark outside until the torch beam showed them the route along the path. The temperature had plummeted once the early spring sun had dropped over the horizon; the chill winds from the Russian Urals might still rage across this place even in March and April, bringing more snow and a fairy-tale picture to wake up to. He knew why his mother and father had loved this place so much, and he was so pleased that for the majority of his lifetime he had been able to share in it.

The door to the Barn was never locked. As they entered, the heat and light made them pause. Familiar faces merged together as he tried to acknowledge all their greetings.

Joshua was suddenly looking much older. His hair was now perfectly grey, and he had a stoop that belied the tall man he really was. He put his arms around David and then held him out at arm's length. There was nothing old about the infectious smile that seemed to light up his face. 'Good to see ya, David.' His deep, earthy chuckle just bubbled out.

Mary pulled him by the arm to get closer to a large open fire where great logs were lighting up the room with the heat they gave off.

David moved towards Rachel. She seemed smaller than he remembered. Since Benjamin had died, she lived alone. Although, whenever someone needed a room for a visitor, she was always ready to take them in. She was still teaching the youngsters to play the piano and also gave some of the local kids lessons. After they exchanged hugs, she gave him a sad smile that spoke volumes.

Glenis and Dai sat at the table with their son whom they hadn't expected to see for several months. The only ray of light to pierce the gloom that they had felt since the moment Dai carried Mo back in from the hill.

Edith and Terry stood with their oldest son, Alan. 'Good to see you, David.' Terry looked very sad. 'Between your dad and old Benjamin, we were given another chance at life. We owed them so much…' He paused and then self-consciously added quickly, 'Alan and I have started a small building company in the area, but there's always something to attend with here as well. Charlie is off travelling – he's in Australia at the moment – but says he'll settle back here with us when he gets back. And Samantha is now doing postgraduate work at Aberdeen University.' His face lost the initial sadness as he proudly told of his family's achievements.

Zufash was quietly leaning against the piano and slightly in the shadow.

David went across to her and spoke softly in Pashto. 'Salam, Auntie, you are well?'

'Well enough,' she replied equally softly. 'Have you any news of Sayyid?'

David's glance took in everyone within possible hearing distance, but they were all busy helping themselves to tea or coffee. 'I've heard that he is alive and well and still in Afghanistan, but that is all I know at this time. Please don't ask me how I know because I'm not able to tell you.' David dropped his eyes, then he looked up as Mary advanced towards him with a mug of tea.

She smiled a sad smile and said, ‘Esther was disappointed that she couldn’t be here when you arrived, but she’s on nights at the hospital and they are very short staffed on the paediatric ward at the moment, but she’ll catch up with you tomorrow. Come on, everyone, take a seat around the table – food’s ready.’

They all seated themselves around the large communal table that Gavin had made when they’d first started to eat together at the beginning. David found himself between Joshua and Dai.

They all bent their heads as Joshua intoned a short prayer. ‘For good food, good friends and good families, thank God.’ They all joined in to say, ‘Amen.’

Two great pots of some delightful spicy chicken dish had been placed on the table, and soon they were all ladling the steaming mixture onto their plates whilst tearing chunks off the plaited loaves that had been baked earlier that morning.

After the meal, the heat from the fire and the constant questions that needed answers, David had to stifle a yawn as the emotional and physical demands on his body started to take over.

His mother noticed straightaway and said softly, ‘I think we should get you home and in a hot bath and tucked up in bed before you fall asleep.’

He nodded his agreement and started to rise from the table. With a chorus of ‘See you in the morning,’ David slipped on his dad’s parka. Putting an arm around his mother, he steered her towards the door.

The next morning, he woke early, but the bed was too comfortable to leave, so he drifted off again. A warm, slightly scented body lotion, a familiar memory, drifted into his consciousness. He opened his eyes as her lips brushed his. His arms shot up and as he crushed her to his chest, she let out a cry.

'It's good to have you home, but I'm so sorry…' Her eyes filled and a tear slid down her cheek to land on his chest.

He hugged her closely and kissed her hair. He pushed her away slightly to kiss her eyes and forehead. He let out a small sigh as he thought that he shouldn't be this lucky.

She pushed away from him reluctantly and sat on the edge of his bed looking intensely into his face. His sunburnt features had become a little more lined, yet his eyes somehow seemed even brighter than she remembered. Ice blue – they seemed to penetrate her very soul.

'When are you going to make an honest woman of me?' she mocked, tilting her chin and slightly narrowing her eyes. 'I can't save myself for much longer. Don't you know how much I lust after you?' Now she had to give an involuntary smile.

He whisked back the duvet and pulled her towards him.

'Hey! Your mum might come in,' she squealed softly.

David let her sit up. Whilst rearranging the bedclothes, he asked softly, 'How are you?'

'Much better for having you home,' she replied, her eyes beginning to fill up again. 'Oh, David, I'm so sorry…' Her voice trailed off as she fought to control her deep sadness.

David drew her towards him, wrapped his arms around her and kissed her again. 'Esther, my dad was one of the most fulfilled men that I have ever known. He lived a great life, with a loving wife and a scallywag of a son, surrounded by friends who also loved him, in one of the most beautiful places on God's earth – growing things and looking after livestock was his passion, I don't think he ever saw it as work.' He leant back on his pillows. 'You and I both know people who think when someone dies that's it, nothing but dust to dust. You and I, I know, don't believe that. If they are right and we are delusional, we will never know! No one will ever know because there will be nothing to know. But if we are right, we will meet my dad and Sophie and old man Benjamin to enjoy even more love and great adventures in the future.'

Esther looked down, then grabbed him and kissed him hungrily with a passion crying out for the life force that screamed 'I need to live now!'

A quick knock on the door heralded Sarah framed in the doorway with a tray of tea and biscuits. After all the pleasantries, Esther went home to freshen up before going with David into Elgin to buy some clothes for tomorrow's funeral.

Esther had never seen David in a suit, with a collar and tie and black Oxford shoes. He could have been a banker, a hedge fund manager (God help us) or a politician. Handsome and so, so cool. She said a quick prayer, 'Please, Father, let him leave the army.'

It was time to have a natural break; a pub lunch would be good. There was a great wee pub just off the high street, but whilst heading that way they had to pass a small antique shop. Esther stopped as something caught her eye as she passed the tiny shop window.

David paused to see what she was looking at. It was an antique ring submerged in a ring box. He took her arm and guided her through the door.

Inside the shop, the very bohemian owner twittered her own excitement. It was an opal (unlucky, some people say) but very beautiful. 'Try it on,' insisted the owner.

Esther slipped the ring on her third finger. She then tried to remove it but was struggling… She started to suck on her finger.

'Stop,' said David. 'It looks gorgeous; I think it should stay.'

The little bohemian lady was beside herself, a special form of rapture. 'Does this mean…you are engaged?' she stammered.

David answered by wrapping his arms around Esther and kissing her before saying, 'This woman has been the love of my life since forever. It's way past the time that I made an honest woman of her.'

The bohemian lady (they never got to know her name) produced a bottle of fizz. David paid for the ring, and they left the shop on cloud seven.

In the pub – whilst waiting for a steak pie, a chicken supreme, a white wine and a pint of Theakston – reality arrived.

'How do you see this happening?' Esther asked in a very small voice.

'I need to finish my tour in Afghanistan, then a few other bits to sort out…'

Esther stammered, 'I-I didn't get time to tell you. I've signed up to work with MSF in Syria. I leave on the twenty-third.'

'Honey,' began David, looking aghast. 'That place is toxic. I really don't want you to go there.'

'Honey! I really don't want you to be a soldier!' she responded fiercely.

'Wait, wait a minute. You've known since we were teenagers that I would take the Queen's shilling and serve in the army,' David pleaded earnestly.

'Hey, and you know that you are the love of my life, but I cannot come to terms with the fact that you are prepared to…' she said, not wanting to say the words, '…kill people.'

David closed his eyes before replying quietly, 'I didn't know how to deal with this eventuality myself, then, in a blinding flash, one day it became obvious.' David took a deep breath and went on to explain, 'If I were to see a person with a knife about to stab someone and I did nothing but walk on by, I believe that I would be an accessory to that person's injury. If I can wrestle the knife off him, knock him unconscious, even – great! But if he comes back at me and he is prepared to kill me as well as his victim, and I pick up a house brick and hit him across the head and maybe kill him, but in so doing I save a life… I have just described the NATO dictum of minimum force.'

There was another pause to let this verbal picture sink in.

'We value our democratic freedoms, and at this time they are more at risk than ever. I do believe you are right, that just killing people is counterproductive. The Nazis killed twenty million to create a Third Reich, the Russians killed thirty million for a failed ideology, the Chinese killed fifty million more for the same communist dream. I want to live in a world that loves freedom, free to love, free to express opinions on anything, free to earn a living, free to produce children within a family environment, free to say no to corruption, free to live without fear.' David smiled, and then went on, 'In our small community, where all the children were nurtured by our neighbours and friends as well as our parents, we had a privileged existence that prepared us for anything and everything that we might want to do in the future. I would like to believe that this could be a pattern in the future for everyone.'

Esther's face glowed with an intensity that David had never seen before. 'Then perhaps you should consider leaving the army to become a politician. Take your vision and turn dreams into reality, just like your dad did.'

David sighed an almost silent breath. 'My dad told me many times that it was your dad's faith in a god, which my old man barely understood, that gave him the strength to make his dreams come true.'

Esther smiled a smile that turned back the years to the day when David passed out the letters from the would-be participants in the great adventure. 'Then perhaps together we can make it happen. When will we announce a date?'

David smiled as he took joy in the ambush. 'I'd better talk to Joshua. He might not want me as a son-in-law.'

Esther dug him in the ribs. 'I think he loves you even more than I do.'

The food had arrived halfway through this soul-searching conversation, so nothing had been eaten. The waitress came back to their table, looked pointedly at their untouched plates and asked, 'Everything all right?'

They smiled back. Esther spoke for both of them when she said, 'Everything is just perfect.'

David had arranged to see Joshua later that evening so that he and his mother could discuss the final arrangements for the funeral due on the following day. It was to be a simple affair. Dai had prepared the ground, and the withy coffin would be carried by Terry, Dai and Rhys together with David and Joshua. It would be a very brief service; Sarah didn't want anything long and drawn out. She was sure Mo wouldn't want that either.

Sarah was beginning to feel very emotional. She had been able to hold everything together so far. Ever since the tragic event, she had been able to centre her thoughts on having her son beside her to give support. The finality of what was now being discussed was just too much to bear. She excused herself and went into Mary's kitchen to see if she could do something useful.

Joshua's infectious chuckle had died, his mouth was turned down, his eyes had dulled. He looked up at David and wondered at the resilience of this young man in the prime of life and revelled in all its wonder. As David began to speak the words he had so carefully rehearsed, it gradually dawned on Joshua where his strength was coming from: love conquers all. *Then through a mirror, darkly...* The words resonated through his brain.

'With your permission, I would like to marry your daughter.'

No words could reach his lips. His eyes, once again, lit up and his lips parted in that expansive grin that only closed to let him chortle. 'You would like me to give you permission to marry the apple of my eye, my Esther? The two of you have been in my prayers for I can't tell you how long. Why has it taken so long? When is this to happen? Better not be too long, I ain't getting any younger, and I want grandchildren whilst I'm still young enough to enjoy 'em. Have you told your mother yet?'

David hadn't expected quite such an endorsement because he surmised that his military career was not the perfect prospect for Esther. 'Well, no, I thought I should speak with you first.'

'I trust you have asked Esther?' Joshua's mind was whirling.

'Yes, of course,' David replied. 'We will get married when I return from Afghanistan. Meantime, she tells me that she has signed up with Médecins Sans Frontières for a year and is set on going to Syria.'

'I have spoken to her about this, but I couldn't persuade her.' Joshua's face had regained the former sadness. 'Perhaps you may have more success, but I sort of doubt it. I will pray that the good Lord will keep you both safe till you come home for your wedding. Save this good news for your mother. Tell her tomorrow straight after the funeral.' Joshua confirmed David's own thoughts.

No one had seen Joshua in his Anglican finery before. The white surplus over the black gown with the white stole around his neck. His arm that reached into the hearse and edged the withy coffin to the edge. David picked up the signal and gripped the handle, and together they moved it towards the back of the vehicle. Dai and Rhys then grasped their handles in a well-orchestrated movement, leaving room for Terry and the space to lift their friend into eternal space.

The wail of a pre-warm-up bagpipe focused all attention as a young lad, one of Sarah's pupils, played the lament – 'Flowers of the Forest'. The young piper took his place at the head of the cortège and led the bearers up the hill towards the burial ground. The rest of the party, including a number of people from the village, moved behind them.

At the graveside, the withy coffin was slowly lowered. Once the young piper ceased playing, the coffin party stepped back from the grave. Joshua collected his Bible from his wife and moved back to the graveside. It had started to rain that soft, very familiar Highland rain that will soak you in no time at all, but you just don't notice. This was not the time for holy words. No one was listening to anything but their own thoughts.

Mo's world was the place he built with his friends, the trees and hedges he planted, the animals he cared for, the wife and son he loved, the peace that he had learnt to accept without needing anything more.

Joshua finished with a short prayer. 'Lord, I thank you for the life of Mo. And I pray that through faith in Jesus Christ, each of us may worship you in his death. May we rejoice in your goodness and power, and in your plans, which are beyond our ability to understand this side of heaven. May each one here, through faith in the person and work of Jesus Christ, experience the joy of being delivered from the fear of death. Amen.'

The young piper filled his bag and commenced 'Amazing Grace' and led the small band of mourners down the hill. Sarah stood at the edge of the grave flanked by Esther and David. They each took an arm and led her back down the hill.

The soft rain continued, but then the sun slid out from behind a dark grey cloud when they reached the bottom of the hill. As David looked back over his shoulder, he saw a bright rainbow linking his father's resting place with the clachan of wee houses. A distant memory struggled to surface, but he could not capture it; yet it didn't matter because an overwhelming feeling of peace seemed to surround him.

David and Esther walked Sarah to the door of her cottage.

'Will you come in for a cup of tea?' Sarah asked Esther.

As David opened the door, Esther nodded her acceptance. 'Yes, that would be good,' she replied.

'David, would you put a couple of logs on the stove? Esther, get your wet things off; they'll soon dry off in here. I'll make us some tea.' Sarah slipped into the kitchen, removed her coat and scarf and leant back against the kitchen sink. She felt like she had suddenly lost all the power in her legs. She paused and took a couple of deep breaths, after which the dizziness gradually subsided and her eyes cleared.

She grabbed the kettle from the stove and quickly filled it, then with one sweep of her hand grasped a tea tray from the dresser and added a teapot and two cups and saucers. The third saucer was laid, and the cup was about to join it when it just slipped between her fingers. She watched as it described a neat parabola and then, in what seemed like slow motion, hit the stone floor and smash into a thousand pieces. She was still staring at the floor when Esther came through the door.

Taking in everything that had happened, Esther slipped an arm around Sarah and gently moved her around the mess on the floor and back through the door where David took his mother to the chair by the stove.

This last incident was the final straw, yet she still tried to smother the emotion that was fighting to come out. It was a heart-wrenching cry that became a sob, which even then she tried to subdue, but it had to be released. Her shoulders rose and fell as the pain of her loss finally became too much to bear.

David was on his knees with his arms around her; his shirt was wet with her tears along with his own.

Esther, having cleaned up the mess, made the tea and quietly brought it to the small table beside them and started to fill the cups from the teapot.

Sarah reached into her pocket for a tissue and dabbed at her eyes before sniffing and then vigorously blowing her nose. As Esther handed her a cup of tea, Sarah thanked her with a sad smile.

David wiped his eyes with the back of his hand. Looking intently at his mother, he launched into the short statement that he hoped might cheer her up: 'Mum, Esther and I are going to get married when I get back from Afghanistan.'

Sarah smiled and reached out to place her hand on Esther's arm. Looking into her face, she murmured, 'I always thought you might; I always hoped that you would. I can't tell you how happy this makes me feel at this moment. Will you get married here? Will you live here?'

David put up his hand to stop further questions. 'We haven't begun to start working out the detail yet. I've got to finish my present tour, and Esther is going to Syria to use her medical expertise for the children. All we know now is that we love each other and want to spend the rest of our lives together, and the rest of the details we will work out as we go along.' He looked at Esther and raised his eyebrows. Esther smiled back in confirmation.

Sarah started to look more like her usual self and said, 'I've made a decision as well. I'm not going to live here on my own. I've been working with Zufash at the refuge and teaching some of the children. Well, she has kindly offered to share her house. There are people coming and going all the time and all sorts of dramas to sort out, so I won't have time to feel sorry for myself. It will also mean, if you two decide you want to come back at any time, that you will have your own home here.'

David looked relieved and, determined to lighten still further the improved atmosphere in the room, asked, 'I think we should have a celebratory drink. Do you have any booze in the house, Mum?'

'Your dad usually kept a bottle of Macallans in the sideboard, and there is wine in the kitchen.' She left her chair to fetch some glasses and show David where the wine was stored.

David slipped his arm around Esther. She turned towards him and kissed him softly on the lips. They both then followed Sarah into the kitchen.

When they had settled down with their drinks around the stove, Sarah asked the question she didn't want to ask, 'When have you got to go back, David?'

'I can stay till the weekend, but I have some business that I have to attend to in London on Monday before I return to Afghanistan on the next flight out of Brize,' David replied with a long look at Esther.

She replied, 'I finish at Aberdeen at the end of the week and leave two days later for Geneva, and then on to Syria, but I haven't got any firm dates yet. It's all a bit chaotic there at the moment.'

There was a silent moment as each absorbed the information and sipped reflectively on their drinks.

Sarah was once again the schoolmistress in charge. 'I can easily move in with Zufash tomorrow, and you two could have the house for your last few days before being separated.'

Esther's self-conscious laugh heralded a quiet, almost whispered response. 'I think that I have loved your son since I first clapped eyes on him when I was about ten years of age. As I grew more mature, my love for him has grown and grown. I knew that the day would come when we would be able to share that love together, fully. All that time, I have kept myself for him and only him. I can wait a bit longer. I want our marriage to be extra special. I would like it to be here. I want the full wedding service outdoors, or in a marquee if the Scottish weather won't allow. I want our union to be blessed by God and witnessed by all our friends and family. Then lots of feasting, music and dancing before David carries me over that threshold,' she said, nodding towards the door. 'Don't want much, do I?' Her eyes had become intense and her face lit up as though some inner light had been turned on as she spoke.

The simple intensity of her statement left Sarah speechless for a moment as she remembered how her wedding had come about. She suddenly had the clearest vision of Mo's conversation with her father at that time. She smiled. 'Sounds beautiful. I just wish it was tomorrow!' She then got up out of her chair and said, 'David, pour us all a refill. I've got something of your father's that I want to give you.'

With that, she disappeared into her bedroom only to return with a box file that was crammed with exercise books.

She passed the file to David. 'Years ago, Joshua suggested that Mo should write the story of how our community came into being and how it progressed. He didn't want to do it at first, but Joshua kept encouraging him. Over the years it became really important to him, and he spent much of his spare time at that desk over there scribbling in those notebooks. I think it was almost as though it became a sort of daily meditation culminating in a few words each day. Anyway, I think you should have it.' She smiled and said, 'On that note, I think I will turn in. It has been a day that I was dreading, and yet you two have turned it into something really very special. I only wish your dad could have been here to share in it.'

'He was, Mum,' David said softly as he kissed his mother goodnight. Esther did the same.

As Sarah closed the bedroom door, they both sat either side of the stove and finished their drinks.

The next couple of days drifted past in a haze of reflections. The weather didn't get any better, but it didn't matter. David and Esther walked the paths of their youth, remembering all the good times and conveniently blanking out the episodes they no longer wished to return to.

They had both toughened up by Sunday morning when it had been decided that Esther would drive David to Aberdeen Airport. He gave his mum a hug, shrugged himself into the field jacket he had bought in Elgin the day before and hefted his holdall with the few belongings he had brought with him, plus the box file crammed with notebooks. He then came back to kiss her once more before turning to let himself out through the front door.

As he arrived at Esther's, the door opened, and Joshua and Mary walked out followed by their daughter.

Mary rushed up to David, hugged him and kissed his cheek. 'Be careful, look after yourself, and come back to us safe and sound.' She released him so that Joshua, who was impatiently hovering beside her, could gather him in a great bear hug.

'May God go with you, my son.'

Meanwhile, Esther had driven her little Fiat from the car park and leant across to open the passenger door. 'Come on, David, I don't want us rushing at the last minute.'

David slid into the passenger seat and smiled at her parents. 'I only asked her to marry me a couple of days ago, and she's bossing me around already!'

Esther gave her mum and dad a wave and moved off up the track towards the main road.

Aberdeen Airport had been built during the heady days of North Sea oil exploration, and that industry still provided the vital pulse of this north-east city. Once it had been granite, then fish. Now the technology necessary to take fossil fuels from the deep ocean bed had made the exponents of this industry world leaders, and this airport transported them to the furthest corners of the planet to deliver their expertise, together with their work ethic and courage.

Rhys had left via this airport three days ago and was even now being picked up and taken back to their lines at Camp Bastion.

David, having nothing to check in, had a coffee with Esther. Then, not wanting to precipitate an emotional farewell, he took her hand and said huskily, 'Sweetheart, I promise you that I will do everything to make sure that I come back to you soonest. I need you to promise me that you will not put yourself in any more danger than is necessary.' Even as he said it, he knew it was a stupid statement. They would both have to do what they both had to do.

There was a brief kiss, then he turned and walked away. She did the same. Fifty paces later, he turned at the precise moment she did. He wiped a tear with the back of his hand. She unashamedly felt the tears gently course down her beautiful face. She sniffed, then waved a final farewell. He waved back and headed for security.

Having found his seat, he pulled out his dad's file from his holdall before stowing it in the locker above. He settled in his seat, opened the file and started to sort through the exercise books. They seemed to be placed in date order with the first one entitled 'Introduction' at the bottom of the box.

He had barely begun to read when the stewardess announced the litany of safety instructions. For a man who regularly jumped out of perfectly serviceable aircraft, it seemed a bit bizarre. However, it seemed rude not to pay attention.

The take-off was routine, and soon the plane had reached its cruising altitude and was heading south. David returned to the neat script of his father's handwritten text and started to read.

Just under an hour later, the plane started its descent into Heathrow. David put the book back into the box file on his lap, relaxed back into his seat and closed his eyes.

There wasn't really time on the Heathrow Express to get the books out and continue reading before arriving at Paddington. On arrival, he decided that he didn't want to finish his journey by tube so grabbed a taxi.

The special forces club is tucked away in a quiet street with nothing on the outside to publish its identity. Every visitor is seen before they even press the doorbell. Once inside, there is the soft hush of a private members' club as his details are recorded and booking confirmed.

On his way up the stairs to the bar, he glanced at the photographs of the 'old and bold' heroes of the past from the SOE (Special Operations Executive), the SAS and the SBS (Special Boat Service, the Royal Marine equivalent of the SAS). Men and women who had given so much in order that the children of today should be able to live without fear.

It being a Sunday, the bar was almost empty. He ordered a large Macallan, poured a little water, and then decided to take it up to his room.

The room was comfortable without being ostentatious. David pulled out the box file once more and placed it on his bedside table, undid his boots and heeled them off. Then taking a pull from his glass, he propped up his pillows and sank back with the first notebook and started to read again, almost as though the full impact of his father's words had not really sunk in at the first read on the flight down.

As he read, sharp images came to life as his father's words told of their great adventure. Often, he paused to read and then reread a paragraph. Time and space had no meaning as each book led him, without hesitation, to the next…

Chapter 2

Introduction by Morrice Stevenson

I was never very good with words. I always knew what I wanted to say but getting those ideas over my lips seemed to give me the greatest difficulty. Writing was even more of a task. At school, a teacher once wrote on my school report: *I suspect that more goes on this boy's head than I can fathom... He must learn to express himself better*. So, when Joshua suggested that I write this chronicle, me of all people, I thought he must be joking. There seemed to be so many others of our group that could have done it better. Joshua smiled, and growled gently that I should read Exodus 3:10–12. I did, but I didn't tell anyone, not even Sarah.

It was the day I took Moss up the hill to see if I could find the ewe and her twin lambs that I had somehow missed when I moved the others, just before the blizzard struck. Suddenly, I had no doubts at all – I knew that I must now make a start.

Our story is about living, not in the past or in the future, but now. Most of the stories that I've ever read usually contain extraordinary happenings; they have a beginning, a middle and an end. Where our story began, I can only surmise. I can only tell you that which I know. Those of us who are still here are living the middle bit, and the end is yet to come. Our story deals with a dream, a vision, and the group of people who were, and are, determined to turn that dream into a reality – and I suppose that, in itself, is extraordinary.

Before I tie myself up in knots, I had better make that start, then you can judge for yourself. Please don't be put off by my style, or lack of it. Simply open your hearts and minds and try to become part of our great adventure. For the real value of a good story, it seems to me, is not that you just read it, you must be part of it:

Exodus 3:11-12.
But Moses said to God, 'I am nobody.
How can I go to the king and bring the
Israelites out of Egypt?'
God answered, 'I will be with you, and
when you bring the people out of Egypt,
you will worship me on this mountain.
That will be the proof that I have sent you.'

Chapter 3

A Glimpse of Things to Come

A kamikaze rabbit skittered out across the road inches from our front wheels. I braked and automatically changed down. The rabbit froze as the engine squealed, and then we passed over the top of him. I looked desperately in my rear-view mirror to see him dive into a patch of bracken, obviously unharmed. I let out the breath that I had clamped between my teeth.

Sarah looked over her shoulder and asked for confirmation, 'Did you miss him?'

'Yes,' I replied, smiling. 'He's on his way back to *Watership Down*.'

David, sitting in the backseat, had missed the drama but instead noticed something else. 'Dad, I can smell burning!'

The old VW camper van had served us well, but this holiday in the Highlands of Scotland had taxed it almost beyond endurance. It had been overheating since we had set out that morning. This was the last day of our holiday, but we had a six-hundred-mile journey back to London to make tomorrow. Now, on this lonely moorland road, I'd asked too much of it when I had changed down to avoid the rabbit. It managed to climb the hill in second gear, and I let it coast down the steep hill to a small lay-by that I could see ahead. I stopped and turned off the engine. There was a second or two when it seemed as though the engine didn't want to stop; it coughed twice and left us in silence.

'I think we'd better let it cool down for a bit,' I said.

Sarah got out and stretched. As she pushed her arms up to the heavens, a soft breeze took her hair and wafted it about her face. She shook her head and the soft curls were swept back. Her tanned face seemed more relaxed than I had seen her look for ages – the last two weeks had been special for all of us.

It had been good to be away from the city. I wondered briefly what the weather had been like in London whilst we had been away. We had purposely not bought a newspaper or listened to the news. I consciously stopped myself from thinking about the gardens that I look after... *Dad can manage for a couple of weeks*, I told myself.

David undid his safety belt and opened his door; his thoughts were where they always were at this time of day, regardless of location or scenery. 'I'm starving,' he said to no one in particular but looking at his mother.

Sarah opened the other door and started to unpack some food and a flask which she put into a basket. 'Will you grab that rug from the back, love?' she asked David.

I locked the doors and gave the old van a fond tap on the roof as if to say get well soon, and then I followed Sarah and David as they strolled down the hill.

At the bottom, a path went off to the left beside a burn that gurgled its way over smooth slabs between two great rocky outcrops. An alder tree, clinging tenaciously to the bank, forced us to step carefully over a couple of the boulders. As we regained the path, I looked up to see the most beautiful panorama I had ever seen. A glen opened up either side of the burn to rolling hills covered in silver birches with rowans interspersed amongst them.

On the edge of this wooded area was a group of three or four geans, resplendent in a mass of foliage that was already beginning to turn red, an early harbinger of the autumn that was to come. The horizon was framed by the Cairngorm Mountains, their lofty tops acting as a dramatic barrier to a drift of storm clouds that were gathering. Whilst here, the sky was clear and the bluest blue you could imagine, and the sun was bright. There was just the hint of a breeze to stir the long grasses.

Sarah helped David to spread out the rug, and then she started to unpack the basket. David grabbed a roll and wandered off down to the burn to explore. I sat down with Sarah as she poured me a cup of coffee from the flask. As David moved down the bank of the burn, a couple of quite large birds flew up and spiralled into the sky. Their warbling cry had a plaintive note as if they were not sure about having their privacy disturbed.

Sarah had a faraway look in her eye, and I knew she was wishing that she had brought her sketch pad with her when we left the van. She had done a lot of sketching this holiday, so I also knew that when we got home, I would see some of those sketches come to life as she reproduced them into large, extravagant canvases. She liked to work with a palette knife using bold strokes layering on the paint and then sometimes scraping it off, creating depth and vibrancy until she would finally step back and say, 'That'll do.' Then, and only then, would I be allowed to look at it.

I had noticed a molehill, so I leant over to take a handful of the soil. I let it sift through my fingers. *It has a rich, loamy texture – you could grow anything with this*, I thought.

Sarah read my mind. 'Are you planning what you'd like to plant?' she teased.

I'm a gardener, and I know that anyone can grow anything – it's all down to the soil. Get that right, and everything happens after that – well, almost.

'This place has been cultivated at some time,' I told her. I answered her raised eyebrow, 'Look at the difference in the colour of the vegetation between here and further up the hill… It's been drained… And look—' I pointed to where you could just make out what was left of a dry-stone wall '—at some time it's been enclosed.' I stood up. 'Come on, let's have a look round.'

By this time, David had moved in amongst the trees and was out of sight. After I helped Sarah to her feet, we left the picnic where it was and followed the path that David had taken. As we moved into the trees, we could see David entering a dilapidated cottage. By the time we arrived at the doorway, he looked out through a broken window on one side of the house and thrust a bundle of postcards at us.

Sarah took them and started to thumb through the pile. 'Hey, look at this.' She spread them out in a fan so I could see them all in a glance.

I looked down and noticed that they each had a black border.

Sarah had turned one of them over and was reading it. 'The postmark on this is 1915… It's a condolences card… I can't read the writing… I think it must be something to do with the First World War.' She turned to look in the window and called out to David, 'Be careful what you are doing in there. We've no right to be here, you know, let alone poking around in someone else's property.'

David's face showed briefly at the window. 'Come'n and see… It's all right. It stinks of animals; I think something has been living in here.'

Sarah and I moved reluctantly towards the door. It didn't seem right somehow. Even if the cottage was a wreck, it must belong to someone.

Inside the hall, the rank smell of sheep made Sarah wrinkle her nose. The floor was wall-to-wall sheep droppings; livestock had obviously found shelter here. As our eyes grew accustomed to the gloom, we could make out an open grate with a cast-iron arm that had been designed to hang a pot from.

'David, where are you?' Sarah called softly.

'I'm here,' his voice replied from a room nearby.

We moved into the room where his voice had come from. With a broad beam of sunlight angling through the window, we could see David rummaging through a drawer in a broken cabinet.

'What do you think you're doing?' Sarah demanded. 'This is someone's property…'

David had his baseball cap on back to front, making him look like an American kid in a Walt Disney movie. He held up a bunch of red, blue and green rosettes. 'Look,' he said, 'somebody won a first.'

We looked on with a certain sense of awe. I remembered the first time I won a prize at the local show for some parsnips. The applause was the first I'd ever received for anything; it set me on a path that still gives me so much pleasure. Years ago, the owner of this house had felt that same feeling as the judge handed over this scrap of silk and they shook hands.

'Can I keep them?' David asked.

'No, put them back, they're not yours.' Sarah's voice had that schoolmistress tone that she didn't often use outside of school.

David knew there was no room for discussion.

'It's chilly in here; let's go back outside,' she said and moved towards the door.

David followed on whilst I paused for a last look around. Considering the cottage had no glass in the windows and you could see daylight through some cracks in the roof, it was amazing how dry most of the place was. The walls, which must have been more than two-foot-thick, were built of irregular pieces of granite that had been wrestled into place by raw manpower.

Outside in the sun, Sarah was sitting on a dry-stone wall that had once contained a kitchen garden. 'It's a beautiful spot,' she said. 'I wonder why no one lives here.'

David had moved on further along the burn. He turned and called out, 'There's more houses here.'

Sarah and I followed the line of the wall and then cut down to the burn which had turned another bend, and sure enough, straddled either side of the burn, we could see four or five more cottages.

We had only meant to have a short break for lunch, but by the time we had investigated, what turned out to be six cottages and two barns, two and a half hours had passed. The dark clouds that we had seen over the Cairngorms were now directly overhead, and it looked as though it wouldn't be long before the heavens would open. With the sun hidden, the freshening wind was chill. We got back to our picnic spot, gathered up our things and started to make our way back the way we had come.

At the alder tree, I turned to take a last look at the glen. Rain was streaming in hatched lines across the tops of the hills above the cottages hidden amongst the trees. A break in the clouds caused great fingers of light to flood down. As they cut through the rain squall, a brilliant rainbow bridged the glen, which finished, or so it seemed, in the trees by the first cottage.

'Look at that,' I called out. Sarah and David both turned. I watched their faces light up. It was as though the rainbow was somehow reflecting on their faces. I caught up alongside and put my arms about them. 'If you painted that like it is,' I said to Sarah, 'people just wouldn't believe it.'

'It's like a bridge,' said David. Which was a strange thing for him to say, but I sort of knew what he meant.

Back at the camper van we packed everything away, then I held my breath and turned the ignition key. It started straight away, so we set off.

The village of Tomintoul was only six miles away, but our vehicle was hissing its disapproval by the time we got to the village square.

The mechanic was kindness itself. He dropped what he was doing to help us get back on the road. There was no way the old camper van would make it back to London without a water pump transplant. Luckily, the mechanic had one in the inner depths of an old Nissan hut that was both his store and repair bay.

Whilst I stayed at the garage to hand tools to the mechanic and generally make myself useful, Sarah and David went off to explore the village and buy some provisions for our journey home.

By the time they got back, Geordie (I had discovered his name) had almost finished the job.

'I was asking about that place we went to this afternoon,' Sarah said. 'I asked the woman in the grocers… She said that all the families left there in the 1920s after a third dreadful winter in a row. They were blasted out by the weather… It doesn't seem possible, does it, when you see it on a day like today?'

Geordie looked up from tightening the last nut and wiped his hands on some cotton waste. 'An' where was this, then?' he asked with a natural curiosity.

I started to try and explain, but he looked puzzled.

He dug in the top pocket of his overalls and pulled out a small receipt book. Tearing off a page, he turned it over. Then with the stub of a pencil that was drawn out of thin air, he started to draw the road where it descended to the burn that we had followed.

After he offered me the stub, I drew the glen as best I could from memory.

'Oh yes,' he murmured I use't to fish fir brownies there when I was a lad… The last families flitted oot of th're afore I was born. They lost a lot of their menfowk in the Great War… An' after the Great War, bad hairsts and worse winters drove them oot. Ma faither's oldest brither used to have th' grazings afore he retired. I hear th' estate's got the place up fir sale noo.' He finished wiping his hands and nodded at the engine. 'That should do it.'

Later, parked beside Loch Morlich, a few miles off the A9, we settled down to spend the last night of our holidays before setting off on our return journey to London.

The rain had finally caught up with us, and the constant drumming on the roof was keeping me awake. Sarah had fallen asleep almost as soon as her head hit the pillow. I pulled myself up onto my elbow and looked across at David, who was mumbling something in his sleep,

'Champion…first.' He had a wonderful smile on his face, and I smiled with him.

It had been a very special day. I closed my eyes and saw, once again, the glen with the rainbow; I knew that I would never forget this place. As I drifted off, the last thing I remember was hearing David's voice again saying, 'Thank you.' Who or what he was thanking, I never did find out.

Chapter 4

The Homecoming

Perhaps it should always rain on the last day of a holiday. We'd all had a great time but now it was time to go home. The persistent drizzle, that had kept me awake for part of the night, had increased to a steady downpour, driven by fierce gusts that buffeted the side of the camper van, which were sometimes strong enough to move us, crab style, across the road.

I needed to concentrate on my driving. Sarah was quiet, wrapped up in her thoughts, whilst David had his nose in a comic. Three and a half hours later, the Cairngorms were left far behind us as we skirted around Glasgow. Mean-looking tower blocks reared out of the driving rain as we bypassed the city. They were similar to the post-war community disasters that typified so much of the area where we lived.

I had never visited Glasgow, knowing it only from several drama series that I had watched on TV. It had a reputation for gangs and hard men, drinking and drugs – what was new? Most British cities seemed to be suffering from a similar sort of desperate hopelessness. Even as I thought about it, I knew I was exaggerating. I pictured the leafy private parks that I tended surrounded by gracious Georgian houses – elegance from a bygone age. *Nevertheless*, I reflected, *you still wouldn't let your kids play on their own – not even there. It was different when I was a boy. I must stop thinking like that; it's a sure sign of growing old*, I thought to myself. *Still, it was true*, I reluctantly admitted to myself.

Sarah had put the radio on, and we were listening to the news. David had finished reading and was fidgeting; it must be that time again. After the exit for Gretna Green was signed, it seemed about time to pull over to feed the lad and stretch our legs.

Back on the road, Sarah and I were discussing how couples used to elope to Gretna in order to get married.

'What does elope mean?' queried David. He had seen the sign in the café with the picture of the old anvil where countless young hopefuls had exchanged vows.

Sarah gave me a look with a raised eyebrow and started to explain how young couples whose parents did not want them to marry sometimes took off to the borders of Scotland, where the law was different, in order to get married without their parents' approval.

'Lots of my friends' mothers and fathers aren't even married,' David announced. 'Wayne's had about three dads,' he said with a hesitancy that usually signalled that he didn't really understand how something could be.

Wayne lived down the street. He was a bit of a 'tearaway' and went to the same school as David. He had two little sisters, and his mother had just produced a baby boy. Wayne's third dad had recently been taken into custody for assault, and it was generally rumoured in the street that he would get six years, this time.

'Why did you and Dad get married?' he asked with genuine concern in his voice, as though perhaps we had done something wrong.

'Because we loved each other, and we wanted to live together… and because we wanted to have you.' It came out in a bit of a rush as though Sarah could foresee how easy it would be to get into areas she wasn't ready for at this time.

For my part, I knew that I loved her from the first time I laid eyes upon her. We had been going out together for nearly two years whilst she had been at college. We thought we'd been careful... So when she blurted, tearfully, that she was almost two months pregnant, it was a shock.

It wasn't a huge problem: whilst unspoken, we had both sort of expected that one day we would marry. It would still be possible for her to finish her studies before the baby was due – teaching would just have to wait a little longer! It was worse for her. Her mum had always wanted her to have a proper wedding: in church, and in white. I can still recall their faces that Sunday evening after tea when we had to break the news to them. It was disbelief, hurt, betrayal.

George, her father, was the first to speak. 'Well, I suppose she's not the first girl to get herself knocked up, an' I doubt she'll be the last.' He moved to the fireplace and leant over to knock his pipe out in the grate. His head was down so I couldn't see his face, but I imagined that he was wielding a hammer to the head of the idiot who had shattered his wife's dream and despoiled his only child.

Under the circumstances, they came around quite quickly. Within no time at all, a date had been set at the local registry office and invitations were sent out to family and close friends. There was just a small reception at Sarah's house. For our honeymoon, we spent a rainy week in Cornwall staying at a small bed and breakfast. Sarah was sick for most of the time, so it wasn't very romantic.

Notwithstanding our inauspicious start, we've had a good marriage. There's been disagreements from time to time, but neither of us sulk or throw tantrums. The arrival of David set a seal on our relationship. We were both in a state of excitement for the weeks leading up to his birth. Sarah had read everything on the subject, and she would read things out to me and get me to help with her exercises. I just loved the way she looked: she seemed like a glorious flower in full bloom. In the evenings, in front of the fire, I would massage her back, at the base of her spine, whilst kissing her shoulders, and she would lean her head back and rest it on my chest.

When the big day came, it all seemed to go like clockwork. There were no last-minute problems and even the van, which was known to be difficult at times, started first go, so we got to the hospital in plenty of time.

Four and a bit hours later, I let go of her hand to take my swaddled son in my arms. I remember looking down at him, then across to her… I was overwhelmed by all that had happened; I was so proud of them both – but it was much more than that.

It is comparatively recently that I realised the English language is very deficient in its ability to describe love. I love the park first thing of a summer's morning when the dew is thick on the ground and the perfume from the blossom fills the air as the day starts to warm the ground. I love winters' nights around a fire when we all sit together and I pore through catalogues deciding on what seeds to purchase for the spring planting. But this love has nothing to do with the deep emotion I felt that evening in the maternity ward. Or, as I looked away from the road to see her face as she answered David, that day in the van on our way back from our holiday in Scotland. I realised that I loved her more than I have the powers to describe.

Our friends, I suspect, thought that we were an odd couple. Sarah is a very attractive woman. She is about the same height as me – I'm five foot eight in my socks. She usually wears flat shoes when she is at school or out and about with me, but she seems to tower above me when she puts on her heels. She has sensitive features, framed by hair that hairdressers despair of. It is too fine to be easily manageable, yet she has a way of coaxing it into a style that softens her face and draws attention to her eyes – which are an unusual shade of grey that changes in certain lights to a deep shade of green. Although she has always been slim, she has, in recent years, developed the sort of figure that girls work hard for by 'working out' three times a week. Sarah doesn't 'work out'; she is the type who can eat what she likes without putting on an ounce. Always clever at school, she sailed through both her O and A levels to get a place at teacher training college to obtain her B.Ed. Whilst there, she needed to take a practical subject so chose to do art… From the moment I saw her first real painting, I wanted her to do nothing else. She also likes to read and has a very wide range of musical appreciation.

By comparison, and not to denigrate myself too much, I'm about as stringy as a runner bean, with a mop of hair that is going prematurely grey and blue eyes in a fairly weather-beaten face. I read about things that interest me, but you could hardly call me well read. I particularly like traditional jazz. I think some of our friends used to wonder what this gorgeous, clever girl was doing with a gardening gink like me.

I've never liked motorway driving, but this journey seemed to be going on forever. The M6 passed us on the final stage to London down the M1. Both Sarah and David had dozed off. The traffic was getting more congested as we drew closer to the great metropolis.

The rain that hadn't given up all day had finally eased off. I didn't realise this at first, but the clunking of the wipers on the dry windscreen gradually made me aware that I had no more need for them.

The relative quiet, now that the in-car metronome no longer beat time to my thoughts, left something of a void. I considered switching on the radio but decided that I preferred the quiet of my own thoughts. I started thinking about home and all the things that I must do in the coming week. *I'll give Dad a call as soon as we get back, if it's not too late*, I thought as I flashed a glance at my watch and realised that it was already half past nine. *There must still be at least an hour to go before we are home – he'll be in bed by then. I'll have to call first thing in the morning.*

Familiar streets gave me a strange feeling of both elation and sadness. It is always good to get home from a long journey, but these drab, wet streets looked particularly bleak against the recent memories of the Highlands of Scotland where those vast panoramas seemed so fresh and clean… They somehow seemed vibrant and alive whereas these streets seemed to have died – their life knocked out of them.

The wail of a police siren caused me to look anxiously in my rear-view mirror. I steered slightly closer to the kerb as the police car wailed itself to the end of the street and bucketed around the corner. There was still some life in these streets yet. A rubber man then weaved across the road waving a can of Special Brew at me in an angry gesture for some imagined wrong that he believed I had been responsible for.

As we turned into Benson Street, I was pleased to find that my usual parking place was still available, right outside the flat. As I pulled up, and even before I could turn off the engine, Sarah opened her eyes and smiled.

'We're home,' she voiced the obvious. 'I must have been asleep for ages… I don't know how you do it.' She was turning in her seat to give David his jacket which had been slung across her knees. 'Come on, wakey, wakey, David – we're home.'

David came sort of awake with a huge yawn; his eyes had a sort of sleepy haze over them as if they were refusing to focus.

'Come on, luv, let's get you into your bed – there'll be no fussing tonight.' She stepped out of the van and helped David on with his jacket whilst I wrestled with the back door to pull out our bags.

'We'd better get this lot inside or there won't be anything left by the morning – come on, both of you, lend a hand.'

The large Victorian villa, in which we occupied the ground-floor flat, had been our home for the past five years. It looked a bit austere from the front, but the rooms were large and airy, and we also had a small walled garden at the rear. The three of us lugged our luggage up the narrow pathway to the front door, and I handed the keys to Sarah before returning to the van to collect the rest of our belongings from the pavement where I'd left them.

'Mo…'

I turned as Sarah called out my name softly. 'What's the matter?' I asked.

She didn't answer but motioned me closer. As I moved back towards her, she hissed, 'The door has been forced!'

I looked at the door – there was plenty of light from the streetlights outside to show the split door frame where someone had jemmied off the Chubb lock. I gave the door a gentle push and as it opened fully, a folded empty fag packet fell on the step. I went to go inside, but Sarah grabbed my arm.

'Don't!' she said. 'They might still be in there.'

I nodded down to the step and the folded cigarette packet. 'They jammed that in the door when they left,' I hissed and pushed past her into the hall.

All houses have a distinctive smell. I've always been conscious of it since I was a small boy. Some homes have a warm, inviting smell, yet others have been known to make me wrinkle my nose. Whenever I return home, I always have that fleeting moment of pleasure as I let myself in and identify that distinctive, and unique, scent of us. Difficult to describe, it's a gentle mustiness of polish and earthy boots in the hall, a sharper hint of acetone from the studio where Sarah paints, and a home-baking smell that comes from her constant battle to keep abreast of our son's appetite.

As I entered the darkened hall, I knew I wasn't at home. The light switch was still where it should have been, but my nostrils were assailed by the nauseous stench of excreta and vomit. Worse was to come as I clicked the switch and the hall was illuminated. For a full second we didn't move as we viewed the devastation. Four different colours of spray paint had been used from the skirting boards to the ceiling. Framed pictures had been smashed in situ and hung tortured against the wall. And someone had 'thrown up' on the hall carpet!

Sarah was the first to move. She pushed past me and moved swiftly down the hall towards the living room and the studio. I followed her. The scene represented a *Robocop* movie when he moves into the land of the weirdoes. Everything that could be lifted and sold had been lifted. Everything else was smashed. Then there was the artwork: at least one of them was quite gifted – great flowing, well-formed letters showing flair and assurance – until you read the words. What minds, what imaginations, what filth concocted this assault of the senses? But words were not enough – they had dropped their trousers and defecated in some sort of ritual to tell us that this was no longer our territory.

When they'd smashed up the kitchen, they had found a couple of bottles of red wine and a few cans of beer in the fridge. They had eaten anything that was vaguely edible in the cupboard and washed it down with the beer and wine – that which they hadn't squirted on the ceiling and walls. They only borrowed the food and drink; most of it had been left for us as a welcome on the mat.

I was between the living room and kitchen when I heard the sobbing. Until then, this wasn't happening to me… I was just an observer in a nightmare. I got to the studio door in time to catch Sarah in my arms. I looked over her shoulder as I cradled her head into my chest to see that every canvas had been slashed! The broken heap of paintings – years of work and memories – desecrated in a pool of water where they had communally urinated on a talent that they would never possess.

The living room door slowly opened. Sarah felt me tense up, her sobbing stopped and she gripped my arm tightly… David was framed in the light from the hall; his face was pale, his eyes were wide with horror. His mouth opened and shut several times but no sound came out. He turned and went back towards his bedroom. We followed his silent plea which acted like a magnet drawing us both along behind him. It was the same picture – total destruction designed to humiliate and wound.

He didn't cry. In fact, now I think about it, he didn't shed a tear throughout the whole of that miserable night, but his face had an expression that I never want to see again. I knelt down beside him and put my arms around him. Sarah was meandering about the room trying to put some things back where they should be, but it was the work of someone deranged – everything was smashed.

I left David to grab her and wrap my arms about her. I edged her closer to David so that I could hold him as well. My frustration at not being able to hold onto both of them culminated in hot, burning tears that coursed uncontrollably down my cheeks. Anger, rage… I wanted, needed, to hurt someone for this. I've never been a violent man, but now I wanted to kill, to maim… If only I could find the people who had done this! The tears and the stench of the room caught in the back of my throat and I started to heave.

Sarah's turn came to take over the family as she gently took my arm and David's hand – for he had now been sick down his front – and ushered us both outside the front door. She dug in her handbag, still lying on the doorstep, and produced some tissues. She stuffed a couple into my hands and started wiping down David whilst saying in a low, even voice, 'We must report this to the police…but I've got to get David out of here… Take me to my mother's… You can call the police from there.'

It made sense, so we carried all our things back down the path and stuffed them in the back of the van.

'Hang on a minute,' I said, and rushed back up the path to the doorstep, picked up the folded bit of cardboard and stuffed it back in the door to keep it shut. On reflection, it was probably one of the silliest things I've done in my life – who could do any more damage!

Sarah's parents were in bed asleep, so it took some time for them to wake from my impatient banging.

'Who's there?' George demanded gruffly. Then as soon as he realised, the bolts and chain came off the door and we were ushered into the cosy warmth of the house.

Meg, Sarah's mother, was on the stairs behind her husband quickly tying the cord of her dressing gown, her face clouded with concern as she realised that something was very wrong for us to be there at this time in the morning.

George ushered us into the kitchen as Meg swept past us, putting the kettle on as she went, in one flowing motion.

I went back into the hall leaving Sarah to explain; I had to phone the police…

Twenty minutes later, I was back at our flat where a police panda car was parked outside.

A young constable with his colleague – a pretty policewoman – were inspecting the door with a flashlight. They both looked up as I strode along the path. 'Mr Stevenson?' the young man enquired.

I didn't answer but gave the door a shove, after which it swung open.

'Try not to touch anything,' the young policewoman warned. 'We've called for forensics to come, but they won't be here for a couple of hours – it's been a busy night.'

We all trooped back into the flat. It was a strange feeling: it was as though this wasn't where I lived and I was somehow detached from it all. I don't remember saying very much; there wasn't much that could be said. The nauseous devastation said it all.

The young couple somehow seemed to get older as I watched them move from room to room. Their faces took on an expression of world-weariness, suggesting that they had seen all this before.

'There's not much we can do here before forensics have been over the place,' the young constable explained. 'You might as well get back to your in-laws and get some sleep,' he suggested. 'Perhaps you could call into the station later on in the morning, and we'll take a statement then.'

'What's the chance of finding out who did this?' I demanded.

The young officer looked uncomfortable. ‘It’s probably a bunch of youngsters… Someone might have seen something… If you can give us a list of what’s been taken, we might pick up a lead when they try to offload the stuff.’ He didn’t sound very optimistic.

Chapter 5

Genesis

They never did find the culprits. The insurance company paid the claim for the things that had been stolen or wrecked. I hired a skip, and we unceremoniously tipped all our broken treasures into it. We stayed with George and Meg, and Sarah and I went back to the flat each night to scrub and clean, to mend and refurbish our home. The problem was that it never ever seemed like our home again. I couldn't let myself in through the front door without my nose wrinkling up in distaste; it was as if my brain had been programmed, albeit for only a fleeting moment, so that I could still smell our unwanted visitors.

Sarah was grieving. It is the only way I could describe her deep unhappiness. During the day she went to school, and every evening, after we had eaten, we went to the flat to continue redecorating. But there was no joy in it, none of the fun that we had experienced at other times when we had worked together to make a home for ourselves. We couldn't bring ourselves to finish the job and say, 'That's enough, we'll move back in, tomorrow.'

Finally, she said what I sort of knew she was building up to, 'Mo, I don't want us to live here anymore.'

I had already been there in my mind, but simply moving to a new house was now a major problem. A few years ago it would have been easy – there had been a good market for flats like ours. Now, at the beginning of the nineties, the property market was in the doldrums.

We'd be lucky to sell it, and even if we could find a buyer, we would be lucky to get what we still owed on the mortgage. 'Negative equity' the pundits called it – I was aware of the problem, but it wasn't a problem for us before as we were not looking to move to a new house, and sooner or later the market would pick up and everything would balance out.

I started to try and explain what the problems were likely to be, but she just looked at me, refusing to accept what I was saying. 'There's got to be a way. We'll find a way!' She was interrupted by the telephone ringing in the next room. She went off to answer it as I finished painting the bedroom door.

When she returned, she looked puzzled.

'Who was it?' I asked.

'Lawrence Denning – David's headmaster. He wants to see us both, tomorrow… I said we could see him at lunchtime… Can you make half twelve?'

I nodded in agreement. 'What's it about?' I asked, trying to get some sort of clue from her expression.

She shook her head in mystification. 'I don't know, but I don't like the sound of it… He asked me not to mention anything to David. I hope he's not been up to anything…' Her voice petered out weakly.

'Who, David?' I said in disbelief. 'I hardly think so… We have left him a bit to his own devices the past few weeks…and he has been upset by all of this.' I waved the paintbrush at the room we had been putting back together. We both remained silent, wrapped up in our own thoughts.

We packed up our gear soon after the phone call and went back to Sarah's parents. George and Meg were still up when we got home;

they were watching a late-night movie. David had gone to bed at nine o'clock complaining of a headache.

For the past couple of weeks we had all been sleeping in their spare room, and David was sleeping on a camp bed jammed into the space at the bottom of our bed. When we crept into the room, he was fast asleep; his face looked drawn and there were dark rings under his eyes. We slipped silently into bed, but sleep didn't come easily. I had a bad premonition about our meeting with the headmaster tomorrow. I don't think Sarah slept much either.

We both tossed and turned for most of the night. When the digital clock radio beside the bed slotted up 5:55, I swung my legs out of bed and went downstairs to make some tea – I was pleased that the night was over.

The headmaster's secretary ushered us into the head's study. He rose and offered us his hand by way of breaking the ice.

'Please, take a seat… Would you like some coffee?' His tone was measured, giving nothing away, trying to make us feel as comfortable as he could. He was a kind man and dedicated to bringing out the best in his young charges – not always easy in this inner-city environment.

We both shook our heads; we wanted to get to the reason for the phone call. He was sensitive enough to realise our concern.

'Look, I don't want to alarm you unnecessarily. David's a good lad, and I've never had the slightest problem with him, but in the last week or so he has become very friendly with Wayne and a few of our more difficult boys. In the past, he has kept himself pretty much to himself. He gets on with the other boys without being one of them…

if you know what I mean. The past few days, he has been very much a part of that group. We had a bit of nonsense yesterday morning in the classroom, and it seems that David was the main instigator. Now, that's not like him. At lunch break, something was going on beside the bike sheds. The playground superintendent went to investigate and found David wandering about mumbling incoherently. It was reported to me, and I went there immediately. By the time I got to him, he had pulled himself together, but he complained of feeling tired. I took him back to this office, and he slept in that chair for nearly an hour—' he nodded towards an old leather armchair in the corner of the room '—then when he woke up, I questioned him… I asked him if he had taken anything. He said no. I had to ask him to turn out his pockets, but there was nothing on him that would explain his behaviour. I asked what he had been doing in the playground – all he would say was that he felt tired. I don't want to alarm you unnecessarily, but I wouldn't be doing my job if I didn't bring this matter to your attention.'

Sarah spoke first. 'Do you think he had taken anything?' she asked, her voice had an edge to it that I hadn't heard before.

'A few months ago, we had our suspicions that some of the boys had been experimenting with solvents… We found some containers in the corner of the playground that indicated some of them had been up to no good. I reported it to Jeff Dobbs – the local community bobby – and he came around the next day and gave the school a lecture on the dangers of solvent abuse. There's been nothing else…but I have to say that I'm worried.' The headmaster leant back in his chair.

'You said, on the telephone, that you didn't want us to discuss this with David—' I started to say but the headmaster interjected.

'I wanted to speak to yourself and your wife first. Sarah, I know that as a teacher you will realise the importance of getting to the bottom of this problem, and the only way we will do that is by getting the children to talk about it. I didn't want everyone clamming up because they were too frightened to speak up. I'm relying on you to get David to tell you about what is going on.'

Sarah's mind must have been racing ahead; she started to speak to me as though we were on our own in the room. 'We can't do anything whilst we're at Mum's. We must move back to our own place, tonight... There's not much more we can do there anyway. Tomorrow's Saturday – we'll find out what's been going on!' She looked up at the headmaster and said quietly, 'Thank you, we'll speak to David over the weekend. Can I come and see you on Monday morning?'

'That will be fine. Try to be calm... There might be nothing to it, but in cases like this we must be vigilant. There are enough problems without things like this.'

We left shortly afterwards. I drove Sarah back to her school. We didn't speak – what could be said? I watched as she walked through the clamouring playground – some of the children, boisterous and full of life, called out to her, but she ignored them and pushed her way through to enter by the main door. I stared at the children. This is the school that David should be going to in a few years' time. *The fabric of the building looks tatty and run-down, and a coat of paint wouldn't go amiss*, I thought to myself.

I took a long last look at the school and set off back to work – I had two sacks of narcissus bulbs to plant that afternoon. I had a brief mental picture of soft yellow blooms carpeting the ground between silver birch trees in the springtime. It was much later that afternoon before it dawned on me that the picture I had in my mind was not the park where I was busy planting the bulbs, but the fringes of the glen we had seen in Scotland the day before we came home.

That evening we moved back into the flat. There was a brittle atmosphere; no one said much. We moved from room to room trying not to break the eggshells underfoot.

It was gone twelve before Sarah and I were ready to turn in. As I turned off the light in the living room, I looked around me. Everything seemed too pristine, unlived in, like a show house at an exhibition.

I don't think either of us slept much again that night: we could hear David mumbling whilst he continually fidgeted and wrestled with his bedclothes.

The next morning, Sarah collected the breakfast plates from the table and turned to put them on the side beside the dishwasher.

I opened the interrogation (I had intended for Sarah to make the first move and watch closely how things developed, but I changed my mind). 'David, the day before yesterday at school, you were unwell.'

He looked at me as though I wasn't talking to him.

Sarah put the dishes down and stared intently at David. There was a silence.

I went on, 'You were found wandering about in a daze… You fell asleep in the headmaster's study.'

His eyes had grown very big, his mouth opened and closed; he turned towards his mother in a silent plea for help.

'I want you to think very carefully. What had you *done* to make you act so strange?' I asked the question quietly, almost as if I didn't want to know the answer. My eyes were looking directly into his from across the table.

'Not-hing,' he stammered. 'I didn't take nothing.'

My hands shot out across the table.

He withdrew back as though I had slapped him.

I caught his hands in mine; I drew myself over the remnants of the breakfast things until my face was only inches from his. I looked inside him and saw the hurt and the fear…then I was sure! I let go of his hands and slumped back in my chair.

Sarah leant over David and grabbed him around the shoulders. 'What was it?' The icy tone conveyed no love.

His face crumpled, the lower lip folding and unfolding.

She turned his shoulders to make him face her.

He turned his head away only to find himself looking directly at me. 'Glue.' He sobbed a single sob.

Sarah dropped onto one knee, drawing him to her. 'What do you mean, glue?' Her voice was still not under control, but she was trying.

'Some of the boys sniff glue… It makes you feel funny…happy. Well, it's supposed to; it just made me go to sleep.'

'Do you know it could kill you?' She was a schoolteacher now. 'A doctor's son, he was a good lad as well, intelligent, did well at school… Well, he experimented with glue sniffing, and they found him dead in his garden shed…'

I remembered her telling me this story when she got home from a course she had taken on solvent abuse.

'Where did you buy the stuff?' she demanded.

'I didn't buy it. Wayne had it… A lot of the boys do it.' It came out as a sorrowful whisper.

‘Where do they get it from?’ Sarah was determined to get to the source.

‘Jessup’s mostly (he named a scruffy DIY shop in one of the local backstreets), some of the boys get it from home.’

Half an hour later we had all the information that was to be had. The front door bell rang. It was my father.

‘I’m going to the allotment to dig some spuds,’ he announced briefly. ‘I wondered if David would like to come along and give me a hand?’ He raised an eyebrow in recognition that there had obviously been some sort of upset going on.

David jumped at the excuse to leave this highly charged location and go off with his grandfather. Boots and coat were hurriedly put on; the door slammed shut behind them.

Neither Sarah nor I wanted to pursue the matter any further at this stage. Dad’s arrival had actually been a godsend.

‘Do you fancy a cuppa?’ I asked as I went to the sink to fill the kettle. Nothing was said whilst the kettle boiled, and I made myself busy putting out a couple of mugs and emptying the teapot. Finally, I turned to give Sarah a cup of tea.

She was sitting hunched up, her arms clasped tightly together in front of her as though trying to stem a deep pain. Tears flowed down her cheeks, running off the side of her chin. She made no effort to wipe them away, as though she wasn’t aware of them.

I put the tea down on the table beside her and dug my hand into my pocket for a handkerchief. A low sob choked its way to the surface. Her hands went up to her face, and I wrapped my arms around her. I couldn’t get close enough to her; I couldn’t somehow reach her. The single sob heralded a succession of silent, heaving sobs, each one worse than the last. Her face was torn by inner turmoil.

I stood looking down on her. My own inability to make things right caused me to bite my lip in angry frustration. First the homecoming… now this! Our comfortable little life was falling to pieces around us, and I couldn't do anything.

Even as I stood there, searching for the words of comfort that wouldn't come, she took the handkerchief from my hand, blew her nose, and with one movement used the back of her hand to wipe her wet cheeks.

She glared up at me through the tears. 'We've got to find David another school. I want to leave this place…' She glowered at the room. 'There's got to be a better place to live.'

I looked on helplessly, still unable to find the words of comfort and reassurance that my mind was groping for. In desperation, I said, 'Look, get your coat on, let's get out of here for a bit.' I knew that the flat was as much to blame for her present state of mind as everything else that morning.

Not needing much coaxing, she meekly followed me into the hall where we both put on our coats. She let me help her as she struggled to get one arm through a sleeve whilst holding onto her shoulder bag.

Once outside we walked together, although apart – normally she would slip an arm through mine. With her hands thrust deep in her coat pockets and shoulders back, she strode resolutely along Benson Street. We paused at the first junction, and I took her arm to cross the road. We turned left. I didn't have a clue where we were going, and neither, I believe, did she. We didn't speak, but our combined unhappiness seemed to hang over us like a cloud. Perhaps it was just instinct, a homing urge, to go somewhere peaceful where growing things produced beauty amidst the grime of this city.

At the park gates we turned into my place of work. Just inside the gates is a small duck pond. Last week I had a party of youngsters doing community service – cleaning up the banks and dredging the accumulated rubbish from the water's edge. Not even a week later it looked like the Sargasso Sea! Beer cans, fast-food containers and the flotsam and jetsam of human disregard had been flung into the pond. The ducks manoeuvred through the debris looking for fragments of special fried rice floating in polystyrene cups.

We didn't pause at the pond, but moved to the centre of the park where I had been planting bulbs – was that only yesterday? By the grove of silver birch, we stopped to sit down on a bench. I was determined that we should talk about our problems. I still didn't have the words, but I knew they would come once I made a start. I took a deep breath in preparation but paused again as a passer-by walked up to the bench and made to sit down.

He was a tall black man. He smiled shyly and said in a low baritone voice, 'May I join you?'

We both just looked at him; he took our lack of comment as a signal of our agreement.

He settled himself on the bench and dug deep into the pocket of his topcoat for a thick, dog-eared paperback book. He opened the book at a page that had been marked by a bus ticket before looking up at us once more.

I realised that I was staring at him, wishing him to go away so we could start sorting out the problems. He was late forties and quite smartly dressed in heavy polo-necked sweater and dark trousers topped by a dark wool overcoat. His black shoes had seen better days, but they were highly polished. He smiled, and his face lit up… The sun streamed through the branches of the trees above us… His crinkly black hair was peppered with silver, as was his thin, straggly moustache. The sun seemed to reflect the light from his face.

The soft resonance of his voice washed over us again. ‘Forgive me, but you look troubled… Would it help to speak about it?’

It was as though he had read my thoughts; I was taken aback. I was embarrassed, angry and, furthermore, I didn’t know what to say.

Sarah answered, ‘Is it that obvious?’ She paused as if weighing up her thoughts, and then quickly came to a decision. ‘How would you feel if you found out that your child was in danger at school…? Your house was wrecked…? No, worse…fouled, ruined…?’ The tears came back in memory of the past experiences. I slipped my arm around her, and she grabbed onto me.

The black man watched all of this without showing any emotion, then he pleaded gently, ‘Let me pray for you.’ After he closed his eyes, I heard the words, ‘Dear Father God, in the name of Jesus, I ask you to come to these people in their time of need. Comfort them with your Holy Spirit, bring peace into their lives and show them the way out of their adversity. Safeguard their child with the power that only you can bring, and bless their home so that it might be a fit place for this family to live and prosper…’ There was a pause as though he was listening intently for an answer. ‘Mmm,’ he intoned. ‘Yes, Father, yes… Thank you, Lord.’ He opened his eyes once more and his smile grew into a grin that would have matched old Satchel-Mouth himself.

Sarah turned her face to mine. Her tears had stopped. (We discussed that first meeting many times afterwards, and we both agreed that it was like a great and terrible weight had been lifted from us.)

'Your child will be safe; no more need to worry,' he said gravely.

'Are you a priest?' I asked hesitantly. I wasn't sure if that was the right word. I knew that different religions had different terms, but I wasn't up on those sorts of things. I hadn't been to church outside of weddings and funerals since I was a kid.

'No,' he answered. 'I came over here as a missionary.' There was a distinct twinkle in his eyes. He enjoyed the puzzlement that must have showed on our faces. 'I came to bring the Word to the godless people of Britain… Bit of a turnaround, eh? Who says the Lord ain't gotta sense of 'umour!' He dug his hand into his pocket and produced a card which he offered to us. Then, as if remembering something, he produced a pen from the same pocket and took the card back to write something on it. 'Do you have a Bible at home?' he enquired.

When I gave a somewhat embarrassed nod, he handed over the card. On the back it said *Genesis ch.12 v.i.*

'I'm sure we'll meet again. If you need to talk in the meantime, call me – my name is Joshua Urquhart.' He rose beaming at us again and, as if judging that we needed time on our own, gave a short bow and strode off towards the park gate.

Nothing had really been spoken about, serious problems still had to be sorted, but our brief encounter had somehow lightened us both. It couldn't be explained, and we didn't try. It would have been easy to pooh-pooh it all, but that would have meant descending into that dark corridor nightmares are made of. So, arm in arm, we quietly made our way back to the flat.

We let ourselves in. My dad and David hadn't returned. Whilst Sarah went off to the kitchen to make a brew, I wandered over to the bookcase and quickly found the small Bible that had come with me when Sarah and I first set up home. I don't think it had been looked at for years.

I opened the book, and on the cover, I read in clipped copperplate 'Morrice Stevenson – St. John's Sunday School – New Testament Studies'. *Did I win this for Bible studies?* I had a dim and vague recollection, but I thought the only prize I had ever won as a youngster was for parsnips. I turned to the contents page and looked up Genesis, then I thumbed my way through to chapter twelve, verse one.

As Sarah came through with a tray of tea and some biscuits, I looked up from the Bible. 'Read this.' I offered the book once Sarah placed the tray on the table. I pointed to the passage. 'That's what the guy in the park wanted us to read.'

She took the Bible from me and started to read over my finger as I traced out the line. *The Lord said to Abram, 'Leave your country, your relatives, and your father's home, and go to the land that I am going to show you…'* She handed the book back to me slowly. 'Well, is that an omen or what…?' She seemed miles away.

I planted my finger in between the pages and closed the book. I wanted my tea, but I didn't want to lose the place. I stuffed my hand in my pocket feeling for something to use as a marker. A scrap of paper came into my hand, which I placed in the page.

'Let me read that again,' Sarah asked softly. I passed the Bible back to her. She read the passage again and was about to close the book when she looked at the marker. Her head snapped back. She didn't say anything but passed the scrap of paper to me. It was a page from a receipt pad. It was headed 'Tomintoul Garage'. I looked at her in puzzlement. 'On the other side,' she insisted.

On the back of the slip was the sketch of the glen that we discovered when we had broken down in the Highlands. At the bottom, in Geordie's spidery scrawl, was a telephone number: the contact for the estate office who was selling the property!

Chapter 6

Time Out

Sarah phoned the estate office. The two hundred and fifty acres of hill farm, with the six derelict cottages in various stages of disrepair, was for sale with an 'asking price' of £125,000. They would be pleased to note our interest. (It doesn't seem a lot of money now, but back then in the early nineties it seemed like a fortune.) They expected to announce a closing date by the end of the month.

This was all gobbledygook to us, but the agent explained the terminology. There's no 'gazumping' under Scottish law: a property is advertised, then if people are genuinely interested, they ask the vendor's solicitor to 'note their interest'. Then they go about raising a mortgage, arrange surveys and all the other things that a would-be purchaser normally has to do. When the vendor's solicitor deems that there is sufficient interest in the property, they will call for a 'closing date'. This could be midday on the last Friday of the month, or some such date and time. On that day, the purchaser's solicitor has to present a 'missive' or firm offer to purchase. At the due time and date, the vendor's solicitor opens all the offers (missives) at the same time, and the offer that best suits the vendor is the one that is taken. Once you have entered your missive and it has been accepted, you must buy that property. Similarly, once a missive has been accepted, the vendor cannot go back on the deal, even if another purchaser comes along and offers more money.

It seemed a very civilised way of going about things. The real problem remained: where would we find £125,000 for the ground, let alone the money to convert one of the cottages into something we could live in?

‘How much would we get for the flat?’ Sarah asked me.

‘Even if we could find a buyer, I doubt we would get much more than sixty-eight, and we owe fifty-three.’ I recalled how a couple of years ago we would have expected the same flat to go for nearer eighty thousand.

‘Could we rent it out for enough to pay the mortgage?’ Sarah kept gnawing away at the problem.

‘That shouldn’t be too difficult. There’s still a crying need for rented properties in this area.’ I couldn’t see where this conversation was leading. Where could we raise £125,000, plus the cost of making a home, when we would both need to find new jobs in a new area…? It wasn’t worth thinking about, but I kept my council to myself.

‘I need to talk to Father – I bet he’ll have some ideas.’ Sarah’s dad had worked for the Prudential at a senior level before he retired last June. ‘Would you mind waiting here for David? Your dad said they’d be back by six.’ She picked up her coat and bag and made for the door.

I couldn’t remember when I had seen her so determined. ‘OK. What are we having for supper? Would you like me to put something on whilst you’re out?’ I suggested.

‘No, how about I bring in a pizza? David will like that, and we could all have a lazy evening in front of the fire.’ She smiled a tired smile. Things were looking much better than they did at breakfast, but I knew we still had a long way to go.

After the door had banged shut, I went over to the fireplace and put a match to the kindling in the hearth and fed a few lumps of smokeless fuel onto the flames. When it was burning, I moved into the kitchen and washed my hands. Then taking a glass, I poured myself a glass of Oddbins 'special'. I moved to the turntable in the stack and fished out a Louis Armstrong LP that the vandals hadn't completely wrecked – *I've Got the World on a String*. Anyway, I liked the scratchiness. His voice flowed like warm honey through the flat: '*Nobody knows the trouble I've seen; nobody knows but…*' I thought of Joshua on the park bench… I saw his face again, glowing in the morning sunshine. The next track by Fischer and Laine, 'We'll Be Together Again', seemed to provide just the right note of optimism. I finished the wine with a gulp as the front doorbell rang.

David and my dad came in through the door carrying half a sack of new potatoes between them. Dad had a basket in his other hand that was full of courgettes and French beans. I peeked into the sack. 'They look good enough to eat,' I joked.

'Those Desiree are a cracking good spud—' he looked at them with pride '—if only the slimmers realised that the way to slim is on a diet of spuds.' Dad was on one of his hobbyhorses. They certainly have less calories than people ever imagine, and a high protein level and lots of vitamins – it's amazing how this wonder food has been denigrated. But if you don't grow these sorts of things, you don't get the opportunity to find out

'Would you like a glass of wine, Dad?' I waved my empty glass at him.

He looked doubtful. 'I'd rather have a cuppa.' He smiled.

'David, would you put the kettle on, son?' I called out as I went back to the sitting room to recharge my glass. I returned to the kitchen. David had gone to his bedroom to change his damp jeans.

'Is everything all right with the lad?' Dad asked, keeping his voice down so that David couldn't hear.

'We had a bit of an upset this morning, just before you came, but I think we have sorted it all out now.' I also spoke quietly.

'He's not been his usual self today, that's all... Very quiet... I think he's worried about something.' Being my dad's only grandson, they're pretty close.

'I'll tell you all about it later, Dad.' I didn't want to go into it all at this time. There was still a lot to discuss before Sarah's meeting with the headmaster on Monday. I finished pouring the tea as David came back into the room. 'Would you like a cup?' I asked him.

He nodded and sat down beside his grandfather.

After my dad had finished his tea, he set off back home. On Saturday evenings he liked to go dancing. After Mum died, it took a lot of nagging to make him see that he should still go out and enjoy himself. He had always enjoyed ballroom dancing, and it gave him the opportunity to meet other people.

David sat quietly as I thumbed through the evening paper. 'Dad, I'm sorry,' he said quietly.

I looked up from my paper and realised that he wanted to talk. I put the paper on the other side of the table and waited.

'I did a stupid thing the other day. I won't ever do it again,' he said, it all coming out in a rush. 'I've never had any real friends at school, and then Wayne was sort of friendly, but the others didn't like me very much... They said I was a "big girl's blouse" and that I wouldn't dare to do anything. Afterwards, they said if I told on them, they would beat me up!'

'Don't worry about it,' I replied. 'We'll sort it out. No one, but no one, is going to beat you up.' I put my arm around him.

'I'm back!' Sarah's voice called out from the hall; she arrived carrying a large boxed pizza.

'Great!' David chortled as soon as he realised that Ninja Turtle food was on the menu.

'Did your father have any ideas?' I called out as she disappeared into the hall to hang up her coat. Her face had lost some of its previous intensity. 'He's got the picture. I had a long chat with him. He wants to sleep on the problem – he never makes snap decisions – he says that he doesn't trust his own intuition, prefers to work it all out methodically. It's an interesting thought. He says it's like having no sense of direction and having to rely on your compass. He maintains that more people get lost because they think that their sense of direction is more accurate than a compass.' She paused to accept a plate from David who was busy laying the table, anxious to get stuck into his favourite food.

'Would you like a glass of wine?' I already had a glass and the bottle in anticipation. She nodded, and I poured.

'Anyway, I've invited them both over for supper tomorrow. I'm hoping that he will come up with something.'

Later, after David had gone to bed, I told Sarah what he'd said and about his fears of being beaten up.

Sarah snorted. 'We'll see about that. I'll be having a word with Wayne's mother tomorrow.'

'I'm not sure that will fix anything – it may even make things a lot worse for him.' I remembered back to an occasion when I had been a boy… This lad down our street had given me a hell of a time. My mother got to hear about it from a neighbour, but instead of flying off the handle, she told me to invite him home for tea! She made hot crumpets with thick butter and jam. Afterwards, we played in the yard. We became quite good friends after that. My mum used to say there's always a bit of good in everybody, sometimes it has to be coaxed out, but it's better than going to war.

I told Sarah that story when we went to bed. I cuddled her back and whispered the words that my mum had said whilst nibbling her ear.

'We'll see in the morning.' She sighed, and I felt her body relax into sleep.

I stayed awake for a bit longer. I thought about my mum and how she would have handled our present crisis – she was the most down-to-earth person I had ever known. No flimflam… *'You know what is right and what is wrong – like you know if your hands are dirty or not!'* She always did things right… *'If a job was worth doing, it was worth…'* Mmm, I missed her a lot.

Over breakfast, Sarah suggested to David that we invite Wayne to come to Jessup's Park where they had just built a rollerblade rink. 'Dad'll come with you to keep an eye on things, then you could bring him back here for a bit of lunch. What d'ya think?'

David looked surprised at his mother's suggestion – no one in the family had ever been a keen fan of Wayne before. But that's what happened.

I waited in the van whilst David went up to the door and rang the bell. Wayne's mother came to the door; she looked harassed with a baby in her arms and two little ones hanging onto her legs. She called out to Wayne. He arrived, scowling around the door. The scowl then changed to a grin, and he was off to get his rollerblades, pads and helmet. Soon the boys were chattering away like budgies in the back of the van.

They both enjoyed themselves careering around the rink whilst I had a coffee from the small café in the park and read my Sunday paper. Autumn was early that year. A sharp north- easterly wind arrived in gusts that sent a flurry of yellow leaves cascading along the pathway. I glanced at my watch to find that it was almost midday. I called out to the boys that we should make a move if we were going to get back in time for lunch. I think they were going to ask for a bit longer but hunger pains, I suspect, overwhelmed the plea. Ten minutes later we were heading back to the flat.

'I think you boys enjoyed that.' Sarah smiled at Wayne as she lifted the boys' empty plates. Bangers and mash finished off with two helpings of apple pie and ice cream seemed to have gone down quite well.

'Can we leave the table?' David asked, hooking his legs round about to catapult himself off his chair.

'In a minute. I want a quick word with Wayne.' She turned from the sink and looked directly at the boy who had been wondering what this treat was about – he was waiting for the crunch!

'Wayne, you know I'm a teacher… A few weeks ago I had to go on a course about solvent abuse   you know, glue sniffing…all that sort of thing.'

Now he was looking very uncomfortable wondering if this could be trouble.

Sarah continued, ‘During that course I found out some very scary things: how constant sniffing can damage the inner lining of the nose and throat, how it can damage the brain, and I read the case notes on a ten-year-old boy who collapsed *and died* after sniffing glue.’ She didn’t give him a chance to say anything, but carried straight on, ‘Last Thursday, at lunchtime, David did something in the playground… He couldn’t speak properly, the headmaster took him to his study, and he went into a deep sleep. Now, it was possible that David might never have woken up again – he could have died. Oh, I know lots of boys muck about with these things and nothing ever happens to them, but we don’t know, even the doctors don’t know, what the dangers are.’

David was staring down at the table whilst Wayne was looking up at Sarah – his face expressionless.

‘David wouldn’t tell us what he had been doing or even who was with him. I understand that all you boys stick together, and I wouldn’t ask you to tell me about it.’

Wayne looked visibly relieved.

‘But I need your help, Wayne. I don’t want any of you to get hurt. You’re all mates, so you must all look after each other. As you get older, there will be other things. People will want you to try pills and other sorts of things. They’ll tell you they’re OK, it won’t hurt, it’ll make you feel good; but at the end of the day, these people only want to get hold of your money. If you get damaged – or even killed – they don’t care! So, it’s right that you stick together; that’s what friends are for. You have fun without taking things, and you look after each other and make sure that nobody, but nobody, lets any of your friends get involved with drugs of any kind. Look, the two of you, will you make me a promise, here and now? If and when anyone wants you to take anything that you don’t think is right, would you come and tell me? I won't do anything about it except give you advice. If you think something should be done about it, then that will be up to you.'

Both of the boys, who had been listening carefully, nodded.

Sarah smiled, and the tension suddenly evaporated. 'Would you like a Coke to take out in the garden with you?'

Both boys nodded again. They still hadn't said a word.

She went to the fridge and handed the boys a can of Coke each, and the boys scuttled off down the passageway. 'I don't know if that achieved anything,' Sarah said with an air of resignation.

I glanced out of the window where the boys were immersed in a game involving cars and tunnels. 'I think you might have bought us some time,' I replied. 'I think you'll find that Wayne makes sure none of the other boys give David any trouble at school tomorrow.'

'I'll see the headmaster and let him know what we have found out and what we have done – that little creep at the DIY shop needs to be sorted out for a start!' Sarah was beginning to look agitated again.

I went across and put my arms around her. 'Easy now, I think we've achieved a lot in two days, but this won't be the last problem we have to face.' I felt her stiffen. 'But it's amazing what you can do with a quiet, sensible approach.'

'I still want us to leave London,' she said quietly, almost to herself.

I might as well go pack a bag, I thought to myself, *I know what she's like when she makes up her mind to do something!*

As I arrived back from taking Wayne home, George was parking further up the street so I could get the van into my usual place. I locked it and waited for George and Meg to walk down to where I waited at the gate. I gave Meg a hug and a peck on the cheek whilst David grabbed his grandfather and led him through the gate. I let us all in and called out to Sarah.

David had eaten with Wayne before I had taken him home, so it was time for a bath, into pyjamas and a quick goodnight to all of us before he disappeared into his bedroom. I got the feeling that he was a lot happier than he was at the beginning of this weekend.

We had finished dinner, and Sarah had just put the coffee out when George introduced the conversation that I know she was waiting so desperately for. She knew her father well, and she knew that he would only start when he was good and ready.

'About that problem you spoke of yesterday,' he said to her but looking at both of us. 'So, you would really like to move to this place in Scotland?'

Sarah gave a small nod and said nothing.

'Well, for a start, it would be a mistake to try to sell this place at the moment. Anyway, you might not like it after you've been there for a while, and you might want to come back to the big city.' There was a twinkle in his eye, and I just knew he had some plan that he was going to present like a magician pulling a rabbit from a hat. He didn't have to make a pitch to us, but he couldn't help himself now he was the manipulator of finance, making the most of forty years of experience in the city. But even with his experience I couldn't see how he was going to produce £125,000 out of the hat.

'Right, then it's agreed that you don't sell this flat – it shouldn't be too difficult to rent out for sufficient to continue paying the mortgage.'

'Do we have to have permission from the building society?' I asked.

'Yes, but don't ask them right away, that will come a little later,' he answered.

'If we don't sell this place, how can we possibly think about buying the land in Scotland?' asked Sarah.

'Even if you could sell this place at the moment, you would almost certainly have to accept much less than it was worth even a few years ago, and that way you would lose your original deposit as well as the money that you have paid back. Don't worry, give it time, it will appreciate again, it's just going to take a bit of time. People still need somewhere to live.' He gave a wry smile. 'Now, here is the meat of my plan. As Sarah is an only child, her mother and I always intended that after we had gone...' he looked across at Meg and gave a small shrug '...we'd leave the house to you, but it seems that your need is now, not sometime in the dim and distant future – for I don't mind telling you, I'm not planning on popping my clogs for quite a while yet. However,' The tension in the room had heightened; he had us all in the palm of his hand. 'You could buy our house from us. You wouldn't be able to get a mortgage for all of it because the amount you could borrow would be limited by your earning capabilities – that's both of you together.' He looked around us all to make sure we understood what he was talking about. I was already a bit lost, and he noticed. 'Our house ought to value at about a hundred and seventy-five thousand pounds, allowing for the recession. It shouldn't be difficult to get you a mortgage of say a hundred thousand pounds – we draw up an agreement for you to pay us the difference over some time in the future. You'll get the house in the end, so it doesn't matter. Now, Mother and I will have a hundred thousand pounds that we will want to invest.' He smiled at Meg. 'So we thought we would like to become partners with you in this land in Scotland. You will have the full deeds of the house, and there will be an equity value of seventy-five thousand still left in the house.' George noted that I had a glazed look on my face again – he looked enquiringly.

'Equity value?' I murmured.

'Yes, the difference between what you have mortgaged on the house – in this case, a hundred thousand pounds – and the current valuation, say a hundred and seventy-five thousand. Any bank should be happy to lend you the twenty-five thousand that you need against the seventy-five thousand extra value there is in the house value.' George patiently explained.

'Wait a minute,' said Sarah, 'let me see if I've got this right. We keep paying the mortgage on this place?'

'Yes,' interjected her father. 'But that should be met by the tenants – you will need a small emergency fund in case you're ever without a tenant for a period of time, but that wouldn't often happen in this area.'

'OK, then we get another mortgage on your house…' She raised her eyebrows. 'Is that legal?'

'Well, suppose you wanted to move to our house and then found out after you had bought it that you couldn't sell this flat… The building society would have to give their permission, but they would much prefer to do that than have to repossess it!' A look of bland innocence spread over his face. I wondered if all big business was done with this look.

'All right, then.' She wanted to know more. 'We get a mortgage of a hundred thousand pounds on your house, and you use that money to invest in the land in Scotland?'

George nodded his agreement.

'Wait a minute, then how do we repay the mortgage and find the money to refurbish the house?'

'First things first,' said George – he was beginning to enjoy himself now. 'First, let's worry about how to buy the land. We'll put in the hundred thousand pounds; you will have to find a Scottish bank that will lend you twenty-five thousand. When that's been achieved, we can worry about how to service the money.'

'Yes, but…' I knew she didn't want to sound negative, but there were lots of holes in this plan just now. She was voicing my doubts, too, when she said, 'Remember that we will both have to find jobs when we get to Scotland.'

'Mmm, I spent most of last night thinking about that, and I ended up thinking that you will have to make a living from the land itself.'

'What, you mean growing things?' asked Sarah.

I liked the sound of that.

'Yes, but it will take time, you need a buffer zone, so I think you will have to do some asset stripping!' He pushed his cup towards Sarah.

She filled it and pushed the milk and sugar towards him.

He continued, 'You don't necessarily need two hundred and fifty acres and five more houses. So, my first thought was for you to sell off some of the plots, but then everyone else is in the same spot – they can't sell their own property… So, how about leasing a plot for development? They could purchase it later on if they wanted to. That would give you income. Income to service the original hundred-thousand-pound mortgage, and more than enough to service the extra twenty-five thousand. If we've got the sums right, you would have enough to work on the house that you want to live in and start some sort of horticultural business to supplement your lease income.' He pushed his cup away, untouched, his face was slightly flushed. You could see that this sort of deal was the stuff of life to him.

'Do you really think we would be able to lease those plots for enough to do all that?' Sarah desperately wanted it to be so. It took barely a second to filter in, then Sarah rushed around the table and gave her dad a big hug.

Meanwhile, Meg looked on. She was proud of her husband – these young fellows don't have all the answers – but also because she had been a part of all this, after she had brought a tray of hot chocolate and biscuits back to bed at half past four in the morning, listening as she always had to George's schemes. She had developed a pretty keen acumen of her own, enough to be recognised by George, who had for years been trying out his multifarious schemes on Meg, over hot chocolate and biscuits, in the middle of the night.

'Do you think it will be difficult to find five families who would want to live in that glen?' I thought it was time I said something.

'Now there's a thing,' said George. 'I don't know, but I have a very strong feeling that you might be very surprised by the replies you get. It depends where you advertise… Remember these are going to be your closest neighbours!'

'We really don't want to go out of the frying pan into the fire – it would be terrible if we imported a load of problems. We would have to be careful to get the sort of people who think like us…' Sarah paused, and even had the grace to blush. 'That sounds terrible,' she said. 'But you know what I mean… We want to start afresh…to produce a good place to live, somewhere to bring up children,' she said in a rush.

Her mother smiled. 'Yes, love, and you will… I can't wait to come and visit you.'

I had to ask the question, 'George, would you sort of act as our financial consultant?'

'I thought I was doing that already,' he gently chided…but it was obvious that this was a project he was going to see through to the end.

'What do we do first, then, Dad?' Sarah would have gone out and done it there and then if it were required.

'Tomorrow, I shall get some rates from the leading building societies. There are a lot of deals on the go at the moment because of the recession. Then you will have to make an application to buy our house. And you'd better get in touch with the selling agents in Scotland and register your interest.'

'Mum, are you sure that is OK with you?' Sarah still hadn't realised that Meg was as much a part of the decision-making in her own house as George ever was – this was only because Meg chose it to be that way.

'Don't be silly, dear, this is the most exciting thing that has happened to us since your father retired – we were in danger of dying of boredom.' She gave a chuckle.

'If you choose wisely,' said George, 'you might even be able to find skills and talents that will be of value to all of you whilst you are building the houses – perhaps, you could all muck in and help each other.'

'Dad, I don't want to live in a commune!' Sarah had some set ideas on hippies.

It fell to Meg to make the most profound comment of the evening: 'I realise that, dear, but think how nice it might be if you could initiate something that could become a real community.'

There was a pause all round. 'Where do you think we should advertise?' I asked.

'Try the *Time Out* magazine,' suggested George.

Sarah turned to the bookcase and reached for a pad and pen. 'What do you think we should say?' she asked.

'See if you can get the spirit of what you were telling your father about yesterday. I'm sure you're not the only one who would like to move out of the city to set up somewhere that was a good environment to live and bring up a family,' Meg answered, directing her remarks at Sarah.

And so it was, the next week's *Time Out* carried the following advertisement:

ARE YOU FED UP WITH LONDON?

How would you like to move to the country,
away from pollution, the stress and the crime?
We are looking for five families to share our dream.
There are five 10-acre plots, each with a house (that will
need to be renovated), in the Highlands of Scotland.
You can buy a plot for £25,000 or lease for £300 per
month – with an option to purchase the freehold at a
later date. You will need extra funds to spend on your house,
and it will probably be necessary to live in mobile homes
during the building period. This is not some weirdo
commune concept, we are simply looking for a group
of families that are interested in helping each other to produce
A COMMUNITY.

Write: P.O. Box 714 Time Out.
Giving details about your family, what you could
contribute in terms of skills and abilities to the group,
and why you think you would like to be part of a
new community. No obligation will result from your
enquiry and no commitment on our behalf before
satisfactory interviews have taken place.

We read the advertisement and held our breath wondering what the post might bring!

Chapter 7

The Flood

It began with a trickle the day after the advertisement appeared, then fifty-seven letters landed on the doormat the day after that. When Sarah got home from school on the Monday, she could hardly open the door: there were 286 assorted enquiries! Our advertisement had certainly touched a chord within the minds of a lot of people. They had come from a wide variety of individuals, including some crackpots, but most seemed very genuine. We dipped into the pile to read story after story; many of which made our difficulties seem very minor in comparison.

By Thursday, the postman had left a note asking would we please go to the post office and collect our mail, for there was simply too much to be delivered by hand!

The weekend came around again. David was playing at Wayne's house – his mother had called that morning to ask if he would like to go around for the afternoon.

Sarah was sitting on the floor surrounded by the letters and looking somewhat bemused. 'It's like playing at being God,' she murmured. 'How can we possibly decide who to approach from this lot?' She spread her hands over the pile.

I didn't know what to say. What could anyone say, or do? A thought came into my head: the last time we had been at our wits' end, a chance meeting in the park had helped to resolve our problems. Once again, I pictured the tall black man, with the sun lighting up his face, talking to us on the park bench. I went across to the telephone table, and there, beside the telephone, was the card that he had given us – Joshua Urquhart and his address and telephone number.

I came back to where Sarah was sitting and thrust the card under her nose. 'Perhaps we should ask our spiritual advisor for a bit of help,' I said with a wry grin.

Sarah took the card and read it. She flipped it over and read the Bible reference that had initiated this adventure. She turned the card back over and handed it back to me. 'Call him,' she said quietly. 'He started this… And anyway, I don't know where to go from here.'

I looked at her again; she seemed somehow lost in a sea of letters. I couldn't think of anything more constructive to say. I went back to the telephone and dialled the number.

The telephone only rang once before the receiver at the other end was picked up. A soft Scottish voice answered, 'Hello, Mary Urquhart speaking.'

It wasn't what I was expecting. 'Is…is Joshua there?' I stammered.

'He's helping the kids with their homework… I'll get him for you… Who's calling?' The rolling of the 'r' in homework confirmed the message that my mind wasn't taking in.

'Mo Stevenson,' I went on rapidly. 'My wife and I met him in the park a couple of weeks ago,' I finished, lamely.

'Give me a minute…' There was a clunk as she put the telephone down and went off to find him.

I was still trying to put a face to the female voice when a familiar baritone crooned down the line. 'Joshua speaking.'

Two hours later, both Mary and Joshua Urquhart were at our house. I hadn't tried to explain the situation over the telephone; it was enough that we needed to speak to him.

We were all a bit awkward to begin with. After the introductions had been made, Sarah took them into the living room and sat them down in front of the great pile of letters whilst I made us some tea. By the time I carried the tray through to them, Sarah had made a start on the lengthy story that would lead up to our present dilemma.

Mary was a neat, no-nonsense sort of woman in her early forties. She had very light blue eyes – which never left Sarah's face. Her auburn hair was plaited and pinned in a bun on the top of her head. Seated next to Joshua, she seemed tiny (I think the right word is petite). When Sarah got to the bit about finding the valley, off the Tomintoul road, she smiled. Her face lit up. An infectious chuckle burbled out involuntarily. She turned to her husband; her eyes were laughing.

He met her gaze with a flashing smile that was an ivory poacher's dream. Sarah and I looked first at each other and then back at the two of them who seemed to be enjoying a private joke.

'Excuse us.' Now his deep chuckle was being controlled. 'It's just that Mary was born in Dufftown, a nearby village to the area that you are describing. We met when we were both studying theology at Aberdeen University; she knows the area well. She would do anything to live there again!'

'Do you know the actual place?' Sarah sounded incredulous.

'I think I know exactly where you left the road… I've never seen the glen that you are describing, but I must have passed it a million times… Please, go on, I must hear the rest of the story.'

Sarah continued with the saga about what had happened when we returned home. I took up the story where I tried to explain how the feelings of violence and frustration had gripped me. Mary's eyes took on a softness that calmed my mind – just retelling the story had brought it all back, and for a second I could feel a thudding in my temples and my mouth went dry. As I sipped at my tea, Sarah took up the story once more.

She retold the episode with David's headmaster and our feelings of helplessness. Then the chance meeting in the park: the prayer… the feeling of a burden being lifted. Sarah seemed a bit embarrassed by this revelation, so I finished the story. When it got to the part that included George's finance plan, I had to exchange notes with Sarah to be sure I had understood the full implications of his complex funding arrangements. Finally, Sarah showed them a copy of the advertisement that we had placed; then she waved her hand over the mountain of mail we had received.

'This is now our problem… I don't want to play God with other people's lives!' she announced.

There was a silence. Joshua looked at each of us in turn. His face had become very serious. 'I'm not sure I know what to say.' He paused and took a deep breath. 'I believe that you have answered our prayers.' At this, he looked directly at Mary, and she solemnly nodded. He continued, 'At times like this, I have learnt that it is better not to be too hasty. It is a time for reflection and prayer… What we need is the gift of discernment.'

I wasn't at all sure I knew what he meant by that last word, but I nodded – it sounded right somehow.

Mary had closed her eyes, but a single tear was rolling down her cheek, which she brushed off with the back of her hand. Sarah reached into her pocket for a tissue and blew her nose. I only knew that the short hairs on the back of my neck were standing up!

Joshua started to pray: 'Father God, we know that you always want the best for us, your children, but sometimes we cannot see the way ahead as clearly as we should, and we know how easy it is for us to get it wrong… We acknowledge our weakness and frailty, and we would like to claim the promise that Jesus gave us before he was hung on the cross: that you would send your Holy Spirit to help us and guide us. We ask now, Father, that in the name of Jesus, you will grant us the blessing of understanding what it is that you would have us do with the opportunity you have laid before us. Grant us wisdom and understanding and bless all that we now do in your name. Keep us safe and let no powers of darkness come between the vision that you have for us and the reality that could influence so many lives. Keep your Holy Spirit close to us – we ask all this in the name of Jesus – Amen.'

This time there was no feeling of a burden removed. I checked with Sarah later, and she agreed.

Joshua smiled a reassuring smile. 'All will become clearer – trust me about this.'

'What should we do about sorting these letters out and replying to them?' she queried.

Mary answered her, 'A day or two either way won't matter… There will be an answer to this afore long.'

They left soon after. They had two daughters, so they would have to get back in time for supper. They promised to call us the next day and said that we should all get together again. Perhaps we would like to take David with us and have a meal with them? David! We had both almost forgotten about him! He was still at Wayne's house…and given the problems that had started with that young man… I left with the Urquharts and set off to collect our son.

The boys were still playing in the backyard when I arrived at the house. Wayne's mother invited me inside. The kitchen smelt of damp washing, and she had been ironing. The baby was asleep in a pushchair whilst the two small girls were watching a kiddie's video in front of a portable television in the corner of the room. They both looked up at me shyly, then went back to watching the television.

Wayne's mother went to the back door and called out, 'David, your dad's here.'

David's head came around the door. 'Oh, Dad, can't I play for a bit longer?'

'Sorry,' I answered. 'It's school tomorrow… I bet you haven't done your homework yet…' I realised I had probably said the wrong thing when Wayne's head came around the door, for his face told me that doing homework wasn't high on his list of priorities. I wasn't prepared to discuss the matter, and David read this in my face. He went off to get his jacket, but his face had taken on the same pouting disapproval that I had seen before on Wayne the first time we had come to pick him up.

David said a quick, 'Thank you for having me,' and we left. He didn't say much in the van as we headed for home, but gradually the tension between us evaporated. And as we arrived home, he asked, 'What's for tea? I'm starving.' He didn't wait for an answer but let himself out of the van and skipped off up the path, presumably to ask his mother the same question.

After we had all eaten, David went off to his room to finish his homework, and I helped Sarah to clear away the dishes. So far, we hadn't had an opportunity to discuss the implications of our meeting that afternoon.

'What did you think of the Urquharts?' Sarah initiated the conversation that we both needed to have.

I frowned slightly; to be honest, I didn't really know what I thought. She paused waiting for an answer. 'I sort of gathered that they might like to join us.' I remembered Mary's chuckle and Joshua's big grin.

'Hmm… I think you could be right…but…' She left the question hanging. She voiced my own thoughts whilst I was still searching for the words. 'They're nice enough people, but I don't know if I'm comfortable with all this religious stuff. Do you think they'll expect us to start some sort of religious community?'

That was the thought that had bothered me as well; although, try as I might, I couldn't see why that thought did bother me so much. Usually, I need to think of what I want to say before I speak, but suddenly I was answering her question before I had even formulated an answer: 'Some strange things have been happening to us lately – and I don't know, but I feel that we are about to embark on some sort of adventure… Something totally different from how our lives have been in the past. Things are happening to us that we don't seem to have much control over. Perhaps we should just go with the flow.' I couldn't remember where I'd heard that phrase before, but it seemed to sum up my thoughts. 'Let's go along with them for the time being. If it doesn't seem right later on, we can always say no.'

Sarah shrugged her shoulders. I could see that she didn't have an alternative plan. She then looked down at the pile of letters on the floor. 'What shall we do with these?' she asked plaintively.

I bent down and started to gather them all together. 'Let's wait until we hear back from the Urquharts.' I continued pulling the letters into one big pile.

Sarah went to the kitchen and returned with a couple of black polybags. As she held one of them open, I unceremoniously stuffed handfuls of letters into the sack. We filled the two bags, so she had to fetch another one before we could finish the job. I heaved them over to the bookcase and stood back looking at our handiwork and thinking of all those people who had taken the trouble to put pen to paper after reading our advertisement.

When we got home from work the following evening, there were another twelve letters from applicants – we didn't even try to read them – we simply put them in the sack with the others. There was also a letter from the estate's office giving the details of the land, including a map of the area with the boundaries of the property delineated in red.

We received two phone calls that evening. The first was George telling us that he had been able to gets all sorts of quotes from various building societies vis-à-vis the proposed purchase of their house. He seemed very bullish about us being able to raise the £100,000 to make it possible to consider the purchase of the land in Scotland. He asked how our advertisement had fared. He was astonished when we told him about the size of the response. I didn't tell him about our meeting with the Urquharts.

Less than a minute later, Joshua called asking if we would like to bring David over to their place for dinner the following evening. He enquired if we had a map of the place in Scotland. When I told him that one had arrived that very morning, he gave out one of his infectious chuckles. 'See you tomorrow,' he intoned. Then, sensing my unanswered question, he added, 'I think I know what we must do... I'll tell you tomorrow.' He wasn't ready to explain over the telephone. 'Do you know where we live?' He then went on to explain, 'The name of the house is Shiloh.' He chuckled again before giving me the rest of the address.

I went into the kitchen where Sarah was preparing our evening meal and told her about the calls. She looked uncomfortable, so I gave her a hug and said, 'Things are moving. You do still want to move out of London, don't you?'

She looked at me with a worried look on her face. 'You know I do,' she said. 'It's just that I don't want us to be steamrollered into something we don't want... It just seems that we are being swept along, and we are not, somehow, in charge of our own lives.'

I gave her another hug and said, 'Let's just relax for now and see what happens.' I didn't know why, but I didn't share her anxiety. It was a bit like propagating seedlings: there comes a time when you must just wait and see. For some reason, I had this mental image of mustard seeds growing – you could almost see them pushing upwards, those tiny specks, in a feverish bid to reach the light – it was strangely comforting.

The next evening saw us driving slowly down the road where Joshua lived. It was a quiet residential area. Most of the houses were named, so we had to cruise along slowly in order to find the house. Nanuki, followed by Nirvana, then the inevitable Dunrovin, then we saw it – the name on a brick gatepost leading into a small driveway – Shiloh.

'It sounds like someone likes westerns,' I joked. 'Wasn't there a cowboy film called *Shiloh*?' I asked.

Sarah was busy organising David and giving the usual warnings about being polite. He didn't say anything. He had heard it all before, and he was usually good when we were visiting.

We pulled into the drive, but before I could turn off the engine, the door opened, and Mary came out to welcome us. She ushered us into the house. Every spare bit of wall space was book-lined, books were everywhere. There was a wonderful aroma of food cooking: it was a spicy, fruity, strangely exotic smell that pervaded the whole house.

Two teenage girls came out of the kitchen. The oldest girl, it transpired, was sixteen, although she might have been a lot older, She was gorgeous, as tall as her father, and although she was only dressed in a T-shirt and jeans, she could have been a top model. She had wonderful almond-shaped eyes set in the most exquisite face, which was a café au lait colour.

She smiled and put out her hand to Sarah as her father, who also came out of the kitchen wiping his hands on a tea cloth, said, 'This is my oldest daughter – Sophie.' Then, turning to the smaller edition – who had a smile as big as her father's – he added, 'And this is Esther.'

The girl turned her eyes down in a fleeting moment of embarrassment. It only lasted for a second before she bubbled back with her smile. She was small like her mother, but she had an exuberance that filled the room. Her hair was braided into a plait that hung like a question mark over her head. Her complexion was identical to her sister's, and she was going to be a stunner as well.

'Esther is our baby,' Joshua said with a twinkle in his eye.

'Dad!' wailed the young lady with a look of mock horror that made us all laugh.

Sarah introduced David, and we all moved into their sitting room.

'If you will give me a couple of minutes, I'll just finish what I'm doing in the kitchen,' Joshua said, flipping the tea towel over his shoulder and heading off for the kitchen.

'Joshua is making us one of his specialties from the island where he comes from,' explained Mary.

'Whereabouts does he come from originally?' asked Sarah.

'The island of Carriacou in the West Indies – it's a little island to the north of Grenada,' Mary started to explain. 'But even Joshua has a Scottish connection,' she said, her eyes laughing again.

'Well, I did wonder about your surname, I must admit.' I waited for the explanation.

'Yes,' she continued. 'Urquhart is quite a famous name in Scotland. There is an estate called Craigston in the north-east of Scotland, not that far from where you were on holiday, at a place called King Edward. It seems that many years ago, one of the Urquhart sons went off to seek his fortune in the new world – it was rumoured that he became a privateer.'

'Is that like a pirate?' David was leaning forward on his chair.

'Yes.' Mary smiled. 'There are not too many details about what he did, but he seems to have made a lot of money, and he bought a lot of land on a small island in the Caribbean and recreated the estate that he remembered from when he was a boy in Scotland. He even called the farms by the same names and built houses in the same style… In those days, it was usual to run these farms with slave labour. Then when the slaves had children, he insisted that they be given Scottish names. He was determined, it would appear, that he should make his new home in the sun as much like the estate he had left behind in Scotland. It seems that these names stuck – and generations later, Joshua was born to the Urquhart family.' She opened her hands in a gesture of mute resignation.

'So, was Mr Urquhart a slave?' David asked. Only David could come up with something like that!

'No,' replied Mary. 'Slavery had been abolished a long time before he was born. It was strange though, after attending a mission school, where he got a very good education, he managed to get a place at a British university…and that was in Aberdeen – less than an hour from where his surname had originally come from.'

As Mary was finishing the story, Joshua came in. Picking up the thread of what we had been listening to, he gave a laugh and said, 'When I found out how close I was to the real Craigston, I had to go and visit the place. The locals were intrigued with the story, but when they asked me the name of my island and I told them it was Carriacou, they were very amused. They pronounce "cow" as "*coo*" in that part of the world – and they thought the place was called "carry a coo"!'

We all laughed, and I couldn't help thinking that sometimes the truth is much stranger than fiction. Before we could ask any more questions, Joshua announced that the food was ready and asked if we would like to move into the kitchen.

It was truly a remarkable meal: chicken casseroled in a delicious mixture of mangoes and sweet potatoes with delicious spices. David's eyes lit up the moment the lid was lifted.

Joshua paused before he started to ladle out the food and said a short grace, 'For good food and good friends, thank God.' Mary and the two girls murmured, 'Amen.'

The food was too good to let conversation get in the way of eating, and it wasn't until we had all finished – David had three helpings – that we started to consider the real reason why we had come to visit.

With the dishes put to one side, Joshua started speaking for the benefit of his daughters. He started to retell the story that we had told him two nights before. I felt guilty, for I realised that neither Sarah nor I had really discussed the matter with David. He knew part of the story, of course, but it did concern him in a major way. It was as though Joshua realised this, as he omitted the part concerning David's problems at school. David had asked questions about all the mail that we were receiving, but we had fobbed him off with a story about advertising and that we would tell him all about it, later. Now he was hearing it all from Joshua.

We shouldn't have worried, for Joshua had the compelling voice of the born storyteller; and he made the story into a wonderful tale of mystery and adventure. So much so, that I was almost squirming in my seat waiting to hear how he was going to resolve the present dilemma so we could move on with the other characters of the story and proceed with the plan of action.

When he had finished the lengthy preamble, he asked, 'Mo, have you got the map of the place?'

I dug into my inside pocket and brought out the letter from the estate office that had the plan of the area attached. I spread it out on the table and pushed it across to Joshua.

He looked at it closely, counting the dilapidated cottages as he went. '…Five, six,' he concluded. 'And you are looking for five families to join you in this venture?' he asked.

'Well, there's six potential sites,' I replied, confirming his count.

Joshua looked thoughtful; he rubbed his hand through his grizzled hair as though something was bothering him. 'Are there any other buildings there?' he enquired.

'There's an old stone barn with most of the roof intact.' Sarah had a faraway look on her face that I had often seen when she was painting whilst trying to recall some detail or other that she had seen.

Joshua gave one of his special grins. 'That's it.' With that terse remark, he left the table and went to get something from the other room. He returned in no time at all carrying a leather-bound Bible. 'I want to read you something.' He started to finger through the pages until he came to what he was looking for. He started to read Joshua chapter 18, starting at verse 9:

'So the men went all over the land and set down in writing

how they divided it into seven parts, making a list of the towns.

Then they went back to Joshua in the camp at Shiloh.

Joshua drew lots to consult the Lord for them, and assigned each of

the remaining tribes of Israel a certain part of land.'

'Where was Joshua's camp?' asked David. Then something rang a bell.

Joshua's voice chimed, 'Shiloh,' and he started to laugh. Soon we were all laughing; it was infectious.

'I thought Shiloh was somewhere in America,' I spluttered.

'And they divided it into seven parts,' said Mary quietly.

'Are we to simply draw lots, then?' said Sarah, almost in a whisper. Any doubts she may have had seemed to have disappeared.

'Not before we commit this to the Lord,' Joshua said equally quietly.

And so, we did. Joshua and I brought in the black polybags full of letters from the hallway. We tipped them out on the table, and all sat around the great pile of correspondence.

Joshua linked hands with Esther on one side and Sarah on the other; we each held hands until we had all linked up around the table. We closed our eyes and there was a hushed expectancy in the room. The world seemed to stand still. I don't remember hearing a sound; there was only a feeling of wonderful tranquillity.

Then I heard Mary's voice say, 'Thank you, Father.'

We all opened our eyes and let our hands drop to the table.

'Mo.' Joshua looked directly at me. 'We want to join with you. I'm sure you both realised that, but we wouldn't take up a house… Could we lease the barn from you?'

I looked over the table to Sarah. She smiled and gave a quick nod of assent. 'Of course,' I replied. The girls squealed their delight.

'Your family will have one of the houses – that leaves five more families to find.' He turned his attention to our son and asked, 'Would you like to do the Lord's work and pick out five letters from all those in front of you?'

It took a second or so for the import of the question to sink in, then he stretched out his hand and carefully eased out of the pile – slowly, and with great deliberation – five of the letters.

Chapter 8
Chronicles

When David had carefully selected the five letters from various parts of the great pile before him, he looked up at Joshua expectantly.

Joshua rose from the table and after picking up the bags from the floor, he started to scoop all the other letters back into the bags. We all helped him until they were all carefully packed away.

'What should we do about replying to all those.' Sarah looked unhappy.

'I thought I would ask Sophie to help me catalogue them all.' He looked up at his eldest daughter. 'Then all the names and addresses could be entered on my PC. It would be a relatively simple task to produce a reply for each of them. We will have to give some very serious thought about the content so they don't feel that they've been rejected... We would still have all their details in case we needed to contact any of them again.'

It was obvious that this was not going to be an easy task, but we were all ready to gloss over this problem in our excitement to find out more about the families who had been chosen.

There was an air of expectancy that seemed to fill the room when Joshua finally said, 'Well, David, let's see what we have. Would you like to pass the first letter to your mother, and she can read it out to us.'

David dutifully passed the top letter to his mother; she looked at it quickly and started to read:

Dear Sir/Madam, 16th April 1992

Re: Your Advt in Time Out *Magazine concerning building a small community in Scotland.*

I have recently retired, after a career of more than forty years as a concert pianist; my wife is five years younger than me, which makes her sixty-one. Regrettably, we have not been able to have a family of our own, although we both love children.

I was born in Germany in 1930, but my parents brought me to Britain before the outbreak of the war. After the war, my parents took me and my older brother to Israel where they became one of the early settlers. As a boy, I was brought up on a Kibbutz – so the setting up of a new community is nothing new to me. Whilst I have played the piano since I was five years of age, I am not worried about getting my hands dirty!

My wife was born in Holland, and whilst still a child, she was separated from her family, who perished in Dachau. She was brought up by an elderly Dutch couple as their own child. We met in London when I returned to study at the Royal Academy of Music (She had come to London to visit a distant relative for a holiday – we met at a concert, where I literally bumped into her!) We were married as soon as I completed my studies. I was lucky, my career took off almost straight away, and for the past forty years we have travelled the world together. Although I suppose we have become quite cosmopolitan (we speak nine European languages between us), there comes a time when you don't want to travel anymore. We kept a small mews house in Chelsea which was our base when we were home, and on retirement we considered living in Israel; however, what we want most in life is to do something useful in a place that is peaceful and quiet.

We couldn't decide where to live, and we had got into a pleasant enough routine living back in London. But two months ago, returning from having lunch at a small local restaurant, we were set upon by a gang of youths (the shaved head variety). They beat us quite badly – my wife is only just out of hospital – and stole what little we had on us. Now my wife cannot face being out on the streets of a big city.

A few years ago, we had a memorable holiday in the Highlands of Scotland, and we both yearn to live in that sort of environment. We are comfortably off. So were you to choose us as one of your required families, we would be able to pay, outright, for one of the plots that you have advertised.

We both realise that you would probably prefer to have younger people with children, but we hope that this will not be a barrier in considering us. As I said earlier, we are both very fond of children and we are sure that we could offer some value to your small community – if only by way of teaching music!

We shall anxiously await your reply.

Yours faithfully,

Benjamin & Rachel Stern

There was a silence around the table as we all digested the contents of the first letter. Sarah was still looking at what she had just read as if she needed to read it again to herself before forming an opinion.

We all waited for someone to say something, but it wasn't an adult voice that spoke first: 'They sound nice,' said Esther. 'They like children…'

'Out of the mouths of babes…' Joshua didn't finish the quote. 'Let's hear the next; pass one to your father, David.'

The next letter was passed to me. My mind was still reeling, trying to absorb the content of what I had just heard. I gave up and looked briefly at the letter before me. It was written in an untidy scrawl that was quite difficult to read. I made a start:

Dear sir,

I read your ad in Time Out *and it was like an answer to our prayers as a manner of speakin. I am married with three kids and my husband is a builder. That is to say he was a builder before the resession. He run his own business as a builder/roofing man. I used to do the books. We were doing very well until we were hit by the slump in building. He was a good builder and had served his time with Bovis.*

Anyway, we were doing alright then the slump came. We had bought our council house and my husband had fixed it up great. We were all happy. Then the building trade was depressed and *we couldnt get any more work. He had to lay off the three boys that worked for us and we sort of managed by doing odds and sods. But we couldnt manage the repayments on our mortgage as well as the gas and electricity to say nothing of the poll tax.*

The court took our house off us and made my husband an me a bancrupt. I cant tell you what that was like. We still have seven months to go before we will be free again. The DHSS paid for us to live in bed and breakfast but its horrible. The kids miss having their own room. My husband is now working for a double glazing company. He can turn his hand to anything - he can do woodwork and welding - anything.

We were both brought up in the east end and you know coming from that area, we are survivors and we want something better for our kids. Our kids are Jerry who is nine, Samantha who is seven and Charlie who is only two. We are grafters and we could help you build your COMMUNITY.

Please get us out of here cos its doing my head in. Id rather work 24hrs a day to get somewhere than stay in this place. I can't spell very good (you probably realised that even if i did use a dictionary for this letter) but Im good at books, with VAT and all that. I was checked out by them and they were surprised that I never made a mistake.

> *The kids school is 90% packis and I dont think the teachers care about the ones that have always lived here.*

At this stage, I couldn't read the next bit. I pushed the letter to Mary, who was sitting across the table from me. 'Can you read that bit?' I had to ask.

Mary looked at the letter closely and continued reading:

> *We need a knew start and we no you could give it to us if you wanted. We could not buy the land but we could rent if the DHSS helped us. I think they would cos that would get us off there books.*
>
> *Please please get us out of here - we need help, but we could also help you.*
>
> *The telephone wont take calls, but if you could even send me a number I could call you and you would see that we are perfectly genuine. 18 carrot.*
>
> *Yours,*
>
> *Edith Thorpe*

Mary was crying. Silent sobs welled up and took her breath away. Sophie put an arm around her mother.

Joshua said to no one in particular, 'Recently, I read that some forty thousand small businesses went to the wall during just one part of this recession – nobody will ever know what that means in human tragedy:

homes lost, marriages broken, children displaced. Our politicians know nothing about some of the realities of an enterprise culture!'

'Well, I could work with people like that.' Sarah's voice had an assurance that I hadn't heard for some time.

Sophie said, 'Jesus loves that family.' What more could be said?

'David, pass the next letter to Joshua,' I requested quietly.

David was being very grown up. He spread out the letter – I think he was enjoying being the deliverer of news – and passed it across to Esther who passed it on to her father. There were several pages written on lined paper.

We all leant forward as Joshua started to read the letter:

14th April 1992

To who it may concern.

Your advertisement in Time Out *magazine refers.*

As you can see, we live in Wood Green where we have our own house which we bought six years ago. My wife and I both came from South Wales originally, where I was brought up on a farm.

When I was fifteen, I started working at the local butchers as it was not possible for me to work on the farm as my brother was working with my dad and it was only a small farm. My wife went into nursing. I had completed my time as a butcher and Glenis (my wife) and me got married.

A few months afterwards the first of the pits were closed down. The effect of the pits closing in the area had a devastating effect on the entire area. Lots of the shops had to close down and it was only a matter of time before I knew that I would be laid off.

Then my wife was accepted for a position at Great Ormond Street Hospital in London. We decided to move to London. To begin with we lived in digs but when I managed to get a job at Smithfield, we rented a flat. That was twelve years ago, and we have done quite well for ourselves if I say it myself.

We have a nice home and a reasonable car, and we have been able to have a few nice holidays. Six years ago, we decided to start a family and we had our son Rhys – he is now five, but we would prefer to bring him up in the countryside.

We have been back to Wales on holiday, but things are still difficult by way of getting a job as most of the people that still live there are on the dole. When we saw your advertisement, we got quite excited as we would like to help in making a good place to bring up our son.

I could easily turn my hand back to farming (or butchery) and I am sure we could make a go of it. We would not be able to buy a plot to begin with as we would have to sell our house first, but we have put some money aside which we work out would probably be enough to get a mobile home and pay you the rent. We have looked into it and it is possible to get a mortgage to allow us to renovate the cottage that is part of the scheme.

We hope we will be able to meet you soon to discuss this.

Yours sincerely,

Dai Philips

As Joshua finished, he was slowly shaking his head. I think the same thought was going around in all our heads: how many other letters like this were still in the bag. Sometimes we become so involved with our own lives, and our own problems, that we don't think behind every door there are families trying to sort out their own lives with their own problems.

David passed the next letter to Mary. This was the first letter we had seen that was typed.

Mary started to read in her soft Scottish accent:

Dear Sir,

Re: Your recent advt., concerning setting up a Community in Scotland.

I have read your advertisement with interest, and I would be grateful if you could send me further details.

I am thirty-five years of age and I am a self-employed designer – I produce bespoke boardroom furnishings for some of the top companies in Britain. I am married, and we have three children between myself and my wife. I was married before, and I look after the two children from that marriage (two boys aged seven and four), and my second wife has just produced a baby daughter. My wife is taking maternity leave, but she is a computer programmer by profession.

It might seem strange that I would like to bury myself in the Scottish Highlands, but I should explain that both my wife and I are very interested in the environment generally and are passionate about creating a design for living where people can live without damaging this planet. I have made a special study of energy efficient housing and alternative energy systems. I'm not just a theoretical individual; I have a 'good pair of hands' and I can make most things, from fine furniture to mundane jobbing carpentry.

I would like us to live a simpler existence, somewhere that my wife would be happy to stay at home and look after the baby. Please don't think by that last statement that I am a chauvinist. I want to be able to take as big a part of those duties as she does, it is just that living, as we do, in London, by the time I get home from work, I hardly get to see the children at all. By the time the weekend comes around, I am often too tired to be much of a father.

I shall look forward to hearing from you in due course.

Yours faithfully,

Gavin Smiley

'I wonder if he has even spoken to his wife about this?' murmured Mary.

I must admit, the same thought crossed my mind. For the first time, I noticed that Joshua looked a bit glum. Mary was still on a high from thinking that something could be done for the people who were living in a bed and breakfast (even though she had said nothing, I just knew).

'He certainly seems to have some of the talents that we could use.' Sarah spoke as though she was trying to convince herself.

There was a pause: we all had our own thoughts on the matter. I couldn't be specific, but I felt that we had somehow been let down.

David looked around the table wondering who he should pass the final letter to.

'Let Sophie read the last one,' Sarah instructed David.

He grinned at Sophie who grinned back, took the letter and started to read confidently:

17th April 1992

Dear Sir/Madam,

I am a single parent (my husband died at the hands of the Russians during their occupation of Afghanistan). I have a son, who will be eleven next month. I was educated in Kabul University where I studied Political Science.

With the Taliban, once again, becoming more powerful, Afghanistan was not a country well disposed towards women, let alone educated women.

Two years ago, I was granted refugee rights in the UK and have been retraining in psychology. I have also been assisting in the running of a home for battered wives in Ealing.

Now, I would like to put down real roots and build a home for my son. Your project sounds perfect for us as we are, traditionally, a hill people.

When my husband died, he left me reasonably well provided for. (He had been a tribal elder and a senior lecturer at the university before he left to join the mujahideen.)

I would be able to purchase a plot and pay for the refurbishment of one of the houses.

I shall look forward to hearing from you in due course, but should you require any further details, please do not hesitate to call me. My telephone number at home is 071 946 0612.

With best wishes,

Zufash Rasheed

Sophie sighed. 'Now the patchwork is complete.'

We all looked at each other around the table – it was far too much information to take in properly at one sitting.

'Sophie, darlin', would you do me a favour?' Joshua gave his daughter a special smile and went on, 'Would you take these letters to my study and photocopy them so Mo and Sarah can take the originals home with them?'

'Would anyone like some tea?' Mary asked the question, rising to her feet. It was obvious that she was going to make some anyway, so we all nodded.

'What do you think we should do next?' I asked Joshua.

He thought for a moment, and then replied, 'We've got to somehow meet these people.'

'Together, or one by one?' asked Sarah.

Joshua looked longingly at his Bible as though seeking guidance from the closed book. 'They will all need to meet each other sooner or later. Let us, with God's help, bring them all together, and let us see what the Lord has in mind for us.'

That was the first time (there would be many more in the ensuing months) that I envied this big man and his sure certainty and faith that his God had a plan for us – to turn our dreams into a reality.

On the way home in the van, Sarah picked up on my thoughts. 'I suppose that throughout the ages people, who couldn't fathom their own destiny, appealed to some god or other to solve their problems… But what makes Joshua and Mary think that their God has some unique power to help us?'

I didn't know the answer to that question, but I felt her need to hear something optimistic. 'We shall just have to wait and see… It must be better to have some faith rather than no faith at all. At the end of the day, the proof of the pudding will be in the eating.'

She smiled, then leant across the seat and kissed me.

A voice from the back cried out, ‘Oi, you two, no snogging. We’ve got to get home – I’m starving!’

I was so pleased that over all these years I kept those letters. I would never have remembered the contents so perfectly otherwise.

Chapter 9

A New Direction

David closed the exercise book and slipped it to the bottom of the box file. His mind was now full of long-forgotten memories. Whilst he wanted to read more, his eyes were tired; all the pressure of the week now seemed to have sapped his energy levels. Tomorrow would be busy: he had to meet the spooks at their headquarters and then arrange his trip back to Afghanistan.

He stripped off his shirt, went to the bathroom and cleaned his teeth. He removed the rest of his clothes, laying them neatly over a chair, and then slipped into bed. Sleep didn't come easily; his mind was still surging with all those boyhood memories. Even when simple fatigue took over, dreams rampaged through his subconscious.

He came awake, his muscled body tense with head and shoulders off the bed, held in position by a well-trained core. His eyes registered no threat and he relaxed back onto the pillows, but the relentless knife thrusts into the body remained in his recent memory as he had tried to drag Sayyid away. He ran his hand over his face and chest and realised that he was soaked with sweat. It took a while, but eventually he drifted off into an altogether different place.

He was with Esther; they were sunbathing and alone.

She rose to her knees. 'I'm going for a swim, come on.' She ran into the water until it reached her thighs and then dived gracefully into the waves. David hauled himself up and followed her at a run.

They both swam far out to sea before returning, but Esther stumbled whilst wading ashore, so David had to reach out to steady her. Esther turned in his arms and kissed him. That kiss triggered more kisses. Touching, tender feeling, fingers drawn through hair. David swept her up in his arms and carried her the last few yards to the water's edge. He laid her down and knelt beside her; he slipped his hands through her bikini strap and eased it down to her waist and kissed her breasts. She turned his head up towards her so that she could kiss him once more on the lips as he slipped her bikini bottom down to her knees where she impatiently kicked it off altogether.

David opened his eyes. Daylight was filtering in through the curtains as he surveyed his room that looked a bit more severe in the pale light of morning. Disappointed that he'd had to leave the sun-drenched beach, he swung his legs out of bed and smiled as he realised that he still had a hard-on. He shuffled into the bathroom to take care of his ablutions. He would be having another full-on day today.

At breakfast, he wolfed down a bowl of porridge with some blueberries on top whilst he waited for the full English to be prepared – two eggs, bacon, Cumberland sausage, black pudding, tomato and mushrooms. This, together with a couple of slices of wholemeal toast and two cups of black coffee, would have to last him until his next meal, and there was no telling when that might be! David treated food like sleep: take it when you can because you never know when the next opportunity might present itself.

Having taken the tube to Vauxhall, he presented himself at the reception of the SIS building, home to MI6. He gave his rank and name and flashed his ID. Security went through his grip, taking a look through the box file. With arms outstretched, he went through the normal search routine as the body scanner passed over his body. He was expected, so minutes later Peter arrived with a ready smile and an outstretched hand.

'How are you?' he enquired. Then, not waiting for an answer, he continued, 'Did everything go off OK at home?' Still not waiting for an answer, he motioned David through a side door.

David ignored the questions as he rightly assumed that Peter wasn't the least bit interested in his domestic affairs.

Peter led the way. Not bothering with the elevator, they trekked up the stairs at a brisk pace. On the fifth floor, they moved along the corridor and entered a comfortable office that looked down on the Thames.

As Peter took his place behind the desk, he asked, 'Would you like a coffee? Tea perhaps?'

David shook his head. 'No, thank you, I'm good.' He wanted to get on with this meeting, find out what it was all about.

Peter settled himself in his chair and leant back. 'Tell me all you know about your friend Sayyid… I'd like you to start at the beginning and tell me everything you know.' He reached across his desk and switched on a tape recorder.

David started to explain how they first met when his family had hoped to create a community of like-minded people who wanted to leave London, set up a mutually supporting community and create a healthy environment where their children could flourish. He explained how Zufash, having lost her husband when the Russians killed him, had brought her son to the UK from Afghanistan to seek refugee status.

Peter asked, 'Why did the Russians kill the father?'

'He had been a tribal elder and was fighting with the mujahideen,' replied David.

Peter nodded. 'Was his body recovered? Was there a funeral?'

David raised his eyebrows at this question. 'No idea, I'm afraid… It was never mentioned.'

'OK, sorry. I'll save my questions until later. Please, go on.'

David explained how there had been seven families when they started. 'Sayyid and I became friends, we were the same age, he is three weeks older than me. We were both only children, so, having no siblings of our own, over time, we became more like brothers. When we went to school, we got a bit of a rough time at first because we were so different from the local lads, especially Sayyid. We took a few bumps and bruises for a while until Dai Philips took us in hand – he was one of the other fathers in our community. He had been a boxing coach in his native Wales and soon had us sparring together. We trained every day and soon mastered the rudiments.

'Eventually, when Dai thought we could handle ourselves sufficiently well and he knew that the bullying had been going on relentlessly, albeit most of what we had to put up with was verbal, he counselled us that now was the time to make a stand. We did, and it worked…even if it was a bit gory. We never had any more trouble after that, but the headmaster was furious, so we were both excluded from school. It was my mother's turn to be furious; she paid the headmaster a visit when she heard the whole story. The upshot of which, and after speaking with Sayyid's mother, was the decision that we would be schooled at home for a while.

'Sayyid thought it would be fun if we could talk to each other without other people knowing what we were speaking about, so he started to teach me Pashto. I seemed to pick it up very quickly, and we could soon have lengthy conversations with only the odd English word or phrase being used. For his part, Sayyid spoke fluent English that his mother had taught him since he was a small boy. My mother introduced him to English literature, and Sayyid's mother started instructing me in some of the ancient Afghani legends.

'Sophie, a girl from one of the other families who was now at university, was roped in to coach us in maths and physics during her vacation. Later, when we were considering further education, it was suggested that we should study languages, as we had both shown an interest. I think it was about that time when we made one of our rare visits to the cinema where we saw, for the first time, *Lawrence of Arabia*. That's what did it; we decided that we would both like to learn Arabic.

'But it wasn't all studying by any means. We had just about every afternoon off to do what we pleased and, in the summer, when the sun rises very early in the Highlands, we were sometimes off up the hill as the sun came up. Early on, we had met up with Gordon, the head keeper on the estate. He was a mine of information. Soon, we were running rabbit trap lines for him and going out with him on the back of his Land Rover on foxing trips.

'When we were sixteen and wanting to earn some pocket money, he showed us how to tack up the Highland ponies with deer saddles. We would then go to a RV and wait for his signal before meeting up where the stalker and guest would be waiting after the kill. It would then be our job to take the carcase back to the larder. One day, the stalker was with a German guest when we arrived on the scene. The guest had shot a ten-pointer, and he was delighted. Sayyid was busy carrying out the gralloch whilst I was getting the pony ready. He was struggling with his small lock knife on this big beast. From a sheath on his belt, the German drew a beautiful Damascus hunting knife and handed it to

Sayyid. This did the job admirably. Afterwards, Sayyid went to the burn and carefully washed the blade and dried it with his shirt tail before returning it to the guest. The man smiled, took the sheath off his belt and replaced the blade before handing it to Sayyid, telling him to keep it. After we had loaded up, the guest came to me with a generous tip as well.'

Peter interjected, 'You boys must have had a great time hunting, shooting and fishing in those hills, but now tell me about how it all went wrong.'

David, not wanting to think about it let alone speak about it, drew in a deep breath before replying, 'We had gone on our run: we had set ourselves a target of being able to run to the top of the big hill behind our place without stopping. There were two false crests, and the best we had managed was the top of the first crest. It was hard.

'That day, we had pushed ourselves until the build-up of lactic acid in our legs was so painful that we couldn't push ourselves any further. We both looked at each other, grimaced, nodded and slowed to a walk before flopping down beside a big boulder. We were both elated yet disappointed. Elated because we had managed to get further than ever before, but still disappointed that the hill had beaten us once again. As we got our breath back, we looked down into our valley. The sun was warm, and the sweat was stinging my eyes when Sayyid, shielding his eyes, called out, "Sophie's at the pool, and there's a man, I think he's hurting her!" He catapulted himself to his feet and started to hurtle down the hill. I followed, but I had no chance of catching him until his foot must have hit a loose rock and he went down, only slithering to a halt as he hit the base of a large boulder.

'I was about to stop to help him, but now I could see below me. Sophie was fighting for her life against a big man who had her by the waist and was trying to fling her to the ground. She was screaming, and that sound made me run even faster. The man threw her to the ground. She must have been stunned, for she was making no move to get up. As I reached level ground, the guy heard me coming and turned to face me. He swung a huge haymaker, which, together with my own momentum, caught me on the side of the head and floored me. I was stunned but not out. I saw him pick up a rock and come at me, and then Sophie launched herself onto the man's back. He shook her off, but not before her nails had raked his face. He raised the rock and smashed it on the top of her head. He turned, with the rock still in his hand, then a flash of light lit up his sweaty face. His free hand went to his throat, and I watched as blood spurted from between his fingers. With a look of total surprise, he dropped the rock and sank to his knees, but by then Sayyid was on him stabbing, stabbing, over and over again. I tried to pull him off, even as the man's heels were drumming on the ground and a half-stifled groan slithered out of his slit throat.

'I ran back to the house to get help. When I got back with my dad and Dai and with Terry bringing up the rear, Sayyid was washing himself in the pool and looking dazed. Our beautiful Sophie was seriously brain damaged – she died a month after the trial. Her assailant had been the partner of one of the women at Zufash's refuge for battered women. He had tracked the woman down after speaking to one of his kids on the telephone. He'd arrived drunk, demanding to see his partner. When Zufash called up our men for backup, he left, went back to his van for more booze and then came back. He must have seen Sophie sunbathing by the pool.

'The police were summoned and Sayyid was arrested. The evidence was put before the procurator fiscal who determined that he should go to court. In the summing up at the trial, the judge said, "Understanding that whilst the threat the deceased had offered to the young people at the time was severe, the excessive violence shown by the accused was totally out of proportion to the level of violence shown against him as a person." He was found guilty as charged. There had been a spate of knife-related killings in Glasgow, so the authorities were determined to wipe it out. Sayyid was now nearly seventeen and sentenced to seven years and packed off to a young offenders' institution, he completed his sentence in Barlinnie.'

'Did you stay in contact?' Peter asked the question.

'In the beginning, all the time. I would write once a week, and he would reply. He was able to study Arabic. They let him have books, and there were some Muslim inmates, one of which spoke Arabic. I had started looking into Stoicism, and I sent him some books on this philosophy – in the beginning he seemed interested. Later, when he was moved to Barlinnie, I went to see him. Within a few months, he seemed to have got much older. Older and more morose. When I told him that I had been accepted to go to Edinburgh University to read Arabic, he didn't seem that impressed.

'I had been thinking about joining the army for some time. Then, at one of the Highland Games that I'd been to, I met a Para Reg recruitment team, and I got to speak with them. It was through them that I first heard about officer selection, service with the university cadet force…possible bursaries. I discussed all this with my mother and father, and then I made my decision.

'When I next saw Sayyid, he had changed. He had grown a full beard and wore an Islamic prayer cap. When I told him of my decision, he said that we could end up fighting on opposite sides. He told me that he was hoping to be paroled in two years' time and that he wouldn't be staying in the country. The next time I visited, he refused to see me. He had long since stopped writing.

'The next few years passed very quickly. I finished my studies at Edinburgh, attended Army Officer Selection Board (AOSB) and was accepted for officer cadet training at Sandhurst. A year later, I had a provisional acceptance for the regiment subject to passing P Company and doing my jumps to gain my wings. That all went to plan, and I joined 3 Para. Less than a year later, I was doing my first tour in Afghanistan as a young platoon commander.

'In those days the Taliban were on the back foot, so we would patrol in depth into their known areas of influence. They would then gather and engage us in strength. Then, with disciplined fire and movement, we would deploy against them. As the firefight built in intensity, we would call in an Apache, and it would be game, set and match. The helicopter gunship would annihilate them. Their tactics had to change, and they did. It soon became more of cat and mouse, where strategically placed snipers caused initial casualties to draw us into urban areas where IEDs and booby traps would cause much larger casualties, and even counterattacks could be mounted against us.

'We still managed to deny them access to most of the towns and villages. By the time I went back for my second tour, I was a captain and working as the battalion IO. Now our job was to ensure the safety of the people trying to rebuild the major infrastructure whilst still denying the Taliban free movement. We were also tasked with helping to train the Afghan defence forces so they would be able to keep the country secure.

'Because I could speak Pashto, I spent a lot of time talking to tribal elders in the smaller villages. It was at one of these meetings I first saw Sayyid. He was sitting at the back of the room, his head covered with a keffiyeh, part of which was also wrapped around his lower face. As small glasses of Kahwah were being offered, his hand reached out and his face covering slipped. I was looking at him at this precise moment, and I just knew it was him. Even as he covered his face again, he knew that I had clocked him.

'The meeting was over in half an hour, and I left with my escort to go back to our lines. As we turned the first bend, I told the driver to stop; and with my covering party, not knowing what the hell was going on and scrabbling up behind me, I raced up a small escarpment where I could look back at the village. I had glassed the village with my binoculars just in time to see a pickup truck leaving a trail of dust as it took off in the opposite direction. My signals corporal had strategically placed himself just behind me. I asked him to get Sunray to set. When the CO was there, I asked where our nearest patrols were to the road going south. It was perfect; our guys were just where I needed them. He said, "Get a roadblock up immediately. Look out for trouble. They will probably be armed – but, ideally, I need these men captured not killed. I will explain all when I get back." The CO then signed off, and we headed back to our vehicle and back to base. It all went like clockwork. They weren't armed, as it turned out – travelling in broad daylight on that road would have been too risky.

'They had all been arrested on suspicion of trying to buy poppy from the village where they had come from. They were all kept apart, and I had Sayyid brought in. I spoke to him in Pashto and drew my knife and cut the cable ties on his wrists. I hugged him and told him how pleased I was to see him. He remained passively on guard, staring at me intently. Then he asked me about his mother; I told him she was well. I motioned him to a chair, and he sat down still absently rubbing his wrists. There was a lengthy silence as we were both battling our own memories. I broke the silence by saying, "You said we could end up fighting on opposite sides. How goes your battle?"

'He replied, "Not good, David." He used my name for the first time. "There is no real leadership. The imams want to bring about a government of religious intolerance, totally authoritarian on the lines of what is happening in Iran, along with the local militias whose headmen are only interested in money and what they can extort or make from selling poppy. For myself, I just want to rid my country of foreign troops, see an honest, stable government installed with freedom of education for all, and freedom to worship Allah. We will never be a wealthy nation, but as history shows, we are strategically placed between a number of powerful countries, so it should be in everybody's interest that we safeguard our sovereignty."

'I had to agree and told him so: "This is the endgame, Sayyid. NATO involvement is coming to an end, there is no stomach in the West to prolong this engagement, but the West also wants to see a true peace return to Afghanistan." We carried on like this for over an hour. At the end, I posed the question, "Couldn't we work together to do what we could, as brothers, to bring about a peace that we both wanted?"

'After a pause, I continued, "I want to see a day when, after you have achieved what you need to achieve here, you could return to the UK to see your mother. You might even be able to convince her that she should return here with you." I actually think that is what really clinched it. I started to sketch a plan whereby he could lead me to the bad guys – the ones on the top of the pile that wanted the ravages of war to continue for their personal gain. I would arrange for them to be surgically removed.

'And that is how things turned out. It seemed that he was regularly in Kabul; I would arrange a dead-letter box there. We arranged to meet there in four weeks' time in the spice market. I would wear a tunbaan and a turban. My face was already burnt dark brown and my beard would be allowed to grow a bit more ragged by then. I would be there at eight in the morning, then once he had recognised me, I would leave the market, after which he would follow me to a prearranged position where I would have set up the drop box. All I needed was the names of the bad guys to be taken out, and where and when they would be at a certain time. I would arrange the rest. When there was a message to be picked up, he would leave a newspaper on the table of the place where he went for his chai every morning. I had this covered by the shopkeeper who got paid every time he reported in. If I needed to contact him, a paper would be left on his normal table. In the event of an emergency, I gave him a telephone number to memorise. I then put a fresh cable tie around his wrists and called the guards to take him away.

'Now I had to interrogate the other two prisoners. I took one of our translators with me to ask the questions that I posed. I had them photographed and kept asking questions about the purchase of poppy. Finally, I had all three brought into the same room. Through the translator, I apologised and said that it was from the sale of poppy that guns and ammunition were purchased, which, in turn, was causing so much damage to this country. I asked the translator to cut their cable ties, and then to see where their vehicle was, and have it brought round to the front of the building. When he had gone, I appeared busy with my papers. The older man hissed in Pashto, "Was he (nodding at me) only interested in poppy?" The other two glanced at me and nodded. The translator returned with the information that their vehicle was ready, and we escorted them to their vehicle. We watched it reach the guard at the gate who had been told to let them through.

'For the next four months our plan worked perfectly. I had reported to my CO, and he decided that this bit of intelligence should remain between the two of us. During this time, we managed to account for five high-ranking terrorists.

Eventually, our tour of duty came to an end and we were relieved by 2 Para. I briefed their IO and explained that there had been no sign of our informant for the last two months. Were this to change, I left him my email address and asked him to let me know.

After a spot of leave, I decided to apply for SAS selection. I was lucky enough to pass the course and four months later I was back in Helmand!

I had been back a couple of weeks when I got a call from 2 Para's IO. He told me that a young boy had turned up at the gate and handed in a note. It was from Sayyid and asked if we could meet at the café on the next day at 10.00.

It all sounded a bit dodgy, so I filtered in some back-up from my squadron before slipping through the side entrance. He was quietly drinking tea as I sat down opposite him. He spoke quietly in Pashto and told me that he was going away in two days' time. He was to meet two senior jihadis who were recruiting fighters to go to Syria to fight with Isis. I asked him where they were to meet up and he passed me a slip of paper. I asked him if there would be others with them. He told me that it would just be the three of them. They have a pick-up and I will travel with them. I told him to make sure that he travelled in the back. He understood what I meant.

As you know, we were able to take out the two commanders whilst Sayyid made good his getaway. The drone strike ensured that there was no evidence. His story was that he saw the drone as it moved into the attack and he jumped and lived to fight another day.

'Interesting.' Peter then started to explain, 'The day before yesterday, your mate surfaced again. GCHQ identified his phone in northern Iraq. Yesterday, another call, this time from Syria – his voice print was positively identified.' At this juncture, Peter leant across his desk once more to switch off the tape recorder. He gave David a long, hard look. 'Syria is a mess at the moment. Thanks to the Russians and Iranians, and the use of chemical weapons, the rebels are taking a beating. Whilst ISIS and al-Qaeda have taken over much of the country outside of Damascus, they declared a new caliphate that was designed to unite all Arabia. However, they are now on the back foot, as the Kurds, and the Syrian Democratic Forces with help from the Americans, our RAF and the French Air Force have driven them into isolated towns and villages.

'We are not supposed to have boots on the ground, thanks to a vote in parliament, but we must have some independent intelligence on the ground. We have some SF in a training role, and we have been able to embed a few guys with American SF on an exchange basis.' He looked at David and smiled. 'I have got MOD approval to post you to an American unit in Syria as an exchange officer. I've spoken to your CO, and he agrees that it will be an important experience for you. The CIA are assisting as long as they get to share anything that you come up with. We will monitor all of Sayyid's communications and try to guide you in his direction in the hope that you can make contact again. David, a lot of British jihadists have been fighting there, and we believe some of them will try to return to use their new-found skills to cause chaos here, with all the innocent loss of life that entails. We badly need information from the sharp end to be able to combat the terror which will surely increase the risk here in the UK.'

David hadn't seen this coming. He was still trying to digest this last bit of news whilst constructing a list in his head of what he would need to do. 'I'll need to go to Colchester to pick up some gear. I've only got what I'm standing up in.'

Peter's voice left no room for debate. 'That won't be necessary – the Yanks will provide everything you'll need. No one is to know where you have gone; let them think you're still in Afghanistan. I will establish a link with you, and I can forward all emails to your family. You will move out tomorrow. I'll send a car to pick you up at zero seven hundred hours tomorrow from the SF club.'

This ended the meeting, and David was escorted back down the stairs to the main door where Peter offered his hand and wished him good luck.

David needed some air and time to think. He walked along the embankment and looked down at the Thames. It was full tide and the powerful current surged. The only craft on the water was a police launch where the helmsman was having to gun the engine in order to make way downriver.

It was lunchtime when David arrived back at the SF club. He wasn't hungry but bought himself a pint and took it to a corner table. He then pulled out the battered box file, picked out the next exercise book on top of the pile and started to read his father's neat, rounded handwriting.

Chapter 10

Exodus

It transpired that George would fly up to Aberdeen with Sarah and myself to complete the contract that would seal the purchase. Whilst we were there, we gave instructions to our solicitors to draw up the contracts that would cover the sale and leases for our new-found friends – this documentation would be completed once we had all arrived.

After the legal formalities had been completed – it was far quicker than I expected – we hired a car and set out to show George our future home.

When we arrived at the place where the old camper van paused for breath, we parked in a small, natural lay-by that would later become the entrance to our site. We had brought stout walking boots for this occasion, and I led the way with an ever-growing feeling of excitement. It had been a cold October day with grey clouds scudding across the sky, but as we started to descend towards the trees, now bare of their red and silver mantle, the clouds parted, and great beams of sunlight lit up the area like a theatrical floodlight. We paused to take in this sight and draw breath.

George, who was normally quite serious, lit up as though the sunlight reflected in his face and a broad smile heralded the quiet whisper, 'Oh my! What a beautiful place. I can see why you fell in love with it – it's amazing. I don't think I've ever seen a place that I can compare it with.'

Later, on the way home, and again when he was describing it to Meg, he kept going on about the breath-taking view and the air of tranquillity – a piece of paradise.

A plan had been devised that required Terry and I to go to the site as an advance party to arrange for the track from the road to the houses to be widened and made suitable for trucks to access the site. Terry was licensed to use a JCB, which we would need to hire from a local plant hire company, and I would have to project manage all the other necessary aspects. We had found a B & B in the village where we could stay that wasn't expensive. Meantime, Edith and the kids would move in with Sarah at home. Sarah had given notice to the school that she would be leaving at the end of term.

Gavin had discovered a local company that produced accommodation cabins which were used offshore for the workers in the oil industry. These pods would provide our sleeping quarters together with a toilet and shower attached to each pod.

It had been decided to take the big barn and make it weatherproof as our first priority. It would have communal cooking facilities and a large recreational area with a big log fire where we could relax when we were not working. During the day, it would be used for the children – organised by Sarah with help from the Urquhart girls. The second barn was also to be made weatherproof and would act as storage space for our furniture and personal effects until our individual houses were ready for occupation.

We all accepted that it would be more than a bit frenetic whilst all this was going on and it would test our ability to all get by together, but this is what we had all signed up to do – it would either make us or break us!

I sold the camper van and bought an old Land Rover pickup that had four-wheel drive and would be more practical in the winter at our new home in the Highlands. Terry and I used it for the first time driving to Scotland to see what was needed to prepare the site for our arrival in the spring. It was an arduous journey, but we shared the driving which helped a lot.

As it turned out, once Terry had cleared the entrance from the road, the original cart track was exposed. It had been metalled with tonnes of granite pieces laid by hand many, many years before, which were now covered with six to eight inches of earth that had accumulated over the years. He also uncovered a flat stone nameplate with the word 'SUCCOTH' chiselled out of the granite.

When Joshua heard about our find, he could hardly speak as he was so overcome and excited. 'In the book of Exodus,' he explained, 'it was the first encampment of the Israelites after leaving Rameses. Whoever lived in that settlement before must have had a good knowledge of the Bible.'

It is strange how that discovery pleased us; the thought that this place had been home to generations of people before us.

Terry worked like a Trojan. When he wasn't working on the road, he was measuring up the barn, determined to make it habitable by Christmas – when he had set his heart on bringing up his family so they could all spend the holiday period together.

The accommodation pods arrived over two very hectic days. Terry and I tried to position them to give each family as much privacy as possible whilst still making them accessible to the barn. I found a spring further up the hill, and Jerry dug three large concrete collars into the watercourse beneath it. The collars would contain almost three thousand litres of water before overflowing into the burn that flowed down the hill. We then had to bury Alkathene pipe to bring the water to our settlement. This needed to be buried two feet below the surface so our supply wouldn't freeze in the winter. With Terry handling the digger, I laid the pipe into the trench. Terry would then return to backfill the trench every so often. It was a slow, laborious task, but a vital part of our plan.

Having provided water to the barn and each of the accommodation blocks, we now needed to address the question of power. I had sourced a diesel generator that would provide sufficient electricity for the barn. Six smaller petrol generators were purchased to provide lighting for each of the pods.

The days slipped past quickly. When we weren't working, Jerry and I talked non-stop about how to develop 'the project', as we called it. I spoke with Sarah each night. It seemed that everything was going well at home, and Edith and the kids were anxious to join Terry as soon as possible. I was missing my family as well. With a week to go before Christmas, I left the Land Rover with Terry after he had run me to the airport. I was leaving in the morning, and Edith and the kids were due to arrive at one o'clock.

The house still seemed strange when I let myself in. It was that neutral smell of fresh paint and cleaning materials, not what I remembered from... It seemed like a lifetime ago; so much had happened since that fateful summer holiday.

'I'm back.' I fleetingly wondered why I didn't say 'home', but I knew why.

Sarah appeared smiling from the kitchen. 'I've missed you,' she said as she wrapped her arms around me and kissed me. 'Come into the kitchen. I've opened a bottle of wine for your homecoming.' She smiled again and drew me into the kitchen.

'Where's the boy?' I had missed him too.

'He's with your dad – they've gone to a fishing shop. Dad wanted to know what he would like for Christmas, and it seems that David hopes to do a lot of fishing when we get to Scotland. So, they've gone to a place that your dad knows. It seems that before he got so involved with his allotment, he used to do a lot of fishing in the canal.'

'What's it been like having Edith and the children here?' I'd asked this question a few times when on the phone, but I was never sure if the answer I got was because Edith was in the room at the time.

'The children are a credit to her – polite and really well behaved. Much better than our son at the same age,' she said with a grin. 'Edith has been an angel. I've been up to my neck in schoolwork whilst handing over to my replacement, but I'd come home to the place gleaming, everything scrubbed and polished, all the washing and ironing done, and a meal on the table. I've been really spoilt. But what about you? I'm dying to hear all the news. When will we go?'

'Well, it's all very basic, but it's all systems go. We need to apply ourselves in getting this place rented out straight after the holiday, but then we can up-sticks and go.'

'Dad says not to worry about finding a tenant; he can do that for us. He says to leave the place furnished apart from personal belongings as we will get a better rental, and you can also safeguard the terms of the lease better. We can buy all new stuff when we get there and are good and ready to have a fresh start.'

'Well, we'd better ring around our new neighbours tomorrow and let them know the good news that we will be ready to rock and roll whenever they're ready in the new year.'

And so it was that we all got together once more, this time at Shiloh hosted by Joshua and Mary. I explained that everything was very rudimentary and basic, but we did have a place to start our big adventure. Sarah, David and I were planning to set out on the first week of January. We left it that the rest would go home, make their plans and let us know when to expect them.

It was a cold, wet Christmas in London. Not even the festive lights could really cheer us up. Speaking to Terry on the phone, it was bright and crisp in the Highlands with frosty mornings that kept the grass white until midday.

Hogmanay changed all that: a fierce north-easterly gale swept in from the Russian Urals. The Cairngorms were the next section of high ground after crossing the North Sea; the heavy snowfall swept off the hills to form drifts that looked like waves across the road.

Terry fought a continual battle trying to keep our new road open. Even so, he needed to keep the Landie at the roadside. Then when the snowplough came through, he would tuck in behind it to reach the village and restock with provisions. There would need to be a quick turnaround to return before the wind blew the snow off the hill and back into drift waves across the road.

We decided to travel up by train this time. We had packed all our winter clothes in suitcases, and all the rest of our personal belongings that we didn't want to leave in the flat were left with Sarah's mum and dad. These could be brought up at some time in the future. The journey up was spectacular. As soon as we entered Scotland, the landscape became white. Hillsides of pine trees were festooned with snow and icicles, and blue skies and watery sunshine lit up each panorama. In the cosy warmth of the train, we were unaware of the severe cold outside.

Terry met us at Aviemore station, but we couldn't all cram into the pickup, so he took the luggage and we followed him in a taxi.

When we arrived at the barn, we were met by Edith with a beaming smile. A huge log fire was crackling in the massive new hearth. A great pile of cakes, which made David's eyes widen, and a large pot of tea was just what the doctor ordered.

Later, I took Sarah down to our sleeping accommodation. The generator was gently throbbing outside, and the heated wall panels offered a comfortable heat as we went inside.

All the other families turned up over the next few weeks. Joshua and his family were the first. He was resplendent in a sheepskin coat and fur-lined flying boots that he'd bought from an army surplus store. Mary's face was radiant with delight at being back in her beloved Scotland. The girls were strangely quiet as they peered up at the snow-swept hills and mountains.

Gavin had brought the family up by car and managed to find us on the map. As soon as he arrived, he announced that having no communications here was going to be a problem.

Rachel and Benjamin flew into Aberdeen and took a taxi. But as the Cock Bridge to Tomintoul road was blocked, they had to take the long detour, which took almost as long as their flight from London. They were very tired when they arrived and looked exhausted.

Zufash had sold her Vauxhall and bought a Fiat Panda 4 x 4 – this turned out to be the best car ever in deep snow, even better than the Landies. They had split the journey and taken two days to get to Tomintoul, but they couldn't find us. Geordie at the garage helped out and jumped into his truck and told them to follow him.

Dai and his family were the last to arrive; they, too, had swapped their car for a serviceable Landie. Not very comfortable for the long journey from England, but it would pay off handsomely in the weeks and months ahead. Dai almost had a permanent grin as he looked up at the hills that were even grander than anything he had seen in his native Wales.

It was the first night after we had all arrived. We had gathered in the barn for our evening meal when Joshua stood up. With his hands outstretched towards us, he spoke in his rich, chocolate, baritone voice. 'You all know that I'm a man of God. I call myself a Christian because I wish to follow the example of Christ.' He went on almost without pausing, 'This Christ was born in a place like this.' He stretched out his hands, turning his palms upwards as though to encompass the space. 'He went on to work with his father, carrying out many of the tasks that we will be carrying out in the days and weeks to come. He loved people and hated hypocrisy. He championed justice and abhorred violence. To those around him, he offered a peace that passes all understanding.'

At this point I looked around the gathering. Even the children had stopped playing and were listening to the compelling tones as Joshua was continuing his message. Most were looking at him directly. Only Gavin seemed to be uncomfortable as he stared into the flames of the fire; his downturned lips suggested that he didn't approve of the words being spoken. Zufash was studying her nails, but her face was impassive.

Joshua's voice lowered to a persuasive whisper. 'Before Jesus died, he made a promise that wherever two or three are gathered together in His name, His spirit (His presence) would be there also.' He carried on, his voice rising gently, 'I would like to claim that promise now. I want to ask the Lord to bless us all, to guard us and keep us safe, to guide us with His love, and to help us make a success of this community, Amen.'

I looked around again. Edith had a tear rolling down her cheek. Dai Philips took a tissue from his wife and blew his nose vigorously. The children went back to their toys. It took everybody else a while before normal conversation swelled up again.

I thought about this later that night as I lay in bed next to Sarah. I just knew that I had witnessed a defining moment in our group's existence. I just couldn't be sure, however, if this was for the good. I put my arm around Sarah and cuddled closer. I certainly felt peaceful and pleased with how our life was growing in a way that we could never have even imagined some months ago. I closed my eyes and drifted away into an untroubled sleep.

Chapter 11

The First Note of Dissent

As it happened, the first real disagreement came about our food supply. Thus far, we had been buying everything from the village corner shop, but Edith had suggested that we would probably get better value for money if we made the trip to a larger town where we could buy from a supermarket.

Grantown-on-Spey was suggested, but Mary said it wasn't big enough to have the range of foodstuff we might want. It would be a longer drive, but a monthly trip to Elgin would mean that we could get everything we would need there.

It was Rachel who asked the question that no one had thought of, 'Do you think we would be able to buy kosher food there? Well, it's the meat really…' Her voice trailed off as everyone turned the question over in their heads.

Benjamin walked over to her and put his arms around her shoulders. 'We've often had to give up on that requirement, but I don't think somehow that God will hold it against us.'

Zufash agreed, 'I gave up Halal meat as soon as I came to Britain.'

Mary smiled encouragingly. 'All the Middle East religions had strict dietary rules two thousand years ago.' She went on, 'Animal husbandry was not what it is today. Pork was considered unclean because pigs were allowed to root around and they would eat anything, including human excrement! All other animals had to be slaughtered by bleeding them to death. Blood had been recognised as the first part of the animal to decompose and most likely to become infected; this, in turn, could cause problems for anyone who eats the meat. To be on the safe side, it was usual to get a priest to say prayers over the slaughtered animal asking God to ensure that the food was safe to eat.'

'Isn't it cruel to bleed an animal to death?' David then arched his eyebrows as he started to elaborate, 'Do they slit its throat?'

Dai spoke up at this question. 'It doesn't happen in our regular abattoirs. The animals are stunned before being slaughtered. Everything is done humanely under the supervision of vets. All the areas are kept immaculate and hygienic.'

The conversation trailed off as the women changed the subject to what would be needed on the shopping trip. Lists were drawn up, and they would take the two Landies. Mary would drive one and Dai the other – if one got stuck in the snow, the other could be used to pull it out. Susan would go with Mary whilst Glenis would accompany her husband. Edith volunteered to look after Rhys and Willow along with her Charlie. The two Urquhart girls were busy reading stories and getting the other younger children to read along with them. Sayyid and David put on their boots, coats, gloves and hats and went to go outside to explore.

Before they left, Sophie called them over and gave Sayyid a foolscap pad and a couple of ballpoint pens and asked if they could come up with a map of the farm. 'Pace out the boundaries and put the values in, then see if you can put all the houses and barns in the correct position. We need to have the burn marked in and our water supply. Bit by bit, we can get you to add things until we have a complete picture of where we live.'

The boys looked a bit crestfallen at first, but Sophie was so enthusiastic that they caught the mood and went through the door as though going on a real voyage of discovery.

The day before we had bought some timber from a local timber yard, and Terry and I were making some trestle tables, which we then put together to become one baronial-sized table where we could all sit together for meals. Later, we'd be able to use them singly in our individual homes and bring them together when we wanted a communal party. We had managed to buy a job lot of chairs from an auction when Terry and I had been working here before the other families arrived.

Gavin had set himself up a small workstation in the corner of the room. He had installed a very clever design tool on his PC and was working on the design of Benjamin and Rachel's house. Benjamin put his book down where he and Rachel had been sitting reading and went across to see how Gavin was getting on.

Gavin looked up from the screen as Benjamin peered over his shoulder. 'Pull up a chair,' Gavin suggested. 'I'll show you what I'm trying to do.' He pointed to the screen where the cottage was faithfully represented. 'You see, these houses were built by hauling large bits of granite into position, then filling the bits in between with other smaller pieces and a rough mix of mortar. Some of those walls are two foot six thick. They thought that would hold the heat from a small peat fire. I'm afraid it doesn't. Any heat you produce inside this shell will pass through even this thickness of wall; granite simply isn't a good insulator. However, were you to clad the outside and between that cladding and the outside of the granite wall you insulate, the inside of the wall will heat up and give that heat back into the room.'

'That is a clever idea, but what would we clad the outside with?' Benjamin asked.

'Well, those trees on the skyline are European larch. I took a walk up there yesterday and by the looks of it, the winter storms seem to uproot a few every year as there is not enough subsoil. European larch is a really useful timber, as it doesn't rot easily even without any form of treatment. Farmers always used it for gateposts when they could get hold of it. Even when buried in soil it's been seen to last for many decades. It also matures to a very attractive grey colour as it dries out. I'm sure we could get permission from the Forestry Commission to fell a stand of that as long as we then replanted the area.'

'Would you need it brought down to the roadside and sent to a sawmill to get it sawn into planks?' Benjamin asked astutely.

'No, we can hire in a mobile sawmill and do it all on site. It will also give us masses of offcuts that we can use for fuel,' Gavin replied.

Joshua entered backwards from the kitchen with a tray of mugs. 'Tea, everybody.' He moved around the room serving everyone as he went. When everyone had been catered for, he went to the hearth and moved around the smouldering logs before adding a few more to get the flames dancing in the grate once more.

Terry took a gulp of his tea before looking out of the window that had been part of his handiwork during the setting up phase. 'It's snowing again. Those boys must be frozen out there.'

Bang on cue, the door opened, and the two lads stamped off the snow on their boots before coming in. The heat from the room caused their faces to flush as they snatched off their gloves and woollen hats and started peeling off their coats.

'Where's my mum?' asked Sayyid.

'In the kitchen preparing our meal for tonight. The kettle has just boiled, so why don't you go and get a hot drink?' Joshua nodded towards the kitchen.

The boys disappeared but soon returned with a steaming mug of hot soup and hunks of freshly baked bread. It was Zufash's turn to back through the door, this time carrying a large tray with bowls of soup for everyone.

Benjamin returned to his seat next to Rachel, who had dozed off and then woke with a start. The snow outside seemed to muffle and cocoon the barn as the afternoon wore on. The babies were asleep on the sofa, and the two older boys were helping Jerry and Robin put the finishing touches to their fort.

It was only four o'clock, but it was dark outside. The snow was falling in great flurries and swirling about outside the barn.

Gavin went to the window. 'I hope our shopping party will be OK.' He let the curtain drop back into place. 'We really will have to address the problem of communications. Were they to have a breakdown or an accident, there is nothing we can do about it.'

'Perhaps we could set up a CB radio station and fit one in each vehicle,' Terry suggested.

'I don't know if we could get sufficient range with all these hills, but it's certainly worth looking into,' agreed Gavin. He quickly added, 'We really ought to have a landline here in case of emergencies, though. There's a line of telegraph poles at the roadside, so it would only be necessary to bring the line down to here alongside our track.'

Another two hours passed.

Zufash had gone back into the kitchen three times to hold back the meal. ‘Perhaps we should feed the children,’ she suggested. As no one said otherwise, she called Sophie and Esther to give her a hand.

David and Sayyid also went into the kitchen and came back with knives and forks to start laying the table.

The small children, having been fed, were back on the couch listening to more stories. David and Sayyid then helped the younger boys put all the Lego away.

Zufash started to lay the table again. ‘We’d better eat this meal before it’s ruined,’ she said quietly.

The shopping party had now been away for some nine hours.

‘There’s got to be something seriously wrong; they should have been back hours ago. Susan knows that the children should have been in their beds hours ago.’ Gavin’s face was a mixture of annoyance and worry.

They all gathered around the table and started to sit down. Once they had settled, Joshua looked around the group and held out his hands to clasp those of the people sitting either side of him. ‘Shall we just say a short prayer for the safety of our loved ones who are out in this awful weather?’ He bowed his head, but before he could continue, Gavin rose noisily from his seat.

‘I can’t take any more of this nonsense!’ He took his plate and stomped off to his workstation in the corner.

Joshua quietly ignored the interruption and continued, ‘Father God, before we eat this food that you have provided, we are concerned for our loved ones who are out in this storm. We ask that you keep them all safe and return them to us as soon as possible.’

The words were hardly out of his mouth when the door was flung open and Dai stumbled in looking like a snowman. Ice and snow surrounded his mouth where his breath had frozen in his beard. He made no attempt to take off his coat and said, 'We're stuck in a ditch about a mile down the road. It's the third time it's happened on the way back, but this time both vehicles are up to their axles! I'm going to take the tractor with the snowblade, but we'll need manpower and shovels as well.' He turned to the bigger boys. 'Will you take the big sledge that we made up to the roadside? We'll need it to get our provisions back down; the vehicles will have to stay there. Oh, and boys, don't stay. Leave a lantern on the sledge so we can find it and then come straight back down here – it's like the Arctic out there.'

There was a general hustle as the men grabbed their coats and pulled on their boots. Dai was already off to get the tractor. Benjamin was also pulling on his coat when Joshua put a hand on his shoulder. 'Would you keep an eye on the boys and see that they come straight back as soon as they have got the sledge up the road?'

Everybody set off. The track to the road was full of drifted snow more than three feet deep in places. The tractor passed them, not even trying to use the snowblade – it would have taken too long to clear a path to the road.

When they eventually reached the stranded vehicles, Dai had shovelled the snow from under the front wheels and managed to get a chain attached.

Mary, her face peering intensely through the windscreen, was trying to gently ease the clutch out in order to get some traction. The chain strained as the tractor reversed and gradually pulled the Landie out of the ditch.

Susan's face was grey, and her lips were blue. Her topcoat had not really been up to these conditions, so she was chilled through to the bone. The other vehicle, in an attempt not to hit Mary's, had swerved and was now balanced across the ditch. Dai had to now attach the chain to the rear and haul it backwards. The front of the vehicle crashed down into the bottom of the ditch before it was dragged up the side, with grass, snow and ice balling up on the chassis.

Eventually, both Landies were back on the road. Dai led the way back using the snowblade to level out the worst of the drifts. The rest of the helpers piled into the back of the vehicle to get to the farm gate. Once there, they piled out and started digging out sufficient space for the two vehicles to be off the road so as not to impede the snowplough when it came through, hopefully the next morning.

At the gate, the sledge, already covered in an inch of accumulated snow, was lit by a lantern that the boys had left. We unloaded all our provisions and piled them on the sledge, and then we all set off to get back to the barn as quickly as we could.

The adventure was over. Susan had mild hypothermia and required swift treatment which Mary attended to. For the rest, a mug of hot soup and then Zufash's curry soon made the last few hours easier to bear. Gradually, we all made our way back to our cabins, but we were aware that there were lessons to be learnt and action to be taken to ensure this wasn't repeated. We had been lucky this time, but it could have ended much more seriously.

The next morning dawned with clear skies and sunshine. The storm we had experienced the night before had left an incredible calm. The entire panorama was a winter wonderland of unblemished white and the trees heavy with snow. It was still cold and there was a firm crust on top of the snowfall. All the youngsters wanted to go and play outdoors, so as soon as breakfast was over, they all got dressed in warm clothes and boots and trooped off outside. The Urquhart girls decided to go with them, *to keep an eye on them*, they said, but they were soon building a snowman and throwing snowballs themselves.

After Edith came around with the coffee pot to replenish everyone's cup, Gavin started on the subject that we all knew was coming. 'We had a lucky escape last night. We could have been sitting here today mourning the loss of some of our loved ones. We need better planning if we are to survive winters like these. This is not London. And if we get it wrong, somebody will end up seriously hurt or dead. Oh, and don't tell me that we'll all be kept safe through prayer. I don't believe in God, and it therefore follows that prayers are only so much hot air! It doesn't help, and I, for one, didn't come here to join a religious sect.'

There was a brief silence around the table before Dai spoke. 'I agree that what happened last night could have been avoided. I, for one, have never seen conditions like that. In future, we must pay far more attention to the weather forecast. Perhaps we should set up our own weather station and record conditions so we can monitor our own very local situation.'

Edith broke in, 'When we have to go out in the winter, we do need the right clothes, and we should take food and hot drinks in case we get stuck somewhere.'

'You're right.' The mellow tones of Joshua's voice always seemed to calm things down when matters became heated. 'We obviously need more planning, better communications, and an emergency procedure if and when things go wrong. I'm sorry, Gavin, if my prayers offend you, but you see I've been doing it since I learnt to speak. I learnt to do this on my mother's knee. An' do you know, throughout all my life I have experienced the love of God and that peace, that I believe, can only come from him. However, I have also discovered that you cannot argue the case for the existence of God; it doesn't work that way. People will only come to the peace I speak of when they want to. I would say when they feel a need to search for the truth. When that day comes, my job is to be there for each one of you, to help and to guide through the study and training I have undertaken. Meanwhile, I have a strong back and a willing spirit. I want to help all of you to build a real land of milk and honey. Oh, but please don't ask me to stop praying because I just can't! Now, where were we? Ugh, yes, planning. I remember something that Zufash said a long time ago.' He looked at Zufash and nodded. 'Edward de Bono's Six Hat Theory?' He smiled his big Satchmo grin and went on, 'I think that this might be a good subject to try out. What do ya think?'

I could see from their faces that some of them had forgotten all about this theory, but gradually, and with help from each other, they began to piece together how it would work.

'First, we need someone to prepare the plan that we can all then consider. Gavin, would you like to prepare something to start us off?'

I got the feeling that this was right up his street, but he frowned and said, 'Well, I'd need a bit of time to do some research.'

'How long would you need?' asked Joshua.

'A couple of weeks perhaps to get all the ducks in a row,' was the answer.

'Then, let's say next Monday week, straight after breakfast. We can get the youngsters sorted and then get down to business.'

I had been thinking a lot lately about planning for the future, and I wanted us all to make a start on that, so I said, 'We have got a great deal of planning to do: the development of our houses, access to drainage and water, fencing if we want to keep animals, a growing tunnel to grow vegetables…' I think I trailed off as the number of things to do in the future overwhelmed me.

Joshua spoke again: 'Mo, would you like to start things off in terms of forward planning in the same way that Gavin is going to do with communications and winter travel? There might be some overlap, but we need to make a start, for there is a great deal for us to do.'

The front door banged open and a melee of red-faced youngsters rushed in to tell us all about the wonders of the great white outdoors.

Gavin worked hard and brought us a plan that would give us communications with the outside by way of CB radio, and an application was made for a BT line to the barn which could be divided into separate lines to each house later. The Landies were equipped with winches on beefed-up bumpers. Shovels were permanently attached on the roof whilst extra clothes, survival blankets, flask of hot drinks and food were always available when journeys in the winter were considered. The question of the weather station was put on hold whilst more research took place. Although, it was considered a good idea to involve the youngsters in gathering and translating the readings into vital information that could affect any of us.

This process of making decisions became the rule for every important decision. One person would be invited to prepare a report on the subject, and then we would go around the table trying to add value to the concept. Then the original author would be invited to find things that he or she didn't like or might go wrong – in other words, to be the first to criticise their own work. Then, once again, we would all go around the table looking for problems with the plan. Finally, we would let the author come up with what actions he or she could recognise that would mitigate any problems before going around the table one last time.

I always came away from one of these sessions thinking what a positive way to solve problems in the real world. I'd think back to some of the scenes I had seen on TV from the Houses of Parliament of braying MPs barracking each other. Instead of combative debate, we had a constructive discussion where the only object of the exercise was to find the best answer for our community.

The rest of the winter passed quickly, the snow went away, and blue skies and sunshine heralded the spring.

Chapter 12

Memories

As he reached for another exercise book, David glanced at his watch. Half an hour had passed, yet he had only sipped the top off his pint.

Memories were flooding back of that pitch-black night with snow sometimes reaching up to his hips and flurries of snow that got in his eyes as he and Sayyid dragged the heavy sledge up the track to the road.

He took a sip of his ale. Then realising it was almost past lunchtime, he asked the barman what the 'special' was today. Steak and kidney pudding sounded perfect.

After his meal, he went to his room and put a call through to his commanding officer. He explained what had transpired with his earlier meeting and asked if his movement to Syria in the morning had been agreed. He also asked if he would use a secure line to advise his unit of the developments.

He had to wait an hour and a half before his phone rang again with the answer that it was all systems go as everything had been agreed at the highest level.

During the wait, he had done what all good soldiers do when no action is anticipated: he had barely closed his eyes before drifting into a troubled sleep.

He and Sayyid had been picked up by the school bus at the top of the track. Trouble started as soon as they got on. It had been brewing for the past couple of weeks, ever since they had arrived. There was one particular group of four boys, led by big Jamie Carr. He wasn't Scottish but had come up from the Midlands with his family a few years ago and had made quite a name for himself as the school hardman.

David couldn't quite remember what started the ruckus, but it soon got out of hand. The bus driver stopped and ordered everyone to behave or they'd have to walk the rest of the way. Things calmed down a bit then until they finally arrived at school.

David was just getting off the bus, and Sayyid was immediately behind him. Somebody gave Sayyid an almighty shove, causing him to cannon into the back of David who tripped and fell. Sayyid swung round and grabbed the boy who had shoved him – it happened to be Jamie. He tried to pull him off the bus platform, but Jamie kneed him in the balls. Sayyid dropped to his knees clutching his groin and quietly vomiting. Jamie pushed past him just as David was getting up and asked if he would like some of what he'd given his mate. Before David could answer, Jamie punched him in the face and split his lip. Even as David spat out some blood and checked his front tooth, Jamie's cohorts joined in, kicking and punching, whilst the rest of the pupils rushed over to see the fight. One of the masters, hearing the uproar, came running over and soon put a stop to the brawl. Both David and Sayyid were a bit of a mess: black eyes, split lips, and numerous grazes and cuts.

Not surprisingly, no one had seen what had happened. David had fallen off the bus, perhaps Sayyid had pushed him, and then some of the others had bumped into them in their haste to get away before the master took their names.

When they got home later that afternoon, Dai Philips had paused what he was doing to have a mug of tea. 'We'd better get you both cleaned up a bit before your mothers see you. Were you fighting each other?' The boys shook their heads. 'No, I didn't think it would be that somehow. Bit of trouble at school was it?' His lilting Welsh voice lowered as he added, 'Well, I hope they, whoever they were, look worse than you.' As the boys looked at each other, Dai gathered from their faces that it was them who had been on the receiving end. 'I've brought some boxing gloves with me for old times' sake. I used to run a boxing club in Wales a while back. I think some lessons in the noble art might not go amiss. What do you say?'

The boys looked at each other again, but this time there was a different look in their eyes. 'Could you teach us to box?' David asked. 'The leader of this gang at school is a lot bigger than us.'

'The bigger they are, the harder they fall,' grunted Dai.

'When could we start?' asked Sayyid.

'Tomorrow is Saturday… What about after breakfast? We can use the storage barn till the weather clears up a bit.'

Both Zufash and Sarah had been upset when they saw their boys' faces, but Dai made light of it by telling them it was a boy thing… They had just been mucking about…

They trained hard in the weeks and months that followed. Dai was a harsh taskmaster, but he knew his craft well. The mornings were getting lighter, and each day started with the three of them running up the big hill. When they returned, they would put on the large sparring gloves to begin with. Dai would have them working out combinations of punches on the pads.

'Why throw one punch when you can follow up with six? Most fighters always seem to concentrate on the head, when a good solid blow to the solar plexus will stop most people in their tracks,' Dai instructed.

The style of the two boys was quite different. David was classic orthodox: a very fast left jab that he could throw from any angle followed with a powerful short right hand once the target had been softened up. Sayyid had great footwork, he moved around the improvised ring like a big cat, and both hands held low with little or no guard. He looked like an easy target, but David soon realised that his friend had very fast hands and could punch from any angle as he ducked and weaved around him.

At school, the boys had decided that they would keep their heads down and stay out of trouble until they were good and ready. Although they never said it, they were desperate to revenge their last action with Jamie and his cronies.

In the end, it wasn't their choice. Jamie had been in trouble again. It was something to do with a homework project that should have been handed in but wasn't. He came out of the classroom mouthing obscenities in the passageway as David was about to put on his coat. Whilst slipping one arm through the sleeve, it collided with Jamie, who promptly gave him a shove that sent him back against the wall. 'Do you want another pasting?' he snarled.

David straightened himself up and removed his arm from his coat; he then took off his jacket and removed his school tie. 'Yes, it's time we had a rematch – behind the bike shed!' he announced before striding off in that direction.

Sayyid, watching the look of surprise on Jamie's face, added, 'Bring your mates an' all. I'll be happy to take on any of them.' He followed David down the corridor.

It didn't take long for Jamie to gather his mates and a crowd of hangers-on that were always ready to see a fight.

Jamie strode into the area behind the bike shed and ripped off his jacket and tie, then he rolled up his sleeves, bunched his fists and snarled at David, 'Let's see what you've got, then, you little squirt.'

David squared up and moved within striking range.

Jamie charged forward but was brought up smartly with a left jab that caught him right on the bridge of the nose. He wiped his nose with the back of his hand and saw the blood. He rushed forward swinging both fists but neither connected because that left had shot out again, then again, and he felt his eye pop.

David had also seen the result and moved to the right.

Jamie, not wanting to receive another jab, lifted his fists either side of his face.

David had planned for this; he feinted a shot to the head but switched to a short right cross to the solar plexus.

Jamie jack-knifed, the wind whistling out of his lungs.

David slid alongside the defenceless lad and with an open hand, he pushed the boy's head a fraction to the side and then brought another chopping right to the hinge of his jaw just below his left ear.

Jamie pitched forward as though he had been poleaxed.

Some of Jamie's followers had been pressing forward, keen to assist him, but Sayyid rushed across to intervene. What followed happened so fast that no one could be sure what actually occurred, but when the discipline master arrived on the scene, two more boys were unconscious, and Sayyid was on top of a third punching his lights out and had to be physically dragged off.

David's phone alarm went off. The dream sequence of those past events made him smile as he remembered the event so well. They had both been excluded from school. Sarah and Zufash went to see the headmaster in what turned out to be an acrimonious meeting. As a result, it was decided that the boys would be schooled at home. The other parents agreed to see how this worked out before doing the same with their children – if Sarah was prepared to oversee their education. It was, after all, what she had been doing for more years than she would like to remember. Sarah would organise the programme together with the assistance from other family members.

Sophie had been their favourite teacher. She taught maths, but it was always interesting. First, it was maths for life: measuring, areas, heights, miles per gallon. Then really interesting stuff: map-reading. Soon, both of the boys could read maps like they could read a book. Every contour created a picture in their minds; all the symbols were committed to memory. Magnetic bearings changed to grid bearings; trigonometry made logical sense when applied to navigation. They planned long voyages. Not just navigation, but stores required, fuel for the voyage, and water. Later, when they got to know Geordie and were interested in stalking, it was Sophie who investigated ballistics and taught them the actual physics of momentum versus gravity.

Dai Philips continued the boxing lessons. He also taught them both to drive one of the Landies on the field at the back of the barn. Zufash had a good grasp of Arabic, and both boys took to learning a new language like ducks to water. Sarah introduced them to English literature, and her love of art soon had them both drawing and painting. Rachel now had a piano, and both of the boys had started to progress musically, whilst Jacob introduced them to the intricacies and subtleties of chess.

The work that Gavin so cleverly orchestrated on their houses for heating and insulation, and the energy and sanitation systems that he installed, were far ahead of their time; but as it happened, it was so logical that all the group learnt as they went along.

Mo divided his time between the growing tunnels, which provided all their fruit and veg, and the livestock: sheep and pigs, and the crops needed to get through each winter.

Gradually, Esther joined the boys, and then Jerry and Samantha with Robin and Peter. A few years later, Rhys and Charlie, then Willow.

At times there were vast differences in age groups within the class, but it didn't matter. Education was a voyage of discovery, so age doesn't have to come into it. In later years, yes, computers and tablets were used more and more, but that only allowed quicker, in-depth answers to problems that the twenty-first century would produce. The older pupils (they were never called that, by the way) simply helped the younger ones. It was not a one-way street, though. Quite often by teaching something, the teacher found answers at an even deeper level. The youngsters even listened in on the group decision-making when the grown-ups utilised the Six Hat Theory to chart their way in a sometimes-difficult world.

He smiled as all these memories tumbled through his consciousness, realising just how lucky he had been.

David was hungry again. He slung his legs off the bed, laced up his desert boots, then slipped into his parka and left the room. Not feeling like dining in the club, he set off into Knightsbridge to find somewhere to eat.

It was a dreich (wet and dismal) night; the rain came in squalls hammering against the pavements. The smart boutiques lit up their expensive wares in an otherwise miserable setting.

David's phone rang. He slid his hand into his inside pocket; even as he lifted the phone to his ear, he saw that it was Esther. 'Hi, honey, how are you?' He had just started the enquiry when he registered a moped in his peripheral vision that had bumped the kerb beside him and stopped immediately in front, boxing him in between the wall of a shop.

A pillion passenger had slid off the back, now cutting off any chance of a retreat. Both wore black trousers and tops with black motorcycle helmets.

David still had his phone in his hand, and as he registered the glint of light reflecting from the shop on the knife blade, he smiled and lifted his other hand in front of him as a sign of total capitulation.

'Gimee yer phone and yer wallet!' the knifeman demanded.

David could still hear Esther's voice trying to find out what was happening. David's smile grew broader as he offered his phone to the assailant. As his left hand moved across his body, the phone slipped through his fingers.

The black-cladded attacker made a reflexive grab, but it bounced off his arm and hit the pavement.

David's counterattack was simultaneous: the left hand that had held the phone dropped naturally and locked onto the man's wrist above the knife. His right hand splayed between thumb and forefinger and came up under the rigid chin guard of the helmet, taking the throat with so much force that it lifted his attacker onto his tiptoes before crashing him into the wall. Had it not been for the protective helmet, that would have been an end to it; but he still held onto the knife until David, whilst choking off his windpipe, drove his knee deep into his groin.

As the knife clattered to the ground, the other would-be mugger dropped the moped and launched himself at David.

Not sure if he had sufficiently incapacitated his first attacker, he became aware that the second man had him in a headlock. David shifted his hips slightly to the right and lifted his right foot before turning the outside edge of his desert boot until he could feel it make contact just below the man's knee. Then, with all his force, he raked his foot down his shin, feeling the skin peel away from the shin bone.

There was an agonising shriek, but David dropped the first man into a heap and drove his elbow into the second man's solar plexus. Both muggers were now on their knees. The first made an attempt to recover his knife, but David read his move and stamped on the hand remorselessly as it reached the blade. The hand would be broken in several places and unable to hold a knife again for a long time. Now, he turned to the accomplice (with the unhealthy pallor of someone who spent too much time indoors) ripping off his helmet – he found himself staring into a face puckered up with pure fury.

David moved the chin with his open left hand before the chopping right smashed into the hinge of the jaw just under his right ear. The man/boy lay unconscious at his feet.

David's phone started to ring again – it had done so twice in the short time it took to subdue his assailants. He picked up the phone and saw that it was Esther once again. 'Hi, love, sorry about that. I had a small problem to deal with.'

'It sounded as though you were fighting!' Esther cried.

'I do need to tidy up a bit here. Look, I was on my way to get something to eat…' David looked up to see the first guy take off his helmet.

Nursing his damaged hand, the assailant started digging into the back of his waistband.

Still talking to Esther, David pivoted, lifted his knee and swung his foot.

The boy tried to duck, but the foot caught him full in the face, nose, eyes and temple. Goodnight!

'I'll call you as soon as things settle down. I won't be long. Bye, hon, bye,' and so saying, he flipped the cover over his phone and slipped it back into his pocket.

The rain had obviously kept people indoors, thank goodness. He needed to clean up quickly – he didn't want to be making statements about special forces, IDs and assignments in hostile countries. He quickly went through their pockets and took their phones. He picked up the knife and sliced through the cable to the sparkplug on the moped. Using one of their phones, he called 999. After giving the location, he said what had happened and that their phones and the knife had been posted through the letterbox of the adjacent shop. He then rang off.

As he turned the corner at the bottom of the street, he heard the wailing sound of the investigating police car. He turned on his heel; perhaps it would be better to have supper back at the SF club.

Having changed into some dry fatigues, he asked if he could have a steak sandwich and a half bottle of red sent up to his room, and then he put a call through to Esther.

'Are you OK? It sounded as though you were in the midst of a brawl,' she asked with concern.

'I'm fine, it was just a couple of worthies who thought they might relieve me of my phone and wallet,' he told her and then quickly changed the subject. 'Any news on your MSF posting?'

'Yes, yes, that's what I was dying to tell you. I have to leave tomorrow and come down to London before catching a flight to Geneva on Wednesday. I thought as we'll both be in London; you might like to buy me dinner.' She laughed gaily.

'Oh, honey, I've got to move out tomorrow at zero seven hundred hours.'

There was a short, disappointed silence.

'I'm beginning to wish we could magic away the next twelve months. I want to be with you all the time. I want to hold you and love you; I'm fed up with waving you goodbye all the time.' Esther's voice had taken on a breathlessness as though she had so much to say yet so little time to say it.

'I know, love, the time will soon pass, and we can stay in touch all the time.' He knew that his attempt at placating her wasn't having much of an effect as he wasn't even convincing himself.

They carried on talking small talk until a knock at the door announced the arrival of his food. They said their goodbyes, each not wanting to be the last to put down the phone.

On the following day, reading the newspaper on the flight down, Esther read the strange account of two young men found unconscious in a shop doorway with their moped having been disabled at the roadside. The owner of the adjacent shop had been called out; in his letterbox was a hunting knife and two phones. The phones showed images and videos sufficient for the police to elicit confessions on a whole string of muggings. The police did not know the identity of the mystery man who had single-handedly seen off these two attackers. They hoped this wasn't the start of vigilante violence. Both men had to be admitted to hospital: one with a broken jaw, and multiple cuts and bruises; and the other with a broken nose, damaged eye socket and possible cracked skull. Esther couldn't help thinking that it sounded a bit like the reports she'd heard when the boys were excluded from school.

Having finished his meal, David poured the last glass of red, arranged his pillows and settled down to read more of his father's journals.

He read about the daily round of shared work that saw them completing all the houses before the next winter. With spring, two large growing tunnels had been built with nursery beds prepared and a small heated greenhouse to incubate the seedlings. Also, an outside fenced area for root crops and potatoes. Mo couldn't help planting flowers that would liven the doorways and paths in due course. Everybody leant a hand, even the small children planted seeds of their own. Later, they proudly harvested and brought them home or made a present for someone of their own choosing. Rachel received lots of flowers; she was loved by all the children.

The summer was spent draining the fields, fencing and buying stock. Fifty grey-faced ewes to start with; later, three tups were added ready to go about their business come the autumn. A couple of Dexter cows were bought in ready to milk with their calves still at foot. A duck pond was constructed providing home for a mixture of ducks and half a dozen geese, along with a vicious gander who would go for anybody that came near his ladies. The chickens were laying far more eggs than they could eat, so a resplendent cockerel was introduced. The purchase of an incubator ensured that they could also grow chickens for the table.

The greatest asset, for the kids in particular, came about secretly when Terry chatted up a guy at the nearby quarry who used explosives to break up the granite next to the burn. He then cleared the debris using the JCB and applied a waterproofed mortar to seal the cracks afterwards. It was then only necessary to divert the burn by less than a metre. Within a day and a night, they woke to find their very own freshwater swimming pool that constantly flowed. It was always a bit chilly, but the kids didn't care.

As more and more memories came crowding in, David closed his eyes and leant back on his pillows. 'We were so lucky,' he murmured to himself. Then he swung his legs off the bed and headed to the bathroom to clean his teeth and get his gear ready for the morning.

Sleep came quickly, but the night passed even quicker; and it seemed that no sooner had he closed his eyes than the phone alarm went off. He got up and made his way to the bathroom. Fifteen minutes later, he had packed his gear and was downstairs in the dining room ordering breakfast.

At seven on the dot, his driver turned up and led him to the car. He gave David an envelope which contained a single ticket with Virgin Atlantic to New York, then a two-hour wait at JFK before flying on to Virginia Beach. A short note explained that he would be met at Norfolk International Airport by a US Navy Seal, who would take him to their headquarters where he was expected. He would spend the next two weeks carrying out intensive training before flying out to Iraq, and then overland into Syria as part of a US task force, further briefings to follow.

David passed through security at Heathrow and made his way to Costa Coffee, ordered a double expresso, found himself a table in the corner and pulled out the next exercise book.

Chapter 13

Epiphany

Monday 28th February 1994.

A letter to my son.

It has been a hard winter and yesterday's storm was the worst that we have experienced. Luckily, I had managed to bring the sheep down off the hill and into Home Park, next to the barn. After my morning bowl of porridge, and a couple of mugs of tea, I wrapped up and set out with Moss to check on any damage the storm might have caused.

There was a good couple of feet of snow, which seemed to muffle all noise. The trees were heavy with it and every so often you could hear it slide off the branches when the mass could no longer escape gravity.

The polytunnels had survived the storm's onslaught. The chickens rushed out to meet me hoping that I might be one of the boys come to feed them. The pond was frozen hard, and the ducks slipped sliding away when Moss went to investigate. He couldn't resist having a game with them whilst carrying out his herding routine, moving them from one side of the pond to the other. In the end, I whistled him to come with me and investigate the hill just in case I had missed any sheep when I'd moved them down yesterday evening.

The wind had stopped and as we crunched our way through the deep snow, I realised that I was actually sweating!

It must have taken us thirty or forty minutes to get to the ridge. I paused for breath and turned to look back down the hill. The sky was the bluest blue with no trace of a cloud. Apart from our tracks through the snow, the hillside was virgin white. In the valley, I could clearly see all our houses, each with a thin column of wood smoke issuing from each chimney.

I became aware of a lump in my throat. I tried to clear it and realised that tears were coursing down my face. I felt incredibly happy. Looking down on our small community, watching the people that I shared my life with going about their daily tasks, I was simply overcome with emotion.

Why were we so lucky? Yes, we all had a dream and, yes, we had all worked hard together to turn that dream into a reality, but lots of people have dreams and nothing comes of them. I knew that without Sarah's dad, none of this could have happened. Then there was Joshua, with his gentle insistence that we keep God in the picture. That wasn't a very popular consideration in this materialistic age where many people had decided that the concept of a God didn't fit with their total belief in themselves.

Even as all these jumbles of thoughts tumbled through my brain, my vision cleared, just like the scene around me after the storm. I just knew.

I also knew that I must write the chronicle that Joshua had been urging me to write all along.

Gavin would laugh if he knew how my decision had come about, but I had seen the Promised Land.

The flight had taken off on time. The plane wasn't full, so David had a bank of three seats to himself. He had just read something about his dad that he'd never been aware of. *Spiritual? Religious?*

David remembered fragments of conversations, mostly between Gavin and Joshua:

'There is nothing new about atheism,' explained Joshua. 'For eight thousand years before Jesus came on the scene, the Israelites – God's chosen people – regularly decided that there was no one God and went off and sacrificed to other idols or gods.'

'I don't need to worship anything,' replied Gavin.

'Not even the cleverness of man? Not the wonders of technology?' asked Joshua.

'I believe that, in time, we will all come to see this planet and everything that lives on it as a simple equation of living matter,' explained Gavin.

'So, the millions of bacteria that inhabit your gut and without which you wouldn't survive, or the intricate workings of your brain, which even the most accomplished neurosurgeons admit to understanding so little, or even the mystery of water – simple H_2O – which covers more than seventy per cent of this planet and makes up more than fifty per cent of your body is still a major mystery to all the scientists on the planet?'

'Give it time,' said Gavin, smiling. 'In time, all will become common knowledge. Would I find the answers to these problems in religion?' he countered.

'Depends how you see religion.' Joshua looked serious. 'If you focus on the gospels, within the ancient stories recounted by prophets, amidst the myths and happenings of antiquity, and if you let the Holy Spirit guide you instead of your personal desire to "know best", you will make a start in the true understanding of religion and all understanding. Just as the ancient "chosen people of God" moved away from God and then returned, awaiting all the time for a Messiah. They built temples, had various levels of priesthood, dressed up in fancy clothes, sold animals to be sacrificed and changed money – in short, got it all wrong! And when Jesus came, he came to tell people that they had got it wrong. And yet, apart from the very early church of believers who risked their lives to spread the word and serve people, men have vied with each other to create vast religious bodies, cathedrals and palaces, monasteries and convents that repeat the mistakes of history over and over again. If I wanted to end the belief in God, I would start by convincing people that religion was fanciful nonsense, and then I would work on destroying the clerics and everyone involved with the church to ensure that it would never rise again. I sometimes think that maybe Satan is winning.'

Gavin looked resigned; he didn't want to argue. 'Each to their own, then.' He smiled. 'I'll just trust the scientists to answer all the mysteries.'

'And I'll continue to thank God for all his wonderful gifts, particularly the friendship and love that we have within our community.' Joshua smiled his most beatific grin.

David closed his eyes for a moment, so many thoughts flooding his mind, but a thought suddenly hit him. There was so much that he wanted to ask his dad, and the thought that he would never see him again… He had to brush away the tears welling up in his eyes.

The stewardess touched his shoulder. 'Would you like anything from the bar?' she asked with an inviting smile.

Swallowing quickly, he replied, 'A large whiskey and soda would be good.' He added, 'No ice.'

She returned quickly with his drink, and he nodded a thank you.

He sampled the drink as his thoughts turned to Esther. Once they were married, would they stay in the community and educate the kids there as they had been? Esther would always find work as a doctor if she wanted to, but what would he do? Obviously, he would carry out whatever was required as far as the day-to-day living was concerned – helping out at harvest, felling trees, that sort of thing – but he would need more. Perhaps he could write. With a bit of a shock, he had just realised that he'd made the decision to leave the army.

Food arrived, and he had a coffee after he'd eaten. He sat back and continued to read.

As each season passed into the next, their community grew more efficient and even more self-sufficient. Now they were practising not only hydroponics but aquaponics – fish being raised in tanks and fed protein, with the effluent from the fish being pumped through the tubes to nourish the salads and vegetables. All their energy was sourced through either their small-scale hydro scheme or the single wind turbine they had built last year.

There were other moments of sadness: the death of his grandfather George from an unexpected heart attack was made even worse with the news twelve months later that Meg had breast cancer. Sarah went down to London to give support whilst Meg went through her initial course of chemo. A year later to the day, she died in a hospice with Sarah and Mo at her bedside.

Closer to home, Jacob had become forgetful. He couldn't remember his favourite opening move in chess, yet he could play the piano perfectly with his right hand but couldn't bring his left into play. Later, he took to going walkabout. Always just at dusk, everyone would join in the search to find him and bring him safely home.

Life, nevertheless, continued year on year. The highlight of spring was the lambing, with everyone giving a hand. There would inevitably be orphan lambs that needed to be looked after. The younger members vied to help bottle-feed them. Willow and her brothers were mad on ponies, so they now had three ponies at home. The local pony club would often meet at the farm, and once a month they would all help to provide riding for the disabled. It was incredible that the ponies, some of which could be quite skittish and others that were downright bad tempered, would be gentle and patient for these children who seemed to gain confidence once in the saddle.

Moss was sent off to a farm further up the glen to an excellent working collie that had just come into season. Four months later, Mo went to collect the pick of the litter, a beautiful little bitch puppy that was eight weeks old. They christened her Floss.

At Christmas time, instead of individual family presents, all the adults got together to provide one special present plus a lot of stuff that was shared between everyone.

Christmas 2000, David remembered it so well. His granddad had come by train to spend Christmas with the family. He hadn't been too well and even had to give up his allotment. He had developed a deep throaty cough that kept David awake on the first night. (That holiday was the last time David saw his granddad. Before the winter was over, the old man slipped away in his sleep. Mo and Sarah flew down to London for the funeral, but David stayed behind at Sayyid's house.)

Sayyid and he were to receive a joint present, but it was all a bit of a mystery until, on Christmas morning in the barn, this long object sat on two saw benches concealed by bed sheets was uncovered to reveal a sleek kayak complete with paddles and life jackets. It was still bitterly cold, but it couldn't stop them taking it straightway to the river to launch it for the first time. They named it Ceto, after the ancient goddess of the sea in Greek mythology.

David smiled as he remembered how cold they were but how they continued to course down the river, only to find it was twice as difficult to come back against the flow.

It was at Easter that year when they first heard about the DW (the Devizes to Westminster Canoe Marathon), which was said to be one of the most arduous canoe races in the world. They decided to race in the junior doubles the following year. The race would take place over four days during the following Easter period. They would have twelve months to prepare.

That summer, they trained hard and their double canoe had become almost a second home. Sometimes they took sleeping bags with them and lived rough by the river Spey. Their major training session took them all the way to the estuary of Moray Firth. Sixty miles of hard canoeing, but this would be nothing to the one hundred and twenty-five miles they would need to navigate from Devizes to Westminster Bridge in the centre of London.

David and Sayyid had both passed their driving licence first time, and they had been allowed to use one of the farm's Landies to take their canoe to the Thames so they could carry out a thorough recce and do some last-minute training.

The weather had been kind to them whilst they had been training, but the heavens opened on the first race day. It didn't stop until halfway through the final day. A number of the juniors had dropped out by this time. They had been pretty much soaked from the first half an hour, and they had stayed that way. With blistered hands, backache and constant hunger, they got to the final day and had moved up the listings to now lie in sixth position. Then, the clouds just lifted, the sun came out, and they bent their backs to finish in style. They would've loved to be in the top three, but they just couldn't make it. They managed to overtake two other teams and arrived at the winning line in fourth position. However, their position didn't matter. They would come back next year – they would still be classed as juniors – and they would go for gold, they told themselves.

They looked around at the Houses of Parliament and Big Ben. The sun lit up the scene, and they knew that this would stay in their minds forever.

Their planned return never happened because that was the summer when their lives, and the lives of all their community, were irrevocably changed. Their dreams were smashed in one single incident that set off a chain reaction altering all their lives.

Chapter 14

Grief and a Faith That Passes All Understanding

This was the chapter that David didn't want to read but knew he must.

It started with the alarm given by one of the children from the shelter that Zufash had set up for women who had suffered domestic abuse. The drunken partner of one of the women had turned up; he was demanding to see her and remonstrating with Zufash.

Jerry, Dai and Mo had all turned up at the house almost together whilst Gavin could be seen running towards them as backup.

He might have been a big man full of Dutch courage, but his eyes narrowed as his drink-sodden mind registered this was a battle he couldn't win. 'You should mind your own fucking business.' He spat a gob of phlegm at the ground in their general direction before staggering off to where he had parked his van.

The rest of the story was burnt into David's mind.

David had been bowled over by Sophie the moment he saw her. She was the most beautiful girl he had ever seen. She was always smiling and radiant, and she wore simple clothes that accentuated her lithe, athletic body. Although completely unobtainable, as far as he was concerned – he was just too young – he nevertheless had a crush on her for all of his early years. Later, when she taught him and Sayyid maths, she was just fun to be with; and they both looked forward to her lessons and always came away with new facts and ideas to store away for the future.

After the ambulance arrived, it was quickly decided that she must be transported to Aberdeen, so a helicopter was summoned. The body of her attacker was taken away in the ambulance. The police took Sayyid away to be held in custody.

Joshua and Mary stayed with Sophie at the hospital. A dark gloom hung over the community as they all waited for news. Two weeks passed by with Joshua only returning for fresh clothes as he and Mary watched over their oldest daughter.

David was playing a game of chess with Esther; she had been staying at David's house whilst her mother and father were away when the call came.

The time had come to say goodbye to their darling Sophie.

The doctors had explained to Joshua and Mary that nothing more could be done, and the life support should be turned off. The family were told to come soon to say their last farewells.

Esther broke down in sobbing gasps that wouldn't let up. David, without thinking, put his arms around her and held her tight. Much later, he realised that this was the first time he realised just how much he loved her. Her pain transmitted itself directly to his body; only by holding her tightly was the hurt made just bearable.

He was holding her hand as they were ushered into the intensive ward by Mary and Joshua. Mo and Sarah followed quietly.

Sophie was attached to any number of tubes and wires that seemed to power the screens behind her. Her eyes were closed, her long lashes lay gently on her cheeks, she was peaceful and still. Esther moved quickly to her side and took her hand. She raised it to her lips and kissed it gently. Nobody spoke. What could be said? Why? Where was God when this happened? What a stupid waste of a beautiful life. We were gently ushered out by Joshua. Mary and Esther remained.

All the families gradually started to arrive, and a few at a time passed into the ward to say goodbye.

Zufash was the last one. She returned supported by Mary and Joshua, all three with tears flowing down their cheeks. As the door opened for the last time, Esther was framed looking towards them with unseeing eyes. David moved quickly across and guided her to a chair where she slumped down with great silent sobs wracking her body.

The life support system was switched off at 20:00 hours. The coroner took a fortnight to deliver his report, and the funeral took place the week after that.

After the funeral, we all gathered in the Barn. Joshua wanted to say a few words – he had already given a wonderful eulogy to his daughter and explained that the gift of her life had made him and Mary so very happy and so proud that this girl, in her short life, had been able to give so much to so many other people. He went on to say that she would not want them to be sad, that he was convinced she was now in a wonderful place where she deserved to be, and he was confident they would all meet together again at some time in the future. He took a deep breath and went on, 'Now, we must think of the living, for one of our sons is presently incarcerated in prison for trying to protect her, and we must see what can be done to ensure that he is freed.'

They were brave words, but they came to nothing.

Five months later, Sayyid was sentenced by Lord Connor at Aberdeen High Court to detention for life with a punishment part of seven years. He said that there had been extreme provocation and the extent of the retribution was disproportionate. 'Your guilty plea has been considered, although, in your own words, "You believe that he got what he deserved, and you would do it again if you had your time all over again" showed clearly that you have no sense of remorse whatsoever for this barbarous act.'

Sayyid looked around the courthouse, lifted his chin and smiled a thin smile. As he left the dock, he winked at David.

For the next few weeks, a gloom had descended on all the families that couldn't even be dispelled by the sunshine of an Indian summer which gradually mellowed into autumn.

David lifted the exercise book and started to read again.

We were all having a Sunday lunch together as we usually did at least once a month when Gavin did a very strange thing.

He clinked a teaspoon on his glass as he stood up. 'Friends, I would like to say something. You all know that whilst I have always enjoyed Mary and Joshua's friendship, I have never entertained their Christian beliefs. As an avowed atheist, I thought it was all a load of mumbo jumbo that flew in the face of science. But I must confess to you now that I believe I was wrong.' He paused to draw breath; he was clearly emotional. 'I have watched a family face one of the greatest sadness that I can imagine, and they have faced the reality of their lives with a peace and a calm that I can only wonder at. If this is what faith brings at times like these, then – even if I don't understand it – I would like some of that faith for myself and my family. Having discussed this with Susan at great length, I would like to ask Joshua, publicly, if he would be prepared to instruct me and my family in that faith that his family have.'

Mary got up from her chair and was the first to go around and give Gavin a big hug before turning to Susan and the children.

Joshua just beamed. 'Will I ever.' He strode around to give him a bear hug as well.

Six weeks later, we had our first service as the family were all baptised.

Thereafter, we would hold a short service every Sunday before lunch. Rachel played piano, and we all sang modern worship hymns. We would have a selection of prayers that the children were invited to produce, and Joshua would give us all a couple of readings and a short family sermon with lots of surprises and sometimes the odd belly laugh. Even Zufash came along and said how different it was from the male-oriented worship of Islam where women were expected to remain in the background. Old Benjamin really enjoyed the singing and banged his walking stick to the beat of the music.

Gradually, our community had come back together with the exception of Sayyid, which left David, in particular, with a great sense of loss as they had become more like brothers.

Joshua would take Zufash to visit her son who was now in Glasgow, but it was all very strained. David regularly did the same journey to visit his friend.

As a group we didn't get much post, but one day a letter arrived for David. There was much excitement when we heard that he had been accepted by Edinburgh University to study for an MA in Arabic and Islamic Studies. Joshua couldn't have been more excited if it were his own son.

The food trolley was on its way around again. David needed a drink!

After the meal he closed his eyes, but his mind was still in the Scottish Highlands as he remembered all the good times. Then, as always, the dark cloud was always on the horizon: Sayyid was now somewhere in Syria living with some of the most dangerous individuals on the planet.

They landed at JFK where he had a two-hour stopover before boarding his connecting flight.

The short domestic flight was uneventful, other than a rather large lady bursting out of a floral dress who was determined to show him pictures of her late husband and a motley group of grandchildren in individual and group photographs on her phone. They had been pictured from infant to teenagers, and all of whom seemed to have inherited their grandmother's ample frame.

He moved swiftly once the plane had landed. With only his grip containing the bare necessities, he forged ahead and only paused at immigration to produce his passport and military ID. When asked the purpose of his visit, he simply told the official that he was on an exchange visit.

As he entered the arrivals area, he scanned the crowd of people awaiting the passengers who had disembarked off his flight. He registered, right away, the young man with the sharp military haircut but wearing jeans and a T shirt. He was holding a tablet with the name 'STEVENSON' on the screen.

David moved towards him. As their eyes met, he gave a slight nod of acknowledgement. The young man moved to take hold of David's grip, but then let his arm fall as it became obvious that David did not intend to let him carry it.

'Sorry for not saluting you, Major, but I was instructed to keep things very low-key and not draw attention to you.' The young man spoke quietly but with authority. 'I'm to take you to DEVGRU HQ; I have a vehicle waiting in the car park.'

In the car park, a dark double-cab pickup truck started up as they drew alongside. His escort opened the rear door, and David threw his grip on the floor and climbed in. As his escort slipped into the passenger seat beside the driver, the vehicle moved off. The journey to NSA Oceana, Little Creek and then on to Dam Neck Annex, the home of Silver Squadron – part of the famed Seal Team 6 – went without incident and no small talk.

David was ushered into the building and through to an office at the rear where his young escort knocked abruptly on the door.

'Enter.'

The command was answered immediately. The door was opened, and the young man snapped to attention. 'Major Stevenson, sir.' He nodded at David.

A tall, lean officer dressed in camouflaged shirt and trousers rose from behind his desk and came to meet him. With a ready smile and an outstretched hand, he welcomed David. 'Great to meet you.' He shook David's hand warmly whilst thanking the young escort and motioning for him to dismiss.

'Come and sit down, Major, or would you prefer me to just call you David?' he enquired.

'We're pretty informal where I come from,' David replied. 'How should I address you, sir?'

'Most people around here usually just call me Commander,' he replied with a smile. 'I understand that you have had a hectic few weeks,' said the commander, kicking off the conversation. 'You were on SF duties in Afghanistan before being called back to the UK as I gather your father had been killed. I'm very sorry to hear that.' He went on in a rush, 'I understand that you have been co-opted by MI6 in conjunction with our CIA because you have been managing an operative who now seems to be operating with ISIL in the north of Syria.

'I've read the full report, and this asset could be very useful to us. I have a squadron that have just moved to Iraq in preparation for an important operation in Syria. I've got less than a week to get you kitted out and fully prepared to join them on this operation. I have assumed that coming from your background you are fit and rarin' to go. I will introduce you to our quartermaster in a minute who will take care of you. He'll show you to your quarters, and then kit you out with everything you will need. Tomorrow morning, he will take you to the armoury, and you can decide what personal weapons you would prefer to use. Later, you will be able to take them on the range and get them zeroed in and get a bit of practice. Tomorrow night you will get an introduction to some of our night vision gear…' The list went on.

The days just flashed past. The quartermaster was a massive guy with a very quiet voice, but he made things happen quickly and efficiently.

David preferred to keep an AK-47 as his personal weapon; it drew no attention anywhere in Arabia where it was the weapon of choice for most fighting men. He chose the Glock 19 over the Mk25 – the Sig Sauer that had been favoured for so long. This sidearm was extremely accurate and could withstand any amount of punishment whilst still being able to function. The beefed-up Toyota Hi-Lux was an eye-opener: it was built like a tank and could even withstand a direct hit from an IED. Looking at some of the kit these special forces had at their disposal, he couldn't help feeling a bit like the impoverished neighbour when he compared some of this stuff with what he was used to, bearing in mind they had the best of the best when compared with the rest of the army.

In the end, it wasn't even a week. There was a flight for Iraq flying out on the fifth day into his induction process, so everything was compressed. It was early mornings and late evenings.

The day before he shipped out, he received an email from Esther:

Where are you love? Is everything OK? I am still in Geneva, but I leave tomorrow for Turkey and then, we hope, we will be able to either help out on the border or even move over the border into Syria. Please let me know that you are OK. Love you lots, Esther XXX.

David responded immediately via the contact address in London:

Sorry, sweetheart, it's been manic for the last few days, had meant to drop you a line but there's hardly been time to sleep. I'm good, but I'm having to do a lot of travelling in places with little or no signal. Will write again as soon as I'm able. Please be very careful, you are going into a very dangerous area. I love you very much, David XXX.

He sat back feeling guilty that he was unable to tell her the truth: they were both going to be in the same country but with little if any chance of being able to see her.

The plane touched down at FOB Sykes at 16:00 hours. David was introduced to Silver Squadron that evening. He would be attached to 3 Troop. They would be moving out at dawn on the following day, and he would be going with them. The briefing would commence in five minutes. Just time to grab a bottle of chilled water and then join the 3 Troop leader, Ben Layman, and his right-hand man, Chief Petty Officer Bill Mathewson.

Ben wasn't very tall, about five foot five, and not heavily built, but what one noticed immediately were the ice-blue eyes staring out from a sharp-featured face burnt a dark mahogany by the sun. Bill Mathewson, on the other hand, was at least six foot four or five with a fiery red beard and a mop of hair to match.

'Sorry, David, everything's a bit rushed, but I want to get this briefing over so that the men can get their stuff together and get some rest. We can have a longer chat once we have got this out of the way,' Ben explained as he led them into the briefing room. 'Gentlemen, good evening, you will know by now that we can stop loafing about getting bored. We have been tasked with an important mission that has been code named "HIGHLAND FLING".'

The chief petty officer grinned at the link to his heritage, and his boys grinned back.

The troop leader continued as he switched on the projector with a thumb button and a map of Syria and her near neighbours appeared on the screen. 'The gentleman on my right is a very experienced officer who has been serving with British Special Forces, and who was serving in Afghanistan before coming here on an exchange visit. He will be joining us on this mission, and I will expect you all to extend the same courtesy to him as you would to myself.' He rose up on his toes as if stretching his calf muscles or maybe to increase his stature that psychologically wanted to be bigger. He clicked the thumb button once more. 'Right, down to business. You will all have gathered the local intelligence from your daily IO briefings together with what is going on in Syria. It is Syria where we will be heading for tomorrow. ISIL are on the run and have regrouped in the Idlib area in the north-west. The Syrian air force backed up by the Russians are saturation bombing the area. The Syrian army is advancing under this air cover together with Russian contractors and a number of militias and Iranians on the side of the Syrian ruler. ISIL have been caught between a rock and a hard place. The Kurds, with our backing, are attacking from the north-west. So, as you can see, things are pretty chaotic there just at this moment. We have been given very strong intelligence information that the leader of ISIL, who as you know recently came to power after his predecessor was killed in a drone attack, is heading for Idlib to rally his troops and also to have a meeting with an important Afghani jihadist.'

After another click, a single sentence in white lit up an otherwise black screen: 'MISSION: WE WILL CAPTURE THE LEADER OF ISIL AND BRING HIM BACK TO IRAQ'.

The clicks continued and the screen kept lighting up with further information. They were to leave in the morning in four of the beefed-up Hi-Lux pickups with a heavy machine gun mounted in the load bed area of each vehicle. The navigator would be able, thanks to a small reconnaissance drone that would scout ahead of the small column, to see ahead for fifteen miles in any direction. Keeping away from any population and main roads, they would make their way to the north of Idlib to set up the OP and await further intelligence. Once the meeting destination had been discovered, they would execute a snatch raid and hightail it back to the border.

All the finer details of what weapons and ammunitions together with the explosives they would carry were discussed. Along with their communication systems between each vehicle and their overall commander back at the base. The rations, which was an eye-opener for David, made the ration packs he was used to look somewhat meagre. Before they crossed the border in the morning, they would carry out bump drills in case they ran into trouble once in Syria.

The Seals looked very fit; the tension in their faces was simply craving for the adrenaline rush that accompanied this type of operation. Cool, calculating, yet with an energy barely hidden. Like top-class athletes in that millisecond before exploding into action.

David left with Ben and walked back to the officers' mess to grab a quick steak and salad before retiring. *It could be a busy day tomorrow*, he thought. Before he turned off his bedside light, David took the next exercise book that his dad had so carefully written and started to read.

David and Sayyid left this morning in one of the Landies with their canoe secured on the roof and all their camping gear to embark on their latest adventure – the Devizes to Westminster Canoe Marathon – one of the most demanding endurance tests anywhere in the world. We wished them well, but I couldn't help feeling that they were bit on the young side to attempt this kind of thing. They were adamant, though, saying this was just a bit of a recce and that their real race would be the following year once they had sussed all the wrinkles.

David lay back on his pillows and closed his eyes. That race seemed such a long time ago, yet it only seemed like yesterday. Tomorrow he would be in Syria, and so might Esther. Was it possible that Sayyid could be there as well? He turned off the light and drifted into a sleep that was showered with vivid memories.

Chapter 15

Operation Highland Fling

The four vehicles left in convey just as the sun lifted over the horizon. Leaving FOB Sykes, they kept in single file as they headed for the border crossing to the east of Al-Hasakah, which was mainly controlled by Kurdish forces – albeit, there was still thought to be a sizeable ISIL presence on the Iraqi border to the south.

Once across the border, they spread out into the diamond formation they had practised whilst carrying out their bump manoeuvres. The navigator stared at his tablet intently giving up-to-the-minute directions concerning the route that he was able to see ahead.

They reached their first bivouac area as planned just as the sun slid over the hills to the west. They dispersed the vehicles, scrimmed up with camouflage netting, in a formation where each group could cover the others. Two men were dispatched up the hill to find an OP where they could command a view of the valley and report any movement by wireless. The others split into two groups, one breaking out the rations and getting some food on the go whilst the others busied themselves cleaning weapons and laying out equipment.

There was no moon, but a myriad of stars managed to light up the whole sky. David lay back with his head resting on his pack. It was chilly but not bitter; he wondered what the weather was like in Scotland.

The all-encompassing silence was split by a single piercing female scream.

Each turned to the other with a puzzled frown or lifted eyebrow. Nobody moved other than to reach for their weapon beside them.

The troop commander reached for the small mic that was clipped to his equipment. 'Number One to set, over.' He slipped his finger off the send button.

'Copy that, over,' came the quiet reply.

'Did you hear the scream? Over.'

'Yes, and saw a light briefly, seven or eight hundred yards and seven o'clock your position if we're at twelve, over,' the reply came again.

'Observe carefully and be prepared to put down covering fire if necessary. We will put a recce party out to investigate. Over.'

The succinct detail was acknowledged with the reply, 'Copy that, out.' The sound abruptly silenced.

'Jonah, Ivan,' he called softly.

The two men slipped silently in beside him.

'Seven or eight hundred yards at seven o'clock. That distance is approximate. Take it slowly. Take night vision. I only want eyes on – no heroics, please. We have a much more important task ahead of us. Do you understand?' The two men nodded silently.

'Chief.' The big man was alongside him. 'Get around the others, full alert, all kit packed ready to move out and heavy machine guns trained on the area of interest. No firing unless sure. I want no blue-on-blue episodes on this watch.'

A quick nod was the answer, and he moved off silently to ensure everything was in place as ordered.

'Could I go with Jonah and Ivan?' David gruffly whispered. 'I speak Arabic fluently – it might be useful.'

Ben paused for thought, then nodded. 'Yes, good suggestion, but keep your head down.'

David nodded an affirmative, nodded again at Jonah and Ivan, and the three moved off into the darkness.

David's early experience of stalking deer in the Highlands of Scotland had served him well when he undertook his sniper course before taking over as platoon officer for the sniper platoon in 3 Para. Now he cautioned himself: *slowly, slowly, no hurry, nothing alerts the senses more than movement.* He looked for the other two and was pleased to see that they were all reading off the same page.

Forty minutes later they had covered the easy bit, but the next two hundred yards would need extra care. For some strange reason, David was thinking about metres versus yards. All his training had been in metres except for cricket. *Now there's Brexit going on in the UK, will we all go back to imperial measurement?* A movement caught his eye – it was less than twenty yards/metres away. He heard a gentle fart as a sphincter muscle relaxed to allow a stream of urine from an overstressed bladder gush onto the path.

The girl stood up and adjusted her clothing.

'Get your arse back in here, you Yazidi whore,' said in Arabic with a real menace that would brook no refusal.

The girl lifted her skirts and started to run back. It was then that David saw the fissure of the cave and the man with the potbelly who was guarding it. Jonah had been unsighted, but Ivan had seen everything as well.

'Get in the back with the other girls – no one else is coming out tonight,' spat the guard as the girl passed him.

David jerked his thumb backwards; two nods acknowledged that there was little more they could do but return to base.

The debrief over, it was decision time. Nothing must happen that might endanger the mission – however, the most likely scenario was that the captors would be Daesh (the less flattering title for ISIL) and the woman or women most likely to be Yazidis, taken as sex slaves for onward sale to other Daesh in the area. The girls might be able to provide some useful intelligence once they had neutralised their captors.

A brief battle plan was produced. They would move down to the cave an hour before daybreak and take up their ambush positions. A cut-off group of two would move down the valley to ensure no one slipped through the net. The main ambush party would number off from the left. Then as the Daesh party came out of the cave, they would take as their primary target the corresponding enemy from left to right. The signal to open fire would come from the first, which would come from the troop leader. David was to stay in cover and call out to the Yazidi women to stay down.

The simple but effective plan worked out as planned: as the first shot brought down the Daesh man on the extreme right, the following fusillade sent the others down like ninepins sprawling in the dirt. The girls heard the call in Arabic and dropped to the floor, but one woman tried to crawl to a small child who was crying out in terror. One bearded jihadi pounced on her, grabbing her by the hair and hauling her to her feet. He dropped his AK-47 and pulled out a Beretta pistol, which he put to her head as he backed away from the carnage.

David slipped out from behind the tree where he had taken cover and let the man back straight onto the Glock which rammed into his neck. David muttered in Arabic, 'Put down your weapon and let the woman go.' As the man slowly let his hands fall to his side, David relieved him of the pistol.

The man was swiftly restrained with his arms behind his back, his ankles similarly pinioned. Now on his knees, his wrists and ankles were cable tied together. The cut-off group had been called back. Sentries were posted on the high ground just in case the short firefight had come to anyone's attention.

David was now talking to the women and translating for Ben. Their story was harrowing. Their village had been attacked several months ago; they had not put up a fight. Their men and boys were taken away and shot. The women were then all grouped together; the older women were taken outside and shot in the head and left on the street. When their small children were being taken away, some of the mothers fought back only to see their children killed in front of them. In one instance, a child's head was sliced off and the head kicked down the street. They were told that they must learn the Quran as they were devil worshipers. They would be sold to jihadis and become their sex slaves. Some of the women had been sold four or five times. They had been beaten and raped on a daily basis.

It was then revealed that they were on their way to a village in the Idlib province where Daesh were gathering for a major battle with the Syrian army. They didn't have the name of the place, but it was somewhere in the north of the province.

A thorough inspection of the dead Daesh members' clothes and belongings produced nothing of any importance. The man on his knees didn't want to say anything at first, until David suggested that he would let the women loose on him. David knew that if a Muslim is killed by a female who is a non-believer, he would never go to Paradise.

Sweating profusely, the man by the name of Abdul, was to meet with the rest of his clan on the 420 Road, about forty kilometres north-east of Idlib. He would then be told where and when he would see their great leader. He informed them with a sneer that the women would have all been sold on by that time.

David was focused on Abdul's mobile, scrolling through the names, looking for any other information that might be of value.

One of the women had started to also go through the belongings of the dead jihadis. She found what she was looking for and folded her arms. She walked over to where David was still asking the prisoner the odd question. She smiled; it was a cold smile which didn't reach her eyes. David started to smile back as she opened her arms wide and her right hand swept in an arc in front of the prisoner's face. Her lips parted and her eyes were definitely not smiling as she stared down at the prisoner.

David moved his gaze to Abdul in time to see the chin drop and a flood of arterial blood flow down his front. Abdul coughed once and slumped backwards. There would be no further questions, and Abdul wouldn't be going to heaven. The woman handed the knife to David, turned on her heel and strode back with immense dignity to where all the other women were sitting in the shade.

Ben came over to talk to David. 'Well, that's solved one of my problems.' He nodded at Abdul's slumped figure. 'We can hardly be slowed down with a prisoner, but I'm not sure what we can do with the women.'

'Can you not get them picked up by a chopper and flown back to Iraq?' David asked.

'Yes, but that will mean us hanging around till they get here to secure the landing zone, as well as alerting anyone in the area of our presence – this is why we motored in the first place.'

David paused before replying, 'Well, the only other thing we can do is take them along with us; there must be vehicles here. If we take some of the clothing off these guys, we might even be able to get closer. As long as you let me do all the talking. Why don't I have a word with the women and see what they think?'

'OK, but let's get this show back on the road. We've got two more days of travel to get to our destination.' Ben gathered his men together and started to clear the area. The vehicles, two pickups and a lorry, were tucked away in the trees. The men brought them back into the clearing.

David, by this time, had questioned the women. None of them wanted to return to Iraq as they had been defiled and could never go back to their families even if any of their families still existed. The only choice was a refugee camp on the Turkish–Syrian border where, if they were lucky, they might be able to enter Europe to start a new life.

There was one very important request from the women: they wanted the weapons from their jailors because they would never allow themselves to be captured again.

With this final point agreed, the convey set out once more. The lorry was being driven by one of the Seals, and everybody else wore headgear and dark glasses. They were a very disreputable-looking bunch that regained the road and headed off for the second RV.

The rest of that day was uneventful; they mostly kept to minor roads or dirt tracks. It was hot and dusty, and they had nearly reached their next planned bivouac area when the leading pickup hit an IED.

The force of the explosion lifted the vehicle up and to the right, where it landed on its side with the wheels still spinning. The lorry ground to a halt, but the other three vehicles spun out either side of the stricken vehicle where their gunners could cover the entire area. The assaulters were out of their vehicles and in positions of all-round defence in a heartbeat. There was a long silence as the dust settled, but there was no follow-up ambush. Ben was sending a situation report back to base as the chief sprinted to the vehicle that had been hit and from which there seemed to be no sign of life.

He called out to big Ivan, 'Give me a hand to get these guys out of here.' By now, he had managed to wrench open the driver's door and peered inside. One by one he managed to lift them out to Ivan, who had now been joined by the troop commander.

They carefully laid them down beside the road. They were all alive but severely concussed. The driver was the first to open his eyes and groaned. Blood was seeping through his trousers.

Ivan drew a knife from his belt and expertly slit the trouser, revealing a bloodstained leg with part of the femur showing through the skin. One by one, they came back to life: The driver's navigator had a dislocated shoulder, but a skilful bit of manipulation by Ivan sorted that out quickly if not painfully. The two assaulters in the rear seats had managed to escape with little more than serious ringing in the ears. And the driver's leg was swiftly splinted and immobilised. All in all, the armoured vehicles had performed well – had it been any other sort of vehicle, they would have all been killed.

The problem now was that the injured driver could not be lifted out before first light tomorrow as they were too close to their secure area. The good news was that the Yazidi females were to be handed over to a detachment of the YPJ at a rendezvous in the north at 12:00

the next day. These all-female Kurdish units were ferocious fighters, some of whom had been on the front line against Islamic militants for the past three years. They were more than just warriors safeguarding their homeland: they were feminists who were determined never to be subjugated by a patriarchy again.

Once more, they settled into their defensive positions. The injured driver was kept comfortable by regular morphine pain control. Nobody got much sleep, so everyone was pleased when a yellow glow lit up the hills to the east. As the glow intensified to a deep orange, a lone helicopter emerged from the sun's rays and moved towards them in a straight line.

A single smoke bomb was lobbed into the LZ, which the chopper slipped into very expertly. The injured driver was stretchered in whilst the Navy Seal with the dislocated shoulder heaved himself painfully aboard before the pilot lifted back off the ground and made a sweeping curve above the treeline.

The disabled truck had been emptied and the heavy machine gun was transferred to one of the other trucks. A phosphorous grenade went off with a *whoosh*, which became a much larger *crump* as the fuel tank exploded. As they drove off, they were still aware of the intense heat.

They kept to minor roads and dirt tracks, but there didn't seem to be much activity in the area they were transiting through.

They arrived at the RV with fifteen minutes to spare and spread out in all-round defence.

The YPG arrived spot on time. They were smart and efficient and certainly looked the business. They were very kind to the Yazidi women and helped them into a bus they must have commandeered from somewhere.

David had a short conversation with the woman who appeared to be in charge – there were no badges of rank to be seen, but she was the one giving all the orders – and the rest moved immediately. In her fluent Arabic, she explained that the more you move north and east, there were numerous groups of Daesh moving in the general direction of Idlib. This all confirmed what he had heard at Ben's original briefing.

That night at their final OP, they set up camp in the hills to the east of Idlib. No lights, no cooking, they were now in watch and wait mode – probably the hardest aspect of life for an active special force operative.

As usual, Ben got together with his signaller at 20:00 hours to send his encrypted situation report (sitrep) to HQ back in Iraq. The reply soon saw the team come together as he called his men for a briefing, leaving only a skeleton watch of two on the hill.

'David, it seems that your man has definitely been tracked to a site in a small village north of Idlib; there is strong evidence to suggest that tomorrow night he will be joined by the man we came to get. Who is this man and how does he relate to our mission?'

'This man is an Afghan; he is an asset of both the British MI6 and your CIA. He has provided us with very valuable information in the past. He must not be damaged. Whatever else happens, he must be allowed to escape in order to continue being our eyes and ears on the ground wherever militant Islam rears its ugly head.' David continued, 'Our mission, as you all know, is to lift this other individual who has declared war on the West and get him back into Iraq.'

Ben now gathered the men around him and spread a map and placed some aerial pictures on the tailgate of one of the trucks. He used a pointer as he traced the whereabouts of the village and the approximate position of a house within that village. Then he spread out the pictures. 'Access to the village should not be that difficult, but the house they are using is bordered by three other houses. This man will have top security, so any chance of creeping up on that house in the night without being discovered is unthinkable. There are two possible exits via the adjoining houses were they to come under attack. This leads to the two small adjoining roads. It is likely that they will have vehicles tucked away in those side streets to move them out of the area if a situation requires it. Chief, I want you to take Team Two and make a frontal assault on the gate to that compound. Roar in, heavy machine gun firing all the way; and as you reach the gates, grenades over the top. Then reverse at full speed to a safe distance and plaster the compound with maximum firepower. I want them to think that we are coming in from the front. Meanwhile, David and Team Three will be lying in wait here just where the small road exits the village. If they come your way, I want you to surgically take them out. Rake the tyres and use your driving skills to disable them.

'I, together with Team Four, will be covering the other road, so we will be ready to do the same thing if they come our way. All networks will be open as soon as the first shots are heard, and whatever vehicles are not involved with the capture of our prize will move to give immediate backup. After the snatch, we will withdraw to this location. We will then need to hold this position until first light when the Sixth Cavalry should arrive with reinforcements and we get to be airlifted back to base.'

The two men up in the OP were relieved of their post and returned to hear the same briefing whilst everyone else ate some cold rations and cleaned their personal weapons.

David had lost count of how many times he had been exposed to firefights, the lead-up to the action, the aftermath, the excitement…

The fear? It's dangerous when you don't feel that dragging feeling in your gut because that's when you can get careless.

He shut his eyes and immediately had a vision of his dad. Mo was on the hill with Floss gathering the sheep. The dark clouds heralded, ominously, the storm about to arrive. No warning, a single surge of energy, the thunderclap came later. Mo lay on his side as rivulets of rain poured down his face. Floss came bounding in and tried to lick his face dry as if this might bring him back to life. The dog lay with his head on Mo's chest until help arrived.

Esther, another vision, she could be here or anywhere in this godforsaken place trying to put broken children back together. His last waking thought for when this was over: *I will take her home and start to lead some sort of meaningful life; this is not how we were meant to live our lives.*

Sleep came because it had to.

David's eyes opened. He stared at his watch only to confirm that it was 04:00 hours. Some soldier's brains become hot-wired to know intuitively the hour and minutes of the day without a wristwatch – which they only wear because they still distrust their own proclivity.

The air was abuzz with little or no noise as the men prepared for battle.

Everyone in place, the first rattle of heavy machine gunfire woke up the entire neighbourhood. The spearhead vehicle screamed down the narrow road with guns blazing. As it reached the gates of the compound, grenades bounced into the yard beyond. Then, for good measure, the chief put an anti-tank rocket into the battered gate, which blew it to pieces. The driver then slammed into reverse and with a bit of excellent driving, he brought the pickup back to the start position with the heavy machine gunfire still hammering into the front of the compound.

Ben listened to all of this through his headset. His vehicle was tucked in beside a small shed as he waited in silence. He hardly heard the vehicle as it barrelled past the shed until it must have been fifty yards ahead. His driver let the clutch in, and they set off in hot pursuit. The Navy Seals' vehicles weren't only armoured for defence, the engines were tuned to perfection to provide the very best in performance.

The gunner on the back of Ben's pickup was focused on the tyres of the vehicle that they were pursuing. The rear wheels were shredded, and sparks flew like Catherine wheels as the rims bounced along the concrete. The occupants of that vehicle were now returning fire as the distance between them reduced.

It may have been a lucky bullet that hit Navy Seal Jonny Johnson in the chest. He slumped over the machine gun and then slid, lifeless, to the floor of the truck. However, by this time, Ben's driver had drawn alongside the pursued vehicle. As soon as he was a third of the way past, he swung the wheel violently to force it into the wall of a building and bring it to a screaming halt.

Ben exited first, closely followed by his signaller. Covered by his backup, Ben wrenched the door open. A young man, unarmed, stepped out and raised his arms in surrender. Another man shuffled his backside across the seat to follow. The driver was slumped over the wheel unconscious, or worse. Ben moved his head over the passenger seat to see if the passenger was also injured. The bang of the discharged weapon in that confined space was deafening, but Ben didn't hear it, for the bullet had already torn through the frontal lobe of his brain and splashed much of the contents on the roof of the cab.

The signaller had taken a step back to reassess the position. The passenger door was pushed open and the signaller raised his weapon to confront anyone who tried to get out, but then a spurt of automatic fire from below the door raked across his ankles, bringing him down in a heap. A heavyset man was sprinting down an alleyway opposite where all the action had taken place.

Team 2 with the chief and his full crew arrived just in time to see their prize disappearing. 'Team Three, Team Three, target on foot heading east through alleyway. Try to engage, over.' The chief looked over at the two now captured prisoners. 'Restrain those two and get them in the back ready to move!' he barked.

His gunner was already administering first aid to the injured signaller. He went to the enemy vehicle and gently picked up his boss and placed him carefully in the Team 4 vehicle. Lights were now coming on all over the town; although, no one seemed inclined to venture out to see what was happening.

'Move out,' rasped the chief.

When David heard the chief's last message he was on the right side of the town, but he thought it was unlikely that their target would leave the security of the town, so he would probably try to move back to where his security detail were, at the safe house. Leaving the driver with the vehicle parked under some trees on the outskirts, he took the other three members of his team on foot back towards where the operation had started.

They moved quietly, each covering the other. As they got closer to the safe house, they could see lights and people milling about. A good ambush position is always close to home base – that is when a returning patrol becomes careless as they get closer to home.

Jonah had taken up a position beside a solid gatepost in the next-door garden. He'd heard a slight scuff on gravel, then suddenly their target was there right in front of him. He didn't hesitate. The right-hand karate chop slammed into the soft tissue covering the carotid artery. He caught the man as his knees folded and he slumped into his arms. Laying him down gently, he immediately restrained him with cable ties, stuffed a bit of a medical dressing in his gaping mouth and sealed it with a piece of gaffer tape. He managed to haul the big man up and sling him across his broad shoulders.

David and the other backup man had watched all of this from a distance. David put his mouth close to his ear. 'Get back to our vehicle and get him back to us as soon as you can. I will cover Jonah.'

Once all of Team 3 were back in their pickup with their prisoner, David got back on the wireless. 'All units, mission complete, return to RV, over.'

The chief's voice came back straightway, 'Team Two, wilco, out.'

Ben's signaller was in a lot of pain, but he managed to encrypt David's message to base.

The Daesh leader had regained consciousness on the way back to the RV and now sat aloof and saturnine. David had not acknowledged Sayyid, who simply sat quietly in the shade of one of the vehicles. David wasn't sure what to make of the younger man, who was probably only seventeen or eighteen, with a pale complexion and large brown eyes and full lips. *He hardly looks like a fighter, far too pretty*, he thought.

'Who here speaks Arabic?' the big man growled.

'I do,' David answered him fluently.

The captive said, ‘I need to piss.’ He looked down to his crotch that he couldn’t reach because his hands were restrained behind his back.

David thought quickly and called out to Jonah in English, ‘Cover this arsehole. If he makes a false move, blow his brains out.’ He didn’t know if the man could speak English, but the prisoner got the message as Jonah chambered a round in his Glock. David came up behind the man and sliced through the restraint with his knife and switched back to Arabic and said, ‘Keep your knees on the ground and relieve yourself on the ground in front of you.’

The man moved his hands to the front and rubbed the circulation back into his wrists. Slowly, he unzipped and drew out his penis and started to urinate. The stale smell wafted up, and Jonah wrinkled his nose in disgust. The flow seemed to go on forever, but eventually the last drop was evacuated. The dry earth absorbed the fluid like blotting paper until only a mild froth was left on the surface. The prisoner was once again rubbing his wrists.

‘Put your hands around the back,’ David ordered in Arabic.

The man appeared not to have heard; he was still rubbing his wrists and further up his arms.

‘Now!’ demanded David.

Jonah was standing over him with the cocked weapon pointed at his head.

The prisoner seemed to relax his shoulders in resignation and put his hands obediently behind his back.

Jonah lowered his weapon as David bent to secure the prisoner’s wrists once more.

Then, out of the side of the captive's hand, an object rolled towards Jonah and the other two Seals who were busy sorting out their kit.

'Grenade!' David dived beside the prisoner and levered himself behind him to shield the blast.

On this cry, Sayyid and the boy made a dash for one of the vehicles. Jonah was down but still holding his Glock. Almost as a reflex action, he fired a short burst that stopped the youngster in his tracks before he, too, collapsed.

From the other side of the vehicle, Sayeed saw the boy drop. Without hesitating, he came back to pick the boy up in his arms, run to the driver's side, slip him into the rear seat, leap inside and roar off in a cloud of dust.

The prisoner obviously had a grenade secreted in the loose sleeves of his outer garment. Whilst rubbing his wrists, he had removed the pin and courageously waited until the optimum moment to roll it towards his enemy. He hadn't reckoned on David's swift reflexes, or he might have wished to try another plan. He was dead now, but he had taken two Navy Seals with him and blown the leg off a third.

David was busy applying a tourniquet to Jonah's upper leg when the chief arrived. 'Chief, you'll need to get back to base and give them a sitrep: troop leader plus two men down, two of our lads badly injured, target killed himself, request immediate assistance. Then organise the rest of the men in all-round defence – it could get quite lively around here before too long. I'm going after my asset; his companion is badly wounded and will need hospital attention. I'm guessing he will make for Idlib. I'll take the lorry that we used to transport the ladies; it won't attract so much attention. When you get back, tell them what I'm doing and that I'll head for the Turkish border regardless of how successful I am. I will get word back via the American embassy.'

The chief nodded and quickly went about carrying out David's instructions. David had done all he could with the emergency tourniquet. He administered a shot of morphine, then scribbled the date and time and pinned it on Jonah's jacket. Checking his AK-47 and slipping a further couple of magazines into the pocket of his oversized coat together with a couple of grenades, he pulled out his Glock and checked it before returning it to the holster beneath his coat. Then, with a nod to the chief busy on the set, who acknowledged his departure with a half salute, he drove off in the lorry in the direction of Idlib.

Chapter 16

Amalak Al'aswad (The Black Angel)

David had to double-declutch to change gear; there was little if anything left of the synchromesh in this ancient lorry. It was a whole different experience from the beautifully engineered Hi-Lux, modified for these roads and tracks, which had transported him to this parched north-west part of Syria. He was just able to trundle along at forty-five miles an hour (if he was lucky); his window was down to allow the arid desert heat to dry the sweat constantly running down his chest. The downside of this draught was the minute particles of dust along with sand blowing in. His face and beard were soon covered in a brown crust.

He had been driving for nearly three hours without seeing any movement on the road at all. However, as he turned a bend, he found himself head to head with a strategically placed roadblock. The soldiers on both sides of the road had their weapons trained on him as the non-commissioned officer at the roadside waved him down.

David judged the odds of trying to ram his way through at about a hundred to one against, so he braked and came down through the gears only to crunch the change from third to second.

The NCO sauntered over to the vehicle. David noted that he was a Syrian army regular soldier. 'Get out and keep your arms in the air,' the NCO barked in Arabic.

David did as he was told.

'Papers!' the NCO demanded, stretching out his hand.

David shrugged his shoulders. 'I'm from Iraq, all my gear was lost when the Americans bombed my village.'

'What are you doing here?' the brief interrogation continued.

David opened his hands in supplication. 'I was paid by some Yazidis to see if I could find their women who were taken as slaves by Daesh when they attacked Mount Sinjar. If I bring them home, they will reward me.'

'Waste of time, I would have thought, they'll all be pregnant by now, and what man would want damaged goods.' He waved at the men who were manning the roadblock. 'Let him through.' Without another word, the NCO strode off.

David climbed back into the driving seat, found first gear, ground it a bit as he mistimed the second, and did a perfect racing change into third and on to the fourth gear like a pro before speeding off down the clear road ahead.

Ten miles further down the road, he pulled into a rough patch at the roadside. He had stored two ration packs beneath his seat and soon had a couple of cans opened. He didn't bother to use the stove that came with them, but forked the bully beef, cold, into his mouth and chomped down. He drew his water bottle from the same place, removed the screw top and sipped from it. The water was warm and had a metallic taste, but it was a much-needed fluid that his body required. From his jerkin he pulled an electronic tablet and used a biometric to engage the GPS that immediately showed the map of the area together with his exact position within three metres. He calculated that, barring incidents, he ought to be able to reach Idlib in about four hours.

He had hardly got going when he heard the steady drone of aircraft. The sound was off to his right, so it was difficult for him to see through the passenger window. The sound had now become a loud, steady drone. He stopped the lorry and got out. Off to his right was a town in the distance where wave after wave of bomber aircraft were carpet-bombing the entire area. *It must be like hell on earth to be under that*, he mused.

He was just about to move off again when a scrambler bike careered from behind some low rocky hills and drove straight at him. He grabbed his AK-47 from the cab, but before he could move it onto his shoulder, the rider swerved away and zigzagged back from whence he came.

David realised it was just a diversion when he looked around to see three pickup trucks full of armed men bearing down on him. Realising he couldn't fight them all, and that it would be impossible to outrun them in his ancient lorry, he raised his hands.

'Who are you?' the tall, bearded and turbaned leader demanded in Arabic.

'My name is Abu-Zar, I'm an Afghani. I was working in Iraq when the Americans attacked. I lost everything during the bombing – my wife and children are all dead.'

'Where are you going?' The clipped question demanded an answer.

'I will be paid if I can reach Idlib and transport children to the refugee camp in Suruç...' Before David could finish, his peripheral vision caught the blur of a rifle butt, then the lights went out.

As he regained consciousness, he didn't make a move. He silently explored his body. He was trussed up tightly, so tight that his hands had gone to sleep. His head was aching, but whether this was from the blow or just dehydration, he couldn't say. The pulse in his spine where he was lodged up against the wall was thumping away, but after a short count he realised it was nothing to be alarmed at, not much over sixty beats per minute. He let his eyelids open just a smidgen. He was in a room and there was a small table in front of him on which his Glock 19 was laid out alongside what was left of the American ration pack and the navigation tablet.

He gathered his wits, formulated something of a plan and groaned out loud as he opened his eyes to tell the world that he was now ready to play.

His original interrogator was now standing in front of him. 'You lie, you are a spy working for the Americans!' The tone of his voice wasn't going to brook any denial.

David replied sulkily, 'The only Americans I have seen during the last few months were four soldiers, all of whom died when their vehicle hit an explosive device. There was nobody else around, so I stole their weapons and rations. I arranged to sell all the guns and ammunition in the market. I just kept one pistol for myself. With the money I was able to buy my lorry, for which I hoped to get some work. I was introduced to a Western woman who worked for saving children or something like that. She said it was very dangerous in Idlib, but if I could get there and get some of the children out, she would pay me one hundred dollars per child when I delivered them to the refugee camp at Suruç.'

The interrogator picked up the tablet and held it under David's nose. 'And what about this?'

David looked at it intensely. 'I can't make it work,' he said lamely. 'You can have it if you want.'

'You shouldn't be wandering around here looking to make money; you should be making Jihad like a good Muslim,' his interrogator sneered.

'But that's what I want to do,' David said earnestly. 'I need to make money to get me back to Afghanistan to fight with the Taliban.'

'What is your favourite passage in the Qur'an?' The tall man stared down on David.

Without a moment's hesitation, he replied, 'Sura eight, verse seventeen. It is not for us who slay them but Allah, in order that He might test the Believers by a gracious trial from Himself.' He quickly added, 'Sura nine, verse thirty-nine. He has made the Jihad mandatory and warns that "unless we go forth for Jihad, He will punish us with a grievous penalty, and put others in our place".' He went on in an enthusiastic voice that quivered with emotion and his eyes burned with passion. 'I want to return to the garden of Paradise and the celestial virgins that will await us there.' He leant back against the wall seemingly drained by the emotion of his belief.

'Send for Ali. Tell him to come here immediately,' the interrogator instructed the guard on the door.

Minutes later a short, stocky man appeared at the door.

'Come in,' he called out to the man. 'Speak to this man.' He nodded down at David. 'I want to know where he comes from and what his father does in Afghanistan.'

Ali hunkered down beside David and said quietly, 'Salaam Alaikum.'

'Alaikum Salaam,' replied David.

Ali then slipped into Pashto to enquire, 'Where are you from?'

David remembered all his boyhood conversations with Sayyid, about where he lived, who his friends were, what his dad was like and hearing about how his father had been killed. Now it all came out in a rush as David took on the identity of his best friend.

When he had finished answering all the questions, Ali looked up at his leader and said, 'It is true – this man is who he says he is.'

The tall man replied, 'You can get back to your bed now, you have done well.' He turned to David. 'I will sleep on this and tell you your fate in the morning.' With that, he picked up the Glock and the tablet and left the room.

The guard at the door remained in his position. After a while, the guard came over and checked the cords around his wrists and ankles. Satisfied that he was securely bound, he went across the room and lay down and made himself comfortable.

David had an uncomfortable half hour until he could hear steady snoring from the other side of the room. As he reached up to the back of his waistband, his fingertips worked away at the roughly sewn patch where he had concealed a razor blade. Ever since his first escape and evasion exercise in the Brecon Beacons, this had become a good luck charm that he took with him whenever he went into active service operations.

It was torturous work, but by reversing his wrists in opposite directions, it allowed him to saw away at the cords that bound him. His own AK-47 was propped up against the wall near the guard. He picked it up and brought the butt down with enough force to break his skull. Then he searched the guard for more ammunition, only to find his own magazines in a bag around the guard's neck.

He crept out into the cold night air; his lorry had been parked just opposite. When he came alongside, he glanced in through the open driver's window and was relieved to see the ignition keys still in the dash. However, he knew that he would wake up the entire camp as soon as he started the lorry, and he would never be able to outrun their four-by-fours.

David moved over to where the pickups were parked hoping to find the keys, but this time he was unlucky, the drivers had taken them when they'd parked up for the night. In the back of one of the pickups he found two jerrycans of petrol. That would do. He quietly doused each vehicle with a generous amount and linked them with a trail of petrol. Then he went back to his lorry to retrieve a bit of old towel and a lighter that he had seen on the dashboard when he'd first climbed into the lorry. He drenched the towel in petrol and flicked the lighter. After the end of the towel caught, he lobbed it into the cab of the first vehicle. There was a *whoosh* as it went up, but David was not waiting to see the fireworks.

He sprinted back to the lorry, jumped in and turned the key. It fired first time. David didn't even crash one gear as he hurtled past the blazing pickup. He had barely passed the first one when the second went up. Five hundred yards later, two more in quick succession lit up the dark night sky.

He had no idea where he'd been taken – and without his navigation aid there was no other way than to head north-west by the stars. As he reached a crossroads, he saw that the road to the left, a minor road, was signposted Idlib. David was pleased to get off the main drag as he was sure that the Daesh group who had held him prisoner would have a welcoming party waiting for him when he reached Idlib.

Dawn was just lighting up the sky as the city suburbs became more populated with bombed-out buildings. As he drove through the wreckage, sometimes having to swerve in order to bypass burnt-out vehicles, a donkey, still attached to a cart on its side, lay dead in the middle of the road. As he passed by, the stench and audible hum of flies made him turn his head away in disgust.

As the first wave of bombers howled over the outskirts of the city, David slid into a small side road. He got out of the lorry and took cover beside a wall where he could observe.

Six Russian Su-34s led the way, followed by a similar wave of Syrian-badged MiG-23s. David watched as they launched their guided bomb loads. He could clearly hear the detonations about two miles to the west. Then the bombers went around in a huge circle. David thought they were going to carry out another bombing run over the target, but they just kept the same circular track. After five circuits, the bombers reduced altitude and came in another run right over the first pass, discharging their payload as they went. Having completed the second run, they veered off to the west and eventually disappeared over the horizon.

David had resumed his journey heading for the centre of the city. People were now streaming towards him carrying all the possessions they could manage whilst supporting old people and holding onto children. One family had stopped by the roadside to make adjustments to their handcart.

David stopped the lorry and went to speak with them, but first he removed the ignition key and slung his AK over his shoulder. He gave the usual Arabic greeting and asked, 'How bad is it back there?' He nodded down the road.

'It is like hell on earth,' the elderly man replied. 'They have hit the hospitals again.' He shook his head. 'As if the sick and wounded could be a threat.'

Not for the first time, David felt sick to the stomach at the thought of Esther somehow being caught up in all of this. *No*, he reassured himself, *MSF would have had their people out long before all of this*.

Nevertheless, he asked a question that he didn't think would be understood. 'Do you know anyone that has seen a female British doctor with dark skin?'

A small voice piped up, 'Yes, she mended my leg.' She pointed at the still bandaged leg.

But before the child could give more detail, an older woman joined in, 'She was at the Tarmala Maternity Hospital, before it was totally destroyed.'

'Did she survive?' David asked in a small voice.

'I think she took the children that survived to the Al Rayan Hospital. The people here call her Amalak Al'aswad – The Black Angel. But after this morning, who would know. They hit the hospitals again.'

'How do I get to this hospital? I must get there quickly.'

A young teenager, maybe thirteen or fourteen, interjected, 'I can take you there, but where are you going to afterwards?'

'Turkey,' David replied.

'I'll take you to the hospital if you will take me to Turkey afterwards. All my family have been killed and I just want to leave Syria.'

David nodded towards the lorry and said, 'Come on then, you've got a deal.'

The boy's name was Sami, and he seemed very old for his years.

A black pall hung over the city. Long streams of desperate people were pouring out of the city like an apocalyptic nightmare scene. When they reached the hospital, smoke and steam still rose from the ruins. Rescue workers were digging, some with bare hands, heaving and pulling bits of masonry in a desperate battle against the clock to reach any survivors before it was too late.

David grabbed one of the rescue workers and demanded, 'Have you seen Amalak Al'aswad?'

The man barely paused what he was doing but jerked his thumb towards a tent just outside the main area.

David strode into the tent and saw her straightaway. She was surrounded by cots, all with at least one child and some with two. All had been hurt and were bandaged with arms in slings and some with no arms that could be seen at all. She was nursing a small baby.

'Esther,' he called softly. She paused rocking the child and half turned her head. 'Esther,' he said again, 'my love.'

At this, she turned and stared up at him. She closed her eyes but tears still flowed down her cheeks. 'I prayed for you to come. I knew the only way these children...' she opened her hand to all the infants in the cots '...could be saved was if you came to help me get them away from this hell on earth.'

He pulled her gently towards him and wrapped his arms around both her and the baby.

Esther let out a single sob of relief, but this was followed by a succession of involuntary heaving breaths as she fought to gain control whilst her tears washed over the baby in her arms.

David kissed the top of her head. Searching to find any distraction that might relieve her anguish, he asked, 'And who do we have here?'

Esther sniffed loudly whilst rocking the baby in her arms and said in a whisper, 'Sophie.' She rushed on to explain, 'I was working with a mobile unit of MSF. They had dropped me off at the Tarmala Maternity and Children's Hospital, when we were bombed by Russian bombers. Many people were killed, buried under the rubble. Even as the people from the surrounding areas came to help us save the people that were trapped, the bombers came back and bombed us again! Later, we continued to search, and this baby was discovered alive – both her parents had been killed and no one knew of any other family. She has been with me ever since. I called her Sophie because she is so beautiful.' The tears began to roll down her cheeks once more.

David realised that she was emotionally all burnt out; he hugged her tightly and kissed the top of her head again. 'Well, my love, I think it's time for you to let me take over. I have a rust bucket of a lorry, but it should be able to get all these children and what parents or loved ones they have to the refugee camp on the Turkish border. All I want you to do is look after our Sophie.' He waved around the tent. 'Are any of these young ladies nurses?'

Esther pointed at a woman who was tending to a young boy. 'Miriam is very good, and she has lost all her family as well.'

David released Esther reluctantly and spoke softly in Arabic to the woman. 'Miriam, I have a lorry outside. I need you to gather what adults you can find to get these children onto that lorry with all the medicines and provisions you can lay your hands on. I will take you to the refugee camp on the Turkish border where you will be safe, but we must hurry. Will you come with us?'

It took a second for the question to register, then she nodded emphatically. She finished the dressing on the boy's leg and went off to find the help and provisions needed.

It took the best part of an hour to get them all loaded and comfortable. Mattresses were laid on the floors and around the edges of the lorry, and bedsheets were stretched over the high sides to give some shade. There were baskets of food and water, baby milk powder, fresh dressings and whatever medical supplies they could find. Altogether, there were nine adults and fourteen children, including Sami, crammed into the back, with Esther and baby Sophie in the front with David. Twenty-six souls were relying on an ancient lorry and all the skills that David possessed to get them to Suruç.

David had managed to find a map of the area. He estimated that by driving one hour stretches and pausing for half an hour to administer to the children and give the old lorry time to cool down a bit, the journey should take about seven hours.

Esther's head was still whirling; she kept looking up at David as he carefully nursed the old lorry through each gear change. She didn't know where to start with all her questions. How was he in Syria when he'd told her that he was returning to Afghanistan? Why was he dressed like an Arab and driving an ancient lorry?

David started to explain that whilst on his first tour of duty in Helmand Province, he had met with Sayyid who had cooperated with him against the Taliban. This had been very hush-hush, and the Official Secrets Act was involved. This information had also been relayed back to MI6. When David returned to the UK after the death of his father, he had been asked to attend their headquarters in London. It was at this meeting he was told that Sayyid had turned up in Syria and that he was to have a high-level meeting with top Daesh leaders. MI6 shared information with the CIA, and it was decided to embed him with American Special Forces operating in Syria to see if he could somehow make contact – the Americans were determined to capture one of ISIL's top generals.

'As it happened, I did see him again, but he was able to make off into the night before I had an opportunity to talk to him,' David explained.

'I have seen him as well,' she said softly.

'Where?' David snapped back.

'In the same tent where you found me…yesterday… It's no wonder I've been wondering if I'm going mad, if all of what's happening is just in my head.' She bent over and kissed the baby's head as if this was her touchstone of reality.

David slipped his hand to her knee and gave it a squeeze. 'You'll be fine, I'll be looking after you from now on, all the way back to Scotland.' He gave her a broad, reassuring grin. 'But I need to know more about Sayyid.'

'He says that the next time he sees you, he will kill you. He turned up with a young man in his arms who was critically wounded. The boy died in the early hours of yesterday morning. Sayyid was inconsolable. He took the body away. It was obvious that they were lovers.'

'What!' David almost choked. 'You are joking me! Sayyid is one of the hardest men I've ever known. You're saying…' He couldn't find the words to finish the sentence.

'Oh, David, when we were younger, he idolised you. If only you could have seen him watching when you were busy with something else. I recognised it years ago. I wasn't a bit surprised when I saw how he looked at that young man as the life ebbed out of him.'

There was a silence as both seemed lost in their own thoughts.

David snapped back into operational mode as he became aware of a string of armoured cars rapidly gaining on him.

As the first two passed the lorry, the other two took up position abreast at the rear. The leading vehicles then slowed to a halt whilst the two armoured cars at the rear came up alongside, boxing them in.

An officer flanked by two soldiers with sub-machine guns at the ready advanced to the driver's side.

'What are you carrying?' the officer asked in Arabic.

'Women and children damaged by the bombing in Idlib. I'm trying to get them to Suruç.'

'Lower the tailgate and let me see.' The officer seemed a bit more affable than usual.

David climbed out from behind the wheel, went to the rear of the lorry and lowered the tailgate.

The officer looked up into the faces of very frightened children and their carers. 'OK, you can move on. By the way, in case you haven't heard, our allies – the Russians and the Turks – have been able to broker a limited truce with the dissidents, so you should have nothing to fear for the rest of your journey.'

They arrived at the teeming refugee camp at five o'clock that evening.

David was able to find someone in charge and explained the situation. They were not enamoured with the fact that he was a serving British army officer and were more than pleased to find him some fuel so he could continue his journey. It took a while to unload everything and arrange the details for all the children.

Esther was close to tears when it came time to leave. 'They won't be bombed here, but this is just another form of hell.' She put the shawl around baby Sophie and hunched over her. David knew that he must move on before Esther cracked altogether.

They reached Adana in Turkey in the small hours and slept fitfully in the cab of the lorry, leaving behind David's Arabic clothing. He still looked very disreputable, but Esther seemed to have survived the journey looking just about acceptable. When it was light, they left the lorry and soon found an ATM. Using Esther's debit card, they were able to draw out 1,400 Turkish lira. They found a reasonable-looking hotel and asked for a room for two.

'We've had our luggage stolen and are waiting for the consulate to arrange alternative IDs,' David explained.

Once they got into their room, David left Esther to freshen up and feed the baby whilst he went back downstairs where he had noted a small room with a computer for the use of guests.

David sat at the computer and brought up the email section. He tapped in the innocuous address that he had been given in London: hotshot098@btinternet.com.

Message: Hi Peter, Esther and I and our baby Sophie are on holiday in Turkey. We've had all our luggage stolen including our passports. We are presently staying at the Otel Senbayrak City in Adana.
Please can you advise Esther's family that we are all OK.
Also, I would be obliged if you would advise my CEO of the situation.
Any help and assistance that you could offer to get us all back home would be greatly appreciated. David S.

David returned to his room and took a shower to wash away the grime of the past few days. Neither of them had any clean clothes to change into, so it was just a matter of washing what they had in the handbasin and loafing around in their hotel dressing gowns until their clothes dried. Luckily, Esther had managed to grab a large pack of disposable nappies when they left and two tins of baby milk. Baby Sophie seemed remarkably unperturbed. The hotel had been able to provide them with a cot and bedding. Now bathed and fed, she was kicking her feet up and cooing at the chandelier hanging from the ceiling.

Esther had fallen into a much-needed sleep on the bed whilst David was reading an Arabic newspaper he had picked up in reception.

The telephone suddenly rang its strident note, waking Esther and causing Sophie to let out a little cry of alarm. As David reached for the phone, Esther leant into the cot and stroked Sophie's cheek, which reassured her immediately and made her gurgle with delight.

'Yes,' David said curtly.

'Is that David?' a strange voice enquired.

'Yes, that's me,' he responded.

'Oh good, I'm Peter's PA, he asked me to give you a call.' The voice went on, 'Peter asked me to tell you that he has arranged transport for you tomorrow. A driver will pick you up at zero seven hundred hours local time, sharp. Don't worry about paying your bill at the hotel; that will all be sorted. He is looking forward to seeing you all when you get back. Your driver's name is Jack, and he will be driving a black Jaguar which will be waiting outside the front door. If there's nothing more, I will say goodbye.'

'No, that's excellent. Thank you. Bye.' David turned to Esther, who had only heard the cryptic end of the conversation. 'They are sending a car for us tomorrow morning at seven o'clock and they are arranging for us to return to the UK.'

'Who are *they*?' Esther asked, looking at him directly.

'I'll tell you all about it when we get back. I'd rather not discuss it just now.' He spread his hands around the room as if to say he wasn't sure how secure they were even in this private hotel room.

They all managed a good night's sleep apart from a brief interlude to provide Sophie with her four o'clock feed. When David's alarm went off at six, they quietly moved around the room and bathroom and were ready with plenty of time to spare. David went to the window where he could look down to the hotel entrance and saw the black Jaguar arrive.

'Time to move out.' He put his arms around them both and kissed the baby and then Esther.

Esther's eyes started to fill with tears again, and David registered just how close to the edge she was as he noticed that her hands were shaking. Then she tucked the shawl around the baby; this simple action seemed to empower her. She put her shoulders back, now carrying the baby on one arm, leaving the other arm free to ward off any other problem.

She needn't have worried, for David moved in front, deftly opening doors, his eyes searching each arc, front and back, as he propelled them to the entrance. Once outside, they strode to the car.

The driver saw them coming and was out of the car and holding the passenger door open for them.

'Thank you, Jack,' David said as he settled himself into his seat.

After the driver slid back into his driving position, they moved off smoothly into the early morning traffic.

Once they were going with the flow for a few minutes, they stopped at some traffic lights. Jack then turned and handed a large buff envelope to David. Inside were tickets for Turkish Airlines from Sakirpasa Airport outside Adana to London Heathrow with a short stopover at Istanbul. They should get into London at about five o'clock BST. There were also temporary passports in the names of Mr David Stevenson and Mrs Esther Stevenson and their female child Sophie. Esther's spirits soared upon seeing this. She let out an involuntary giggle and clutched onto David's arm. Finally, there was a booking for the Dorchester in London for a twin-bedded room together with a cot. This took the smile from her face for just a fleeting moment.

The front of house staff at the Dorchester had seen all sorts of people come and go at this illustrious hotel, but few looked as travel weary and rumpled as this young couple with the absolutely divine baby.

Chapter 17

To Have and to Hold from This Day Forth

Sophie didn't even wake them for her four o'clock feed. It was a quarter to seven before she started to make her presence known.

Both accepted that this was the first full night's sleep they could remember since they had left the UK. Nevertheless, they didn't wake full of get up and go. If only they could turn over and close their eyes…

Sophie's wail was more effective than any alarm clock. Esther swung her feet out of bed and moved across the room to put on the kettle to make a bottle.

David wasn't far behind as he found the necessary makings for two cups of coffee. Whilst Esther was busy feeding Sophie, David was scanning through the breakfast menu. 'What do you fancy? Full English or something a little bit more exotic like eggs Benedict?' he asked.

'Scrambled eggs on brown toast with some crispy bacon sounds good to me… Oh, and a pot of tea please – Earl Grey.' Esther smiled.

David nodded in agreement, picked up the telephone and called room service. Having passed on Esther's order, he decided to go for the full Monty: the full English with Cumberland sausages, smoked bacon, black pudding, no hash browns or baked beans, but a full rack of wholemeal toast and some marmalade. He would also like a pot of coffee.

They had finished their breakfast and put the dishes outside their door. Sophie was back to sleep with a beautiful contented smile on her face. Esther stepped out of the shower and into David's arms.

He only had a towel wrapped around his waist and as he kissed her, gravity edged his towel down. He reached out with one hand to grab it but was too late. He pushed her gently back into the roomy shower and suddenly they were glued together. Her eyes were closed, and her head thrown back; as he kissed her breasts, her nipples became erect. His hand came up to caress her breasts and his thigh pressed in between her legs as their lips locked together once more. It took the strident telephone a full four or five rings for the couple to disengage.

David moved into the bedroom to answer the call. 'Room 247,' he said quietly, looking down to see his erection dissolve into perverse flaccidity. He couldn't help but smile.

'David, it's Peter. I'm in the lobby. Can you come down?'

'Give me a couple of minutes to get some clothes on and I'll be down.'

Esther had come out of the bathroom; she looked tense again.

'The man who arranged all this is in the lobby and wants to see me,' he explained.

Esther looked close to tears again.

'Honey, it will be all right. I need to clear a few things up, but then we will be on our way back to Scotland.' He smiled. 'We've got a wedding to plan and the rest of our life to look forward to.'

She nodded but couldn't raise a smile even though she tried so hard to do so.

Peter got up from the comfortable leather chair in the foyer as David approached. He shook hands warmly, not letting go as he gestured to the door beside the concierge's door. 'I've arranged for us to use an office to give us a bit of privacy,' he explained in a stage whisper.

The office was on the ground floor and had bars on the window. There was an ancient desk, which had seen better days, with a captain's chair behind it. In front was a single solid wooden spindle armchair. The desk was empty, as were the shelves. It looked as though someone had cleared all the evidence from a previous function.

'Well then, David, you've had an epic journey. I'd like to hear all about it from the time you arrived at DEVGRU HQ.'

David patiently retold his story, only omitting the episode with Sayyid and Esther.

Peter listened attentively, occasionally rubbing his chin when the story had little or no significance to the operational detail.

David internally analysed his handler's body language and the questions that followed. When the long, convoluted story was over, there was a short pause before Peter was ready to continue.

'You will be pleased to know that your comrades in arms were casevac'd back to Iraq. Whilst the operation did not achieve its total objective – in that we had wanted to capture the ISIL commander, not kill him – you did rid that theatre of a very dangerous adversary. Apart from the members of that squadron who returned in body bags, the rest have survived.' Peter leant back in his chair, dug in his pocket and pulled out a battered briar pipe and a tin of Samuel Gawith Bothy Flake. He concentrated on filling his pipe then tamping it down before thumbing his Zippo lighter over the top. He blew a stream of whiskey-smelling smoke before tamping it down again, relighting and then settling back. It would all have seemed a perfect backdrop to a winter's evening beside a log fire with a good book and a generous whiskey alongside. Instead, David thought it came across as a hammy attempt to impersonate a Sherlock Holmes character. *Should have smoked a Meerschaum*, he thought yet keeping a straight face.

'It seems the Americans are planning to give you a Navy Cross,' Peter went on in between puffs. 'I rather think that you might be the first Brit to have received such a prestigious decoration.'

David remained impassive. All he wanted to know was where they went from here.

'So, your mate Sayeed...' Peter's pipe had gone out again '...where do you think he is now? Who was the young guy with him? Do you think he was hit hard when Ivan opened fire?'

'If you remember, a grenade went off at the time – my priority was to stop a man bleeding to death and arranging for backup.' David moved to the window and opened it to allow the pipe smoke to exit. The traffic noise muted his next remark. 'I suspect that Sayyid can no longer be counted on as an asset.'

'What makes you think that?' Peter's question was like a rapier thrust.

David was still exhausted from his recent travails and decided at this juncture that he must relay everything Esther had told him to end this interrogation. He forgot in that moment the special dictum of the successful interrogator: it is every small detail that eventually adds up to the algorithm of the truth he is looking for.

'So, Sayeed is as bent as a bottle of chips?' Peter dug deep for his lighter again.

'I can only tell you what I told Esther: I grew up with this guy. He is one of the hardest men you will ever meet. We have fought each other, and we have fought together. He is clever, intellectually very bright, a good linguist, resourceful and as hard as nails.' David paused. 'Before you ask the question, no, he didn't show much interest in girls, apart from Sophie. But did I ever suspect for one moment…? No, and I don't think I do now.'

Peter came in softly, 'But from what you say, he now wants to kill you.'

David had no answers; he just wanted this interview to end. He didn't reply.

'Well, my friend, I think it's time for you to take your young lady… and the baby home. What are your plans?'

David replied almost without thinking, 'I'm going home to marry Esther and start living a meaningful life within my community.'

'Are you going to resign your commission?' Peter asked quietly.

'I think that I must. It's all I've known since I was eighteen, but it's time to move on.'

'I wouldn't ask you to join us, for that would mean moving to London, but I could offer you a post as a consultant to research certain things and give us the benefit of your experience.' Peter let that sink in before adding, 'I think we could match your military salary and pension rights.'

'Can I have some time to think about it?' David asked.

'It's Thursday; I need to know for sure by next Monday.' Peter stood up, moved his pipe to his left hand and offered his right. 'You can stay here for another night if you wish. You might want to go shopping for some fresh clothes before you meet your respective families.' He dug into his inside jacket pocket and brought out a Manila envelope. 'There's your tickets to Aberdeen – I guess you can arrange to be picked up – and there's some shopping coupons.'

David glanced in the envelope and noted that there was a substantial amount of money inside. 'Thank you. I will call you before Monday and give you my decision.'

Peter gave one of his totally insincere smiles that was meant to impart a genuine bonhomie. 'I look forward to hearing from you. Have a nice day. I'd stay on the extra night if I were you; I'm sure it will all be a bit emotional when you get back. Oh, and don't worry about the bill here, it will all be attended to.'

Once David returned to the room, Esther opened the door to his knock. She looked tense and stared into his face. 'What did he want?' she asked quietly.

'Well, he has given us loads of money to go shopping so we might look presentable when we meet our folks. He suggests that we stay over another night to rest up, all paid for by HM Government. And we have two tickets to Aberdeen for tomorrow at midday. I think you should call home now and put everyone's mind at rest.' He drew the tickets out of the envelope, glanced at them and added, 'See if someone could pick us up from Aberdeen, ETA thirteen fifty hours. Oh, and you had better tell them about Sophie before they think there's been another immaculate conception!' He chuckled. 'Talking of Sophie, I think the first thing we must shop for is a decent pushchair. Can't have you trying on expensive lingerie and pretty dresses with a baby in your arms.'

Mary answered the phone. David could hear the squeal from where he was lounging on one of the beds. The telephone had been put on speaker at the other end, but they were all talking at once. Gradually, things calmed down, and Joshua had gone off to find Sarah so she could speak with David. There was just too much to discuss over the phone, so it was agreed that they would explain everything when they got back. Esther did, however, tell them about Sophie. The silence that followed was difficult to interpret.

At this juncture, Sarah arrived talking excitedly. When would they get home? What were their immediate plans? David explained that the most important thing in his life just now was to marry Esther. Then to officially adopt Sophie. Esther's face lit up with delight as they hadn't even discussed this important element of their future life. The rest could be sorted out in the next weeks and months.

As suddenly as these conversations exploded into life, there was now a silence whilst all parties realised that the matters for discussion were too important and too complex to be discussed over the phone. They would have to wait until they were all relaxed and comfortable back at home to really understand the complexities that they must all deal with.

It was agreed that Joshua would collect them from the airport, and Mary and Sarah would arrange a small welcoming party together with all the other families.

David was not a great lover of shopping. It suddenly struck him that the last time he had been shopping was when he and Esther had gone to Elgin to buy him a suit for his father's funeral.

They had a fun day. They bought a pushchair with chunky tyres that could easily convert into a carrycot. Tucked up in a new shawl, with a supply of pretty clothes to change into once they had got back to the hotel, Sophie was taking in all the new sights and sounds and appearing to love every minute of it.

David and Esther decided to go for 'smart casual', and soon David was laden down with bags of all shapes and sizes. Eventually, they had to return to the hotel as Sophie needed to be fed, and David's arms were dropping off.

They had missed lunch as it was now mid-afternoon. David called room service and ordered two club sandwiches and a pot of tea.

Esther interrupted, 'Could we have some scones with strawberries and cream?' She gave a little shrug.

David passed on the request before replacing the telephone and leaning back against the pillows.

A sharp knock on the door heralded their much-awaited lunch. As Esther finished feeding the baby and settled her back in her cot, David set a table for them both.

'What would you like to do this evening as it's our last night in London before we go home?' he asked whilst pouring the tea.

Esther thought for a moment before answering, 'Well, I know it sounds odd, but we have got Sophie with us, and that limits us a bit… I'd really like to get dressed up and take baby for a stroll around Hyde Park, feed the ducks, then perhaps we could find a small Italian, family-run sort of thing where they don't mind children, and have an early supper. What do you think?'

David got the picture almost before she had posed the question. 'Sounds good to me. We could do with an early night as we will be travelling tomorrow.'

It was a pleasant late spring evening, vast drifts of daffodils swayed in the breeze, but it wasn't cold. The park wasn't busy, just a few people jogging and the occasional couple enjoying an evening stroll. Sophie was wide awake and thoroughly enjoying all the new sights and sounds. The trees had yet to come into leaf, which caused a filigree of spring sunshine to splash a golden glow over the couple and the child that wasn't theirs but certainly was.

Esther looked up at David and smiled; she couldn't remember when she had ever felt this happy. The trauma of the past weeks had been pushed to the farthest corner of her mind, and she would pray that in time it might be forgotten altogether.

They found just what they were looking for in Shepherd's Market. A small, family-run Italian restaurant. They made a huge fuss over Sophie who chuckled and smiled at every face that smiled at her. Esther had even brought a made-up bottle for Sophie, and the waiter rushed off to the kitchen to have it warmed up. This resulted in the chef and two of his assistants coming out of the kitchen to see this golden child.

After some delicious antipasti, they both decided to have the veal escalope, with an extra-special bottle of Valpolicella to go with it. David rarely ate desserts, but he kept Esther company as she wanted to taste the zabaglione with berries. He ordered a lemon ricotta granita, which wasn't too sweet as the lemon cut the ricotta and made his taste buds zing.

Over their expressos, David had ordered two Stregas. Esther had never tried this Italian digestif before, but this amber fluid with a complex flavour complemented the meal perfectly.

After David settled the bill, they started to walk back to the Dorchester. It was dark now and a brisk wind caused them both to turn up their collars.

As they arrived at the imposing doorway, a crackle of thunder introduced a rainstorm. They scuttled inside, collected their key and went up to their room. None of this caused baby Sophie to bat an eyelid.

Whilst Esther was busy changing Sophie and getting her ready for bed, David called room service and ordered a vintage bottle of Dom Perignon 2004. Well, he hadn't billed HM Gov. for an evening meal, and if it was good enough for 007… There must be some rewards.

Esther had taken the opportunity to freshen up after seeing to the baby and had slipped into a baggy white T-shirt that just covered her panties. With a knock on the door to announce the arrival of the champagne, she slipped her legs under the counterpane on the bed. David went to the door and stood to one side whilst the waiter deposited the tray with ice bucket, bottle and two glasses on the small table.

David slipped the waiter a note, smiled and opened the door once again. On closing it, he said, 'Just imagine, we couldn't possibly have thought a few days ago that we would be sitting in the Dorchester sharing a bottle of the best.' As he was making this pronouncement, he had been removing the seal and *muselet*, then he carefully eased the cork which came away from the bottle with a gentle plop.

He leant across and poured them both a glass. Giving one to Esther, he proposed a toast. 'To us and our baby and all the others that, please God, may come. Let us hope we can have a good and happy life together.' He sipped his champagne and continued, 'I think we have had enough adventures to last us the rest of our lives, don't you think?'

Esther smiled. 'When do you think we can get married?' There, she had finally asked the question that had been running through her head for so long.

David took another sip to give himself time to think. 'I'm completely torn in two on this. We have both waited so long; I don't want to wait any longer. Then I know that weddings take time to arrange properly. My guys don't get back for another three months, and I'd like them to be there. I was going to ask Rhys to be my best man.'

'I have an idea.' Esther drew her knees up to her chest and went on in a conspiratorial tone, 'I decided years ago that you were the man I wanted to spend the rest of my life with, but I was determined that we wouldn't fulfil that love until we were married. This is very important to me, but I also know that with every day that goes by, I just yearn for you to take me in your arms, and soon I just won't be able to resist – but then I know that if we are not married, I will have somehow failed myself.' She laughed and carried on, 'We could just ask my dad to marry us as soon as we can get the paperwork done, and then have the celebration when we bring everyone together.' She suddenly looked deflated as she knew this would be cheating on her ideals.

'I guess we have both waited this long; another few months isn't going to kill us.' He smiled and leant over and kissed her.

She placed her flute carefully on the bedside table, put both hands around the back of his head and pulled him down onto her. It was a long kiss, and they both clung to each other in a mutual desperate need to become one.

David's bulge at the crotch couldn't be disguised, and the silky softness of Esther's panties had become creamy with the moisture that her body knew would be needed to lubricate the entry and expose her ultra-sensitive clitoris to his thrusting penis. All this would have to wait a little longer, but sleep didn't come easily after they had retired to their separate beds.

The next morning the doorman ordered them a taxi. They arrived at Heathrow with plenty of time to spare. Sophie slept for most of the flight and only woke up as the aircraft decompressed prior to landing. She let out a howl as the pressure in her ears became painful. Esther rocked her backwards and forwards and bent her index finger so that she might suck on it. This seemed to do the trick, and soon she was smiling again.

Joshua was impatiently waiting as the other passengers moved past him towards the exit. David and Esther had to wait for the pushchair to be unloaded, so they came in behind the rest.

Joshua's face split into his trademark grin as he caught sight of them. Esther let David continue to push the pushchair as she rushed over and flung herself into her father's arms. Eventually, Joshua let her go in order to wrap his arms around David. Then it was time to see the baby.

He moved the shawl away from her face. She was truly beautiful. His eyes filled up. It was almost as though his daughter Sophie had somehow been miraculously returned to him. He slipped his huge hands around her body and lifted her up to gaze into her eyes. He hugged her to his chest and kissed her forehead as large tears rolled down his face.

As they drove into the Succoth, the entire community was there to welcome them. Mary rushed to sling her arms around her daughter; Joshua couldn't wait to pick up Sophie from her carrycot and hold her aloft.

Sarah was rooted to the spot with tears streaming down her face. David strode over and hugged her, then he took the silk scarf he had around his neck and wiped her tears away.

Soon, they were all inside the barn where beers and wine were poured, with lemonade for the younger members. Some of the ladies from the shelter had brought their families to greet the young lovers and their yet-to-be adopted baby.

Sophie was just loving it. She cooed and smiled at everyone and captured all their hearts. Everybody wanted to know how the two had managed to meet in the middle of a warzone.

David and Esther had previously discussed this at length and had prepared a very brief summary of the episode. Esther began by explaining that she had arrived in Syria with an MSF mobile team from a base in Turkey. She had then volunteered to stay at a maternity hospital in Idlib as there was a desperate need for a paediatrician. They had been continually bombed until the hospital could no longer function. She had then moved to another hospital, taking the children and their carers with her.

Once again, the Russian and Syrian bombers targeted the hospital. They would hit it once, then, when the local population were trying to save some of the occupants trapped in the rubble, they would come back and bomb it again, trying to kill the emergency service personnel and all the local people desperately trying to save the children's lives.

During one frantic rescue after a bombing raid, a man heard a child crying. They tore at the rubble with their bare hands and found the mother in the arms of her husband. They had been killed instantaneously when a concrete beam had fallen across them, but the baby had slipped from the mother's arms and slid between her thighs as she'd raised her arms to protect the child. Esther had tried to find out if there were any other living relatives for the child, but it appeared that the rest of the family had been murdered by Daesh.

Meanwhile, David had been assigned to an American Special Force's unit as an exchange officer. They had just completed a reconnaissance mission when he heard stories about a young British doctor who was tending to the children. He left the assignment when it returned to base and went in search of Esther.

David arrived in the nick of time. She explained and managed to rescue all the children and what parents or carers who had survived and got them all to a refugee camp on the Turkish border. David was able to pull some strings and got the three of them back home.

David then took up the story explaining about deciding to leave the army. That he and Esther were planning to get married, here at Succoth, in the summer. Also, that he wanted to play a part in the everyday life of the community whilst hoping to do some writing. And they would, as soon as possible, be talking to social services about officially adopting Sophie.

After the story had been told, the questions came thick and fast, but Joshua brought them to a close when his dark chocolate baritone voice said, 'Folks, today our prayers have been answered. Not only have two of our family been brought home safely, they have brought with them a beautiful child who carries a name that we will never forget. Let us thank the Lord for His gracious mercy by praying: Lord Jesus, you once made us a promise that wherever two or three people are gathered together in your name, you would be there also. Father, we want to thank you for keeping that promise; we want you to know how grateful we are that you have kept our children safe even when they were surrounded by danger. We are pleased that they have also brought us the gift of a child whose natural parents have perished. We promise, as a community, that we will keep this child as one of our own, and we will teach her to love You as we all love You. Finally, Father, please keep everyone of our community safe from harm so that we may continue to love one another and provide a secure community for all our people. Amen.'

They all echoed, 'Amen.'

Chapter 18

Preparation for Dystopia

10 September 2019

Sayeed got off the train at Cambridge, walked the quarter of a mile to the offices of Jason & Glennie, a firm of old, established lawyers, where he had an appointment with a Ms Wilson, a very bright young lady who specialised in commercial property.

Sayeed's journey from Syria had been an interesting voyage of some complexity…

Having left the hospital tent where Esther had been tending the children, he carried the body of his young friend back to the pickup truck. He placed him in the passenger seat and used the seatbelt to hold him in position. He paused to ask directions to the souk, where he left the vehicle briefly to buy a long-handled shovel, a Kaffan, a water carrier and some linen wash towels. Having returned to the vehicle, he drove out of town and further into the northern desert country.

He drove off the road and into the swirling sand of the dunes. The torrid heat was advancing the decomposition of the body, and clouds of flies seemed to have materialised from nowhere. He stopped the car and got out pleased to be away from the cloying scent of death. He took off his shirt and, turning his back to the now setting sun, started to dig the grave.

When he was sure that the grave was deep enough, he lay a blanket beside the vehicle and carefully placed his friend upon it. He gently undressed him, and as he removed the shirt, which was stuck to the body with congealed blood, the wounds opened up again. Bitter tears ran down his sweat-streaked face and into his beard.

He rose and brought a bowl which he filled with water and started to carefully wash the body. Finally, he wrapped him in the Kaffan and gently lowered him into the grave, where he laid him on his right side looking towards the east and Mecca. He took handfuls of sand and wet them with water and compressed them in his hands. These balls were then used to prop the head and shoulders in the correct position.

It only remained to refill the grave and pray. He stayed in silent prayer for a long time. By the time he left, the tears had dried up; and there was now only a dark and fearsome anger in its place.

It was a long drive to Ankara, where he had a number of important contacts.

Sayyid had removed his beard but left a moustache. In a smart, lightweight navy-blue suit, white classic shirt and brown leather loafers he looked like a successful young executive in the renewable energy business, which was what he professed to be. He had obtained a cloned passport (the true owner of which had been well paid) that gave his name as Richard Jeffries, born in Germany, where his father had been in the RAF, educated at the international school in Cologne and finished off his education studying renewables in Switzerland. His luggage was expensive, and his shoulder bag contained his laptop. He carried a modest amount of cash in euros and sterling, settling most bills with a debit card. Surprisingly, he didn't carry a smartphone.

A few weeks in the sun had coloured the delicate skin where once a luxuriant beard had been. All the preparations had been attended to; it was time to move on.

He booked a domestic flight from Ankara to Marmaris, and then took a taxi to Datça, a pleasant coastal town where he managed to get a room at a small three-star hotel. It was coming to the close of the season, so the town was a lot quieter than it had been a few weeks earlier.

His choice of using Datça as a springboard into Europe was interesting. Barely two and a half miles off the Turkish coast is the Greek island of Symi. At the end of the Second World War the island was up for grabs, but as it had no water, it would be incumbent on whichever country laid claim to it to provide water for the island on a regular basis. The Turks decided that it would be more trouble than it was worth; thus, the Greeks laid claim to the island. The Greeks and the Turks had not been good neighbours since the invasion of Northern Cyprus by the Turks, therefore little or no commerce took place between the two territories. Sayeed was certain there would be some illicit trade going on that he would be able to tap into to give him passage over that vital two and a half miles.

In the event, it was easier than he had imagined. A casual question in a waterfront café led him to a conversation with a Turkish Gulet skipper, which resulted in money changing hands and he went aboard the next day on the rising tide.

The approach into Symi is via a perfect deep-water channel that ends in a natural harbour. Not many tourists stay on the island, but large numbers visit for day trips from the larger island Rhodes. Sayeed, aka Richard, booked a passage on the ferry for that evening. By the end of that day he was at Rhodes International Airport booking a flight to London Stansted.

He took the 'red-eye special' first thing the next morning. Whilst he was waiting for his flight to be called, he did some research and found a legal firm in Cambridge that he thought would suit. He emailed them to try to arrange a meeting later that day.

By the time his flight landed in Stansted, an appointment had been offered for 3 p.m. He immediately confirmed. Booking.com provided him with the accommodation he would need until he'd found somewhere to rent.

The immigration checks had all gone smoothly, and he was now feeling quietly confident with his new identity.

Ms Wilson – 'please call me Helen' – was a smart, attractive young lady in her late twenties. She provided a firm handshake and motioned Richard to a comfortable chair and smiled encouragingly before asking, 'Well, Mr Jeffries, what can we do for you?'

He smiled back. 'Please call me Richard.' He went on, 'I represent a renewable energy company based in Switzerland, and I've been given a project to start a pilot scheme for producing biodiesel from used cooking oil here in the UK.'

He passed her a business card with all his company information. It was, in fact, an accommodation address manned by someone who would confirm his appointment. The company was a shell company professing to be an incubator fund that invested in start-up companies in renewable energy initiatives. They banked with Credit Suisse and had recently set up an account facility in London to fund future investments in the UK.

'I will be looking for premises within an hour or so north of London, north Hertfordshire, Cambridgeshire. I'm looking for about twelve to fifteen thousand square foot with sufficient parking for twelve tankers,' he added.

Helen thought for a moment and said, 'A number of farms in that area are taking advantage of the farm diversity scheme to provide premises for start-up companies like the one you have in mind. Ah, but I'm getting ahead of myself. Before we can go any further, I'm afraid I must carry out some security checks. Do you have your passport with you?'

He nodded and drew it out of his breast pocket.

She pulled a face. 'Normally I would need to take a copy of your proof of address – a utility bill or bank statement.'

He smiled. 'Well, I'm afraid that I have been pretty itinerant for the past six months or so, living in hotels mostly. I do all my banking online, and the address I give my bank is the office address. In fact, my next question to you was going to be can you assist me in finding an apartment to rent? I would quite like to live in Cambridge.'

'Let me just go and photocopy your passport.' She smiled again and left the room. She was soon back and explained, 'KYC, Know Your Customer, is an anti-money laundering measure that we all have to abide with these days, but I can see in your case the difficulty in providing the evidence that we would normally require. However, once we have found you somewhere to live and have organised the utilities, we can conclude these matters in due course.' She returned his passport across the desk. 'Have you got a budget for the premises you are looking for?' She raised an eyebrow with the question.

'Well, I'm guessing that I will have to be looking at somewhere between eight and twelve pounds a square foot. So, I would imagine somewhere around a hundred and twenty to a hundred and thirty thousand per annum. I would want to pay quarterly in advance if possible.' His eyes didn't waver as looked at her directly.

She wrote a brief note on the pad in front of her. 'I'll do some research for you this afternoon.' She looked up and asked, 'What about accommodation?'

He looked thoughtful. 'Nothing ostentatious, a one-bedroom studio. I'll probably eat out most of the time. I tend to work most evenings when I'm working on a project.'

She glanced down at his business card. 'There doesn't seem to be a mobile number.' She looked at him enquiringly.

'That's because I don't have one. It happens to be one of my idiosyncrasies. If you want to call me, you will have to call my company number in Switzerland, and they will email me. Much easier if you use my direct email address on the card, and I'll get back to you as soon as I am able. Meanwhile, I shall be staying at the Hotel du Vin.' He gave a small shrug of his shoulders. He wasn't going to explain that more miscreants are captured and successfully prosecuted from the evidence on their mobile phones than any other factor. He communicated within his shadowy milieu thanks to the encryption that Wickr offered. For more detailed instructions, he would be using Dropbox which had been set up via a secure VPN.

Their conversation at an end, Richard/Sayyid rose to his feet and offered his hand. As they shook hands, he said, 'I'll look forward to hearing from you in the next day or two.'

The Hotel du Vin was very comfortable, and the food was excellent. Sayyid spent a lot of time in his room remaking contact with many of the people that he had shared time with behind bars, others who had fought in Afghanistan and Syria. He also sent a lengthy encrypted email to a learned imam who he'd first met in Afghanistan but who was now secretly living in Pakistan. Sayyid needed a fiery preacher who could move his jihadi soldiers into an act of martyrdom that would shock the Western world to its very foundations whilst rewarding the brave few with all the pleasures of Paradise.

Sayyid checked his emails every hour on the hour. It was a great discipline that not only did he review his messages, but it also meant the rest of his time was used productively without the diversions that can so easily steal time in the course of a day.

He was just about to go into dinner that evening when a young man came to the bar and ordered a gin and tonic. As his drink was being prepared, he looked around the room and gave Sayyid a penetrating glance that spoke volumes.

'Are you dining alone?' It was Sayyid who broke the ice.

'Why, are you offering?' The stranger spoke in a soft whisper.

'I don't enjoy dining on my own. Why don't you join me? That is if you're not waiting for someone.'

'No, I was going to have dinner when I've finished this drink,' he replied.

'Well, then, bring your drink with you and join me.' Sayyid spoke with an authority that would bridge no rebuttal. 'My name's Richard.' He thrust out his hand.

It was grasped hesitantly. 'Francis,' came the reply.

They had a pleasant enough dinner and talked about trivialities. Francis was surprised that his new-found friend was teetotal, but then again, he didn't drink much himself, preferring to have the occasional snort when he wanted to boost his confidence a bit.

It was later, in Sayyid's room, after they had made love, that the interesting facts came out. Francis was a logistics manager, but he didn't like his job. His boss was always making jokes at his expense, so Francis was thinking about looking for a new appointment.

'I might be able to help you there,' mused Sayyid. He would need someone he could trust to buy the fuel tankers and hold the fort whilst he returned to the Middle East for the final ingredient of his master plan.

Two days later, Helen had emailed him to say that she had three apartments he might be interested in and that there was a farm diversification scheme with a warehouse and a large parking area available which was situated in north Hertfordshire. If he was available on Friday, he could visit the industrial unit in the morning and return to Cambridge to view the apartments. He immediately confirmed that he would meet her at her office at nine in the morning and he would be pleased to follow her itinerary for the rest of that day.

It all went to plan perfectly. The industrial premises were ideal. He had to haggle a bit over the price, but by the end of the morning he was able to give Helen instructions to ask for the lease and to advise on all the terms, rates and conditions.

The afternoon was even better. The first apartment they visited was exactly what he was looking for, so he decided not to view the other two. After phone calls were made, he took Helen off for a celebratory lunch.

Francis moved in that weekend. He had decided to start work for Richard on the following Monday, even though he was supposed to give his present employer a month's notice. Richard said that if they were going to work together, they would have to start right away.

For his part, Francis couldn't remember when he felt this happy. His first job would be to source twelve second-hand tankers. Richard didn't mind if they were non-compliant; they were simply going to be storage containers for methanol which would be used to produce biodiesel from used cooking oil that would be collected from restaurants, cafés and pubs. Not only would it solve the problem of getting rid of a difficult waste product, but it would produce a clean fuel with no particulates.

Francis was impressed. He had always wanted to do something worthwhile and be part of a team that would produce something ecologically beneficial, and this eco-friendly fuel project was like a dream come true. To have Richard as his boss would be fantastic. He rushed about the apartment cleaning and tidying before settling down with his laptop to work his way through *Autotrader* looking for tankers.

Richard explained where the new premises were and showed him on Google Maps. He asked him to take his car, which was a smart blue Audi A3 parked outside the apartment, and visit the site in order to measure the space above the roller doors where Richard wanted a sign produced ASAP: 'THE GREEN DEAL: Biodiesel for Cleaner Air in London'.

It took less than a week of Richard chivvying Helen before the lease was ready for signing. But with the lease now executed, the extra funds from Geneva had hiccoughed, so Richard would have to go over and sort out the pros and cons.

He had arranged for BT to install the landlines and broadband connection… 'Would that be OK?' he had asked… He didn't want to lose his place in the queue.

Helen thought that as long as he could sort out the finance side in a couple of days, it should be all right.

Francis had been busy buying tankers. These had to be paid for, but when he asked about insuring them, Richard said that he was negotiating a complete insurance package with some Lloyds brokers. He was to use drivers from a temp agency to get the vehicles to site. Their own staff would be recruited when he got back from Geneva.

While all this was going on, Richard was busy viewing narrowboats. He finally found what he was looking for on a mooring in Broxbourne on the River Lee. He wanted to rent it for the autumn months from October 1st. until November 31st as he was writing a book about the importance of the River Lee and its relationship with the Thames. He would be prepared to pay three thousand pounds a month – paying monthly in advance. As the young couple who owned the narrowboat were particularly hard up, six thousand pounds would provide a much better Christmas. They would be able to stay with friends and family for those few weeks.

Sayyid sent a message to Jarrah, a fearless jihadi who had revelled in the slaughter of Kafirs. An oddball individual, he had experienced a torturous life as the result of consistent physical abuse from his stepdad. It only stopped when one day the boy hit him with a claw hammer.

Whilst in Barlinnie, after a Glasgow bar fracas that resulted in some serious GBH, he was taken under the wing of the resident Islamic mullah.

Sayyid had a black book in his head. He had the ability to remember not just faces but, more importantly, email addresses of the faces. Some of these received a perfectly encrypted message via Wickr.

On opening, Jarrah read a terse call to arms. Would he offer his miserable life to destroy the Kafir government and martyr himself for that special place in Paradise? *If this is the right time for you, you must reply immediately. It is time for all Muslims in the UK to come together to strike at the centre of this corrupt state, to advance Sharia law that will make this place a sanctuary for Muslim people throughout the world. Don't just take my word for it, see what Imam Omar bin Hussein has to say – Dropbox: Omar777. google.com.*

The choosing of Jarrah wasn't random. Jarrah aka Cullum, aka 'Wee Man', described a small-boned individual of about five foot five inches, who had been known to deck five aggressive individuals outside a Glasgow club by use of a Neolithic forehead structure that could strike at the speed of a vomiting cobra. Later, in Iraq, he demonstrated an ability to slice throats with an Arabian sword, razor sharp – his record was seven in one slash. He tried many times to beat his record without success.

It was a strange fact that they had both shared a cell in Scotland and later in a makeshift interrogation centre on the Iraq–Syrian border. Sayyid remembered another story, told in the dark when they shared a cell – telling each other stories would make the realities of life go away. Cullum had been born on a narrowboat on the Union Canal in Scotland. Notwithstanding the beatings, and the drunken rages of his mother's partner, he loved the life on the water. He could manage the boat, take her though the locks, tie up and make some grub. His mum was most times below deck, collapsed on her bunk, pissed out of her mind.

Cullum replied to the Wickr message two minutes later: *I have prayed to be called. Just tell me, Bro, and I'll be with you all the way.*

Sayyid replied: *I need you to find another brother who thinks like you. He must be secure, or we will all die for nothing.*

Again, the reply was back in minutes: *I have a friend who believes as we believe. Will there be just the two of us?*

Sayyid's reply was terse and to the point: *Inshallah (if God wills it), this will be the beginning of our great revolution. Alhamdulillah (thanks be to God).*

Cullum replied: *I will speak with my friend today. We should be able to move later this week.*

Sayyid replied: *Go online and open a bank account with one of the online banks, then send me your sort code and account number and I will arrange funds for your journey. I will send you details of where you must go when I next hear from you.*

Their brief exchange of messages was over for the time being; Sayyid revisited the couple on the houseboat and completed the arrangement.

Three days later, he received a confirmatory Wickr from Cullum with the required details. It was signed 'Jarrah'. Sayyid made a note to refer to his friend by his Islamic name in future.

He put the required funds in his bank account to take the train down south, and enough money to feed the two of them and fuel the narrowboat for the journey. He wanted them to cruise down the River Lee through the canals and locks to Bow Creek, and thence into the tidal Thames and on to Brentwood. They should take their time, memorise the route and pay close attention to the tidal aspects of the Thames and how long each part of the journey took to complete. After a one-night stay at Brentwood, they were to return using the same route and bring the narrowboat back up the River Lee. He would arrange a further RV in due course.

Before they left Glasgow, they were to purchase two pay-as-you-go smartphones. No calls were ever to be made on these; they were only to be used for data and then only by Wickr. The only other app they needed to download was What3words – they would use this to navigate to their RVs when needed. Their own phones might have already been compromised and must be left in Glasgow.

Sayyid paused before removing the USB stick which linked him to the Tails app (The Amnesic Incognito Live System), and thus via Tor to provide complete anonymity with every message deleted as soon as it was sent – all browsing history became non-existent. He needed an e-visa for the journey that he knew he must take in three days' time.

The next day, Sayyid received a message from Jarrah: *We will be there tomorrow. Need the name of the boat and location.*

Sayyid replied: Queen of the South. *Three words: 'volume, credit, visits'. Keys: Geranium pot on the roof. Your cover story: You have been employed by me (Richard Jefferies) who is writing a book about the River Lee and its relationship with the Thames. You are going to take the narrowboat down onto the Thames on a recce before returning to collect me in a few weeks' time. Report daily at 6 p.m.*

Jarrah's confirmation just said: *No drama. Will keep you posted.*

Sayyid's next message was to Imam Omar bin Hussein: *We will be ready to move at the end of next month. I need twelve drivers who wish to find their place in Paradise. They must be true soldiers who are battle hardened, who love Allah and who are prepared to die for Him.*

The imam's reply came back almost immediately: *There are ten times that number of men in Britain who have returned from our holy wars. I will gather the best. You must let me know when and where you want them.*

Sayyid replied: *I will know more in a few weeks. Inshallah.*

Back in the apartment, Francis had made a spaghetti bolognaise and put some freshly cut flowers on the table. He thought it might be nice to open a bottle of red wine, but remembering that Richard didn't drink, he chilled some sparkling water instead.

The last few weeks had flown by; he now had his fleet of tankers already to be delivered to site whenever he gave the word. He had spent an awful lot of money, but it didn't seem to faze Richard one tiny bit. He couldn't wait to get into the offices so he could start organising their administration and learn about the process of producing biodiesel from used cooking oil. He had googled it so had some idea of how the process would work, but he was keen to get into the detail. How many people would they need to employ?

Over dinner, Richard explained that he would have to go to Geneva to sort out the financial side. This would probably take a couple of weeks, so he wanted Francis to hold the fort until he got back. He would stay in touch via Wickr and wanted Francis to drive him to Heathrow in the morning.

The next morning, Richard asked Francis to drop him off without coming into the airport; he wanted him to get back to Cambridge and ring BT to see what the hold-up was in setting up a landline and internet connection.

Sayyid had no intention of going to Geneva and instead went to the Azerbaijan Airlines' desk to buy a one-way ticket to Baku, the capital.

Two weeks before, he had emailed a long, encrypted message to a certain Iranian cleric who was the head of the Intelligence Organisation of the Islamic Revolutionary Guard Corps. The email was marked 'Top Secret' in Arabic and headed 'Operation Rolling Thunder'.

There followed a very detailed operational plan for a major attack on London. The credentials of the author had been checked and was regarded as a topflight jihadi who had been fighting in Afghanistan, Iraq and Syria. His father had been killed in Afghanistan fighting the Russians. The son had been brought up in Great Britain, but he hated the infidels and was ready to pour fire and brimstone into the heart of their, so-called, democracy.

The plan gave the exact detail of how the operation would play out. An industrial plant in the countryside, one hour north of London, had been established. Twelve tankers, each two-thirds filled with methanol, were ready to go. Explosive charges would be set ready to blow when the drivers operated a switch. The oxygen and methanol mixture would combine with the detonation in an enclosed space, causing a massive explosion. The author was an experienced bomb maker since his days in Afghanistan. Imam Omar bin Hussein had chosen twelve drivers who were ready to die for Allah.

On a day chosen, when all Members of Parliament could be expected to attend, Operation Rolling Thunder would be executed.

The tanker on the Queen Elizabeth Bridge would detonate, as would the tanker in the Dartford Tunnel. Then each road bridge would be blown at two-minute intervals, including the central span of Tower Bridge, culminating with the first span of Westminster Bridge together with a tanker in front of the Houses of Parliament.

This ancient building was falling apart, so work had started on a major refurbishment. The roof and much of the upper part of the building was covered in scaffolding, but a major blast would bring down tonnes of masonry upon the heads of the incumbents.

A barge had been obtained and would be moored upstream. At the appointed time, it would swoop down on the ebb tide. It would be packed with explosives. At the last moment it would change course and ram the bank in front of the Houses of Parliament. It would be detonated as it hit the explosives.

Special forces had tested the possibility of an attack from the river and had reported on its vulnerability. As a temporary measure, engineers had sunk concrete blocks with cable mountings to entrammel the propellers of any craft trying to reach the vulnerable bank.

However, due to the jihadi barge weighing more than fifteen tonnes and with the maximum momentum given from its powerful diesel engine together with the ebbing tide, these cables would not be sufficient to stop the barge striking the bank. Even if it did, the blast in such close proximity to the building would be sufficient to produce the required effect.

So, what did this young jihadi want from them? Explosives, EPX-1, a very powerful plastic explosive together with detonators and switches. Then the difficult request: sufficient radioactive material that, when disbursed by the barge explosion, would contaminate the entire area of Westminster for years to come. Furthermore, he wanted these materials to be transhipped on a coastal vessel en route for Norway or Sweden. He would go with the cargo, and he wanted a small detachment of Revolutionary Guards to ferry him ashore on the east coast of Scotland. This simply wasn't going to happen. The risks were too great.

However, the American reversal of their nuclear arrangement, together with further sanctions, had hardened opinions. Then, after a detachment of Royal Marines boarded an Iranian oil tanker, it was decided to show the world that it was still capable of biting back.

They agreed to meet Sayyid but not in Iran. It was decided that a safe house would be set up in Azerbaijan. A suburban house on the outskirts of Baku was chosen, and the meeting was arranged for the last week in August.

Sayyid left the Winter Park Hotel that morning and walked to the Denizkenari Milli Park. He wasn't in a rush; he just wanted to make sure that he hadn't picked up a tail.

When he was sure, he walked back into town where he had spotted a taxi rank. He took a ride to the funicular. When he got there, he rode to the top, waited and came back down to the bottom. The house that he was looking for was a ten-minute walk from where he had left the taxi.

When he arrived at the property, he continued and walked past to the next corner. The area was just a quiet, peaceful suburb, so he strode up a small path and rang the bell on the side of the door.

The door was opened by a young man who looked like he could handle himself. He smiled and nodded his head as an invitation to enter. Another older man waited inside the passageway. He raised a finger and instructed Sayyid to put his hands on the wall.

Sayyid put his laptop down on the floor and placed his hands on the wall as instructed. The older man placed his leg between Sayyid's legs and forced them out and back, so all his weight was balanced on his hands.

The older man stepped back and swiftly and efficiently ran his hands over any and every possible hiding place where a weapon might have been secreted. As he finished his search, he grunted and instructed in Arabic for him to follow.

Further down the passageway was a door on the left. The guard, for that was surely what he must have been, opened the door and held it open for Sayyid to enter. On a couch opposite was a thawb and a sirwal, the traditional robe and loose pants to wear underneath. He was then instructed to undress, to take everything off, and then put on the clothes provided for him.

The two guards watched him closely as he got undressed and put on the Arabic garments. He was then told curtly to leave everything, including his laptop, and to go with them. They returned to the passage and followed it to the end where another door faced them. The younger man knocked on the door, and this was returned with a single command.

It was a large airy room, and through the windows Sayyid could see a well-tended garden. There was a desk and a chair in front of him, but the owner of the voice that bid them to enter was standing by the windows looking out. He turned slowly and stared intently at Sayyid. He was dressed traditionally, had a hooked nose under dark penetrating eyes, and a neatly trimmed beard. He somehow reminded Sayyid of a peregrine falcon.

He said in fluent English, ‘Please come and have a seat.’ He waved a hand to a chair at one side of the desk. ‘Would you care for some tea?’

Before Sayyid could reply, he started to pour tea into two small glass teacups.

‘I won’t introduce myself; you don’t need to know who I am, and I...’ he smiled a cold smile ‘...know who you are.’ He settled himself behind the desk and opened his hand towards Sayyid as if to introduce him. 'I've read your battle plan, of course, and now I would like you to take me through every aspect of it.'

Sayyid told how he had set up the biodiesel plant and that twelve oil tankers had been purchased which would then carry methanol. He went on to explain how he had managed to lease a narrowboat that would be able to navigate the River Lee to the Thames. And how that, even as they spoke, one of his most trusted lieutenant together with an experienced jihadi were carrying out a recce that would take them past the Houses of Parliament at Westminster; and by the time he'd returned to the UK, they would be back to a mooring on the River Lee waiting for his next move.

He went on to explain how the twelve martyrs were being recruited. On his order, they would meet at two secret locations away from any CCTV cameras. They wouldn't even use public transport to get there. All their personal possessions, including their phones, would be taken off them. They would then be ferried by minibus to the factory. He explained that before the martyrs arrived, he would have made up the initiating explosive devices which would be operated by a simple flick of a switch on the dashboard of each vehicle. He assumed it was known that he was an experienced bomb maker.

Choosing the day of the attack required a time when the Houses of Parliament would be full, and the time would depend on the timing of the tide on that day. The blowing up of the bridges and tunnels, apart from killing and maiming very large numbers of people, would act as a diversion for the main attack, which would take place by one tanker being blown up at the public entrance to the House whilst simultaneously the first span of Westminster (nearest to Big Ben) would blow.

He explained how these ancient buildings were presently being refurbished as they were barely safe for the occupants, therefore it was cocooned in scaffolding whilst sections of the roof were being removed. Even major pieces of masonry were unsafe. A major explosive blast at this time would bring the entire building down upon their heads. The narrowboat coming down on the ebb tide would veer across the river to explode as it hit the bank beside the main hall. The main addition he had asked for was to ensure that no rapid rebuild programme could ever take place – the Mother of all Parliaments would become radioactive ashes!

He concluded by explaining, 'I do not intend to go to Paradise on that day. I have an escape route planned that will return me to Iran. I have more plans in my head to cause mayhem in the West, and to further the expansion of Islam and the implementation of Sharia law throughout the world.'

His stony-faced interrogator smiled a thin smile. 'Explain to me how…if we provide you with everything that you have asked for, will you get it onto the British mainland?'

'I was brought up for much of my young life in the north-east of Scotland; I know many lonely bays where it would be possible to land our merchandise. I can arrange to have a vehicle stood by to transport everything. I only need you to help me get the stuff ashore from the coastal trader, and then they should be able to return to the ship and continue their voyage to wherever.'

At this juncture there was a knock on the door. A studious-looking man with glasses entered with Sayyid's clothes and laptop. The boss pointed with his beard and raised an eyebrow slightly in an obvious question. Sayyid thought the man with glasses spoke in what was probably Farsi. Sayyid wasn't worried; he knew he was clean and that they wouldn't find anything on his laptop.

This was confirmed, as during the brief chat he heard the English words 'Tales' and 'Linux system' and 'Tor' being mentioned. These systems allowed him to browse the net and send encrypted messages. Having backed up with a memory stick, everything would be deleted without a trace once removed. The man left the clothes and laptop and gave a brief bow before leaving.

'One last question,' his examiner asked. 'Who is the Kafir you share the apartment with, in Cambridge?'

Sayyid didn't bat an eyelid. 'I'm pleased to see that you are as thorough as I would be. He is my cover, and when we are about to strike, I will ensure that he cannot jeopardise our operation.'

'Very good, you have done well, I will authorise your request. It will take a few days to arrange all the particulars, but I will communicate the details to you as before. In the meantime, return to your hotel and live quietly. Change your clothes now and leave through a side entrance that Hamid will show you. May peace be upon you, Alhamdulillah.'

Sayyid left as instructed and waited the next four days before the instruction came that he so badly yearned for.

Chapter 19

To Love and to Cherish

David had officially resigned his commission, but he had plenty of accrued leave. Along with his resettlement entitlement, he would be paid for the next three months at least. He had not yet made his mind up about the MI6 offer.

Meanwhile, there was plenty to do: lambing was coming to a close, but now the planting season was progressing well in the growing tunnel. Without Mo being there to organise things, there was a lot of reading to be done to go with the information that his granddad had given him on the allotment when he was a boy.

The news on the TV was focused almost entirely on Brexit, and David realised that he really didn't know too much about the background to this. His military duties in Afghanistan and elsewhere had taken all his study time. He'd always thought that Britain had joined a trading organisation, but now there were strong hints coming out that this wasn't so – that the intention was to produce a United States of Europe. He thought it was about time to carry out a bit of research to get a better understanding on what the EU was all about.

The more he read, the more he began to realise that a united European state had been a dream for some people since the 1920s. Adolf Hitler put a stop to the movement, as he believed that he could rule the whole continent with his victorious armies. However, as soon as the war was over in 1945, the idea was floated again as the European Coal and

Steel Community, designed to bring lasting peace. The six founding countries were France, West Germany, Italy, The Netherlands, Belgium and Luxembourg. In 1973, the United Kingdom, Denmark and Ireland all joined this group of inter-trading countries which seemed beneficial to all.

With the fall of the Berlin Wall, many other countries were keen to join this grouping. Vast amounts of money were lavished on everything from major infrastructure to cultural and environmental initiatives. The rules and budgets were brought about by commissioners who, it would seem, were not elected but somehow came together by a cabal established by an old boys' network of politicians from a selection of European countries. Some of whom had been less than successful politicians in their own countries, and some who had even been suspected of serious fraud. Backed up by a highly paid group of bureaucrats, they initiate all legislation. The Council of Ministers are co-opted members from the member states who can influence any proposed legislation by qualified majority voting (QMV) – the veto is soon to be withdrawn.

The EU Parliament is nothing more than a talking shop; some people say its elected members can do nothing to enforce real change. The entire EU apparatus costs its members €165 billion for the budget this year. The amount of waste and suspected fraud is immense, as such, the audited accounts have not been signed off for the last ten years!

David continued to read and research: How could a common currency be managed without a common treasury, common fiscal rules, retirement ages…? There is an EU flag, and there is an EU anthem, and they would like an EU army and an EU foreign policy. In effect, what is required, it seemed, was a 'United States of Europe', where all national sovereignty would be relegated to the wishes of the president and his commissioners. NATO would be lost as part of the collateral damage.

Many British politicians couldn't accept the ever-growing power base that the EU was developing whilst reducing the ability of parliamentarians to govern. The left-wing Labour minister Tony Benn had been vehemently opposed to the concept of a European state, as was Margaret Thatcher, the arch-Conservative prime minister.

The Eurosceptics, as they came to be called, were quite prepared to trade with Europe, but they didn't want to be governed by Brussels. However, with each succeeding treaty signed in the name of the EU, the respective member parliaments had to obey the diktats of the European commissioners. Political parties could not agree on the benefits or otherwise of remaining a member of the EU.

Finally, David Cameron, the British Conservative Prime Minister at the time, tried to obtain some changes to the structure that would make the EU more palatable to Eurosceptic MPs and many of the disgruntled electorate. He was singularly unsuccessful, so he called for a referendum to let the people choose in a once-in-a-lifetime vote. A majority of more than 1,300,000 people voted to leave the EU. Yet – here they were, more than three years later – and it still hadn't happened.

The people who voted to remain in the EU tried to call for a second referendum on the grounds that the people who voted to leave didn't know what they were doing. Scare stories were put out on a daily basis. Economists were marshalled to tell how catastrophic it would be for the economy. David mused that he had rather more faith in weather forecasters. Of course, big business wanted the status quo. They were making good profits – why change anything that might disturb the market? Strangely, the extremely left-wing opposition were siding with big business – but then, they had a different agenda to address.

With the result of the referendum, David Cameron resigned, and Theresa May took over as PM. Although she voted to remain, she had spent the last three years trying to negotiate a deal with the EU to leave.

Theresa May's ultimate deal was unacceptable to the British Parliament, so eventually she also resigned. Boris Johnson was a leading contender, but he would face an uphill struggle to get any sort of deal through Parliament. With claims and counterclaims, and demonstrations by both sides of the argument, the whole fabric of British democracy seemed to be in peril. A minority government that was only held together by ten DUP members. A Speaker who many believed was totally biased towards the Remainers (when the true function should have been to act as referee between the opposing parties). The Scottish National Party whose only real aim was independence, but who thought that from out of this chaos they would be able to cast off the four-hundred-year association with England.

The government of England could no longer govern; it was stalemate. It would be usual, under normal conditions, for a general election to be called, but even that didn't happen. The 17.4 million people who voted to leave the EU felt disenfranchised, disgusted with politicians in general and just waiting for a general election to make their presence felt.

The Remainers, on the other hand, spoke of another 'People's Referendum', whilst everybody knew this was simply in the hope that the result of the first referendum could be overturned.

David couldn't but think of how the people in his community had solved their problems by working together, as opposed to lining up behind class-based political parties run by professional politicians. David wrote a couple of well-researched articles on the subject that were published in the broadsheets.

Meanwhile, Esther was working flat out to organise her wedding and look after Sophie, as well as putting in three mornings a week to help the local GP.

She had decided against the marquee concept in favour of a giant double tepee that were made in Perth and could be hired for weddings and other celebrations. With two great wood-burning stoves for guests to gather around if it started to get chilly in the evening, she felt this would fit more into the scenery of the Succoth, and David agreed. The date was the last Saturday in September, the twenty-eighth of the month, to give the guys, who would have just returned from Afghanistan, time to decompress.

All the food would come from Home Farm: a poached salmon (?) starter, and slow-roasted lamb, pork or venison with new potatoes, fresh asparagus and garden peas. A simple dessert of Tarte Tatin with home-made vanilla ice cream. An excellent cheeseboard to finish off with. Then coffee and the traditional port or Madeira, beer by the keg, along with whiskey and other spirits to ensure that nobody went thirsty during the dancing.

Her dress would be simplicity itself. In ivory as opposed to white, it was a classic dress that her mother helped to design, and then a wonderful seamstress in Aberdeen had made the dream come true.

David would be in dress uniform, as would his guard of honour. Two of the youngsters from the refuge would act as flower girl and pageboy. Willow would be her maid of honour.

Music had been a bit of a problem until one of her patients in the village told her about an incredibly talented band who called themselves

'Reel Aliens'. A fusion of traditional and modern with wild fiddlers, banjos, guitars and percussion. They had a girl lead singer who was fabulous. They looked like wild gypsies, but everyone joined in when they struck up with their jigs and reels. She and David had spent an evening in Aviemore to see them perform before booking them for the wedding.

The honeymoon was to be three weeks in Kenya. The community at Succoth had decided that their gift to the couple would be their dream honeymoon. The couple had chosen and booked a beautiful beach hotel on the Indian Ocean for ten days for them to relax after all the hectic arranging of their wedding. Then a safari for a week in the Masai Mara. Esther had always wanted to visit East Africa, and David was keen to go back, having been there on joint exercises with the Kenyan army.

Mary was going to look after little Sophie whilst they were away. Esther knew this would be fine, but it still felt strange to hand over this child for what seemed an awfully long time to be away. Mary was already looking after Sophie when Esther went to the surgery, but that was only for a few hours at a time.

The days passed into weeks, the weeks into months, time just seemed to be accelerating. The weather in August was amazing, sunshine and blue skies, not like Scotland at all. With the onset of September, the weather changed. Dark clouds brought gusting winds and frequent rainstorms. Esther prayed that the weather would improve for the last weekend in the month.

All of David's friends had returned safely from Afghanistan and were looking forward to this romp in the Highlands with their respective wives and girlfriends. Some of his other friends that he'd made at university had also been invited. Esther wasn't short of friends either. Girls that she had known at medical school and a few colleagues she had worked with in Aberdeen. They were all quite keen to come as a number of single Para and SAS officers were going to be there!

Joshua wanted to walk his only daughter down the aisle, so he put a call through to the chaplain of the University of Aberdeen, they had both been in the same year as students. The Reverend Udny said that he would be delighted to officiate.

David declined a boozy stag with his mates on the night before his big day, knowing just how easily it could get out of hand, as he didn't want anything to mar this special day.

The day before the wedding was overcast but at least the rain had held off. The tepee had arrived, and the riggers had it fully erected within a few hours. Esther had been worried that it might not be big enough, but it was truly a magical space, with the floors laid and sparkling lights draped from the poles, and tables and chairs positioned around a dance space in the middle. All the ladies of Succoth were busy decorating the tables. The cooking area was an open-sided marquee with propane gas stoves that the caterers had provided. Everything seemed to be going to plan, except the weather.

The day of the wedding dawned without sun. Dark clouds scudded across the sky and rain never seemed far away. David walked around the tepee checking the tension on the guy ropes, but everything seemed secure, even though the canvas was stretched taut with every gust of wind.

He left the venue area and walked to the last resting place of his dad, Sophie and old Benjamin. Dai had built a picket fence around the area and planted some trees. The silver birch leaves made a sparkling backdrop for the red leaves of the geans. Gavin had built a bench where people could sit and wonder at the beauty that surrounded them.

David sat; his thoughts were with his father. How he wished that somehow, he could have his dad back with him even if were just for today. He remembered the words that his dad had written in the last exercise book he'd read: *The most beautiful aspect of this complex universe, it seems to me, are the changing seasons. After you no sooner gather in the harvest and store and preserve the fruits of your labour, it is time to start preparing for the spring. Planning and early planting, soil preparation and manuring. Putting the tups to the ewes on Guy Fawkes Day so that lambing could commence around April the first. The 'last sting of winter' when a snowstorm roars out of the north-west in May! The sunshine of June to maybe get a first cut of hay, and those long days when the sun doesn't hardly seem to set before it starts to rise again.* David had never thought of his dad as a philosopher, but he did have some wonderful insights into what really matters in this life.

His thoughts moved to Sophie. How could anyone see a purpose in the loss of this vibrant, clever, beautiful young woman by a drink-crazed bully of a man? He closed his eyes and immediately had a vision of Sayyid, covered in arterial blood, stabbing and stabbing in a frenzy of hate. He had to shake his head violently to dismiss the vision. And where might he be now? He answered his own question – still in Syria or Iraq, or maybe back in Afghanistan.

Even as he sat there, the clouds had moved on, the wind had dropped, and the silver birch leaves had stopped their silver rustling. The sun came out, and gradually the air warmed to a perfect Indian summer as the sun rose higher in the heavens. He had better get back and start getting ready.

As he snapped the gate shut, he could just hear the notes of a beautiful piece of piano music. As he came closer to Rachel's house, he realised that he was listening to Liszt's arrangement of Schubert's 'Ständchen'. He remembered a saying but could not remember who said it: 'I'm not a melancholy man, but I do enjoy melancholia'. He smiled and walked up the path to his house.

The church in the village had been decked out with flowers. The officers in their dress uniforms and Sam Browne's with ceremonial swords looked very dashing. A very athletic-looking bunch with suntanned faces removed their headdress as they entered the church with their wives or girlfriends. The ladies all, optimistically, wore light summery dresses and large brimmed hats.

David and Rhys stood together in the front row of pews. Rhys did not wear a red beret (although he was perfectly entitled to) but wore the plain khaki beret with insignia of the winged dagger and the motto 'Who Dares Wins'. He was the only non-commissioned officer in the assembly, but everyone knew that this young man, who had already won a MC, would swiftly rise through the ranks when he returned to the regiment.

Rachel, having been asked to play the church organ, had been rehearsing on a daily basis for weeks. The sounds that she coaxed from this ancient instrument was a seduction of the senses. There was a short pause as she glanced into the conveniently placed rear-view mirror, which gave her a clear view of the bride arriving with her father and being greeted by the Reverend Udny. She struck up with Mendelssohn's 'Wedding March'.

As Esther moved down the aisle on Joshua's arm, the sunlight from the still open church door produced a luminescence around her that somehow seemed to emanate an otherworldly sense of pure beauty.

David, looking over one shoulder, caught his breath in wonderment. This girl, who he had known since they were both children, was now a woman who he wanted to share the rest of his life with.

Joshua smiled his trademark grin, and David took her arm. As Esther lifted the small veil, he saw her mischievous smile and her large dark eyes. She parted her lips in a smile that hinted dark secrets.

They both agreed that they would obey each other… Not a problem, they had long ago agreed that whatever serious differences they might have in the future could be resolved. They had a rich community within their community, and by using de Bono's Six Hat Theory (they argued that it had worked for all of them for the past twenty-odd years) it would be better than relationship counselling.

The vows were made, and hymns were sung. Reverend Udny then gave a very interesting sermon that spoke of the real lives of the bride, who risked her life in Syria (no one will ever know the explosive power of death and destruction whilst working with Médecins Sans Frontières), and David, who arrived in the nick of time to save not only his wife-to-be, but to move other vulnerable people to safety and to bring a child with no other relatives back to the UK. 'What we do know is that David and Esther love God and will do everything in their power to live a good life in the love and security of the Lord. Amen.'

I doubt that anyone left that church without being uplifted and believing in a future that was to be celebrated.

David recognised the two dark grey Garrons with the eel stripe that pulled the open landau from his deer stalking days; they were impressive in how they rose to the occasion. Her Majesty's Windsor Greys could not have produced a more royal journey to the Succoth.

The meal was an elevation beyond Michelin stars: The salmon (where did it come from? Should have been put back, whoops!). The venison, only the haunch, bared down to the 'pavoirs' (French for cobblestones), those eight muscle groups suitably skinned of their cling film muscle containers that would not now be require slow cooking but were available as the most tender fillets. The lamb was amazing; the beef tomahawk steaks beat even the appetite of all the young officers.

With the meal complete, the port started to circulate, as did the Reel Aliens. The fiddle playing was devilish, the banjos added a multiplicity of jocular notes, the squeezebox squealed harmony, and the voice of the girl singer was sometimes teasing and sexy yet at other times sad and vulnerable. This then lifted to a joyous celebration of life itself. Traditional it most certainly was, but a real reflection of people who just want to live and love. The young gypsy lady with a baby cocooned in a shawl upon her back showed them how to dance in a way that celebrated life. Some of the other young ladies then found the confidence to challenge their young heroes to join the dance.

The best man, Rhys, spoke of the extraordinary chance that let him know both the bride and groom since he was a 'sprog'. He spoke about his hero – as a boy, as a man, as a warrior (make no mistake about that) – but added the necessary depreciating story: 'One year, the salmon were not running on the Spey. The river hadn't had enough water – then after a week of rain, the river was in spate. The fishers had caught nothing. The boys from the Succoth went fishing at first light with home-made spears. They got very cold but speared a few eatable fish. Boys will do what boys do, but I will say to estate managers and landowners, just look around you, it is from the real-life adventures that boys have which produce the men that go to war in the defence of our small island state. Pray that God will continue to smile upon us and give courage to these lads and forgive us our trespasses.' He ended with a devilish grin.

He continued, 'The other half of this equation is Esther, not only is she beautiful, funny, a great sport, but she is very clever. As you all know, she studied medicine and is now a paediatrician. Her work with Médecins Sans Frontières saw her saving the lives of children in war-torn Syria, where her now husband not only managed to gain one of the most prestigious US medals for heroism, but he was also able to save his wife and their adopted daughter, along with a lorry load of refugee children, and bring them all to safety. I am sure you will all realise that these two people are my all-time heroes, but I would like to add this caveat: All of the children that grew up in this place have been extremely privileged. The Succoth and the people who made it created a paradise for children and grown-ups alike. They produced a real community without class distinctions, without a need to accumulate possessions, with a duty of care for one to another. I am so proud to have been a small part of this experiment, and my prayer is that someday the dream that became a reality here might be replicated throughout our country.'

Everyone had listened intently, then waited in vain for the bawdy joke. They all grasped the thrust of the message. When Rhys finished, there was a brief silence, then there was a simultaneous movement of chairs as all the guests rose to their feet to provide a standing ovation, before toasting the bridesmaids.

The eating and drinking, dancing and merrymaking continued. David and Esther moved outside to get a breath of air.

'Shall we take a walk down to the river?' David asked. Esther nodded, and they walked arm in arm.

A huge harvest moon was lighting up the sky, so it was easy to see where they were going. When they reached the river, they could still hear the wild fiddle music.

Esther smiled, went up on her tiptoes and kissed him. 'Thank you for a wonderful day,' she whispered.

'We can thank all our friends and neighbours. In other places, guests produce wedding presents from pre-prepared lists. Our lot cooked food, put up tents, made a car park, served drinks, made us laugh and shared in our celebration. I love these people and I love this place.'

'And our honeymoon,' Esther added.

The community had wondered what to give the couple for a wedding present, and Sarah had mentioned going to Kenya. That was it – business class all the way and five-star treatment in hotels and safari lodges.

They started to walk back up the hill. 'Shall we just slip away now and go home; we have to make an early start in the morning?' Without waiting for an answer, she continued, 'Mum is looking after Sophie tonight, it's all been arranged.'

When they reached their house, David picked her up in his arms, opened the door and carried her over the threshold just as he had promised.

Both exhausted from the tensions of the day, they slipped into the large king-sized bed and snuggled. They had talked this bit out as well. Having waited patiently for so long, they'd decided they weren't going to spoil their first lovemaking when they were tired. Tomorrow would be spent travelling to Nairobi, and the following day they would reach Malindi on the Mombasa coast. After a day relaxing on the beach, their time would come.

The next morning, David's phone rang. It was Rhys. 'Sorry, guv, but I thought I'd better give you a call…in case.'

'No problem, we're putting our stuff together, grabbing a coffee and a slice of toast – do you want to join us?'

'No, I'm sorted. Pick you up in fifteen?'

'That'll be great, see you then.' David made a mental note that he must stop Rhys calling him 'guv'nor'. He finished his coffee and moved their cases to the front door.

All the community came out to wave them off. Some of the younger members had written messages on the car in shaving foam and attached tin cans. As they opened the door, they were festooned with rose petals. The car had been rented by Rhys to take them to Aberdeen. Then there was a last hug for their parents and a loving kiss for Sophie before they left.

As they drove off, they saw Zufash standing on her own. She gave the couple a small wave, but her sadness could not be mistaken. It was the only off-key note at their departure.

Esther asked the question that David had also been thinking, 'Where do you think Sayyid might be now?'

'It's difficult to say. The Turks will move against the Kurds before long, especially if the Americans leave. The Syrian army, with Russian backup, will mop up Idlib and displace Daesh. It's all a mess. My guess is that he will move back into Afghanistan or Pakistan.'

The flight to Heathrow was on time, and they only had a wait of two hours before their BA flight was called. The eight-hour flight in business class was wonderful. They drank champagne and ate royally, watched movies, snoozed, and before they knew it were landing at Jomo Kenyatta International Airport.

When they arrived, they quickly checked in to the Hilton Garden Inn next to the airport so they could take their early flight to Malindi the next morning.

The next morning, as the plane circled Malindi, they could see miles of white sand and palm trees. The breakers on the reef showed white as the tide came in. The thought of snorkelling on that reef gave David an adrenalin rush, but this was quickly extinguished due to the thought that had been bearing down on him since the moment he'd walked into that tent and taken Esther into his arms. He had waited patiently, but the time to consummate their union had to be close.

The Leopard Point Beach Resort was magnificent in every way. They didn't wait to unpack properly; they just grabbed some bathing things and headed for the beach.

It was high tide, and Esther hit the breakers a millisecond before David followed her. Both powerful swimmers, it was as though they needed to release a tightly wound spring. Eventually, Esther rolled on her back and simply floated with arms outstretched. David came up beside her and trod water.

'Isn't this fantastic?' he said, more as a statement than a question.

Esther smiled a secret sort of smile. 'Not as fantastic as what comes next.' She turned and, with her powerful freestyle stroke that was poetry in motion, headed back to the shore.

She reached the place where they had left their towels well in front of David and had towelled herself off as he arrived. 'Beat you back to the room,' she whispered.

David didn't bother to dry himself and set off in hot pursuit. As he came through the door, Esther had taken off her bikini top and was just removing the bottoms. David grabbed her, and they both fell back on the bed.

'I'm all salty, I was going to have a shower,' she explained softly.

'I'm quite partial to salt,' he replied with a wicked smile and started kissing her breasts. He lifted his head so their lips could meet. Their tongues searched in an aching exploratory meeting, and then David's middle finger slid across her thigh and found its mark.

His first probing attempt seemed dry and uninteresting, then suddenly everything changed as hormones and bodily fluids combined to ensure union. David was now very excited, and he moved on top of Esther whilst supporting his weight on his muscular forearms. They kissed again, and then David guided his now erect member into her vagina. He came up against a barrier; he watched her face change as he entered her.

Her eyes grew wider, a small gasp escaped her lips. David had never been this excited before. He thrust once, withdrew almost, but as he thrust again… He could not control it… It was amazing… It was way too quick.

Esther put her arms around his neck, drew his head to hers and kissed him tenderly and said, 'We've both got a lot to learn…hey, but it's going to be a lot of fun learning.'

And it was; they made love a lot. They didn't just have a lot of sex. They made love a lot, and there is a big difference.

The chemist's assistant stifled a smile when Esther asked if she had anything for cystitis. A cream sort of helped, although a bit of abstinence would have been more proactive, but our lovers were on a journey of discovery.

After their sojourn on the Indian Ocean, they moved to their planned safari into the Masai Mara. The Fairmont Mara Safari Club was breath-taking.

The morning after their arrival, they were met by their guide who said, 'Jambo, bwana (Hello, sir).'

David, without thinking, replied, 'Habari za asubuhi (Good morning).'

The guide smiled. 'Unaelewa Kiswahili, bwana? (You understand Swahili, sir?)'

'Mimi ni mtoto anayejifunza (I'm just a kid who is learning),' he replied. He couldn't remember much more Swahili, but their guide seemed impressed.

Their safari was an incredible journey of discovery. They stopped in the jeep beside a herd of Kudu quietly grazing, yet the head would come up with every bite, a glance spanning the area for any possible danger.

The first they knew that danger existed was as a lioness moving into vision, using the scent of the vehicle to subdue her own. One of the peripheral Kudus caught a scent of danger as it lifted its head. The herd paused as one. A second lioness came out of the long grass on the other side. The herd moved away together. And then the frantic panic as the black-maned lion charged from his ambush position in front of them! He caught the targeted Kudu in the throat and hung on, trying to bring the beast down and allowing the rest of the pride to move in for the kill. The Kudu wouldn't go down. The herd stopped running, it turned on the perceived enemy and charged the lone lion. The lion lost its grip and, in the face of the Kudu community, hightailed it back into the long grasses.

That night they watched the Masai dance. Tall, athletic people who live by an ancient history predicated on courage. From the age of sixteen, they are separated from the rest of the tribe to be trained as warriors. Unlike most other warrior tribes, their fortunes are counted in cattle. Their diet is a mixture of blood (leached from the cattle's throat) and milk; their enemies are any animal or person wishing to take their cattle.

For their initiation into warriorhood, they are armed with a shield and an assegai (a short stabbing spear). They advance to an area where lions are present and encircle it, they then reduce the circle until the lion must attack. The circle must stay strong. When the lion leaps, the warrior must hold his nerve and guard himself with his shield whilst offering the blade of his assegai. If struck correctly, the lion will slide along the shaft whilst the warrior holds his position. The lion was the enemy of their community, so together they had to formulate a strategy that would allow them to prevail.

However, as David explained to Esther, these were very intellectual people. Some had been educated at mission schools and gone on to universities all over the world. However, when they returned to their tribe, they would don their red blankets and go back to guarding the cattle. At night, they would tell stories of their experiences in other countries. Stories are always told in parables: two parts of the story are told, and then listeners must discover the third part to understand the complete interpretation.

Each day was filled with new understandings and each night brought new delights. David and Esther had now forgotten how to be shy or uptight let alone fearful. This was their time to celebrate life and living. Sex was meant to be, a God-given gift. They were enjoying the gift as they explored each other's erogenous zones with a total belief that to enjoy was to give enjoyment. This was a moment in both their lives that would live with them forever.

This wonderful but brief honeymoon had to come to an end, and they returned to Brexit Britain on a miserable, rainy October day.

The news was all about political stalemate. The country was supposed to leave the EU at the end of the month, but legal challenges had disrupted the parliamentary process. The new PM had tried to prorogue parliament to, presumably, close down actions like this. All manner of subterfuges ensured that the will of the people who had voted to leave the EU would not get their wish. The opposition called for another 'People's Vote', which only seemed like another way of getting the first referendum reversed. In all this debate, friends had turned on friends, and families had been irrevocably split. The country was totally divided.

David and Esther returned to Aberdeen to find Joshua waiting for them. Rhys had returned to Hereford to embark on a specialist course.

Their return to the Succoth was yet another celebration. Baby Sophie gurgled with delight when Esther took her in her arms. Everyone gathered in the Barn to welcome the couple by enjoying a meal together.

David's phone went off at seven the next morning.

'David, it's Peter… There have been some important developments concerning your boyhood friend. I need you back here, in London, today. We are facing a very serious problem, and I need you here. I am sending a helicopter to pick you up. Please be ready, ETA ten thirty hours.' The phone went silent.

Chapter 20

The Ayes Have It, the Ayes Have It!

The helicopter landed on the helipad at MI6 HQ. Peter was there to meet and greet. He took David by the arm and led him to the stairwell where they descended into the building and eventually reached Peter's office.

'Sorry to take you away from your nearest and dearest, David, but we are in a bit of a bind.' He quickly continued, 'It seems your old mate Sayyid has been hobnobbing with some serious players in the Iranian Revolutionary Guard. We have some very sound evidence that he has got his hands on rather a lot of explosive material – and, worse, a strong possibility that he also has access to some very nasty reactor-grade plutonium. The combination of which could devastate the centre of London and cause many thousands of deaths. We also understand that his target is Westminster.'

'Is this material in the country already?' David looked very worried.

'That's the point, we don't know. How do you think he might move these materials?' Peter reached for his pipe and struck it up with a few rasping sucks.

David considered for a moment. 'My best guess would be that he'd use the old IRA route and move the stuff into southern Ireland and then by container to the mainland.'

Peter nodded his head. 'That is our considered opinion as well; we have that possibility covered. But suppose he switched to the west coast of Scotland instead?'

David shook his head. 'Doubtful, we had no contact with that part of the world. Unless he met up with someone in Barlinnie that had contacts there, but I doubt it.'

'What about the north-east coastline?' Peter blew a stream of smoke to emphasise the question.

'With all the offshore oil activity, I wouldn't expect it,' replied David before shaking his head. 'But you never can tell.'

Even as this conversation continued, a dirty Turkish coastal trader buffeted her way through the English Channel and into the North Sea. She was actually eleven nautical miles east of Yarmouth when David left MI6 HQ and headed for his usual billet at the SF club.

It was 01:50 when the fully laden RIB (rigid inflatable boat) set off from its mother ship. As long as the ship was at the correct longitude and latitude when they set off, a bearing of 270 degrees magnetic would have them arriving on the small beach at Pennan, a small village that once rose to fame as the location for the feature film *Local Hero*. A flash of two headlights proved that they were exactly where they needed to be.

Twenty minutes later, one of the Revolutionary Guards slipped into the shallow water to bring the boat ashore. Out of the shadows, two figures arrived. As the boxes were carefully handed ashore, they were carried up the beach and stored in the waiting Vauxhall Vivaro.

Once everything was stored away, the RIB took off back to the mother ship. The other two helpers disappeared into the shadows; the roar of a motorbike was the only evidence as they made their way back to Glasgow.

Sayyid settled himself behind the wheel and drove sedately to New Aberdour. In a secure lay-by with no CCTV coverage, he drove the van into a container lorry. He then went into the back, made himself comfortable and went to sleep.

He came awake as the doors rasped apart. He was secure in the warehouse in north Hertfordshire. Once he drove the van out, the HGV moved out. It took less than half an hour to change the number plates and attach the decals that announced 'Joseph Philips – Window Cleaner and Chimney Sweep' with a local telephone number and web address.

Sayyid needed more sleep before he was to set out on the final movement. He settled back on the makeshift mattress in the back of the van.

He immediately sank into a deep sleep that was only rudely disturbed by someone shaking him vigorously and demanding to know, 'What the fuck! What are you doing here?'

Sayyid smiled. 'I'm your new window cleaner.'

Francis was not amused. 'I've been worried sick. I've heard nothing from you for days. The lawyers want us out of here as we haven't paid for our lease. The lorries are all outside, but they will probably take them away if you don't arrange payment in the next couple of days!'

Sayyid smiled a disarming smile that hinted at a special promise. 'Are all the tankers fuelled up with methanol?'

'Yes, you told me to make sure of it.'

'Right then, my love, go and make me a nice cup of tea, and I will explain everything. There's nothing to worry about.' As Sayyid looked around the workshop, his eyes fell upon an extension lead.

Francis came back and turned to place the tea on the bench. 'Well, come on then, tell me what is going on.'

Those were the last words he ever spoke, for a loop of the extension cable was expertly flung around his neck by Sayyid, who then crossed his hands behind his soon-to-be dead lover's neck.

Francis's eyes started to bulge as he was pulled backwards to the floor. No sound emanated from his lips. The only noise came from his heels drumming on the floor until silence reigned. Sayyid pushed him to one side, picked up his cup and sipped his tea.

Sayyid spent all the next day arming each tanker with an explosive device that would initiate a massive chemical reaction as the methanol became subject to a sympathetic explosion. The result was a simple switch fastened to the dashboard. Depress, and reach Paradise!

The narrowboat was back at the What3words RV with lots of important intelligence. He decided that a meeting was necessary. He hadn't felt this vulnerable since he winked at David as they led him down to the cells in Glasgow.

Sayyid listened carefully as they described each part of the journey: every lock, every possible mooring; the outlet to the Thames, the tides, the river police; and the camouflaged RIBs which were probably manned by the SBS. They hadn't missed much and had detailed notes to explain everything that they had encountered on their voyage. They were also confident about breaking through the temporary barrier in front of the bank beside the Houses of Parliament.

Sayyid decided that timing would be all. The Brexit debates were taking all of Parliament's time. The PM had tried to bring his negotiated deal to Parliament, and even when the House finally agreed to back the deal, barely fifteen minutes later they refused to back the timetable!

Sayyid thought the final vote, the one that would involve a full house, would come on Halloween (31st October). However, other events overtook this event. With much ado about something, the House finally agreed to consider having a general election in December. This debate was to take place on Tuesday, 29 October 2019.

The three of them worked to get the explosives aboard and the isotopes stored in the bow.

Sayyid instructed them to return to Brentwood and await instructions.

Now was the time to assemble his other jihadis. The tankers were distributed in different parts of north Hertfordshire and Cambridgeshire in lay-bys with no CCTV by temps who were told that this was a company logistics exercise.

The jihadis all arrived on time and started out to their secondary RV points – all of which were within a five-minute drive to their target bridge or tunnel.

It was expected that the vote would take place at about four thirty. This was excellent news as the narrowboat was close to Vauxhall Bridge and the tide would start to ebb at just before five o'clock.

Operation 'Rolling Thunder' would commence on Sayyid's instruction; each bridge would thunder at two-minute intervals until Westminster Bridge became the final diversion. The whole of London and the Thames should be chaotic at this juncture, and the coup de grâce would be the narrowboat as it crashed into the waterside barrier and exploded.

David lay awake in his room at the SF club and tried to imagine what Sayyid's next move might be. He remembered their shared journey down the Thames in the Devizes to Westminster Canoe Marathon (they had probably never been closer). It didn't matter that they didn't win a medal; they would come back and do better.

Suddenly, David knew quite definitely that the attack would come from the river. He waited until five o'clock to advise Peter. 'I need a helicopter – I'm looking for canoes or small boats. I will also need at least two RIBs with an SBS crew, fully operational, under my command from the air.' His request brooked no negative response.

David was back at the MI6 heliport at six that morning where he briefed both SBS teams before he took off at first light. It was a police helicopter with a sergeant advisor as well as the pilot.

David had explained in his briefing what he was looking for. Firstly, any small boats on the water. Then, more likely, anywhere small boats could be launched onto the river without too much difficulty. Anything that looked vaguely suspicious from their bird's-eye view would be investigated by the SBS.

They had established communications and were now moving upstream. The helicopter was spotting from above whilst the RIBs took one bank each investigating anything that looked untoward. Passing Lambeth Palace, they inspected every possible point from which an assault might be made. They passed Battersea Power Station with its famous chimney stacks, paused and then circled carefully over Chelsea Harbour. Thence to Fulham and past the Hurlingham Club – but not before two SBS men had landed and given it the once-over. Barn Elms boathouse had a facility where people could learn to row or kayak. There was nothing suspicious there. The search went on all that morning and into the afternoon.

It was nearly two o'clock in the afternoon when Sayyid parked the BMW R1200GS motorbike outside an internet café in SE1. He removed his gloves and helmet but left his beanie hat and tinted glasses on. He walked in and ordered himself a pot of coffee and a cheese salad roll and moved to a workstation.

He slipped his laptop out of his shoulder bag and powered it up. Slipping his memory stick into a USB slot, he then pulled his earphones out of a side pocket and plugged them in. As his laptop came alive, he powered up 'Film On', moved to the UK channels and hit 'News'.

As he took a sip of his coffee and a bite from his roll, the screen showed the debate that was happening in real time inside the House of Commons.

How could grown men and women argue about which one of three days to hold a general election, allowing millions of people a say in how their world might be in the foreseeable future? Two hours later, nothing had changed that much, and they would soon have to make a decision and vote. It looked like the date they would have to vote on would be the 12th December.

However, 'time and tide wait for no man'. He had no idea who first promoted that thought, but he mused that it was absolutely right. The River Thames was rising even as he sat there. He knew it would reach high tide at 16:37, and his secret weapon must be ready to move as the tide began to ebb.

Sayyid sent the first message to confirm that all units were in position and ready to go. Thirteen acknowledgements came back thick and fast.

It was beginning to get dark when David finally gave the order to return to base; they had seen nothing that was even mildly suspicious.

Sayyid's sent his next message to Number 1: 'Attack now – Allahu Akbar!'

Five minutes and thirty-seven seconds later, the tanker blew up about one third of the way across the Queen Elizabeth Bridge.

All the next messages followed at two-minute intervals. The second explosion within the close confines of the Dartford Tunnel was devastating – methanol burns, but you don't see a flame. The confined searing heat extended throughout the tunnel, causing lorries and cars to combust. It became a fiery blast furnace consuming everything in its path. It was only quenched as great cracks appeared and the cold water of the Thames flowed in to smother the flames.

David noticed a brief glow in the sky as they flew downriver, but it was only when the emergency channel opened up that he realised what was happening. He had got it wrong. The attack was downstream!

The SBS roared off with searchlights screening every bank.

The *Queen of the South* slipped her temporary moorings. The lighterman received a shout of thanks as he had let them moor up to change their fuel filter which had become blocked with some dirty fuel.

Meanwhile, 'Rolling Thunder' rolled up the Thames, destroying bridges and tunnels as it went.

Sayyid only had a hint that his masterplan was working when a breaking news flash cut across the bottom of the screen. The politicians continued with their braying about what date was most beneficial for the country.

David saw the explosion that destroyed the North Tower of Tower Bridge, and he knew that worse was yet to come.

'Back to Westminster,' he snarled, and the pilot swung the chopper in a carving arc that would reverse their direction. The sudden realisation that he had 'fucked up!' was confirmed as the final tanker blew on Westminster Bridge.

They came in over the top. Using the searchlight switched on by the pilot, he clearly saw a narrowboat sweeping down on the ebb tide, veering across the current and coming in at a forty-five-degree trajectory, about to hit the bank nearest to the House of Commons.

Sayyid was still watching his screen and listening to the inane instructions that required the teller to give his result of the count through the lobbies.

'The Ayes four hundred and thirty-eight; the Noes twenty.' He handed his papers to the Speaker, who replied giving the same number and then stated the obvious, 'The Ayes have it. The Ayes have it!' It was then that the roof caved in.

The ancient masonry, which had known many appalling acts and actions, that had been neglected for far too long, gave up the ghost as the combined blast of high-explosive charges and methanol produced a shock wave that bent the supporting scaffolding and created a heave that was to finish off this tired, ancient Mother of all Parliaments. No one knew until much later that they wouldn't even be able to search for survivors because of the radioactive material which now permeated the site.

The world was made aware of the enormity of this terrorist attack when a single TV camera that had been reporting on the debate, which must have been protected by some part of the structure, filmed the explosion that brought down the roof on the heads of everyone inside. It captured the enormity of this crime against humanity even though the cameraman had been killed by the blast.

As the major blast somehow seemed to stop real time, whilst the world looked on, just like they looked on at 9/11, a lone figure jumped from the fuselage of the helicopter just before it also hit the bridge and exploded.

A police launch, coming to investigate the explosions, was alongside the man in the water in less than a minute. They pulled the man aboard and called for paramedics as they brought him alongside the riverboat pontoon, but there was little sign of life.

Chapter 21

Hide and Seek

Sayyid paid his bill and left the internet café. He put on his helmet and pulled down the visor before kicking his bike into life and moving into the stream of traffic.

This was going to be a long ride, but he would stop for a break every two hours. He had good friends in Glasgow where he could shelter until he was ready to finish what he had promised to do.

He pulled into the Welcome Break service station. He wolfed down a chicken curry that he would have left had he not been so hungry. He powered up his laptop and sent an encrypted message.

He didn't stop again until he was on the M6 near Warrington. A reply was waiting for him when he went online again: *You've made the headlines. Your face is all over the TV. They are on to the base in Hertfordshire and they found a body there. By the way, you managed to kill most of the bastards in the House of Commons. They've taken twenty or so to hospitals, but most of them are badly injured. You're a bloody hero, mate. Not only for our cause, but I think quite a lot of Brits would like to say thank you! You'd better keep your head down. When you get to my place, bring your bike up the path beside the house. The garage will be open. I've fixed a place for you to stay at the back where there's a false wall – push on the right-hand edge and there is a door sufficient to wheel your bike in.*

On arrival, it was exactly as Yousef had described. In fact, it was much better than Sayyid had anticipated. There was a small galley kitchen with an electric hob and a sink with both hot and cold water and a small (but adequate) fridge. There was a toilet with a handbasin and a small walk-in shower. And a bunk that was high enough to sit on with a small table. Also, a selection of books to read, and most importantly a Qur'an.

This was to be Sayyid's home for the next month, but he didn't mind.

His days passed quickly as he kept to a strict routine. There was a skylight in the roof, so he awoke every morning just before sunrise. He prepared himself for prayers and laid out a small prayer mat facing east that Yousef had kindly provided. After prayers, it was time for exercise. He put himself through a brutal regime of isometrics before showering and getting dressed. Thereafter, he read the Qur'an and spent a long time in meditation. He then prepared some food and watched the news on his laptop.

Yousaf was his only visitor. He came every third day during his lunch break to bring fresh food and any requests. He would only stay for a few minutes to hand over the food and pass on any news.

It seemed that the security forces had been to the Succoth and searched the place thoroughly, and it was rumoured that special forces were combing the area where he had been brought up.

He was disappointed to hear that David had been in the helicopter that flew into the blast and crashed and that he was still in intensive care; he had dreamt of killing him slowly and painfully, but that would have to wait for another time now. He still intended to return to the Succoth to insist that his mother returned to Afghanistan. But before the final phases of his plan could be enacted, a number of issues needed to be sorted.

Through his network, a Tunisian undergraduate studying at the LSE had agreed to sell his passport for a thousand pounds and not report it lost or stolen for three months. He was a bit younger than Sayyid and wore heavy-rimmed glasses. By the simple expedient of buying a similar pair of glasses, he would be able to pass muster.

Three weeks later, Reuters picked up an account from an Iranian newspaper that the hero of the London bombings had himself been blown up whilst teaching a group of jihadis bomb-making techniques. The piece told how he had been born in Afghanistan, where his father had been killed fighting the Russians. How he had then been taken to live in the UK but had fought against the Kafir back in Afghanistan as soon as he was old enough, and later in both Iraq and Syria. It was his planning and courage that had brought Britain to its knees. He would now take his place in Paradise where Allah would reward him for his sacrifice.

MI6 and MI5 both picked up the information on the same day and advised the chief of staff immediately.

Two weeks later, after prayers, Sayyid wheeled his bike out of the garage, walked it a couple of hundred metres down the road, kicked it into life and drove sedately down the road. There were very few people about at that time on a Sunday; before long, he was out of Glasgow and heading towards Perth.

After Perth there was a maze of small roads with passing places that he took through the hills to within a mile of his old home. He drove the bike along a track through some spruce trees until he came to an old bothy. He put the bike to the rear, and then stripped off his motorbike gear and left it all with his helmet inside the bothy.

All was quiet by the time he reached his mother's house at the Succoth, and he remembered that she would still be having lunch at the Barn. He let himself in and settled into an armchair by the stove.

He heard the outside door open; a chill draught swept in as the inner door opened to admit his mother. She was partway taking off her coat when she saw him. Her hand flew to her mouth.

'Salaam Alaikum, Mother.' He stood up and put his arms out to embrace her.

She finished taking off her coat and laid it over a chair. She whisked a strand of hair that had fallen over her face before staring at him with unconcealed anger. 'Were you responsible for killing all those innocent people?' she demanded.

'Everything that I do now, I do for Allah, Subhanahu Wa Ta'ala (Glory to Him the Exalted),' he replied.

'Then, why have you come back here?' she asked softly.

'To insist that you return to Afghanistan, where I will join you in due course,' he said with authority.

'That will never happen,' she snapped back. 'Go back – to what? To be subjected to daily humiliation. To wearing a burka! And needing a male relative to accompany me to go shopping!' she snorted.

'It's not like that anymore—' he started to explain, but she interrupted.

'The Taliban may not be back in complete control, but they run much of the country – and mark my words, they will soon be running the country again with their self-righteous, cruel Sharia law. Can't you see, our country – indeed, most of Arabia – will never match the greatness of the Western world until the religious bigots are put in their place and women receive a proper education.'

'So, you would rather live with these Kafir and bring disgrace upon our family?' he snarled.

'These are good people, they are kind and help each other, they share their lives and their possessions. I am also able to help people who are in trouble and use what talents I have to make their lives better.' Her lip trembled as she began to realise that this conversation would not go anywhere. 'Will you continue to plot and plan to kill more innocent people?' she added.

'One day, Islam will rule the world, inshallah (if God wills it), and all our sacrifices will have been worthwhile,' he patiently explained.

Zufash circled the table and went to the sink where she poured herself a glass of water. As she sipped, her eyes focused on the work surface that held a knife block. She reached out and snatched a boning knife and turned towards her son, slipping her hand behind her back.

He had read the movement. Even as she turned, he blocked her knife arm and was in the process of removing the knife from her nerveless fingers when he heard a gentle, deep baritone voice.

'Let your mother go – we need to talk.'

Sayyid let her go but retained the knife.

'It seems that you are responsible for the slaughter of many people including women and children. Are you proud of that?' Joshua looked grave.

'Muhammad, may he rest in peace, instructs that "I shall cast terror into the hearts of the infidels. Strike off their heads, strike off the very tips of their fingers". So, what if I cast off the politicians from this blighted country. Make no mistake, this is just the beginning. The true men, who love Allah, will one day rule this world.'

Joshua stepped a little closer; he must not show the fear he intuitively knew. 'So, answer me this, is Allah the same God that I worship?'

Sayyid looked blank and did not answer.

Joshua continued, 'From my studies of Islam, I remember that Muhammad met with the angel Gabriel in the cave, and from that meeting we learn that Muhammad acknowledged the evidence of the prophets from the Judaic Testament up to and including the Ministry of Jesus. He just didn't accept that Jesus died on the cross and was later resurrected, right!' Joshua went on quickly, 'If I could prove that Jesus did die on the cross, and that he did return to this world after death, might you just question some of the demands that come from the Qur'an?'

Sayyid half closed his eyes; he could feel that tension in his stomach he always felt before he unleashed his violence. 'Speak on, old man, convince me.'

Joshua looked sad as he explained, 'Do you understand flagellation?' He took the silence to mean that either he didn't, or it didn't matter. 'The roman legionnaires used flagellation or scourging as part of the crucifixion process. The whips had small pieces of metal or bone at the tips designed to strip the skin off a body. Sometimes the abdomen was split open and the organs dropped out.'

Joshua added, 'Then, nailed by wrists and ankles to a cross would not just be agonising, the arms could not support the upper body and the chest would fall. It would become difficult to breath, so it would be necessary to try and rise up on the nails that had been driven through the ankles.' Joshua let the vision sink in. Sayyid's face was impassive whilst his mother's looked aghast. 'The next day was to be the festival of the Passover. This spectacle must be finished. A Roman guard thrust a spear into his side. An observer later wrote in a gospel account "Blood and water came from the wound".'

Joshua leant his weight on the back of the sofa. 'It has only been in recent years that we have come to understand the importance of that observation. Now, any heart surgeon will tell you that if the pericardium is ruptured, you will observe a colourless liquid and blood, but that observation will most certainly indicate that the person is dead.'

Sayyid became very animated at this stage. 'There's not one imam that I have ever met who would accept that.'

'That may be so,' Joshua replied quietly, but he moved on to the next sequence of recorded events. 'Jesus then appeared first to a woman who was grieving at his grave. He later met with his former friends who examined his body and were finally convinced that Jesus had been resurrected for there was no other possible answer. These were the same people who only a few hours earlier had been in fear of their lives. Even Peter (the rock) had denied knowledge of him three times. These were the same people who then went on to spread the Word and who would give their lives so that others might understand the value of following Jesus.'

Joshua let that sink in before continuing, 'Six hundred years later, as Christianity was beginning to flourish in the Middle East, an illiterate man, who was married to an older woman, disappeared into the back of a cave. When he came out, he announced that he'd had a meeting with the angel Gabriel. Scribes were summoned to take down the substance of those meetings. He claimed to be the last prophet. He set down a set of rules that were to define Islam. He was militaristic, he sent out raiding parties to attack caravans. They were successful and everybody got rich. The movement grew. With wealth, he took more wives, including a girl child which he consummated when she was nine years of age! So, tell me this, Sayyid, is your God the same as my God? My God wants me to love my neighbour as myself, my God rides a donkey, my God gives his life that I might live. He sees women equal to men, He loves justice… Allah is a cult figure that has only grown through authoritarian male domination. With rules about what food to eat and how to wash before prayer yet says nothing about wiping your arse with your hand! Sharia law has reduced those countries that approve it to Third World status.'

Sayyid could take no more. He struck Joshua in the chest twice, causing Joshua to sink to the floor.

Zufash launched herself onto her son's back, but he shrugged her off and she fell, face down on the floor. The short boning knife was struck twice more into her back. Her backless dress showed clearly the blood and the 'water' that oozed between her shoulder blades, proving that the blade had pierced her pericardium and proved what Joshua had said.

Breathing heavily, Sayyid pulled both bodies into the bathroom. He sluiced his hands under the tap and wiped them on his trousers. He moved to the back door, looked both ways and, all being clear, set off in a loping run back to where he had left his motorbike.

Four hours later, he was at a storage facility in Prestwick where he bought space for a month and lost his motorbike. Back in town, he bought a set of golf clubs and later a ticket at the Ryanair desk to the Algarve for a golfing holiday.

On arrival at Faro, he took a taxi to a sports centre where he managed to lose the golf clubs in a wheelie bin. He then purchased a mountain bike with panniers, a lightweight tent and sleeping bag, some cooking gear, and cycling wear in fluorescent yellow and black with a helmet to match.

He was soon on his way towards the Spanish border.

He really enjoyed the trip to Tarifa. The rhythm of breaking camp, cycling, stopping to make a quick meal and reaching the next destination. There was plenty of time to think and plan the next day. Each day was a gift to be cherished and time to look forward not back. To look back was too late to change. His destiny, he told himself, was to bring about a World Caliphate of Islam.

His crossing into Morocco on the ferry was simple. No one questioned this young student who wanted to cycle through Arabia.

Chapter 22
Rods of God

Four weeks earlier in London, a hastily arranged press conference waited impatiently for the chief of the defence staff and the other members of the Defence Council to arrange themselves on the platform. There was a hush as the general moved towards the lectern.

'Ladies and gentlemen of the press, good morning, I have some important information for you. I have just returned from a meeting with Her Majesty. At that meeting, I explained that as the result of the heinous crime that was carried out against our people and against our Parliament, we are presently without a government. The Defence Council acted immediately, when asked for help by the Metropolitan Police and other police forces throughout the country, to guard against other terror attacks and to curtail any civil disobedience, rioting or looting. A total curfew during the hours of darkness was put into place immediately. During daylight hours, there must be no demonstrations of any kind. These are dangerous times, and the civil population must be aware that they risk their lives if they do not heed these instructions. Her Majesty has accepted that these actions have to be taken in the short term, but she trusts that we can devolve power back to the people as soon as possible.' He paused to let the import of that announcement sink in and then continued.

'The perpetrators of these terrorist actions have all been accounted for as a result of their suicide mission. However, the person behind this attack has been identified as Sayyid Rasheed, a citizen of the United Kingdom (a picture of Sayyid holding his prisoner's number was flashed on the screen), he was born in Afghanistan but brought up in Scotland. He served a custodial sentence as the result of a manslaughter charge whilst still a teenager. Once released from prison, he returned to Afghanistan and later fought with Daesh in Iraq and Syria. It is thought that he is still in this country, but all exit routes have been alerted. Please circulate this photograph but ensure that no member of the public tries to approach him as he is extremely dangerous. A security contact number is being circulated with this press release.' He paused again and looked around his audience. 'I'll take any questions. Please give your name and who you represent.'

The first question came from a young woman in the front row: 'Marie Blazer, BBC. Sayyid Rasheed, was he on anybody's watch list?'

The general looked uneasy but replied, 'We're not sure at this juncture, but this is presently being investigated.'

A man at the back rose as the general pointed at him. 'Geoff Grinstead, *The Sun*. Do you have a total number for all casualties?'

The general looked grave. 'It is very difficult to ascertain true figures; we know that the casualties in the Dartford Tunnel alone were several hundred. The overall death toll we expect to be in excess of three thousand, with serious casualties running into three or four hundred. All the hospitals in the area are working to capacity.' The general nodded to another woman in the front row.

'Mary-Ann Bligh, *The Telegraph*. There have been riots in the East End of London, Birmingham, Luton and Glasgow. Asian communities have come under attack from far-right groups and have retaliated in kind. Looting, with shops being set on fire, have been observed and reported on social media. What is being done about this?'

The general looked grim. 'We have troops stationed in all these areas and others on standby to deploy anywhere in the country as required. In the event of any further criminal activity, drastic action will be taken.'

'Does that include opening fire on demonstrators?' she asked.

'Let everyone be quite clear about this, anyone ignoring the curfew or assembling in numbers or threatening certain communities will be putting their own safety at risk. I have given orders to my commanders that they are entitled to use all necessary force to stamp out any possibility of a civil war in this country.'

There was a long silence as the audience digested this latest piece of information.

An arm was raised somewhere in the centre of the hall.

'The gentleman in the blue raincoat,' the general made the invitation.

'Alan Bridges, *Daily Express*. We were about to have an election. We were about to find out if we would have a Brexit. We all hoped that we would have a government that governs. Where do you expect we will go from here?'

The general looked grave. 'Life must go on. Our adversaries might like to think that this will bring us to our knees. Even as I speak to you now, plans are afoot to set up another administration. It cannot be in Westminster, as it has been established that the entire area has been planted with radioactive material.'

There was a gasp from around the room as this new bit of news hit home.

'Our civil servants will all be moved to Canary Warf, where offices are presently being requisitioned to ensure that our day-to-day administration continues.' He smiled a rather wry smile. 'Going forwards, there will be a daily briefing so you will be able to keep the public informed. It will not be given by myself; there is a press team being formed to update you on all relevant developments. I'm afraid that I can take no further questions.' He left the stage with his entourage.

The CDS (chief of defence staff) left for a meeting with the Defence Council, senior members of the army, navy and air force, together with representatives of MI6 and MI5.

An intelligence brief was given by a suit from MI5: 'All the evidence points towards the explosive and radioactive material originating in Iran. We're not sure how it was brought into the country, but it most likely came ashore off the north-east of Scotland from a Turkish ship out of Azerbaijan. The attack was launched from a small industrial estate in Hertfordshire – a raid on this location provided evidence of a biodiesel production facility, albeit with no equipment other than deliveries of methanol. The dead body of a male was discovered at the site. It would appear that he had shared an apartment in Cambridge with the terrorist we know as Sayyid. The deceased was a known homosexual in the area, and it is assumed that he acted as a cover for Sayyid. Gentlemen, we are extremely vulnerable at this time. A pariah nation with the help of a few fanatics have managed, in the world's eyes, to bring this country to its knees. To redress this lack of confidence in our ability to defend ourselves, there needs to be an act of powerful retribution. Iran has a sophisticated military capability, so it would be difficult to mount a conventional attack without major losses.'

The CDS rose to his feet and took over the briefing. 'We have spoken many times about the potential of our "Rods from God" facility. I know our scientists would like more development time, but I would urge the Defence Council to approve this weapon. First create a political necessity for the ayatollahs to gather in the Islamic Consultative Assembly buildings, then we should hit it at precisely the same time that we strike the nuclear reactors at Bushehr. As far as we know, no one is aware of our Rods from God programme. We will spread the word that Russia used our vulnerability to test a major weapon of mass destruction and hoped to blamed us for it. On the same day, in Russia, we should assassinate the two suspects who we believe were responsible for trying to kill two Russians on our soil, but instead killed an innocent English woman. We will not own up to this action either. It will be enough that the world will still know we can defend ourselves and punch above our weight.'

The Rods of God (so-called) is a formidable weapon. They are simply rods of tungsten weighing 2,000 lbs each that are housed in a satellite at 1,000 miles in space. When they are released over the target, gravity powers this missile at a speed of 6.85 miles per second. Their supersonic speed makes it impossible to intercept, and a simple guidance system guides it accurately to the point of impact. On impact, the kinetic energy is similar to a small nuclear bomb but without the disadvantage of the nuclear fallout.

'With regard to the secondary objective, I'm sure that Porton Down can provide us with a suitable substance for retribution?' The MI6 director left the question open.

Over the next few days, the TV coverage and papers were still reporting on the carnage achieved by the terrorist attack and the inability of the authorities to capture the author of this earth-shattering crime.

Four days later, the ambassador of Iran was called to the Foreign Office, now situated in Canary Warf. He was met by a senior admiral in the Royal Navy and a senior Foreign Office official. He was told in no uncertain terms that Iran was responsible for the terrorist attack, and that all their staff had been designated as *persona non grata* and must leave the country in the next forty-eight hours. This action was soon reciprocated, and the United Kingdom embassy staff were on their way back to the UK. This declaration usually heralded a declaration of war, but we live in different times.

The ruling ayatollahs had gathered in the Islamic Consultative Assembly as expected when the first missile struck. The second missile arrived seconds after at the nuclear enrichment plant at Bushehr.

The Iranian people had been rioting for days over the cost of fuel, but like gilets jaunes in France, this was just the catalyst that exploded as a result of years of austerity brought about by an incompetent government. The drive for a new democracy had begun.

The news on social media was that the Russians had orchestrated this to test its own weapons knowing that the United Kingdom would be blamed.

The Iranian people would never let the autocratic mullahs run their country again. The Revolutionary Guards moved to retain order, but the sheer mass of the people's rebellion made this impossible.

When the world got to hear that the two accused Russian assassins had died mysteriously on the same day, the world leaders wondered if the Machiavellian Russian machinations had gone into overdrive to point the finger at the UK.

The President of the United States summed it up with a tweet: 'Mess with the Brits at your peril!'

Day after day, an uneasy truce was maintained between the immigrant communities and some militant right-wing agitators.

By the end of the month, life was beginning to get back to something like normal: children were back to school, people were back at work, but there were still military forces on nearly every corner of each major city. The night-time curfew was still in place, and one of the unintended consequences was the massive reduction in crime, with knife crime disappearing altogether.

Reuters reported that the international terrorist Sayyid had been killed in Tehran whilst instructing jihadis in bomb making – however, there was no concrete evidence available.

This story was soon found not to be true when it was discovered that he had returned to his mother's house in Aberdeenshire where he had killed her and seriously injured a minister of religion who was in intensive care.

The entire country was on high alert; members of the public were advised not to approach this extremely dangerous man.

A reward of £1M was offered for any news that would lead to his capture.

Chapter 23

A New Direction (Information in Retrospect)

David had no recollection of the actual crash; it was as though his brain simply refused to acknowledge the trauma.

As he opened his eyes, his first recollection was that he had arrived in a place of perfect tranquillity. Then, as he went to move, he discovered that his lower body was tied down on the bed. His arms were free, so his hands searched for something to pull himself up with. Another hand rested on his shoulder and gently eased him back into the mattress. He recognised the smell of her body lotion even before his eyes registered her face. Esther bent over him and gently kissed him on the lips.

Gradually, he processed the information and realised that he was in a hospital. He was attached to tubes and wires which were connected to stands and electronic devices. He went to speak but only a croak came out.

Esther slipped a hand behind his shoulders and gently eased him up until his lips met the glass of cold water she held to his lips. He sipped several times and let out a small sigh. She eased his head back onto the pillows and put the glass down on the bedside table.

'I can't feel my legs,' he complained.

'Darling, it will be all right.' She wanted to sound positive, but the slight catch in her voice gave the game away.

He closed his eyes; the replay came back in violent technicolour. Westminster Bridge exploding in a gigantic flash of light and a powerful surge of red-hot air. Then a fractional glimpse of the Palace of Westminster and the narrowboat streaming across the ebbing tide. Then the mind-bending blast that took the helicopter and made it spin like a sycamore seed – first up and up, and then down into the darkness. He groaned out loud.

The door to his room opened, and a young doctor breezed in. 'Ah, our patient is awake. How are you feeling, Major Stevenson?' The doctor busied himself looking at the chart at the end of the bed and then consulting the electronic gadgetry that was displayed.

Esther was now sitting on the bed holding David's hand.

'Not too bad.' Reaching out to stretch his right leg, then doing the same with his left, he tried to rub his feet together. 'I can't feel my legs.' His face screwed up with the effort and the statement came out almost as a groan.

'Major, you are very lucky to be alive. Let me rephrase that, according to what I've heard from eyewitness accounts, it was your rapid reflexes that saved you. I regret to have to tell you that the pilot and observer were both killed within milliseconds of your leap into the Thames. Unfortunately, you were still a long way from the water, so the impact was severe.'

Esther spoke: 'My love, you have badly damaged your back, and it's going to take time to get you back to your usual self.'

David had seen enough people with blast damage who had ended up paralysed. He screwed his face up as though he couldn't get the words out. 'Am I going to be a paraplegic?'

Neither Esther nor the doctor answered the question; their combined silence said it all.

David forced a smile, thanked the doctor and said, 'I'll see you later, no doubt.'

The doctor left quietly.

David managed to hold the smile a bit longer and said softly, 'I'm really tired. I need to sleep. Can we discuss all this sometime tomorrow?' Then, as an afterthought, he added, 'Where are we, anyway?'

Esther stroked his head. 'King Edward VII's in London. I'm staying close by, and I'll be back in the morning.' She kissed him on his forehead. 'You get some rest now.'

He didn't get back to sleep, though. The actions of that day were burnt into his brain. He had got it wrong, and he could not imagine what the outcome had been. He pressed the buzzer draped over the side of his cot.

The door opened to admit a motherly-looking nurse. 'Well, young man, what can we do for you?' she questioned brightly.

'How long have I been here?' he asked.

'You were brought in on Tuesday evening, after the bombing.' As she spoke, she made herself busy tiding up his table and moving the chairs.

'And what day is it now?' he asked.

'Friday, you have been sedated for the past few days.' She answered his query with a smile. 'But you needn't worry your head about any of that just now. Once we get you fit and well, we will help you put all the pieces together about what happened. The most important thing for the moment is that you rest and focus on getting strong again.' The nurse's voice was like listening to a hypnotist.

His eyelids became heavy and his mind refused to think any more as he drifted into a troubled sleep.

The next day, he awoke as his door opened and an auxiliary helper brought in a tray of tea and biscuits.

'And how are we feeling this morning,' she asked cheerfully as she put down the tray and helped him into a sitting position by manipulating the controls at the side of the bed. She moved the bed table across the bed so that the tray was in front of him. She plumped up his pillows to make him more comfortable, then asked, 'How do you like your tea? Milk? Sugar?' She smiled encouragingly.

'Milk, no sugar,' he replied.

She poured the tea and stood back whilst reaching for a menu on the side cabinet. 'Are you feeling hungry? What would you like for breakfast?'

He listened carefully and decided on porridge followed by a boiled egg, with some coffee and toast and marmalade. He then sat back and quietly drank his tea. His mind was quite calm as he took stock of his present situation. He needed more detailed knowledge regarding the doctor's prognosis. If he hadn't misunderstood the brief exchange from the previous evening, and the evidence he was experiencing even as he sat up in bed, there was no feeling in his lower body.

As his breakfast arrived, he asked the young man who brought it if there was any chance of getting a newspaper.

'What would you like?' the young man enquired.

'*Telegraph*, if you could get one,' David replied.

The paper arrived just as he finished his boiled egg and was pouring his coffee. The toast and marmalade never got eaten as David scanned the headlines and was soon burying into the inside pages. The paper was still full of the atrocity that had taken place earlier in the week.

The police forensics were combing through the industrial unit near Royston where a body had been found. Another team was carrying out a similar search in the apartment in Cambridge. A young couple had come forward to state that they had rented their narrowboat to a well-spoken author who, they were told, was writing a book about the River Lee. The jigsaw was coming together, and it looked as though Sayyid had been the controller behind the attack. Very little was known about the other members of the plot at this time, as each one had been at the epicentre of each explosion and in most cases had been liquefied. The papers went on to say that searches were taking place in the area of his mother's house in Scotland.

David closed his eyes and laid the paper down. *Would Sayyid be stupid enough to return to the Succoth?*

The doctor arrived, cheery as usual. He read the charts and asked him how he was feeling.

David replied, 'Apart from no feeling in my lower body, I feel fine. What I really need just now is information. I would like your prognosis, as accurately as you can give it to me.'

The doctor was visibly taken aback by the directness of this questioning. He stalled for time. 'It's very early days, far too early to be sure. You are a very fit guy, but it's too soon to say. Now that you've had some time to get over the trauma, we will start a thorough investigation today. This will include X-rays and a CT scan. We need to establish how much damage has been done to your vertebrae, and, more importantly, what damage has occurred to your spinal cord. I'm afraid that before we get the results of these investigations, it is impossible for me to give you any sort of meaningful prognosis. All I can ask at this time is for your patience and that you try to relax as much as possible. I promise that as soon as I get the results of these investigations, I will convey them to you straight away. Meanwhile, you are presently on a regime of pain relief, but if you are uncomfortable at all, please let the nursing staff know and they will be able to increase the dose.'

As the doctor left, he almost bumped into Esther who, after the usual pleasantries, asked the same questions as David, but on a doctor-to-doctor basis. Notwithstanding their shared professional status, nothing more could be readily exchanged until the results of all the testing scheduled for later that day.

Esther breezed into the room, moved quickly to his side and kissed him. As she emptied a plastic bag of fruit into a bowl and placed a bottle of sparkling water next to a tumbler beside him, she saw the newspaper. 'Have you read all about it?'

'I hardly think he would be stupid enough to go back to Scotland,' he started, then changed his mind. 'I grew up with this man, for a long time we were as close as brothers, we shared the same dreams and ambitions, I thought we would be friends for life. Now, I just don't know. It's almost like I'm reading about someone who bears no resemblance to the boy and man I used to know. What the hell happened to him that could bring about such a radical change?'

Esther sat on his bed before replying, 'Although I was only in Syria for a relatively short time, I heard enough gruesome stories about ISIL – or Daesh, whatever you want to call them. I heard and witnessed some terrifying aspects of their cruelty. Who knows what that might do to you if you were part of that unrelenting barbarism day after day? It seemed that it wasn't enough to kill, it was necessary to torture, maim, defile, to become something less than human.'

David's face softened. 'Let's change the subject. How are you? How is Sophie?'

'I'm good. I was worried stiff when I saw the news at first – I saw it on TV. I saw you jump. I didn't know it was you, but I somehow just felt it. A phone call confirmed it, so I got Dad to drive me to Aberdeen and was lucky enough to get a flight that night. It took me a while to find out exactly where you were, but I managed, and I was here at the hospital that same night. The nurses here were great. When they knew who I was, they managed to find me a bed. You were sedated, so I couldn't do much. I've now found a small hotel ten minutes away. Your mum knows that you are OK and that I'm with you. My mum is looking after Sophie, of course.'

A black male nurse arrived at the bedside and smiled at Esther. 'I'm afraid that I must take you husband down to X-ray, Dr Stevenson.'

'Of course, I'll stay and read the paper until he gets back,' she replied.

That is pretty much how the morning went, with the scan afterwards, then neurological tests and finally an MRI scan to ensure there wasn't too much damage to the soft tissue.

Lunch arrived, which David picked over, using the same words as his soldiers when the grub was bad – that same quip from *Crocodile Dundee* – 'Well, ya can live on it!'.

Esther made a note to use one of the delivery services to make sure her man had enough to eat.

David slept most of the afternoon. Esther sat next to him reading. Sometimes when his dreams caused him to cry out, she would stroke his arm to quieten him. Sometimes when his upper body wanted to thrash around uncontrollably, she leant over him with her body until his darkest remembering passed.

David had been a devotee of Stoicism since he first read Marcus Aurelius' *Meditations*. Death comes to all, so make the most of the days you have. 'Amor fati' – making the best of everything that happens. Pain and suffering are the forge that creates the greatest strength. Most of all, strive to be the best person you can be in this life. Honest, caring, humble, giving, courageous, loving all of life and not fearing death. Change what you think needs changing, but do not fret about things that happen which are beyond your control.

The doctor came to David first; he wanted to get this visit over before the rest of his rounds took place. After the usual greetings, the doctor believed that he had read this patient correctly – no beating around the bush.

'Right, Major Stevenson,' he started.

'Oh, for goodness sake, call me David, please.' The voice seemed quite relaxed.

The doctor looked down at his notes. 'It's not good news, I'm afraid.' He paused briefly before saying, 'Your vertebrae has been fractured – that's not a big deal, we are able to repair that. The problem seems to be that your spinal cord has been badly damaged.'

David rubbed his nose reflectively. 'You're telling me that I'm to spend the rest of my life in a wheelchair.' He didn't wait for an answer. 'I will not, I must not, accept that outcome. I will not only walk again, I will run. At this moment I don't know how; I only know that I will.'

He turned to Esther, who had silent tears slipping down her cheeks. 'Go home and tell our daughter that this is a race to see who will walk first, her or me!' He seemed to be on a roll. 'Doctor, please repair my spine and do what you can to patch me up. I want to go to Stanford Hall as soon as possible.' He referred to the DMRC (Defence and National Rehabilitation Centre) facility that had recently taken over from Headley Court as the place where all military personnel went for rehab after being badly injured.

After the doctor and Esther had left, it was time for some serious thinking. All his physical energy must be focused on the repair of his body. However, it was not just his physical body that needed treatment; he must now look towards generating the creative use of his mind for both his physical and mental well-being.

Chapter 24

For the Love of God

David insisted that Esther returned to the Succoth when he was transferred to Stanford Hall on the grounds that there wasn't much she could do whilst he was going through the mill of rehab. 'It's not like I can even shag you,' he said with a mischievous grin.

She had never heard him use the word before; she put her hand to her mouth to stifle an involuntary giggle. Nevertheless, she had a flashback of their wonderful honeymoon: the nights beside the Indian Ocean and later on safari and listening to the African night sounds as they cheerfully gave up sleep to continue making love as the sun rose over the Masai Mara. Could that unbelievable joy she had felt then ever be repeated?

Both her mum and dad met her at Aberdeen. Mary was holding Sophie, but as Esther came into view, Sophie rocked so violently that Esther had to reach out for her even before accepting the hugs and kisses that her mum and dad rained upon her.

On their journey back to Succoth, Esher brought her parents up to date on the situation with David.

Esther suddenly thought that what was amazing about this community was that they all seemed to grow stronger when trials and tribulations bore down upon them. For most of the time, even under lowering dark clouds, or vicious thunderstorms, or softly falling snow that nevertheless produced its own menace, the sun would always trump the darkness. Theirs was a pocket of spiritual sunshine that seemed to emanate from each person; who, like a member of a hive, each supported an important function to support one another. Sadness had no place here; it was totally supplanted by optimism. A joy of living, a joy of caring, of loving unconditionally.

If it is true that there is a power of goodness in this world, is there also a power of evil? Esther didn't know why that thought had entered her head as she was spooning the first solids into Sophie's mouth – who, by the way, was enjoying every mouthful.

She had been back for nearly two weeks now. She had spoken to David every day (more accurately, many times a day). He was always positive and enjoyed being back amongst guys with shared experiences.

Esther always enjoyed the Sunday shared lunches. This week Zufash had offered. She showed all that were interested one of her favourite Afghanistan dishes called Kabuli Pulao – rice and lamb. It wasn't hot with too much chilli or, indeed, bland; it was that perfect mixture of spiciness with incredible flavours. With naan bread to mop up the juices, the meal was perfect.

All the families started to drift home at about three o'clock. Mary and Joshua gave Zufash a big hug as she left to return home.

The weather had deteriorated during the day and the temperature had dropped. Mary was tidying up as the last of the group were leaving when she noticed the gloves. She immediately recognised them as belonging to Zufash.

'Joshua, Zufash has gone home without her gloves.'

Joshua looked up from the tray that he was filling with empty glasses. 'Don't worry, I'll drop them in once I've finished clearing the decks. I was wanting a walk before I plant my backside in the chair with a book.'

Esther was putting Sophie down for her afternoon nap. Mary didn't hear the door close on Joshua as he walked through the snow to deliver a pair of gloves.

Four days later, Joshua died on the operating table as the surgeon tried to replace the severed valve that had been partially sliced through with the first knife thrust to his chest.

An imam from the Aberdeen mosque had agreed to officiate together with Rev. Udny, who had not so long-ago married David and Esther. The funerals would take place at the Succoth as soon as the post-mortem examinations had been completed.

It snowed again the night before the funerals were to take place, but by the morning the sky was blue, and the sun shone brightly.

The imam spoke about the community at the Succoth and how it could show the rest of the world how it was possible for two different faiths to coexist in harmony.

The Rev. Udny chose to speak from 1 Corinthians 13:2. 'For now we see in a mirror dimly, but then face to face. Now as I know in part; then I shall know fully, even as I have been fully known.'

Mary bravely offered, carrying on with 1 Corinthians 13:1, 'If I speak in the tongues of men and of angels, but have not love, I am a noisy gong or a clanging cymbal. And if I have prophetic powers, and understand all mysteries and all knowledge, and if I have all faith, so as to remove mountains, but have not love, I am nothing.

'If I give away all that I have, and if I deliver up my body to be burned, but have not love, I gain nothing.

'Love is patient and kind; love does not envy or boast; it is not arrogant or rude. It does not insist on its own way; it is not irritable or resentful; it does not rejoice at wrongdoing but rejoices in the truth.

'Love bears all things, believes all things, hopes all things, endures all things. Love never ends.

'As for prophesies, they will pass away; as for tongues, they will cease; as for knowledge, it will pass away.

'When I was a child, I spoke like a child, I reasoned like a child. When I grew up, I gave up childish ways.

'So now faith, hope and love abide, these three; but the greatest of these is love.'

The Muslim Zufash and the Christian Joshua were buried side by side – facing Mecca and Jerusalem. Both were loved by this community for the good people that they were.

David had been devastated by the news; the feeling of total helplessness brought him to the lowest depths that he had ever experienced.

Chapter 25

Mental Gymnastics

He came awake. He reckoned that it must be about three in the morning but was disappointed when he looked at his watch and it was three twenty – twenty minutes out!

He was sweating, and then he remembered why. He had been having a kaleidoscopic dream. He was doing P Company, running through ankle-deep mud with a metal stretcher on his shoulder trying to mask the pain by encouraging the other stretcher-bearers. Then, pounding around the assault course, and then the bruising minute of 'milling' (a toe-to-toe slug it out with a man roughly your own size and weight) to see if you have the aggressive spirit for real combat. The first parachute descent. Then, the Fan Dance in midwinter (the all-important test for selection into the SAS). All this mixed up with escape and evasion and interrogation!

All the challenges of the past were nothing compared to the challenge that was before him. The day he was able to have an unaided shit was incomparable with any other challenge he had achieved in his life so far. He hated the catheter that was implanted in his penis to allow him to control his bladder, but that, unfortunately, would have to stay in place for some time to come.

His upper body strength was developing amazingly, but sometimes this was self-defeating. He wanted his legs to work, not just being able to drag himself around a room with a frame or a chair. Every day, including the weekend, he was in the gym. Even the physios were impressed; they had never seen such dedicated motivation.

Esther arrived for a surprise visit. The physios then realised where that motivation came from.

However, there is only so much energy that can be utilised in the gym or the pool. David had a good brain, and he needed to find a path to fund his wife and family. He'd already had some success as a journalist with a few articles published, and there was certainly much to be commented on.

His first acclaimed piece was predicated on the question, 'Do we want to go back to political parties?' David argued that they were a throwback to a class system that no longer existed. Ask anyone who professes to be working class to show you their hands. If they are rough and calloused, agree with them, for they are few and far between these days. Some politicians are still trying to resurrect the truth that existed in the formative years of the Industrial Revolution – but now, if analysed, it has become the politics of envy over endeavour. If you risked all and won, we'll take it off you. Yet, you don't have to be Einstein to realise that there are fat cats who will milk the system, and cheat and promote corrupt practices that need to be reined in.

The revolutionary system he proposed was to go back to the historical county boundaries. Place the majority of powers into the hands of county councils – not on a party-political basis, but by a simple random selection of councillors in the same way that we select our juries for legal proceedings. Let them do the job for a year at a time. If they are selected but don't feel comfortable in the role, they may refuse. They would have civil servants to assist, but they would work on the de Bono Six Hat Theory: working together to find the best answer.

David further suggested that a central committee could propose subjects of significant relevance: Our children are the greatest asset this country has. So how do we prepare them for the future – as infants, as adolescents, as young adults?

When each county council has agreed a workable plan, they nominate a representative to bring it to the council. Then, using the same de Bono principle, these plans will be developed with everyone working in unison.

The SNP hated it. They could see all their machinations for independence going up in smoke, as this exercise in true devolution caught the imagination of most thinking people: Moray having the same powers as Surrey.

David had never taken any real interest in politics, but now it was time to rethink everything.

The article drew the attention of a BBC producer who invited him to appear on TV. Of course, his history and service were described in the introduction. A thorough researcher even managed to discover that he had a US Navy Medal of Honour.

However, it was his revolutionary political ideas that fired up his audience. He was an overnight success.

David could now get himself to the bathroom and shuffle with a walking frame to a sitting position on the toilet (which the rehab staff thought was amazing). The catheter was still a problem. Sometimes when he was being super active, his knee would hit the tap. Suddenly, he would find that his lower leg was wet and there was a pool of piss on the floor.

The staff all agreed that there was probably no more they could do; it was time to go home and make the most of it.

Esther drove down to take him home in Zufash's Fiat Panda. Her house and car had just become the property of the community. It was only when they arrived home that the limitations of his manually propelled chair became apparent. To simply navigate from the car to the front door was almost impossible.

Once there, he immediately noticed that someone had made wooden ramps everywhere that was needed. The chair, though, just couldn't hack the rough terrain. He remembered the now bittersweet memory of carrying Esther over the threshold on their first night together.

Manoeuvring into the sitting room, he was surprised to see another wheelchair. This was an entirely different beast. He called it his four-wheel drive monster truck. It seemed that his old CO had called Esther to see if there was anything they could do to make his life easier. She had foreseen the problem getting around at Succoth and explained the problem. All his brother officers had contributed, but the motorised all-terrain wheelchair was very expensive, so Para Charity were asked to assist. Between them all, David had a perfect vehicle to ensure his independence. Although, he did wonder if a rotor blade could be attached to give him a Heliborne facility!

The BBC director who had invited him on the show called. He wanted to know if David would be interested in doing a daily TV podcast on relevant day-to-day matters.

David didn't need time to consider; this was the answer to his prayers.

It was Esther who had the last bit of news to blow him away.

She put her arms around his shoulders and drew his head to her stomach and ran her fingers through his hair. 'How do you feel about becoming a father?'

He pushed her away and stared up into her face. ‘Are you kidding me?’

‘No, it was confirmed on Tuesday, but I thought I would wait till you got home,’ she whispered. ‘We did manage to practice quite a lot on our honeymoon… What did you expect?’

He drew her back and kissed her stomach. ‘You have just made me very, very happy.’

She bent down and kissed him passionately on the mouth.

Chapter 26
Revolutionary Visions

The destruction of Parliament with all the loss of life had elicited much sympathy from the leaders of the EU, but they were very unhappy about the retribution served out to Iran without their agreement. Some of the partner states thought that the action taken against the Russians was a bad move. They were still pressing for answers about Brexit: was the UK going to remain or leave?

David produced a podcast that was to serve as a catalyst for what followed. It was called *Time for the United Kingdom to Redefine Itself.* It proposed that the UK should make a clean break with the EU. He refused to call it Brexit, preferring the longer, but more descriptive, term 'British Independence from Europe'. Economists could argue all they want, but the burning question was, 'Do we want to be governed by Brussels as a department of the EU, or seek our own independence to make our own rules, seek our own justice, trade with whoever we want and defend ourselves whenever we consider it necessary?'

He then broke down each area.

The judiciary needed to be overhauled (our penal system was not fit for purpose and the war against drugs was a war that was being lost) and our homeland security had to be reformed.

Customs borders could be done away with entirely (with homeland security only guarding against people trafficking, weapons smuggling and any other illegal activity). VAT could be replaced by purchase tax

(PT). Tariffs would be zero per cent for imports from anywhere in the world. However, anytime reciprocity was not accepted by countries that the UK exports to would be met with substantial hikes in PT for equivalent imports. It would then become beholden on any exporter who wanted to sell their products in the UK to pressure their own governments not to impose heavy tariffs on goods from the UK.

For example, given that the UK had a trade deficit of £66 billion with the EU (the EU exported three times more to us than we exported to them), it has to be nonsense that an equitable arrangement cannot be found. '*If trying to punish the UK for leaving their club is their only motivation, then we will be better off with new partners*,' he opined. Instead of six 'free trade areas'. With corporation tax having been reduced to 12.5 per cent, most companies in the world would love to have a base in the UK.

The social media pages became red hot as millions followed this podcast.

Since the terrorist attack, and the retributive response (still not admitted), defence had become a very hot topic. David's take on the matter, as an ex-military man (and most people knew something of his exemplary military record and active service exploits from press reports and TV interviews), made a strong case for a change in direction.

He maintained that the UK should not be trying to police the world. He questioned spending vast amounts on aircraft carriers – which have become nothing more than very large targets when up against a sophisticated enemy. That tanks are about as relevant to twenty-first century warfare as cavalry charges in the First World War and biplanes in the Second World War. Wars of the future will be fought in cyberspace, being supported by supersonic guided missiles, and on the ground by robotic killing machines that are directed by operators in safe areas and using AI once in the killing zone.

However, why should the UK become involved in such wars of the future? As the natural geographic bridge between the United States of America and, soon-to-be, United States of Europe, it could be described as the Hong Kong of the North Atlantic. It would be much better to follow the example of Switzerland and claim absolute neutrality whilst maintaining a credible defence capability.

Focus the naval might on a tactical submarine force capable of delivering a range of powerful weaponry to deter any adversary who thought they could bully us into submission. A fleet of frigates backed up by inshore craft and drones to guard our coastline. Sufficient fighter/bomber aircraft to patrol the skies and give support to the navy. A fighting force of special forces to deal with the defence of citizens at risk outside of the country, backed up with transport planes and attack helicopters.

'*NATO*,' he explained, '*was no longer viable as illustrated by the actions of both the Americans and Turks in Syria. Anyway, does anyone really expect that if any of the European nations were under serious attack, an aggressor would allow the Americans to use the UK as a massive aircraft carrier, a springboard to launch into Europe like they did in World War Two? Any aggressor would mount a pre-emptive attack and ensure that the British Isles were no longer habitable!*'

This last podcast might not have won him too many friends in the higher echelons of the MOD, but the interest it drew from the people was immense.

His next podcast entitled *The Case against Prohibition – How to Lose the War against Drugs*. The thesis was quite straightforward: There is absolutely no evidence that prohibition has ever worked anywhere in the world. It has spawned massive profits for organised crime. It has accelerated petty crime as abusers need to fund their habit. And knife and gun crime have soared as ever-younger individuals struggle for territory to sell their shortcut to hell.

Portugal had shown the world how to start the process. By decriminalising drugs for personal use, they had seen a forty per cent reduction in usage within a year of its implementation. But there is so much more that could be done. Every town should have a drug clinic where free drugs are available and administered. Yes, the same warning that you find on cigarette packets, 'Smoking Kills', should be put on display, and if, like smokers, who wish to ignore the warning…

The natives were getting restless. It doesn't sit well with most traditional Brits to have the military governing their daily life. They were still too close to the deadlock that had frustrated everyone to want to go back to a two-party state, but they wanted to move on.

David's podcast *Governance for the Future* revamped his 'Seven Pillars of Governance':

1. A National Trade Plan (If You Can't Make the Money, You Can't Spend It).
2. Lifelong Education
3. A National Housing Plan
4. The Best National Health Service in the World
5. Policing and Penal Reform
6. Homeland Defence
7. Simplified Taxation

All of these would be subject to the intelligent use of resources to combating climate change. Once these important topics had been resolved, there would be the time to produce a written constitution.

This podcast created a media furore, but now everybody wanted to know how all this could come about without the traditional party system.

David explained in his next podcast. A small central committee of experts in each field would challenge the country to find the best answer to a particular problem. Each borough, each county council, would create an investigative group using de Bono's rules – working together to determine the best available plan for a given reform. They would then bring the agreed plan to a given location, somewhere agreeable, and share their findings using the same process as their home constituents. Then they would work together to tease out the best answer available for the country.

Thus, for example, 'The Housing Crisis' where at least 300,000 new homes need to be provided in the short term.

The experts might produce the following questions:

- Where can the land be obtained?
- What should be the balance between privately owned, social housing and privately rented?
- What new building methods could be utilised that were both cost-effective and environmentally sound?
- What extra infrastructure would be needed?
- How could planning be streamlined?
- How could all this be funded?

David answered all these questions, and then added that all this means nothing if we don't have a real and purposeful feeling of community.

It was as though everything that was needed or broken came back to the community. The days when the State was expected to meet every responsibility from the cradle to the grave had to stop. '*There will always be people,*' David explained, '*that will need help and assistance, and as a local community we should be ready to assist. In days long gone, every village had its village idiot, but they were not a figure of fun for the children of the village, they were looked after and protected. In the same way, old people were provided with accommodation and food. In the twenty-first century, we ought to be able to do so much more.*'

He had a somewhat less appreciative audience on the subject of spiritual belief. He produced a podcast entitled *God or Gods Are Hot-wired into Our DNA*. He attested, '*From golden calves to totem poles, from Judaism to Christianity, from Islam to Hinduism. There are more sects and beliefs than the hairs on a pie-dog. Anthropologists will tell you that all known groups of people throughout the ages have found it an important facet of life to have faith in some extra celestial power.*'

He argued that all of our driving forces, our aggression (to have arrived at this juncture in our evolutionary development proves beyond doubt that none of us can be described as Mr Nice Guy), and our ability to love and look after our loved ones has promoted our ability to procreate and build families. And that in Great Britain, for nearly two thousand years, the Christian religion had provided a framework for living – never perfect but evolving to a stage where it almost became irrelevant.

David was happy to give his testimony. His Christian faith had served him well. He had found himself in a number of hotspots, but he had observed that you don't find many atheists in a slit trench under fire! However, he wasn't an evangelist; and he had observed over the years that nobody is converted by argument. Faith only arrives when the recipient personally wants it.

Nevertheless, his Christian belief had tempered his serious concern about the hundreds of thousands of Christians who had been killed and displaced from their homes in the Middle East during 2019. This brought forth a declaration (given also the degree of Islamic fundamentalism that had occurred within British mosques) that our diplomatic service should produce an edict to all Arabic states stating every British mosque will be closed forthwith until permission is granted to build Christian churches in all of their countries and that they will guarantee safety for their congregations.

It was after his podcast which stated 'Multiculturalism in Britain has failed' that the death threats began in earnest. David spoke about certain ethnic groups who were living in the United Kingdom but not really a part of it, other than to collect the benefits of a liberal society. Their refusal to integrate; the patriarchal mores that belonged to their homelands rather than the place where they had chosen to live.

Arranged marriages; women not allowed to venture out of the house without a male member accompanying them; honour killings. Sharia law had no place in British society. As a nation of animal lovers, the killing of animals by slitting their throats was an abomination. This was not a rant against Muslims – David spoke in glowing terms of the Asians that had fled Uganda and who had settled into the very heart of British life, or the Sikhs or Nepalese Gurkhas who had served loyally in two world wars. But for all the others who dreamt of an Islamic state of Europe, there had to be changes.

The changes would start at infant school. Faith schools should not be allowed, although every day would start with an assembly where all the children would stand and sing 'God Save The Queen', and they would hear a reading from the Bible and say a short prayer. This process would continue through middle and upper school. At eighteen, all youngsters would be conscripted for National Service. This would have nothing to do with militarism but would be a multi-ethnic force to provide community service. They would all dress in the same issue denim and earn a basic weekly wage. They would live communally, and discipline would be vigorously administered.

Our international aid in future would not be provided in cash, but in people and materials to assist in infrastructure projects where the recipient country would supply equal numbers of their young people to work with ours. Much-needed technical training would be given that would reflect the needs of industry when they were ready to join their own communities after their tour of duty had been completed. Also, university courses would be reduced to a two-year intensive course that could be achieved with the self-discipline and experience gained during National Service…

The phone rang, it was Peter, his MI6 handler from the past. 'David, dear friend, how are you?' He barely paused for an answer. 'Look, the CDS would like to have a meeting. Could you be available on Thursday? We'll send a helicopter.'

'Do you know what it's about?' questioned David.

'No, sorry, old chap, but he doesn't confide in me, just asked me to fix it up.'

'OK, I could do with a change of scenery. What time should I expect my lift?'

'ETA zero nine thirty hours. Don't offer the pilot coffee or anything. You will be lunching with the boss, I understand.'

'I'll need room to take my wheelchair,' reminded David.

'Not a problem, I'll see it's taken care of,' replied Peter.

David was putting his phone away as Esther came into the room.

'You look very thoughtful – penny for them.' She grinned.

'The chief of the defence staff wants to see me in London on Thursday. They'll be sending a helicopter.'

'Wow, that sounds a bit special. I trust they won't be sending you overseas again. I've only got a couple of weeks to go now before our big day.'

It was David's turn to grin. 'I think I've discovered that the pen is mightier than the sword. No, I'll insist that they send me back the same day.'

Chapter 27

Big Decisions

The helicopter didn't fly to the MI6 HQ as David was expecting, but instead veered to the east until he was looking down on the skyscrapers that rear out of what used to be the East India Docks. They landed on a helipad on the top of one of the buildings. He was met by a small group of men and women, all in smart casual clothes, but David didn't miss that they were all discretely armed. They helped him out of the helicopter and into his wheelchair and escorted him through a maze of corridors until they reached a pair of solid wood doors. One of his escorts knocked on the door and opened it to announce David's arrival.

David drove his wheelchair expertly into the CDS's office, which had been designed as a luxurious penthouse overlooking the Docklands and surrounded by high-rise offices mostly belonging to international banks. Whilst the setting was breath-taking, the interior was fairly austere with wall maps and a very uncluttered desk on which stood five monitors.

The general rose from his desk and came to meet David; he looked relaxed in a pair of dark corduroy trousers, an open-necked tattersall check shirt and dark brown Jodhpur boots. He waved to a comfortable chair in front of the floor-to-ceiling window. 'Before we settle down, can I get you a tea or coffee?' he asked kindly.

'No thank you, I'm fine. I'd rather like to get on, if that's all right with you.'

The general smiled. 'Is it OK to call you David,' he asked genially.

David shook his head. 'Not a problem,' he replied.

The general went on, 'I'm sorry that I had to drag you all the way down from Aberdeenshire, but I have got rather a lot on my plate at the moment, so I can't be away from my desk at all, I even sleep in the adjoining room.' He waved a hand at a door opposite and pulled a face.

'That's fine by me. We're due to have our firstborn within the next couple of weeks, so I do want to be with my wife when that happens. I told her that I would even try to get back this evening if it were possible,' David explained.

'Good, I'm sure that we can complete our business and still have time to get you back home tonight.' He continued, 'I've taken the liberty of ordering lunch here.' Not waiting for an answer, he added, 'Lamb chops and all the trimmings sound OK?'

David bowed his head in a very slight bow. 'That sound just fine.'

The general leant forward in his seat and steepled his fingers and then moved them to his mouth before starting. 'I probably know more about you than I do about my own son. MI6 has a massive file on you, and I'm bound to say that it is all good. I have read every word of every script from your podcasts over the last eight or nine months. I am particularly interested in your ideas about communities. As you know, in order to maintain the peace, we decided to revert to borough and county council areas that could be managed instead of trying to put out bush fires all over the Union.

'To a greater or lesser extent, this has had a certain amount of success – certainly the crime rate has dropped significantly. However...' his clasped hands came back to his mouth and he wrinkled his nose '...this situation cannot continue indefinitely. I've been apolitical all my service life as I felt that this was the only position to take as a serving officer, but in the past few years I am bound to say that I've been not just unimpressed but positively disappointed by the antics of some of these, so-called, professional politicians.

'Now I find myself in the position where I must offer an acceptable answer to the Defence Council, and if they accept it, then I must take that proposal to Her Majesty.' He let that sink in before continuing again. 'I would like you, David, to explain to me why you think it possible to take your experience of living in a close-knit community and somehow expand that into a series of much larger communities.'

Before David could answer, a knock on the door heralded lunch. A table had been set up at the other side of this huge space. As the head waiter gave a small bow, the general rose and led the way to the table. David navigated to a position opposite the general.

A wine waiter brought over a bottle and showed it to the general, who fished in his shirt pocket for a pair of half-moon glasses and read the label.

'Would you partake in a glass of Gevrey-Chambertin?' he asked with a twinkle in his eye.

'You have done your research, sir, that is probably my favourite French red,' he replied.

As the general poured, he asked, 'So, if this your favourite French red, what is your all-time favourite?'

'If I told you that,' David said with a grimace, 'I would probably have to kill you. Enough to say that it comes from the Douro Valley in Portugal, and it is a sublime red wine at a very reasonable price.'

It was a truly excellent meal, and the general was sufficiently civilised not to expect detailed conversation whilst they were eating. He had determined a long time ago that the best conversations came after a good meal, not during.

Neither of them wanted a dessert, so instead opted for a plate of cheese with some fruit. David declined a glass of port, being quite happy to finish the wine in his glass. Over coffees, the conversation sharpened.

'In your utopian dream, you see a central committee – sounds a bit like the EU,' the general baited David.

'Yes,' agreed David, 'but the wheel has to start somewhere. There are some great educationalists out there, just as there are dedicated GPs, surgeons, nurses. These are what we need to guide the people in their ultimate decision-making. There are entrepreneurs and climatologists, agriculturists and environmental experts. Diversity is both a blessing and a danger we all need to be aware of. Multiculturalism is not working in many parts of the UK. Even defence, I believe, needs a radical rethink.

'We all know that everything we do needs funding, and those funds can only come from the people. For too long, politicians have borrowed, leaving the next generation to pick up the tab. Subsidiarity – ring-fencing specific amounts of money raised to spend on specific projects – has been a dirty word for the politicians of the past who always preferred to talk in billions that wash around in the ether and mean nothing. Within my community dream, all would be visible, and God help the member who put personal gain in front of community well-being. Our tax system has grown in complexity year on year, and it is way past time for a complete simplification.'

The general, who had been listening attentively, now asked, 'But, David, how would this committee frame their questions to the individual committee groups around the country?'

David thought for a moment, for this was a very complex question. 'Take the NHS and try to see how it might work within a county community set-up. The "experts" might ask the following: How many patients can one GP manage on his register? Can the surgery from which he operates have a practice nurse answerable to that GP or should that practice nurse look after more than one GP's patients? Within that surgery practice there needs to be a receptionist covering administration from nine to five, five days a week, and he or she or even a small team could look after the needs of a number of GPs. During out of hours, we should have a response service. We might wish to provide bespoke transport to bring older patients to the surgery in time for their appointment. The function of this primary care group, in addition to providing general medical cover, would be to advise on all forms of preventative medicine.

'The object of the exercise is to provide a general level of primary medical cover that doesn't require people to use A & E services at the hospital except for the emergencies they were designed for. All of these questions need to include how to fund premises, and the remuneration of doctors and nurses, locums and receptionists. We all know that you tend to get what you pay for, but at the end of this joined-up thinking, each subgroup in every area brings its conclusions to the county council where the same principles apply. Finally, the CC group will come to a central location and work together to provide a national plan, which will then pass into legislation to make it lawful. This concept can be used to operate hospitals; provide a few centres of excellence to carry out hip replacements or knee surgery; bespoke eye clinics for the removal of cataracts; and loss of hearing clinics. We have main streets that are dying out because of online shopping, but these cost-effective premises could be much better used to house these areas of health and wellness.

'It's just a matter of setting the question and letting the representatives of the people find the answers. I am not the person to set the questions on health issues, but there are plenty of GPs, practice nurses, medical administrators, surgeons, consultants et al. who would be able to share their knowledge and experience. Most people are not stupid, and if they have to pay taxes, they have a right to participate in a real way to get value for money; and by working together, not arguing against any proposition, only seeking the best way for their community, good things can be achieved. I accept that sometimes what is considered to be ideal simply cannot be afforded, so compromises must be made. However, special needs for children and young adults, mental health, and care for the older members of our community all need to be costed separately and be at the forefront of these deliberations.'

There was a pause as the general digested all of this information, then he leant back in his seat. 'I was pretty much aware of everything you have told me, but I wanted to hear it from you. Now I can see why you have such a large following on social media and why you are so popular in the media. Your passion for the concept of ordinary people working together for the common good shines out. I know why people believe and trust in you – I certainly do. I would like to put a proposition to you. I would like you to put together the necessary group of experts for your Seven Pillars of Society. They would work together under your tutelage, and I would like you to chair each committee. You would be supported by whatever civil servants you require to carry out your duties. You would need to live in London with your family, I'm afraid, but you would have a penthouse suite, the mirror image of this one at the other side of the building – you'll have the sunrise whilst I have the sunset.' He laughed and then continued.

'You will be provided with a car and driver and sufficient security – I even wondered if you would like your best man, now serving with the SAS, to take care of your security. I propose that you simply be called Mr Chairman, though you would carry the authority of a Prime Minister in the previous regime. As such, you would have to meet with Her Majesty every week and keep her abreast of what is happening within her realm. Your initial tenure would be three years, and we will see where we go from there at that time.'

David was speechless for a moment. He had little idea of why he was brought to London, yet he could not have imagined this outcome. 'I feel very honoured by what you are suggesting, but it is a bit of a shock. I would need to discuss this with my wife – and as you know, we are expecting our first child any time in the next few weeks.

The general's eyes sparkled. 'Of course, nothing is certain yet. You will need to discuss this with your wife and family. I would hope that you could give me an answer in the next few days, as I will then need to take this proposal to the Defence Council. If they agree, which I think they will, I will then see Her Majesty and, hopefully, gain her approval.'

The Puma helicopter passed over the Succoth at about 20:18, on target for the 20:20 landing. David had called ahead to make sure the home paddock was cleared for landing; Dai had seen to it and was waiting to help once the helicopter was on the ground. He was carrying a powerful flashlight and when the helicopter could be heard approaching, he pointed the light to the clouds and gave three blips (dot, dot, dot – Morse for 'S' for 'Succoth'). The pilot switched on his landing lights and started his descent.

Perched on the front of his reading chair, with Esther sitting on the footstool between his legs, David was busy massaging her neck to relieve the tension. She had not had a good day; she was worried and anxious about David's call to London. Sophie had picked up her vibes and was being very clingy and demanding her full attention. The chilli she had on the stove caught whilst she was busy trying to get Sophie on the potty. Luckily, her mother called in at that time. Recognising the tension growing, Mary offered to take Sophie back to the barn for tea. Esther felt, all of a sudden, that she was very blessed.

Even as the tension eased, she could not believe what she was hearing, and then an internal kick made her gasp. 'This guy's gonna be a footballer.'

'Hope not,' came the reply. 'I was hoping for a boy who would represent his country at rugby.'

'Seriously, is this something you really want to do?' she asked.

He stopped massaging her neck for a moment. 'You know, I just think that we've been extremely blessed with what some folk might call good luck, but I do feel that this might now be the time to give something back. I don't know if that makes any sense to you.'

She looked thoughtful. 'I've followed you through much darker places than this. It's only for three years, you say. A certain First Lady of America did it.' She giggled slightly, then another though crossed her mind. 'Have you really got to see the Queen every week?'

‘Apparently, yes, she has always taken a very great interest in the day-to-day workings of her Parliament. Now it no longer exists, she is anxious to know just what will replace it.’

Another thought crashed across her mind. ‘I hate the thought of leaving Mum here on her own. Since Dad’s death she has coped really well, but I think Sophie has helped a lot in that process.’ She tailed off mournfully.

‘I don’t see any reason why she couldn’t come with us. You would need more help with the new baby, and there will be functions, I’m sure, that we will be expected to attend.’ David continued to massage.

Mary returned with Sophie as it was time for bed. Once they retold her all the news of the day, she was completely overwhelmed. When they asked if she would help and go with them into this new adventure, her joy turned to tears and she said yes.

Esther and David didn’t get a lot of sleep that night; they talked and talked and planned for everything they thought could go wrong. David was bound to say in the wee small hours, ‘I thought I was the Stoic in the family, but now I know that we are both of the same mind.’

The next day, David called the general on his personal number. GCHQ monitored the call, but no one in the rest of the world would ever know what was said.

‘David, I’m delighted that you have decided to accept. I can now go to the Defence Council on Monday and assuming they agree with my proposition, I would hope to meet with Her Majesty on Tuesday. As soon as I know, I will call you.’ There was quite a long pause, almost as if the connection had been broken, then the general’s voice started again. ‘David, I have another problem that I would like your advice on. The EU president has demanded to know what is going to happen when the extended period for decision runs out. I'm not sure what should be said at this juncture.'

There was a strong, confident timbre to David's voice as he replied, 'Tell our EU ambassador to inform the EU that the United Kingdom will leave the EU on 31st December 2020. If the EU believe that the UK should be punished, as has been suggested, so be it. However, they should be reminded that we are at our best when our backs are against the wall. Furthermore, if they ever want a friendly relationship with the UK going forwards, it will depend on what we would describe as "good neighbourliness" when we are facing difficult times.'

The general was as good as his word; he called on Tuesday afternoon. 'I met with Her Majesty two hours ago. She has accepted our proposal and seems very keen to meet with you as soon as possible. I explained that you were awaiting the birth of your firstborn. She replied, "Duty comes first," but I have to say that she sounded very enthusiastic.'

David was unusually curt. 'General, please advise Her Majesty that whilst I have been prepared to give my life in Her service on numerous occasions, I will be at my wife's side when this child is born.'

Esther's waters broke as he retold the story. It had always been agreed that Mary would assist a home birth. Esther was fit and strong and a trained paediatrician, Mary had birthed both her girls at home. Nevertheless, it was three o'clock in the morning when this child arrived on the scene.

David had been there throughout holding her hand and audibly coaching her as he encouraged her to breath. 'In, two, three. Out, two, three.'

Esther's face was pure concentration. The sweat rolled off her brow…

David's face was a reflection of what he was looking at.

They both knew that a final effort was needed.

His hands squeezed hers as he willed that ultimate giving of life as her hips stretched to beyond anything that she could imagine.

Then from her vagina appeared a head, which only David could see, then the shoulders.

With an almost silent slip, the baby arrived in the welcoming hands of Mary. She held the child away from her body and announced quietly, 'You have a son.' Mary quickly did the necessary with the umbilicus, wrapped him in a soft towel and used the edge to take a smear of blood from his face. She leant over Esther, offering the child.

But Esther's whole body was shaking, her legs were rattling with the shock of the final effort. 'Give him to his dad,' she whispered. 'I'll have him when I stop shaking.'

Mary smiled and placed the baby in David's arms.

He drew the child to his chest and kissed his head very gently.

It was only as he looked across at his wife that Esther noticed the tears coursing down his cheeks.

The summer solstice was just an excuse for another party. The refuge was full, with seven mothers and eleven children. Mary had given over her kitchen to Edith, who was going to coordinate everything. Everyone knew the news about David's appointment and were absolutely overwhelmed by somehow being part of it. The news hadn't been made public yet, so they had all been sworn to secrecy.

An email arrived from Gavin. He and Susan had returned from Bangladesh where Gavin had finished his latest assignment to teach the Rohingya Muslim refugees how to build low-cost houses. David replied immediately saying yes, of course, and offering the Barn, as Mary would be staying with them.

David and Esther managed to slip away for an afternoon in Elgin to do a bit of shopping. Joshua, for they had both decided to name their son after Esther's father, was an exceptionally good baby. He smiled and gurgled at all the people rushing around, all of whom managed to stop what they were doing to pull faces and make him laugh, but his parents had to rush back as Esther was still breast feeding.

When they got home, a special surprise awaited them. Rhys, all booted and suited and looking very smart, knocked their door.

Esther opened the door and gave a squeal before wrapping her arms around his neck. She grabbed his hand and led him into the living room where David was loading the wood burner with logs.

'Look what the wind blew in!' she cried out.

David spun around his wheelchair and roared, 'Rhys!'

'Merry Christmas, boss.' He came across with his hand outstretched.

'Help me out of this damn thing. I want to give you a hug,' David roared.

After things had quietened down a bit, and Joshua had been passed around so much that he decided to sick-up a bit of his last feed, Rhys handed him back to Esther who magicked a tissue and wiped his face and laid him back in his pushchair.

'The powers that be offered me the job of looking after your security – they said you had OK'd it if I was interested. Was I ever!'

David smiled. 'Well, the news is not out yet, and I'm hoping it will stay that way until after New Year. Then we can start making plans for our move to London and all the complexities that we will have to sort out. But, for now, let's just enjoy all our friends and remember what this festival is all about.'

Gavin and Susan didn't arrive until June 20th. Gavin's two boys were techies in Silicon Valley; both were now married but no grandchildren just yet. They had all managed to get together and spent some family time at Lake Tahoe, as Gavin and Susan had come back via California. Willow, their youngest, now twenty-five, was living with an artist in the South of France where she had published two books of poems in French, to much literary acclaim in her adopted country.

That evening, with everyone present for a the Summer Solstice supper, David clinked his wine glass for silence. 'Before we start our meal, I would like to ask Gavin if he would care to lead us in prayer.'

Gavin looked into space and didn't move for what seemed an age. Then he stood and said, 'Father God, in this house I was taught that where two or three are gathered together in your name, there you will also be. On behalf of all of us here tonight, I would like to claim that promise. I would like you to know just how thankful we are to you for all the many blessings that you pour down upon us. Thank you, Father, and please continue to spread your Holy Spirit amongst us to guide us and to help us share your love throughout the world in everything that we do. Amen.'

They all chorused, 'Amen.'

After all the festivities were over, David had a long chat with Gavin. He told him everything that had happened and asked if he would come to London with him and act as his chief of staff. 'There will be lots of flunkies, I'm thinking, and as many civil servants as we need, but I will need a sounding board who is not afraid to tell me when I'm going wrong. I'll need someone that I can trust at all times, but who will always be ready to… I hate the expression, but it says what I mean, "think outside of the box".'

Gavin had that faraway look in his eye again. 'I'll need to talk to Susan about it. Where would we live?' he asked.

'We'd be neighbours in a luxury high-rise apartment in Canary Wharf,' David replied.

'OK, let us sleep on it, I'll give you an answer tomorrow.' Gavin then went off to find Susan.

Susan agreed, and everything was arranged quickly. David and Gavin, shadowed by Rhys, would fly down on the following Monday – a helicopter would be put at their disposal.

Esther and her mother would bring baby Joshua and Sophie down whenever David gave the word. They would talk every day. Similarly, Susan would stay on at Succoth until it was time to take up residence in their new home.

Chapter 28
Seven Pillars of Governance

The first morning in their work area, which was a huge open-plan office space with no desks or communications, was bizarre to say the least. Forty people, men and women, of whom a few older ones stood out against the majority of people in their early twenties. A complete racial mix; they were definitely colourful.

David started by introducing himself (most of those gathered had read much of his recent output), and he described Gavin as an innovator that he had known, and been in awe of, for more years than he would like to remember.

Every individual present had been hand-picked against a template that he and Gavin had produced.

David kicked off: 'Our objective is to produce a different form of democracy where ordinary, everyday people may determine how our community survives and prospers whilst creating a better world. Do not be afraid to fail. Do not think that you can't tell your friends and families what we are doing here. We don't deal in secrets, apart from when we are working on national defence matters. The media will hound you and try to trip you up to get you to say things that you may wish you hadn't. Just be truthful, and it will be their problem if they cannot see what it is that we are trying to achieve. This will not be a nine-to-five job; you will be expected to perform and produce results regardless of personal commitments. That said, go out now and organise this space amongst yourselves. We need desks and communications – I don't like filing cabinets and would prefer to be paperless. We will need a coffee area where we can get sufficient sustenance to keep us going when we work late. If you could organise a small gym and a sauna whilst you're at it, that would be ace.'

No particular person had been nominated for any specific task, but it was noted who took charge of these necessary requirements.

The first 'Pillar' was 'Lifelong Education'. David had a banner made and strung across their Ops Room: 'The Greatest Resource That This Country Has Are Our Children'.

He split his researchers into eight groups. 'Find me – with evidence to support it – the most charismatic primary school head teacher you can find in the country, then I want the best middle school teacher, and finally the best sixth form teacher.'

A hand went up. 'Why a primary head teacher and not just a teacher?'

Gavin answered for David, 'This is where the foundations of all education takes place; the best head teacher will make sure that his or her teachers are the best that can be found.'

David took up the story again: 'Find me a university academic who is as interested in his or her teaching as much as they are in their own research and who believe that better things could be achieved at their university.'

The researchers scribbled frantically.

'The last candidates will be more difficult to find. I want you to look for people who've had the initiative to seek further serious training later in life,' said David.

Once again, Gavin brought the researchers to order. 'This will not be a competition. We need them all to work together to tease out the essence of educational perfection. Get them all working to de Bono's Six Hat principles.' Gavin added, 'As a vital side issue, I want a remunerative table produced giving these people's annual salaries compared with a solicitor, a barrister, a senior management executive, an accountant and a stockbroker. I want to know just how we value those people who are in charge of our country's most vital resource.'

The 31st December 2020 was the day the UK left the EU.

The first ferry from Calais arrived on time. The vehicles rumbled off; life went on as usual. Sadly, when the ferry returned to Calais, the inbound vehicles were taken to a parking lot where they remained. They were then checked for CE approval and countless bureaucratic procedures were carried out. No diplomatic activity was brought into play. A ferry bound for Folkestone was advised that its inbound foreign lorries would not be allowed to discharge their goods. The same message was sent from all channel ports to European ferries bound for UK ports.

The cut flower producers of the Netherlands were not happy; the salad producers of France and Spain were in spasm. The French, Italian and Spanish wine industries were furious. The continental automotive industry, suffering from the sea change of moving from fossil fuels to alternative energy, needed the loss of the UK market like a hole in the head.

Britain, it would seem, was not interested in anything other than solving the problems that had come about from losing its entire legislative body.

It was the French president, who had become the ipso facto leader of the EU when the German chancellor was involved in a power struggle within her own party, who finally ordered the release of all the incoming transport from the UK. The actual president of the EU seemed powerless to broker any sort of deal between the UK and the rest of the EU.

German industrialists were up in arms, as were the Dutch, whilst the French government were still trying to placate the gilets jaunes. Intelligent Italian businessmen were moving their wealth to Germany in euros. They believed that Germany would finally exit the euro and return to the Deutschmark, and they hoped to be able to exchange their euros into Deutschmarks at the rate for the day.

David broke the impasse: 'Let the EU know it is business as usual as far as we are concerned; all our trade standards and agricultural standards are the same as before. Why can't we just get on with life?'

The professional civil servants threw their hands up when they heard this – they really do hate simplification.

David remembered hearing a Scottish mother say to one of her kids who couldn't make up its mind about which ice lolly he wanted, 'Do ya wan' a lolly or not!' This mother's words to her child were quite profound, and politicians and diplomats should copy it more often.

It was the WFTA (World Free Trade Agreement), newly announced by the United Kingdom, that cut the mustard.

David explained on the BBC news that evening: 'Tell me what country wouldn't want to do business with this country? We have one of the best financial centres in the world, a fantastic tax regime for encouraging entrepreneurs to initiate new start-ups, and a legal system that is the envy of the world. We are prepared to trade with any country on the planet with zero tariffs. If I had to invest my money anywhere to get the best return, it would be the UK, and why?' He left the rhetorical question hanging. 'Because the people of this Great Britain have the ingenuity and the bloody-mindedness to overcome problems that others see as insurmountable.'

The phone on David's desk rang, and he was advised by an aide that the President of the United States would like to speak with him… 'Mr Chairman. I've just come from a meeting with our security advisors who would be very keen to work with your weapons innovators. Your 'Rods of God' system is something we would be very interested in.'

David paused for a moment before replying, 'Well I would need to discuss this with our Defence Council, but I feel sure that once we have agreed our trade deal, which I gather is all but agreed apart from the tax to be levied on those companies that make vast profits from online business in our territory…' There was another brief pause for that information to be fully understood before he continued, 'Oh, and Mr President, whilst I'm aware that our people do eat salads that have been washed in chlorinated water, it would greatly assist me if chlorinated chicken be taken off the table!' We will never know what the President's answer was to that request as it never appeared in the archive.

Later that evening, back in David's apartment, the space was spectacular, but nothing was filling it. David knew that Esther would make this space their home once she was here. God only knows how much he missed this woman.

Then she called, 'David, listen, listen… I've just been speaking with a surgeon. He wanted to speak to you, but you were unavailable. It's really important. I want you to talk to this man. He believes that he can regenerate your spinal cord by using stem cells.'

David suddenly felt very tired; his entire body rebelled. *No more fucking hospitals*, he thought.

She gave him the surgeon's number, and he promised to call him the next day.

They said goodnight, and David drew himself from his chair to the bed. He slumped back against the pillows and closed his eyes. He remembered that he would have to go to the bathroom to clean his teeth, and he would need to empty that wretched bag again.

He pulled the chair towards him and as he awkwardly got himself into it, his conversation with Esther came back. It would be a miracle if this surgeon was for real and that he could somehow give him back the power in his lower body.

Ever since James Goujon had made contact and professed the highest regard for David and said that he was confident in rebuilding David's body by implanting stem cells, Esther prayed intensely that he would be proved right.

Esther, her mother and the children arrived ten days later. They were let into the apartment by Rhys who had brought them from the airport.

As they arrived, a thunderstorm broke. David came to greet them whilst Rhys went back to the basement car park to bring up the luggage.

They stood in front of the huge floor-to-ceiling windows that still needed drapes and watched fork lightning flash across the dark clouds. A huge clap of thunder made Esther clutch the baby to her breast, and then Sophie began to cry pitifully.

David bashed his chair into the door in his haste to get to her side. He hauled her onto his lap, and then he knew that if there was even the slightest chance this surgeon could put him back together again, he must do it as soon as it could be arranged.

David called the surgeon the next morning.

Over the next few weeks, Great Britain's independence from the European Union was quietly happening, not with fanfares of trumpets or lurid headlines, but simply by companies that were trading together before Britain left the EU finding the ways and means to continue trading.

What politicians don't get is that governments don't trade with governments: companies trade with other companies, regardless of location, when it makes financial sense for that trade to happen. Europe simply could not afford to lose the sixty-six billion of net exports to Great Britain as well as the net gain they had previously received from Britain's contribution to the EU budget.

The Irish border problem seemed to be in a state of stasis. Great Britain stated that it didn't require a border as it was operating a zero-tariff arrangement for Ireland. The EU didn't seem very keen to put up a customs border either – so what had all the fuss been about?

Other trade deals around the world were blossoming. A zero tariff with no VAT and a purchase tax levy that was minimal as long as reciprocal terms were on offer to British exporters. Many new companies had set up shop when it was announced that not only was it possible to use the facility of working in a tax-free zone, but that corporation tax had been reduced to 12.5 per cent. Unemployment had fallen to two per cent, so the biggest problem was finding workers who had the necessary skills. The points-based immigration system that had recently been introduced was working well, but housing still had a long way to go before the housing targets that had been set were realised.

The community councils were working well after a few minor hiccoughs were talked through. The NHS review was coming up with some really exciting proposals, as were the discussions surrounding education. The area of penal reform was getting quite heated between the 'flog 'em and hang 'em high' standpoint to the replacement of existing prisons.

The first priority was a mental health filter that would identify individuals who should never have been incarcerated in prison in the first place. These people would be housed in special secure accommodation for treatment and rehabilitation. Then, first-time offenders should not go to jail. Instead, they should be placed in special units in an attempt to assist them from reoffending through literacy and skills training.

During this time, it was proposed that they should visit the floating prisons. These barges were designed for habitual criminals who showed no sense of remorse or any intention of living a crime-free life within the community. These people would be incarcerated in single-room cells with toilet and shower facilities. These floating prisons would be serviced by robotic assistance that would be programmed to cook, administer medical assistance and restrain when necessary. The entire operation would be monitored by CCTV at all times. These were scary places designed to ensure that people would think carefully before carrying out any criminal act. First offenders were warned that should they reoffend, this is where they would end up for a minimum sentence of five years.

On a lighter note, the experts (mostly accountants) were beginning to wonder what they were going to do if the tax situation was simplified to the extent that many people wanted. Income tax would be capped at a flat rate of fifteen per cent; there would be no personal allowances. An NHS tax would be levied on a per person basis. Similarly, a state pension – that would be funded by five per cent government bonds (used for infrastructure development) – would involve each person upon reaching working age saving ten per cent of their salary towards their future retirement. A hardship fund was proposed to be run by each local community. Funds would be distributed in accordance when a perceived need could be evidenced. Purchase tax would be the only progressive tax levied, with food and children's clothes exempt. The scale would rise in terms of the perceived luxury of the item purchased. Therefore, wealthy people who wanted to purchase luxury items would pay the most tax.

The House of Lords had been disbanded as there was no longer a function for them. They were allowed to keep their titles, but they received no remuneration.

All of the devolved committees were in England. Scotland, Wales and Northern Ireland were still being administered by their own parliaments. However, as the news of the true devolution through all the English counties began to percolate throughout the rest of the UK, there were calls from Scotland, Wales and Northern Ireland to have the same totally devolved treatment, with no professional politicians. Another referendum seemed necessary.

Rhys had gathered a small group of hand-picked men and women, some of whom he had served with in different parts of the world, to ensure that David and his family were kept safe at all times. There had been an upsurge in hate on social media that was liberally laced with death threats since the directives to close all the mosques until agreement to build Christian churches in Muslim countries had been established and the well-being of Christian communities had been guaranteed.

David had arranged an appointment with Mr Goujon, the surgeon. One of Rhys's men was driving. Rhys was in the front passenger seat whilst David was trying to juggle his appointments on his iPad on the back seat.

'Heads up, boss, I think we've picked up a tail.' Rhys had been watching a small screen relaying pictures from a rear-mounted camera. As he finished speaking, the driver started to slow as the traffic light ahead moved from amber to red.

The white Mercedes drew up on our offside. The passenger in the van was staring in their direction through the open window, then the barrels of a sawn-off shotgun were pointing straight at David.

'Take cover!' Rhys was still focused on the man with the gun.

The driver saw a gap in the traffic and went for it even though the lights were still on red.

David could only fling himself sideways as the gun went off; he was showered with glass.

The white van tried to follow, but a black Porsche slid through the lights and collided directly on the driver's side.

'Stop! Stay with the boss,' shouted Rhys as he leapt out of the passenger side. Once he reached the crash scene, he drew his Glock 19 as the passenger came out of the van with his shotgun curving up in an arc as he recognised Rhys from being in the car.

Rhys dropped to one knee and fired a double tap to the chest. As the man went down, he moved in and made sure by putting another round into his head. He moved to the driver's side. When he opened the door, the driver slid out. He had a massive head injury and was obviously dead.

It was at this juncture that the police arrived. Rhys flashed his card and explained the circumstances briefly before returning to where David was waiting patiently, leaving the police to sort out the mess.

At the hospital where he met Mr Goujon, they had a pleasant enough chat. The surgeon couldn't be one hundred per cent sure that the treatment would work; he would need to carry out an examination and perform a scan before he could make a reasoned prognosis.

Four hours later, David left the hospital with the knowledge that the surgeon was confident an improvement could be achieved. He couldn't guarantee all the functions of the lower body could be repaired, but surely it was worth a try.

The Stoic in David believed that there were certain things that happened in this world which couldn't be understood because we can't see the big picture. Some things have just got to be endured. However, when he thought about what had happened earlier in the day, and how he could do nothing but roll over when his life was being threatened – suppose Esther and the children had been with him at the time – his mind was now made up. He would go ahead with the treatment.

Chapter 29

Esther's Last Words

After dinner each evening, David would usually take himself off to his desk where he would write for a couple of hours. I would take him a drink at some stage and look over his shoulder at what he was working on. I had become aware that the book he had been writing, the one his father started, had come to a halt.

I knew a lot of exciting new developments within the community councils were taking off in quick succession. There seemed to be something on the news every day, and it was incredible how quickly the general public had taken up the 'Challenge for Change'. There was a groundswell of really good ideas that the public had put forward which were being acted on in a constructive manner.

Nevertheless, I must admit that I did feel a pang of disappointment that the story was no longer progressing. When I asked the question, he replied with a wry face, 'Writer's block, I suppose. I just don't know how to end it. There has to be an end, but I just can't see it.'

I had read his dad's exercise books right in the beginning, and something was tugging at my memory. I walked over to the bureau where the box file was kept, opened it up and pulled out the topmost one headed 'Introduction'. I read through the first page and found what I was looking for.

I voiced the thought that had suddenly come into my head: 'Would you mind if I wrote the end in my own voice?'

David thought for a moment before replying, 'Well, as long as you don't turn it into a Shakespearean tragedy where we all fall on our swords at the end.' He smiled up at me and said slowly, 'I think that would be a good idea. You've been part of this adventure as long as I have, and a different perspective might be a very good way to bring this story to a close.'

I have now had the opportunity of reading the entire book up to this last chapter. Some of it made me cry. Some of it scared me so much that I couldn't sleep properly for a week. The memories of our special wedding day; our honeymoon in Kenya; the joy of discovering what being a totally fulfilled woman was like; the day our adoption papers for Sophie were completed; and the day my son was born. I thanked God for all his blessings.

Then that awful day when David was blown up in the helicopter. I saw him jump from the blazing aircraft before it crashed into the bridge. I didn't know for sure it was David; I just prayed.

I have witnessed him struggle to have some control over his lower body for months. Just watching this man, the love of my life, stumbling to get to the bathroom before it was too late. This man who had been so strong, so fit, so agile, reduced to needing help just to take his socks off. However, this is not a man who relishes sympathy. He is a true Stoic; he takes whatever the world throws at him and gets on with living the best way possible. He channelled his energy into journalism, then into podcasts using digital means. Soon, he had an audience of millions.

I remembered how our community at Succoth solved their problems by working together and by using Edward de Bono's 'Six Hat Theory', but in my wildest dreams I would never have imagined that you could govern and manage an entire country by these principles.

David did, and gradually his audience began to see that it was possible to have a better form of democracy than the combative proposition versus opposition. Free from all that had gone on in the House of Commons, an enthusiasm for these ideas grew rapidly.

As substantial numbers of the general public warmed to the idea, the Defence Council, who wanted to hand over control, took their chance by appointing David as Head of State with the title of Mr Chairman! The thought of my husband having a weekly meeting with Her Majesty the Queen was somehow unreal.

David, with Gavin always at his side giving support and timely advice, along with Rhys and his team ensuring that they were kept safe at all times, all worked like a well-oiled machine. However, the work was relentless.

When Mr Goujon first called, I was so excited. I couldn't wait to tell David, but I was upset when he didn't seem to want to know initially. He has explained, in the previous chapters, how and why he changed his mind and decided to have the new stem cell treatment. It was a revolutionary process which is not suitable or effective for many people with similar conditions.

The good news is that research continues even as I write this. I pray that in time all people with spinal cord damage will be able to look forward to a complete recovery.

My prayers for David were answered. Within eight weeks he began to have some feeling in his feet and legs. Every morning at five o'clock, Rhys would be at the door and they would go off together to the gym. As we moved into summer, David bought a double scull; and the two of them would be on the river at first light. By the autumn, they had their running shoes on and ran for an hour every morning. That Christmas we went back to Succoth for a two-week break, and the two men decided that they wanted to see if they could run up Cairngorm!

To all extent and purposes, David was as good as he had ever been. Unfortunately, for both of us, everything was not perfect. Physically, he had recovered amazingly; but there was a piece of scar tissue that couldn't be removed surgically or trained away with physical activity. The catheter and all that horrible paraphernalia had long been dispensed with, but sexually he was totally unresponsive.

He was warm and loving, caring and affectionate, but the passion that we had both shared in those few weeks before he was injured had gone. We are not shy with each other. We spoke about it. We spoke about it a lot. We just wanted our life back to where it was before it was torn apart.

The doctors told us that ED (erectile dysfunction) was very common and that we should try Viagra or Tadalafil. Neither made any difference, although it seems to be very successful for the majority of men with this problem.

We had reached the third year of David's tenure. When it was over, he'd promised me that we would return to Succoth where we could have a more easy-going existence. Here he would be able to spend more time with the children and perhaps, I could resume my medical career.

It was a gorgeous summer morning, just after seven thirty, when I heard the front door open as David got back from his run. The children were both asleep as they had been up late the night before. David came through our bedroom to get to the bathroom and gave me a passing kiss as he went for his shower. I decided that it was time for me to get my shower before the children woke up.

As I moved into the bathroom, David came out of the shower. He was glowing with health and well-being; the steam was still rising off him as he towelled himself dry. I stood impatiently in front of him until he'd finished. Then I wrapped myself around him, standing on my tiptoes to kiss him. He dropped his towel as his arms came around me. I lowered my heels to the floor but continued to kiss and nuzzle his chest. I think we both realised at the same time that something was coming between us.

I lowered my right arm that had been around his neck and moved to what space there was between us. It was erect, not quite as hard as I once remembered, but it had potential. I stroked it gently, and David gave a low moan.

I slipped my hand into his and gently led him to the bedroom. Leaning over him as he lay on the bed, I started to gently stroke him. I got strangely excited myself watching it grow harder and harder.

I slipped off my nightdress over my head and as my mouth was now only inches away, I placed my lips about his now perfectly erect phallus and started to move my moist lips up and down. There is a time to be modest and there is a time to be lustful – this was the time for the latter. I moved on top of him and guided him inside me with my hand. I then started to slowly and rhythmically move as I felt his hips rise to meet mine so that he might penetrate me more deeply. To answer your unspoken question, no, we didn't finish together. David's groan of pleasure was all the reward I needed. There would be, I just knew many more loving moments when my time would come.

The last six months of our sojourn in London was wonderful. The new educational bill had been adopted, as had the total reorganisation of the NHS on a county level. The economy was booming as technology, utilising robotics and AI, ensured that whatever jobs were lost in some areas, more jobs were available through retraining in other areas. As a country, once again we were leading the world in innovative technology, with renewable energy being at the forefront – nuclear fusion, the science that no one in the world could quite master, had been successfully trialled in Oxford.

The British independence from the EU, on which we had wasted more than three years, had eventually been resolved. There was too much at stake on both sides for trade to discontinue. However, there were many ongoing problems within the EU as demands increased for more democracy and greater autonomy for members' own governments.

We were showing that climate change itself could be slowed down and subsequently reversed. God gave man dominion over the world, but we have to learn that individually we are only here for a short time. We are not meant to squander what we are given; it is up to us to husband all our resources so our children and grandchildren may be able to enjoy life on Earth.

Probably one of my proudest moments was accompanying David Buckingham Palace where he was knighted by Her Majesty the n. For someone born in a small Caribbean island where the entire on considered the royal family as a wonderful fairy story, this s memorable.

that I remembered, once again, Mo's words in his

'Our story is about living, not in the past or in the future, but now. Most of the stories that I've ever read usually contain extraordinary happenings: they have a beginning, a middle and an end. Where our story began, I can only surmise. I can only tell you that which I know. Those of us who are still here are living the middle bit, and the end is yet to come. Our story deals with a dream, a vision, and the group of people who were, and are, determined to turn that dream into a reality – and I suppose that, in itself, is extraordinary.'

Epilogue

Eighteen months later, Esther gave birth to another son whom they christened Morrice, which was immediately abbreviated to Mo.

On their return to Succoth, David became busy with the day-to-day business of running Home Farm. He and Dai also planted the whole hillside with native trees. One day in the future it would be a joy to behold, if only the rabbits and deer would give it half a chance. In the end, they had to fence the entire boundary in order for the young saplings to have any chance of survival.

Meanwhile, Esther was working as the village doctor. The previous GP had retired, and it had been difficult to get a replacement in this isolated part of the country.

Gavin kept them up to date with how the great experiment was progressing; it seemed to be working extremely well. The media was struggling to find enough bad news to sell newspapers. David had taken over the old storage barn and turned it into a small video editing suite with Terry's help.

He then put the word out through social media to all the TV camera 'stringers' who worked around the world that he would pay for any 'good news stories' they came across whilst they were reporting disasters. He then edited these clips and was able to sell them on to most of the world's news services. He soon got to know many of the news teams that operated in some of the most dangerous areas in the world.

It was from one of the cameramen who had been working in Kabul that he heard a story about someone called Sayyid. He had been found in bed with another young man, and they had been dragged to the hotel roof by the Taliban and flung to their death. There was no way the story could be corroborated, but the local rumour was that one of them had been the leader of the jihadi martyrs who had destroyed the British Parliament.

Rhys decided not to re-join the regiment but took his skills in close protection to LA where he worked as an independent security operative. Last bit of news was that he was dating a very beautiful young actress and was intending to bring her back to the Succoth for Christmas.

The End

Printed in Poland
by Amazon Fulfillment
Poland Sp. z o.o., Wrocław